PUSHING BLAME

PUSHING BLAME

A TWISTED PSYCHOLOGICAL THRILLER

T. S. RUBIDOUX

Pushing Blame: A Twisted Psychological Thriller

Published by Underbite Books, LLC.
Golden, CO

Paperback ISBN: 979-8-9878722-0-8
Hardcover ISBN: 979-8-9878722-1-5

FICTION / Thrillers / Psychological

This is a work of fiction. All of the characters, organizations, and events portrayed in this novel are either products of the author's imagination or are used fictitiously.

A special thank you to H. Baker and P. Gruszka, your insight is immeasurable. Dain Williams, artist extraordinaire, I am in awe of your talent. Bryan Canter, you deserve an award for your patience, and to my Pipeline People, thank you for your love and support.

Je dédie ce livre à mon mari.

Thank you "Honey,"
for always encouraging me and being proud of me
regardless of whatever crazy endeavor
or nonsensical adventure I drag you through.

MAIN CAST OF CHARACTERS

Alan Stanhope - Businessman
Laurel Stanhope - Actress
Dr. Joel Kane – Psychiatrist
Dr. Kathryn Kane - Psychiatrist
Frank Reed – Software Designer
Margo Reed - Bookstore Owner
Randal Lucas – Auto Dealership Owner
Dana Lucas - Chief Technical Engineer
Eric Harper – Financial Advisor
Olivia Harper - Office Manager
Curtis Thompson – Laurel's boy toy
Madeline – The Stanhope's housekeeper
Dr. Bob Flanagan – Dentist
Cynthia Flanagan – Wife of Dr. Bob Flanagan
Dale Warner – Laurel's love interest
Sophia Torres – Detective
Ken Freeman - Detective

Drinking wine and discussing the latest read is harmless
entertainment until it isn't. Be careful who you allow into your
inner circle; befriending strangers can be fun but also fatal.

ONE

Breaking News

Splashed across the front page of the San Francisco Chronicle are the words, *"Alan Stanhope Found Dead." Yesterday at daybreak, the body of Alan Stanhope, a prominent businessman and husband to actress Laurel Stanhope was found dead in San Francisco Bay. Horror-filled passengers aboard the Harbor Bay Ferry first sighted the body floating toward the channel during their morning commute and described the scene as extremely disturbing. The crew promptly called 911 before securing the lifeless man while waiting for assistance. Marine Patrol arrived on the morbid scene in minutes and transported the body to the dock where they were met with the screaming sound of sirens from several squad cars.*

The Harbor Master recognized the deceased man, as the couple is well-established in the local boating community as well as in the public eye.

Police officers descended on the Stanhope's yacht, where they located Mrs. Stanhope asleep in their stateroom. The distraught actress claimed to be unaware her husband was missing. At this time, it appears the incident is considered an accident. However, an autopsy and further investigation are necessary to eliminate the possibility of suicide or foul play, with no other comments offered by authorities.

On the morning in question, the coroner was called to the scene to take possession of Mr. Stanhope's body. This was against the wishes of a combative Mrs. Stanhope, who insisted her husband needed an emergency room. The EMTs had their hands full, convincing the infuriated woman to come with them to get checked out. But she's having none of it, resorting to aggressive flailing, bordering on assault. Finally, an officer stepped in, offering the option of the police station for questioning or the hospital for medical attention. Selecting the latter resulted in a swift escort off the yacht. One stipulation to her compliance was a phone call; she wasn't about to go through this ordeal alone. A few close friends showed up at the hospital, where they tried sympathetically to console their grieving friend.

A full toxicology screening would take weeks, if not months. However, a quick blood test positively identified the presence of narcotics and alcohol. But ultimately, the discovery of saltwater in the bloated man's lungs confirmed the cause of death as drowning. These findings and the lack of defensive wounds or any unexplained bruising suggesting a struggle aided in ruling out a possible homicide.

A gash across Mr. Stanhope's shin was the only visible injury.

This type of laceration could have resulted from a stumble into the railing, causing the man to fall into the water and nothing more. All thoughts of suicide were dismissed after speaking with his wife, business partners, and intimate friends. With no substantial evidence, the investigation stalled. The authorities stated they would pursue any leads that may arise, but all indications pointed toward an unfortunate accident.

Squeezing vital information from witnesses is foreplay for most investigators, but this time, they failed to extract the results they anticipated. In the actress's brief statement, she confessed only to dining on their deck to watch the sunset. The decision to spend the night came after consuming too many Manhattans. Neighboring yacht owners corroborated that this was a common practice, so detectives didn't find their decision to stay on this particular evening suspicious.

When questioned, Laurel said, "Alan suggested staying the night at the last minute; we didn't prearrange the sleepover."

She added, "We retired around eleven p.m.; Alan disturbed me when he got out of bed in the middle of the night. But I assumed he went to retrieve a glass of water or use the toilet."

For her husband, "using the boat's facilities" equated to going out on the deck and urinating over the side. She defended her stance on such a disgusting ritual, only allowing him to engage in this behavior when she wasn't present.

Not fully awake and not the type to wait for her husband to return to bed, she had fallen asleep and rested peacefully until the police woke her by banging on the cabin door. The officers stepped back when initially greeted by the disheveled and annoyed diva, who fiercely demanded an explanation for the early morning intrusion.

One patrolman on the dock noted in his report, "Mrs. Stanhope exhibited strange behavior, not concurrent with the traumatic death of a family member. The woman appeared hysterical, yet she didn't shed a single tear. Again, there was crying and wailing, but no tears."

Other noted observations: she hadn't asked what happened to her beloved, nor did she request to view the body. Furthermore, she had refused to identify her husband, insisting the officer contact their friend Dr. Joel Kane and instruct him to do the honors.

The detectives also questioned the paramedics and the ambulance driver, and all personnel interviewed at the scene conveyed the same account: no tears, no questions, only hysterics.

Empathy never ranked high on Laurel's list of attributes. She would be guilty if the absence of expressed emotion or failure to inquire how a loved one perished constituted a felony. Lucky for her, any overdramatic reaction or lack thereof in a stressful situation is strange but isn't a criminal offense.

Investigators had little to go on without a way to differentiate between medication taken voluntarily versus without one's knowledge. The drug and alcohol levels found would render one under the influence but not blackout drunk. This situation leads one to believe a man drank too much, took some pills, and fell overboard, unfortunately resulting in his death.

The detectives hit a dead end, leaving the actress as their only person of interest. With no other options, they attempt to incriminate Ms. Stanhope but fail. They went so far as to insinuate that her interview was nothing more than a theatrical performance.

Seasoned investigators later described the lack of compassion in the widow's statement as "frightening," even for them. They can't find any reason to believe the victim did this to himself. But worse, they can't prove his wife wasn't sleeping when the mishap occurred.

The hospital ran the same blood tests on the husband and the wife, producing matching results. So, if she ingested the same combination of intoxicants, who's to say they didn't take the pills deliberately?

Which is the story the Mrs. is sticking to in her account of what happened. After exhausting their interview list and with no compelling evidence warranting a continuance in the investigation, Alan Stanhope's death went into the record books as an accidental drowning. Case closed.

News outlets and tabloid rags ran wild with the juicy story, where the famous movie maven positioned herself front and center to bask in bereavement glory. Of course, at times, she is overcome with grief at the loss of her husband—a disastrous turn of events for sure. Thank goodness public recognition is where Laurel finds true solace. The outpouring of fan dedication takes her mind off reality, and she is most grateful.

Envisioning the Stanhope family fortune becoming hers and hers alone also aids in course-correcting any negativity attempting to cloud her mindset. In addition, a generous life insurance policy purchased by her late husband with love and affection will provide a sizable security blanket. These factors make the rebounding process oddly easy for the deceased's wife. She will be fine; some might even say she appears rejuvenated. Yet, in the interest of pleasing her adoring fans, from now on, the actress will wear what becomes her signature color palette, monochromatic black.

The grief-stricken widow maintains this dark fashion statement for months. She makes every effort to mirror Audrey Hepburn as if she were the one having breakfast at Tiffany's.

To soften the harshness of the couture noir, she fastens a "Wearing Memories" locket to several strands of pearls dripping from her neck—a fitting piece of jewelry for the self-proclaimed queen of champagne. The silver locket holds the proprietor's cap found atop the cork on one's favorite bottle of bubbles. Conscious of perception and public opinion, the signature cap is often switched out to emphasize a subtle difference in each photo appearing in the press. The bling lends a regal touch, and the pop of panache lends a spark to every black ensemble.

The poignancy of black reminds everyone that Alan is dead. At the same time, the playfulness in the locket reassures Laurel's audience that she is very much alive. The customarily colorful scarf wrapped around her head and neck went black, as did the sunglasses propped high and proud on her face. A minimal amount of makeup is worn, relying heavily on her supposed natural beauty—all these subtle particulars aid in playing the role of the victim exceptionally well. Suffice it to say, the mourning of her late husband's untimely death is lost in the photo-op drama.

Eager to put Alan's passing to rest, the actress's agent spread the word regarding the funeral. A well-known name has a way of finalizing arrangements in rapid succession. The "festivities" would commence within four days. The private gathering would occur in a small white chapel on the cemetery's grounds. An intimate graveside ceremony would follow a traditional lengthy Catholic Mass, ending with an invitation-only reception at the Stanhope manor.

A security detail befitting a president ensured both services remained restricted, with only family and the inner circle of friends allowed in attendance. The internment's limited access made the event a more sought-after affair. Of course, not being invited would be perceived as a scandal by some—"the some" being Laurel. A written request for your presence meant you hit the A-list. This invitation allowed one to mingle with peers and guaranteed your face or at least your name appeared in the morning's paper or online magazine spread.

———————

A few little-known facts about Mr. Alan Stanhope: a well-respected name in the city's financial circles, he owned several businesses with a vested interest in many more. The allure and endearing qualities were his financial success and social standing, not his intemperate intelligence or warm benevolence. His connections fit nicely into Laurel's life plan, so she did some research. After much due diligence, she aligned her universe to overthrow her adversary, the reigning Mrs. Stanhope, and positioned herself to become Alan's second wife. As if it were a scene straight from the Leona Helmsley story. They met "by chance" at a fundraiser, and by the end of the evening, Laurel had decided that she would marry this man.

Another woman coveting the current role of "wife" made no difference to the actress. For all she cared, that person living in his home was merely a stand-in. Not long after the new couple met, Alan returned home from the office, an evening like countless others, however, tonight, he asked his unsuspecting spouse for a divorce. But she wasn't willing to join the first wives' club without a fight and publicly objected to being discarded. Instead of bowing out quietly, she used her societal influence to ensure the elite and the press fully understood the ramifications of her replacement's little stunt. Who can blame her? The decades of sacrifice and hard work amounted to nothing.

Ultimately, Helen Stanhope may have taken one to the gut, but rest assured, her lawyers guaranteed her soon-to-be ex-husband and his little home-wrecker got an unexpected one-two punch in return. And rightfully so, their self-indulgent ordeal vanished Helen's fairy-tale existence; her cherished companion and family lifestyle were lost. So, please take comfort in knowing the original Mrs. Stanhope walked away with several million opportunities to love her new life much more.

One would think the generous terms of Alan's divorce provoked his new fiancée's now sour attitude. But no, Laurel convinced herself the reluctant ex-Mrs. went one step further by dragging her feet to interfere with their upcoming wedding day. Poor Alan liked Laurel's feisty spirit, but he was getting more than he bargained for in this situation. Circumstances deteriorated rapidly for the groom, who, by default, earned the nomination of telling his future bride his divorce papers had yet to be signed. Therefore, the date she reserved for their upcoming nuptials would need to be changed.

The heel-dragging worked; the courts wouldn't finalize the papers freeing Alan to remarry in time for the big day. The bride, not accustomed to waiting for anything, became inconsolable. Alan couldn't fix this, but he could lessen the pain she would inflict upon him. A red box with curly gold trim containing something expensive and emerald studded ought to do the trick. Realizing she wouldn't win this battle, Laurel retreated with her consolation prize and selected a new date for their matrimonial extravaganza.

Regardless of the date, the Stanhope ceremony would be billed as nothing less than spectacular. The most sought-after industry providers lined up to highlight every detail, from the engagement to the "I do's." Weddings generally revolve around the couple and their union, but the actress had more in store. She used this season's social event to double-dip: gain an influential husband and enrich her acting career simultaneously.

Every paper described the thespian's occupation as "an actor or actress, period."

Publications never printed whether she starred in movies, stage, or television productions. Instead, everyone with a pen or keyboard received iron-clad instructions regarding acceptable content. If they expected to be invited or given an exclusive, words and phrases describing celebrity status, the bride's beauty, and the day's event would suffice.

The groom received a brief mention in most articles, but you must hunt to find that simple blurb on page six. Nevertheless, she intended to make their wedding go viral. After this inauguration, Mrs. Laurel Stanhope would be a household name.

That's how their love story began, and this is how it ends.

––––––––––––

The Stanhope estate, adorned with hundreds of white lilies, accommodated two hundred of Alan's grieving relatives, friends, and associates in a grand fashion. The chosen came and went, exchanging honest opinions privately while voicing faux concerns and obligatory condolences in open conversation. Time management, however, soon became an issue. While the widow mastered speaking in equal increments to the attendees, she forgot to acknowledge her actual friends, Kathryn, Margo, Dana, and Olivia.

––––––––––––

Kathryn is Laurel's oldest friend, and the others came along after the actress achieved recognizable status but was not yet star-on-the-sidewalk famous. These women are the only people privy to the diva's innermost secrets and many shortcomings. The inner circle ranking was essential to the friendship; an established bond before Laurel's celebrity sealed her trust. She's convinced any new friends harbored ulterior motives, inserting themselves solely to infringe upon her fame or dip their fingers into her bank account.

The hierarchy places Kathryn first on the friend scale, followed by Margo, Dana, then Olivia. Laurel shares with them because she believes she can manipulate them, but they understand her motives and love her anyway. Remember that she's a much bigger star in her head than on the stage. Recognition for the starlet tends to come from public outbursts, her demanding personality, iconic couture, and now Alan's death more than any of her dramatizations on the silver screen.

The saddened circle of ladies and their husbands took residence in the sitting room after the service, reliving "Alan" stories they had all witnessed firsthand. After partaking in what they deem a respectable amount of grievance time served, they gather their purses and jackets in an attempt to leave without detection. This maneuver doesn't escape their host, who rushes over, apologizing for being rude.

To express her sincerity for ignoring them, she extends an invitation for dinner Saturday night, "Only us, no strangers, no cameras."

She says this with a straight face as if the group believes the paparazzi would swing by for pork chops and applesauce. Laurel unconvincingly adds, "It will give us time to grieve Alan's passing together."

Everyone accepts the invitation, but their host is off before the last confirmation to suck the life out of the few dwindling well-wishers.

Margo finds it hard to contain her opinion and blurts out several observations regarding the authenticity of the attendee's relationship with Alan. Adding, "This is nothing more than a midweek social, as the host apparently forgot she's supposed to be the grieving widow."

Olivia chimes in with, "Spectacular people-watching. Is Laurel flirting?"

On the way out, Margo, who owns a neighborhood bookstore near Presidio Heights, asks who is hosting the next book club meeting; she also would like a show of hands to see who read or, better yet, started the current book.

"Please finish reading *A Piece of Cake* by next Thursday."

Kathryn states, "Yes, I read the book, and it's my turn to host; bring wine."

All pretend to check the calendars on their phones, and everyone confirms they will attend both events in the coming week. Then, with final hugs and kisses exchanged, they slip out the door unnoticed by the remaining guests.

———

Kathryn Kane is a psychiatrist, as is her husband, Joel. Dr. Joel Kane is Laurel Stanhope's therapist, and the actress will continually test this dynamic. Joel works out of an office in the city, whereas Kathryn set up her practice on the first floor of their home. The doctor-patient relationship began between Laurel and Joel a little over a year ago. The overwhelming stress of fame is her "issue."

Often complaining, "People don't understand the limelight; simple tasks such as grocery shopping may erupt into a fan frenzy."

Although public incidences do arise occasionally, they don't tend to get out of control; gawking, on the other hand, is a common occurrence. A scarf wrapped around her head is customary, or she fashions her hair in an updo, complete with a fascinator or garish derby hat. She never goes out without a pair of black shades to hide behind, insisting this style is a choice and not done to draw attention.

The actress stands at five foot nine with an exceptional build. A woman with her stature would draw stares wearing a plain white t-shirt and faded jeans. But add four-inch Christian Louboutin's, a Burberry coat, any number of designer handbags, and voilà, a spectacle to behold.

Not long after Laurel began therapy, Joel figured out she sought counseling to say she consulted with a therapist. She never denied being a classic narcissist and, therefore, unapologetic for her actions. Laurel doesn't care whom she offends or if someone's toes get crushed under her stilettos. She will do whatever it takes to become the center of attention wherever she goes. The entitled drama queen always gets her way, and if getting her way is at your expense, you should know better. She is who she is; she won't pretend to be anything less.

Joel and Laurel agree on most benefits of traditional treatment, and she claims she requires his guidance for those reasons. The excuse he gives for allowing her to come in is so other therapists won't take advantage of her. Well, this notion justified his initial thought process. Soon their mental health appointments turned into scheduled sex. The little voice in Joel's head warned him that his patient wanted his wife to discover their secret. But his ego ignored the internal lecture, thus accepting the odds.

The doctor's wife and the actress resemble sisters sharing a love-hate rivalry, a perplexing bond they've endured since grade school. They don't like each other as much as they amuse themselves with the frivolity of the other's life. However, seducing one's husband may be deemed more than frivolous. Joel is content being a mere tic in Laurel's bedpost because he craves her escapades. Her risqué random encounters excited the bored therapist. A typical counseling session begins with the actress describing her sexual exploits and ends with a reenactment of said depravity on his couch. As a patient, one might consider obtaining a new doctor if, after several sessions, your husband never surfaced as a topic of conversation, even after he died. Joel is uncomfortable discussing his deceased friend, never pressing her about him; perhaps he considered this a conflict of interest to ask questions about a man when his wife is on top of him.

The man lying in the closed coffin had filled a void for Laurel. But don't be fooled by his past compliance; he was fully aware of whom he married. After all, she broke up his longtime marriage to his first wife as nonchalantly as canceling a dinner reservation. So, nothing much about his new spouse's character came as a surprise to Alan. He never questioned the men she entertained; he sometimes found the fill-ins a relief. The public aspect of being with the diva brought about a youthful excitement; he loved their adventurous life. Yet, being thrust into the limelight occasionally didn't appeal to him, or a calendar conflict would interfere. In this event, an escort would take his place. Alan paid no mind; he willingly accepted being Mr. Laurel Stanhope.

The reception ended, and Laurel embarked on a desperate search for Curtis as the last guests made their way out. This young man and the actress supposedly worked on the same project two years ago. They remained "close" long after the film was in the can. He did make an appearance but realized it was not the time or place to expect affection. Not today, but for now, this suitable replacement for the dearly departed comes in the cliché better known as Curtis.

The staff finishes cleaning up, putting the house back together as if no one had stopped to pay their respects. Then, Laurel sits alone in her empty home for the first time since her husband's death. Finally, with the security alarm set and the lights downstairs turned off, the tired actress changes into her dressing gown and settles in like an heiress. She slides under her puffy duvet, turns off the bedside lamp, and sleeps until noon the next day.

Thursday's headline reads, *"Stars Wore Black Attending Funeral of Alan Stanhope."* Next, the article went into detail regarding fashion and who's who, followed by a short but sweet bio on the guest of honor.

Laurel adores the press and the attention they pay her. The tagline, not lost on her, and much to her delight, features Alan's unfortunate death playing third to her and her guests' black attire. So, of course, not wanting to be "out blacked," the actress arrived in a black limousine with what doubled as the cast from *Men in Black* at her side. The widow wore a black hat, veil, and sunglasses to compliment her little black dress. A black Hermes handbag, tights, and pumps completed the mournful outfit. The only exception to her monochromatic ensemble was the shiny red soles on the bottom of her shoes. Which sadly received more press than Alan.

TWO

The *Friend* Dinner Party

Under normal circumstances, a dinner party would not be deemed appropriate in the wake of a tragic death, but no one would expect anything less from San Francisco's most recent widow. Everyone is still in shock over losing their dear friend, Alan, but Saturday night's gathering will offer Laurel the stability and togetherness she needs right now.

The founding of this eclectic collection of ladies occurred by chance, with their husbands attending dinner engagements and the like out of obligation more so than friendship. Being an avid reader, Kathryn would frequent Margo's bookstore, sometimes stopping long enough to enjoy a cup of coffee from time to time. A title Kathryn purchased happened to be the topic for that month's book club, so Margo extended an invitation. The RSVP marked "accepted" also indicated a fine wine would be her plus one.

Much to her delight, Kathryn enjoyed herself. One would assume finding a "normal" woman to associate with wouldn't be complicated; however, you are incorrect in that assumption, and a collective of rational females is even more extraordinary. The nice thing about this little party of literary enthusiasts is that they choose to be who they are versus portraying someone they are not. A refreshing change to the patients the doctor converses with all day.

Comfort in numbers is foreign to Kathryn, yet the casual setting in the bookstore allows them to conjure up diverse opinions generating a safe mind-stimulating space. Of course, the alcohol distorts the ability to decipher whether the women read the novels or just skimmed over the CliffsNotes online, but it matters not. Participation tends to be the objective, with the more obscure points of view correlating to the amount of Merlot consumed. Intoxication also promotes the insertion of random chatty encounters having nothing to do with the read. Some talk about their day, family, or current fling. The evening often inadvertently turns into a sideways approach to group therapy. The monthly meetings turned out to be a welcomed distraction for Kathryn, a chance to get out of the office and an evening escape from Joel. Olivia and Dana were already regular attendees who encouraged newcomers. Laurel received an overwhelming reception after accompanying Kathryn to a gathering. The worship and free-flowing alcoholic beverages guaranteed the starlet's future attendance. The other bookstore patrons came and went, yet somehow these five participants forged a bond.

After a while, they stopped inviting others on the evenings they met and eventually started taking turns hosting at each other's homes. They soon became a close-knit tribe, everyone contributing something eccentrically different.

These friends meld swimmingly; however, their husbands have less in common, but they tolerate outings at the request of their wives. Dinners and noninvasive social engagements tended to be low-key, and the food was worth enduring the drivel. The gatherings continued for years until "attention" reared its ugly head. This network worked exceptionally well until it didn't.

Madeline, the Stanhope's housekeeper, is quick to answer the door at the sound of chimes. The need for a guest to press the button twice is considered rude. A faux pas such as this would send the madame running through the house, screaming, "Off with her head."

Madeline leads each couple to an alcove, where tonight's hostess waits to greet her guests. The "greeting room" is small, a mere indention off the foyer only big enough to house a flamboyant settee providing Laurel a place to rest between entering attendees. The whole procession is nauseating. But this ridiculous, albeit customary routine, is about to take a surprising turn, as standing alongside Laurel is an unexpected escort. Standard protocol dictates a blatant infringement here; not abiding by the traditional bereavement period makes everyone uneasy. Moreover, the need to commandeer a date soon after a spouse's passing goes against moral etiquette and breaks the most basic human code of decency. Cocktail, anyone?

First to arrive are the doctors, Kathryn and Joel Kane, followed by Margo and her husband, Frank Reed. Frank is a software designer specializing in video games. But rather than labor on a new design, he prefers to stay home and play with himself. Frank's former employers will agree that the latter is his strong suit. Thus, his work ethic, or lack thereof, has become the underlying strain in the Reed's marriage. In general, obtaining employment requires an active search—his failed efforts are only surpassed by his mediocre interest in being the breadwinner.

An overinflated view of his skill set is a recurring argument, coupled with most pay grades laughably beneath his acceptable level. Freelance work is what Frank claims occupies his days; this appeases his wife for the time being. The Reeds have one son, Tyler, who attends high school with future aspirations of playing baseball in college—anything to distance himself from his dysfunctional father and codependent mother.

Next at the door are Randal and Dana Lucas. Dana is the chief technical engineer for Skyhill Technologies, a computer company, and Randal owns and operates a Range Rover dealership in the city. The Lucas's are blessed with two kids, a son, and a daughter, attending separate universities out of state.

The last to make an appearance are Eric and Olivia Harper. An administrator by trade, Olivia is employed by Dr. Flanagan, a dentist with boundary issues, and Eric is a financial adviser. The Harper family wrangle three children, twin boys in their senior year of high school and a middle school daughter who brings home every stray animal she can find.

Enter Olivia; she crosses the threshold only to be stopped in her tracks. The scraping noise from the metal spike protruding from her shoe pierces Laurel's ears. The little black piece of rubber wore off at the base of her heel, exposing a tiny little dagger and making the distinct sound every woman dreads.

To allow this "fashion don't" to go unaddressed is not a consideration.

"Stop," shouts Laurel, "Olivia, would you please remove your insipid footwear and go upstairs and select a decent replacement, preferably a pair with the heels intact."

Next, she scolds her guest for the scratches she left on the floor in the entry, like a mother reprimanding a child for tracking mud across a white carpet. One would think this comment would offend the accosted guest.

On the contrary, Olivia seizes the opportunity and dashes to the dressing suite, taking her time to make her selection meaningful. Then, thrilled with scoring new expensive pumps, she parades her newly adorned feet past the host, singing, "I do love my new Jimmy Choo's."

An eye roll tumbles across Laurel's face before commending her friend on her excellent choice. Please remind me to give you the number of my cordwainer; he can fix anything. The expression on Olivia's face prompts further insults.

"A cordwainer is a shoemaker, a repair person, a cobbler," barks Laurel while holding Olivia's old shoes between her thumb and forefinger as if they are contaminated. The tattered discards are handed to Madeline with hazmat care. "Bag these, please."

Over the years, wearing the same size as the famous actress has proved advantageous for Olivia. Laurel's impressive shoe collection and the ritual of never being caught wearing anything more than two or three times, trading insults for high fashion, is a deliberate and conscious choice. Not much time passes before the next "must-have" pair catches the diva's eye, thus the need to make room for a new arrival. Olivia appreciates and anticipates gently used secondhand goods like an excited kid on Christmas morning.

The men make their way into the library where the libations reside. A shimmering ice bucket is on display, surrounded by various fine spirits. Silver tongs to place the two-inch frozen spheres into the thick-bottomed crystal tumblers reminiscent of a 1920s whiskey bar lay on a sterling tray. The study offers a more manly environment, which is suitable since this is the first time the men or anyone has had the pleasure of meeting Curtis, Laurel's new beau.

Frank and Curtis become fast friends; after all, they are both dedicated to the art of gaming. A few of Frank's older projects are games Curtis is familiar with, which ignites their bromance. These two grown men resemble adult children bragging about their latest round of Dungeons & Dragons.

The toy talk is going to require cocktails. Randal, Dana's husband, can't stomach the banter. A conversationalist, he is not, but he does talk for a living, so feigning interest is a natural attribute, but this game talk is too much. Most of his day revolves around conversing with the privileged at his dealership. Spoiled housewives, entitled young adults, and partners who want the premium off-road vehicle are a daily occurrence. Although the male clients provide the best source of entertainment, these men won't ever permit their new tires to hit real dirt, and the only water they will traverse is a puddle produced by the last rain. Alan's abandoned fine assortment of scotch is inviting, and Randal grabs a glass and pours himself three fingers. Then, with a drink in hand, he settles into a comfortable chair and prays for the evening to end.

Eric, Olivia's husband, listens to the guys talk, but his mind is on his kids and how this evening wastes precious time that could be better spent with them. His only hope is that his sons don't turn out like these middle-aged delinquents and that his daughter doesn't date one. Worries about his family are commonplace; he struggles with not doing more to relieve the pressure his wife endures working at the dentist's office. Finding a new workplace before she can quit her position is the problem. Gold handcuffs are a genuine issue. Dr. Flanagan pays well, so walking away into what they all assume will be a lesser-paying job is a burdensome call. The Harpers treat their money the same way squirrels store nuts, putting every penny in the bank as they prep for the cars and college looming on the horizon. Hoarding their earnings isn't a joke; those dimes to dollars are serious everyday budget concerns. Olivia, the unselfish soldier she is, does what she feels is best financially for the family but not necessarily the ideal option for herself.

In hushed tones, the ladies discuss the inappropriate addition to the group as the host goes to check on dinner; correction, Laurel checks on Madeline, who will, in turn, check their meal status. Questions ricochet like rogue bullets, making it hard to decipher who is asking what of whom.

"Who is this guy?"

"It's obvious; this relationship started before Alan's death."

"Well, he didn't start dating a widow today."

"Do you think he's involved in Alan's… ?"

These and many other rapid-fire inquiries are being spat out at warp speed in hopes of being asked and answered before their host returns.

Back into the circle of confused companions, Laurel addresses the elephant in the room, "OK, I'm sure you are all wondering about Curtis; we worked together on a movie a while back and remained 'friends,' he is helping me cope with my recent bout of depression."

Then, quicker than she stepped in, she stepped back out to gather the gentlemen to the table.

The word *depression* leaves the women dumbfounded. Kathryn suggests, "To suffer is a skill every actor masters early on in their career, so performing the role of bereaved with dignity wouldn't be a stretch for Laurel. But she most likely disguises her outward signs of trauma for our benefit."

"Oh, please stop!" Margo snaps.

"She hasn't shed one tear, not the day Alan died, not the days before the funeral, not at the service or now."

Margo continues without coming up for air, "And her incessant flirting is outrageous; if this is depression, I want some."

"Everyone grieves in their own unique way, and we don't know what she is going through when we aren't around. Death affects everyone differently; if this is her way of coping, we must support her. Is it right? It's not our 'right,' but perhaps it's hers," says Kathryn.

The tinkle from a bell summons the invited to the dining room. A beautiful table setting deserving a *Bon Appétit* magazine cover lays before them, complete with handwritten place cards indicating who must sit where. First, accolades are accepted for the gorgeous arrangement of tableware and foliage. Next, the perfectly plated main course receives equal billing, and yes, the host also claims responsibility for the meal. The women at the table make a mental note to thank Madeline later.

Everyone is seated, proper introductions concluded, and after a brief but heartfelt mention of Alan, Laurel switches gears and wants to talk to Eric about her portfolio. She casually says, "Your assistance would be greatly appreciated; I need some guidance investing the funds from the life policy payout.

The insurance company is still waiting for the death certificate; the coroner must confirm the cause of death before disbursing funds."

Almost shouting, and hopefully, in jest, she quips, "The case is closed and ruled an accident, so what's the hold-up?"

Her frustration is blatant, and being put off by why this is taking so long is understandable, but her approach is alarming. Everyone is bewildered by the annoyance dripping off her tongue with every word she speaks.

Stunned by her tone on the sensitive subject matter, Eric says, "Let's talk in private, call my assistant and make an appointment, at your convenience, of course." Laurel reluctantly concurs with this not-so-subtle end to their conversation.

Oblivious to the flow in the room, Curtis can't stop talking about Frank's virtual masterpieces. He doesn't hide his desire for a new gaming console so he can be a test subject for Frank's upcoming endeavors.

Laurel quickly shifts to her next order of business. "Well, Frank, should I phone your office so you can pencil me in your day planner too? Openings in my calendar are filling fast, so Randal, I'd like to talk to you about selling Alan's Mercedes for me. I can't bring myself to drive it, so why keep the thing? What are your thoughts on trading it in for a new SUV?"

In keeping with the pattern of appointments, Randal also tells Laurel to call his office or come by at her leisure, and he'll take care of her.

The husbands at the table are being manipulated for entertainment more than need. But Laurel can't help herself. To achieve a complete twist from the blade attached to her remarks, she adds, "I love your men making themselves available to me; I'm so alone."

The timbre in her delivery makes it sound as if she's auditioning for the part of a bereaved widow rather than being one. Regardless, her remarks send shivers through the room. Madeline stops mid-stride while collecting plates but quickly regains her composure before anyone picks up on the stutter in her step.

To pump blood back into the stunned group, Dana suggests they adjourn to the den for coffee and dessert. Madeline is grateful to leave the room and return with this epicurean adventure's sweet and final course. In an attempt to diffuse the current momentum, Margo announces an in-person author book signing soon. But unfortunately, no one shares her enthusiasm as Laurel steps on her words.

The chaise lounge Kathryn occupies eases the tension hanging in the air, at least for her. She sets her coffee on the side table and puts her feet up, taking full advantage of the comfortable recliner. Undetected by the others, a wicked wave pulses through the room. While expressing her opinion on the benefits of listening to audiobooks, Laurel explains their value for busy people like her. Her speech is a diversion tactic, dulling the awareness of her guests with yet another self-centered viewpoint. Catlike and with malicious intent, she stalks her prey, casually making her way to the back of Kathryn's chair. Margo takes the liberty of interjecting to justify the therapeutic powers of holding a piece of bound literature in your hands and touching the pages as you read. Everyone's focus shifts to Margo, momentarily leaving their host ignored.

The alluring pose of the reclining doctor is one the actress can't resist. She begins by pulling her friend's hair back into a messy bun. An almost undetectable euphoric sigh emanates from Kathryn's body, catching Joel's ear. Next, Laurel's hands run over the relaxed woman's shoulders; while fanning her fingers as they run down the front of Kathryn's chest, grazing her breasts. Not too far, but far enough. Then in a smooth continuous motion, she glides her palms back up her friend's neck with a firm flat stroke. Next, with her thumbs pressed together, Laurel draws a line down to the base of Kathryn's spine. Her massaging fingers spread wide when she reaches now tense shoulders to repeat the process, just like Joel does.

From across the room, the Kanes lock eyes. Helpless and petrified, Joel stares in horror while his mistress silently reveals all his wife needs to know. Incensed, Kathryn stands and states she is leaving. She says good-night with purpose, not allowing the other guests time to put two and two together. Unable to reach the door fast enough, Joel trips all over himself. Before the abrupt departure, the ebb in the party had already put a cramp in the flow; therefore, everyone takes this to signify that the evening is over.

Margo and Dana start clearing the dishes; Laurel slaps their hands. Directing them to leave those for "the help."

In disgust, the ladies resume helping "the help" gather the plates of half-eaten food and collect handfuls of silverware that were never touched.

As expected, the car ride home for the Kanes is uncomfortable. Kathryn appears fixated on the blackness of night, but she is studying the sadness of her reflection in the passenger side window. The eyes peering back at her aren't tear-filled; they're hollow; emptiness is all she recognizes. Too many times before, she turned the other cheek. No more chances, no more humiliation; her decision is final; the marriage is over.

Joel remains speechless, hoping to talk this out in the safe confines of their home. But, come to find out, the environment has little effect on the evening's outcome or the rest of his married life. Once at home, Joel simulates a scolded dog, heeling tightly behind his wife. He attempts to follow her up the stairs, but she turns around, and without saying a word, she presses her hand on his chest to stop him. He fixates on his wife for the second time tonight, but now it's to watch her climb the staircase for the last time. Disappearing into their bedroom, she closes the door behind her. The click of the lock signals defeat. The single step downward for him is equivalent to a ten-foot drop before turning to face the mile-long hall to make up his new bedroom, the space intended for guests.

The night is restless; sleep isn't a luxury afforded to the guilty or embarrassed. Visions of what he is about to lose impose a far more significant impact than any tryst with Laurel. Weak is the only word he assigns himself; there are no words he can attach to his wife. However, the anticipated repercussions change the word weak to frightened for a good reason. After sixteen years of marriage, Joel is aware of his bride's true strength, and he understands Kathryn isn't someone you can cross and walk away from unscathed.

Streaks of sunlight make their way into the kitchen, where Joel sat most of the night. Breakfast may help, so he prepares a pathetic peace offering while rummaging through his brain for a viable explanation for Laurel's behavior.

The smell of coffee is the only thing strong enough to pry Kathryn from her room, and the aromatic bliss of fresh brew wins, drawing her out. Neither of them will be going to work on a Sunday morning, so she goes downstairs to face the music. An unkempt Joel wants to talk, but Kathryn doesn't.

His desperate attempt to salvage their union with pancakes is insulting. On what planet did he believe a short stack dripping in syrup would save his soul?

Preparing food for her is not an ordinary consideration; her husband doesn't make meals. This loving-kindness is a little too late. In a calm voice, she says, "I love you, but this situation can't continue; I've tried to ignore your actions, and considering our friend's short attention span, I figured she would grow tired of you sooner or later. I bet sooner, I lost. The message she sent last night demonstrates she's banking on later."

He pleads, trying to make her realize Laurel isn't who he wants. Yet, in his desperate plight, he neglects to convey that it is she whom he desires. Defeated, Kathryn says, "It's best to part ways while we can still redeem what remains of our friendship."

Coffee in hand, she goes to her room, gets dressed, calls her lawyer, and starts her day.

After last night's festivities, each person, if asked, would recall a different scene to describe the dinner party's sudden conclusion. For appearance's sake, a lovely gathering, yet one minute the conversation revolved around books and a decadent dessert; the next minute, your coat replaced your tart plate.

None of them pinpointed the truth, nor would they believe it if you told them. Seeing the exhibition with their own eyes made no difference; no one realized anything had happened. To catch the slight, you need to be privy to Joel's intimate touch and know his foreplay routine to understand that the simple gesture on display was a prelude to much grander intentions.

THREE

Lonely Like Me

Laurel's dramatic personality aided in masking her neglected heart before expressing to her closest friends that she craved affection outside her marriage. It was a mistake to share that her husband is selfish in bed, and she can't help but think he is saving his energy for someone other than her. This remark was a justification of sorts and yet another creative way to interject the gentlemen she wrangles on the side into every conversation. She does this to combat monotony, but the ladies no longer find it amusing. Alan, strangely enough, had given his blessing to this bizarre behavior and went on seemingly unaffected; whether intentional or not, his idle concern defeated the thrill of his wife's extramarital activity. So, without any other turmoil to feed upon, Laurel searched for a multifaceted situation, a risk sure to keep her adrenaline pumping for quite some time.

The perfect circumstance presented itself when Dr. Horwath, Laurel's previous therapist, terminated his services. However, before closing the door on their last session, he furnished a register of potential replacements for her consideration. Dr. Joel Kane's name appeared halfway down the reference sheet; perhaps she didn't scroll any further as her dear friend Dr. Kathryn Kane was listed on the following line.

Intimacy between Joel and Laurel wasn't immediate; the shift progressed gradually, one indecent couch visit after another. At first, he evaded the seduction but couldn't ward off a persistent albeit aggressive assault by a gorgeous woman for too long. His ethics and a sworn oath provided a paper-thin coat of armor, a barrier never meant to withstand this type of heat. Nevertheless, rendezvous by appointment made hookups discreet as well as extremely efficient. The good doctor didn't spring for dinner or book hotel rooms, and he avoided being seen by conveniently never having to leave the privacy of his office. An awkward bonus came when it was time for payment, an insurance company covered the bill, but in essence, Laurel paid for her couch time.

Kathryn wasn't without her suspicions, professionally or privately. She was aware Dr. Horwath terminated his services with her friend, but Laurel never wanting to discuss her new physician sparked concern. Confirmation came when Laurel handed over a pill bottle with Joel's name as the prescribing doctor. Like all other tabloid darlings, Laurel claims she will become a statistic if the pills are taken unsupervised. But if she reveals her concerns to her doctor, he won't continue to supply her with drugs. So, the solution was to cry to Kathryn, "I can read the headline now; Dazzling Turns Distraught, Laurel Stanhope Goes to Rehab."

Outcome: Joel prescribes the medication to Laurel, who in turn gives the containers to the other Dr. Kane for safekeeping. The medication is personally dispensed one pill at a time when deemed necessary. To enable the drama, Kathryn plays along, acknowledging at least to herself that this phobia is two-sided.

This deliberate maneuver intrigued the other Dr. Kane. Most women would confront either the husband or the friend, but mind games are Kathryn's area of expertise. Quietly amused by Laurel's audacity to intentionally inflict misery into her life doesn't mean this affront will go unchallenged.

A private investigator confirmed Kathryn's original uncertainty and revealed that her friend sought out others besides Joel. Men like dominoes lined up to topple over at the slightest tap, all in the name of self-serving entertainment. Kathryn often wonders how far Laurel will go to fulfill her insatiable needs. *As far as I would or have gone in the past? No, she doesn't have the dedication or courage and only pretends to be truly cold-blooded.*

However, Laurel's priorities have shifted, escalating her risky behavior. To the actress, her lovers or participants have always been irrelevant. The dismantled families and the brokenhearted suitors are abandoned without a second thought before the unempathetic seductress moves on to the next poor bastard. But intentionally jeopardizing her bond with Kathryn points to a slip in her mental stability.

Early Monday, Laurel sits at the breakfast table and commences constructing her weekly agenda: Finances are her biggest concern, so Eric is her first call.

To be told by the perky receptionist, Lilli, that he won't be in the office for another hour makes Laurel's annoyance receptors stand on end.

The verbal assault that follows the typically minor inconvenience startles Lilli. Not hearing what she wanted and loathing perky, Laurel barks, "Mark the calendar, Mrs. Stanhope, ten a.m., Tuesday, May twenty-first. Inform your boss that my location schedule occupies the month, and this is the only time I am available. Please provide confirmation no later than this afternoon."

After the actress rattles off her phone number, she abruptly ends the call without offering a departing salutation. Lilli shouts, "Rude," into dead air space.

Next on Laurel's itinerary is Randal; she makes arrangements to sell Alan's Mercedes and select a new car for herself. The specifics are straightforward, black on black, and state-of-the-art needs no mention. When preferences are confirmed, she informs Randal that she wants him to inspect the car, after which she expects him to deliver it to her home. The thought of a movie star on a car lot is ridiculous. She then dictates how this will play out: "The pink slip is ready to go. After dropping off my new ride, you can drive the Mercedes back to work."

Transaction complete.

It's hard to fathom Randal and Dana as a couple. Upon meeting Dana, a natural expectation is to assume her partner possesses similar characteristics: genuine, intelligent, and hard-working. Unfortunately, Randal is a disappointment, personifying a slick stereotypical smooth-talking car salesperson. His posturing reads as friendly or innocent flirting when dealing with female clients. But the phony façade is there to mask harassment while trolling for potential hookups. Most women find this conduct unbecoming; regrettably, Laurel is excluded from the group of "most women."

In his best auto retailer voice, he assures her he will customize the perfect automobile just for her as they speak. And because she is a VIP client, he will pull some strings guaranteeing her new ebony chariot arrives on her doorstep tomorrow. A rush from the instant gratification of a new purchase courses through Laurel like a drug.

The royal treatment is expected, but being pampered during large transactions is euphoric. Lucky for them both, the exact vehicle she "special ordered" is in stock, sitting right in front of him "as they speak."

The final item to address is arranging some time with Frank. Laurel places a call to enlist his assistance in selecting and installing the game system Curtis would like. Happy to oblige; Frank estimates the wait time as a few days; he needs to order some components. Then he'll connect with her when he is ready to come over for the installation.

———

Eric returns to his office to find his agitated assistant screaming about Ms. Stanhope's pending appearance. Lilli begs, "Don't make me call her to say you're unavailable."

To comfort Lilli, Eric says, "Laurel is harmless; she likes to intimidate people. She doesn't hear the word *no* often and loves to create situations where the last thing you want to do is anything other than what she requests. Better yet, you're afraid to tell her no."

"I'm not calling her; that woman scares me," whines Lilli.

He'd like to explain to his shaking assistant that is the point but lets it go.

Eric accepts that Laurel is gaslighting him and his secretary. He assumes soliciting his services revolves around her current money manager growing tired of dealing with her drama and will no longer supply the amount of attention she demands.

Another possibility being he reinforces the validity of her wealth or the assets she alleges to possess. The confidentiality agreement adds an extra layer of lie protection. Eric won't contradict her claims; his integrity will stop him from breaking her trust. This bond forces him to sit and listen to exaggerations, unable to confirm or deny her grandiose status. But again, this is no different from any other day with their overbearing friend.

Lilli's been chewing her fingernails all afternoon, waiting to be thrown a lifeline. Eventually, Eric relents, "Go ahead and let our client know the time she requested is fine."

"Thank the Lord" leaves Lilli's lips as she rushes to her desk to place a call to confirm.

———

Tuesday morning's tedium joins impatience, launching an internal struggle for Laurel while she waits for her latest acquisition. Randal finally rolls up a little after noon in her brand-new car, delivered as promised. Unable to contain her excitement, but oddly before inspection, Laurel proposes a toast. "Come in, so we can celebrate."

A scotch is poured while he takes the liberty of popping the cork on a bottle of champagne, which just so happens to be chilling in an ice bucket.

After several drinks, the small talk wanes. After exhausting all cheesy questions, Randal asks, "So, do you think you will ever remarry?"

"Why would I restrict myself?" snaps Laurel with a curl in her lip.

He tries flattery by stating, "I figured an attractive woman like you would want a man around."

She laughs at his ignorance. "Why should I settle for one man when several are much more satisfying."

"Several?" This single word is beyond thought-provoking.

"Sure, why not," says Laurel, who delights in the fantasies sure to be spinning in this man's head. "The internet makes dating a breeze; you can put men in a queue; finding men couldn't be easier."

She continues her shock and awe presentation by explaining, "Imagine I want to go to dinner; I open a file of vetted prospects and click. Think of it as speed dial dating. Let's say I need an escort for a function requiring an intellectual conversationalist; a few gentlemen saved in that folder fit this bill. Sometimes I only require a piece of old-fashioned arm candy for a premiere; I open the boy toy tab. On other occasions, I want an Adonis who can make me scream in bed without strings attached. I'm constantly interviewing for that position.

"Alan disapproved of my app-based catalog of men, but he couldn't expect me to step out of a limousine unaccompanied at an event. My late husband didn't always embrace the limelight. Sometimes he preferred to stay home rather than attend fundraisers or galas. I find being with someone who wants to be present more enjoyable, someone who can appreciate and bask in what I worked so hard to achieve."

The rant ended with Laurel announcing, "Now, I will reserve a man for every occasion."

Intrigued, Randal asks, "How do you determine a man's area of expertise?"

A slight hesitation triggers the mood, then, in a seductive whisper, she answers, "Well, if you and I went on a date, we would share a couple of cocktails like we are now. And we would talk and enjoy each other's company."

Glass-raised, Laurel finishes her drink. "Personality is important; he must be intriguing and pique my interest. Sex appeal is a given; if he checks the boxes, I will refill our glasses like I am now. I would sit close to him and place my hand on his if I'm attracted to the man. The gentleman may pick up my hand and gently caress it, holding my grasp momentarily. Pulling away at this juncture signals that I am no longer interested in the foreplay, and going no further is implied. To remain is an invitation. The suitor may kiss my hand, perhaps nibbling up my arm to my neck."

The visual to the spoken word runs simultaneously with the seductress acting out her fantasy. First, her fingertips glide from her wrist to her chin and down the front of her body. Then, in a breathy tone, she conveys her desires. "He would hold my jawline with a tender hand and place soft kisses on my lips. All women and I presume this instantaneous reaction is the same for men; upon an introduction, one can sense from first glance if they would sleep with the other. But one can tell a lot more from a person's lips."

Laurel's teasing excites Randal.

"For me, at this point, I would harbor little doubt whether I wanted to proceed. The effects of a kiss are an excellent indication of the activities to come. Again, if I don't draw away, I'm sending a clear sign that I would like him to nibble my neck again, opening my shirt a little and partially exposing my breasts. I seldom wear a bra if I anticipate an evening going in this direction. I like the touch of warm lips on my skin as the rest of my blouse is unbuttoned, leaving me naked and exposed."

While she speaks, he picks up the hand she placed on his and starts to lay the sequence of kisses she described. With her shirt now open, he views her braless bare body. The slippery silk resting on her shoulders falls to the floor, and he finishes as instructed.

Randal's debut performance resulted in unexpected pleasure. As they lay bare on the plush rug in the library, Laurel responds with, "Oh, this is going to be fun!"

Pleased with the day's outcome, Laurel asks if he would consider lunch sometime.

"Of course; how about next week?" he says, biting her nipple through her shimmery top.

"How about tomorrow, noon, at the Yacht Club?"

"You're on."

He isn't sure if he accepted a request or a command, and what came next was a bit of a blur. She took his hand but only to smash the keys to Alan's old car into his palm. If that didn't signify their rendezvous was over, the signed title and a check for her new vehicle slapped against his chest before being ushered out made it crystal clear. Randal's confusion and dejection are a unique experience for him; he's accustomed to being the user, not the used.

FOUR

Wednesday, May 8 — Yacht Club, Nooner

Fashionably late, the actress makes her entrance, where the Club's hostess greets her with a cheerful yet professional salutation. The young lady confirms that the preferred table requested is ready without being asked. Then announces, "Your associate is already seated and has been appropriately attended to while awaiting your arrival." Laurel saunters past the girl at the pulpit without acknowledging her. There is no eye contact, but the actress does deliver the coveted approving nod.

Randal demonstrates he can be a gentleman by standing as he welcomes his tardy companion when she approaches the secluded table. Today's seating assignment isn't random; the couple is strategically out of the sightline of the other members. Smiles and kisses are exchanged, insinuating joy, but the happiness doesn't last. Awkward moments hang in the air as they sit amidst uncomfortable pleasantries. Saving the moment is the server who appears from out of thin air with the scotch Randal ordered and the champagne Laurel didn't request yet expected.

The server inquires if she will be having her usual today or if, perhaps, she would prefer the chef create something special for her or her guest. Not wishing to prolong this day date, the special offer is declined. Instead, she requests another glass of bubbles and a lobster salad before motioning to bring whatever "he" is ordering off the menu.

The day is beautiful; the conversation flows smoothly enough, but Laurel is fading. Agitation creeps in halfway through the fruit cup portion of this dismal meal, causing extreme restlessness. She is kicking herself for blurting out the lunch invitation. A call to Postmates would have eliminated the dreary small talk with this person who clearly can't articulate anything of interest. Another tragic disappointment, she can't share the insults floating in her brain regarding her date's inept social graces with anyone. Keeping his only redeeming quality, his mattress maneuvers, quiet is also frustrating. A between-the-sheets tell-all trumps any other topic of discussion at book club.

The thought bubble hovering over Laurel's head pops as soon as she spies the paparazzi. Then excitedly, she says, "Thank God; I had begun to believe dying of boredom was a thing."

However, the burst of enthusiasm is short-lived as the realization of the press seeking photos of someone other than her becomes obvious. From her vantage point, she can't make out who they are actively pursuing; the bald spot on the back of a man's head is all that's visible.

Laurel pushes her plate away, grabs her purse, and excuses herself to use the lady's room. The wide-eyed hostess catches sight of the determined actress heading straight for her; a hundred-dollar bill slides across the podium in a single motion. And with an intense stare, she whispers, "I don't think the media is aware I'm here. Let's fix that, shall we?"

The stoic girl pockets the money with discretion, using the circumstance to return the approving nod she's grown accustomed to only receiving.

Back in her seat, Randal asks if everything is all right.

The question he poses is ignored and replaced.

"Care for dessert at my house before returning to the office?"

Not waiting for a response, Laurel excuses him from the table.

Randal hasn't digested his food or the dismissal before he spots the photographers rushing toward their table. Laurel isn't attempting to protect her relationship with Dana or her lunch date's marriage. Instead, her psychopathy screams, "Get out of my photo!" The flashes from a dozen cameras snap as they swarm. Under his breath, Randal says, "Meet you at your place," and disappears through the bar.

The bright, popping lights and a barrage of questions engulf the seemingly surprised star; she is in heaven as she picks up her flute and tosses back the last of her drink.

The frenzied group ushers the actress to the valet, where she waits for her car. The shouts stating how stunning she looks and how everyone is excited about her upcoming release bounce off the tall walls of the Yacht Club's foyer. Her shiny new ride pulls up, and the attendant opens the door as the diva smiles and waves before making her exit.

For the second time today, Randal is waiting on his afternoon entertainment. He is growing impatient as he scans the street, but this time he isn't the only one who lies in wait.

A few months ago, Dana sensed her husband's personality shift. But one heartbreaking clue finally got her attention; animation in the bedroom. He initiates sex more than usual, and this week he is playful. Randal is not playful.

Suspicion grew further when the unaccounted-for late evenings and several unexplained missing weekend hours became routine. So, a tracker installed on his car assisted in monitoring his whereabouts during the day. It wasn't a stretch to assume her now fun-loving husband acquired his new titillating tricks from his pals on the pole, as strip clubs surfaced as the revolting habit of choice until today. She assumed hookers were involved but couldn't stomach the thought of Randal actually screwing prostitutes. She never thought the day would come when she hoped her husband would be satisfied being the recipient of a lap dance somewhere.

From her office computer, Dana stares at a map. A small diagram in an open tab in the top left corner of her screen displays a little flashing red dot. She followed the car-shaped icon from the dealership to the Yacht Club. OK, his client is a member; that's completely justifiable. What is not defensible is the tiny red marker leaving the previous location and stopping in front of Laurel's house. "Why is he waiting with the engine still running outside her home?"

Ten minutes later, the dot continues to flash red. Fourteen minutes in, the red dot turns blue, which indicates the car is off. The spot on her screen stays blue for fifty-three minutes. Dana yells at her screen, "Fifty-three fucking minutes, with her, during the middle of the day!"

Randal stated she picked up her car from the lot yesterday. So, what is he doing at her place for almost an hour today?

Her husband went too far when he described the chaotic scene the actress caused in the showroom. Then, the whole bit about the special treatment, custom ordering a vehicle already in his possession.

Well, the joke is on me. He was waiting for her. He would only expect her now because Laurel was his lunch date.

The facts funnel in too fast, and Dana realizes she's talking aloud at her desk. Finally, after the agonizing fifty-three minutes, the tiny blue dot blinks red and doesn't turn blue again until the car stops at the dealership. The blue dot remained parked there the rest of the day.

After work, Randal walks through the door to the inviting scent of his wife's home cooking. In this retro 1950s scenario, his dutiful bride waits at the table, holding his martini, and asks about his day. "Busy," he says before making a beeline upstairs.

Ordinarily, before they dine, he changes his clothes or removes his shoes and tie. But showering before getting near his wife is another glaring modification to his routine.

Randal reappears after fifteen minutes, posing the same question about her day. A simple "OK" won't suffice today. She adds, "I'm working on a program that requires tracking; the project is time-consuming and mind-numbing. I'm developing an algorithm to eliminate a bug wreaking havoc in the system; this update will make daily activity monitoring obsolete. I implemented an experiment this week, which is working, but the full-scale plan still needs tweaking. I want it to be foolproof."

His remark is comical, "You're the smartest person in your office; if anyone can kill a pesky bug, you can."

He kisses the top of her head and sits across from her.

Randal fails to mention a car-related errand involving their close friend or his midday rendezvous during dinner. Pleased with the meal his wife prepared for him, he eats in silence while her plate remains untouched; she fears she won't be able to keep her food down. Temples throbbing, she stands complaining of a headache, leaving her lying husband sitting alone with the dirty dishes.

The image of the man she married and her friend intertwined in sheets repeats on the back of her eyelids. But then, a jolt sends her upright in bed, screaming, "Stop fucking!"

A second after the words leave her lips, her hand slaps across her mouth. Randal is downstairs; one would expect audible profanity would prompt an investigation. He didn't bother. She didn't want him to rise to the occasion, but the opportunity to send him away would've been somewhat gratifying.

Early in their marriage, suspicions were dismissed as paranoia. But his increase in action, however, pushed the limit. She overlooks his tasteless preference for bars, late nights, and later weekends. *For what? So you can sleep with hookers as well as my friend?*

The thought of separating isn't new. She revisits the idea often, especially after each drunken stupor, when the odious stench of dancing girls still lingers on his clothes. Those are the times when the thoughts of leaving him become the strongest.

She feels trapped and wonders if Randal also considers himself stuck. One would prefer he felt bound by suffocating financial obligations versus her, but it's hard to tell. Somehow lacking the ability to vacate the relationship softens the blow of her nonresponsive actions toward his deplorable behavior. But the rationalization of her husband acting a fool because she can't leave him is repulsive. Divorce, as tempting as it is, is not an option. Their two kids in college and a mortgage she can't afford alone put the brakes on a split.

Randal makes a decent salary, but she earns more. Together they live a comfortable life. But, alone, she won't be comfortable at all, and to add insult to injury, she may end up paying him alimony. There has to be a better way out.

FIVE

Book Club Meeting, May 9 —
A Piece of Cake **by Cupcake Brown**

The Kane house is a wonder spilling from the pages of Architectural Digest, exhibiting the classic traditional San Francisco bone structure mixed with high-end contemporary chic accents Kathryn refers to as transitional. The dwelling reflects her style while, at the same time, exudes comfort. A calm, welcoming aesthetic is crucial as the residence doubles as her workspace. The home setting is her niche; patients wanting a pretentious or sterile environment should pursue assistance in a conventional office building or clinic.

San Francisco is famous for the tall, thin houses lining the bay; Kathryn's spacious three-story walk-up exemplifies the typical stereotype. Located on the first floor is Kathryn's practice. Again, the surroundings maximize her patient's mental well-being. Her office offers a reception desk, a serene waiting area, and a small kitchenette for tea and sweets.

Recently the property underwent a massive remodel, converting several small rooms into an open-concept floorplan, with each level reflecting what one would expect: eclectic, pampered elegance. The kitchen's large center island provides ample workspace any baker would envy, yet some appliances remain unused. A spare bedroom, never enjoying the pleasure of hosting a single guest except for Joel, hides in the back of the flat, and a dining table completely set for no one flows into an antiseptic family room. A grasp on genuine hospitality seems to be missing from the upper floors. One may conclude that not much living happens in these rooms, regardless of the interior design.

The third level is the grand finale; the primary suite rivals a retreat at the Four Seasons. The décor is gorgeous but suffers from a "don't touch" showroom feel, indicating not much goes on in this room either. An adjoining spacious bath resembles a spa; the floor-to-ceiling marble boasts gold fixtures, incorporating a hint of old-world charm laced with modern romance.

Closets in the city are typically small, but Kathryn transformed an extra room into her private armoire. However, her wardrobe is a mystery, exclusive only to her. This little corner of the world is off-limits, even to her husband.

Book club gets underway as soon as Margo and Dana arrive. Olivia popped in early, hoping to help in the kitchen but, in reality, to get out of her office. She vacated her station alongside the last patient to avert being left alone with the dentist. A limousine drives up ten minutes later, allowing Laurel to make an entrance. A driver indicates she'll consume more than two glasses of wine this evening. She exits the car with true star power, but only after a large man in a black suit opens her door. A spiked heel slinks out first, followed by a pair of long legs; her dress is a vintage replica from the forties. Next, a hat balanced atop her head emerges as she raises her face to show off her bug-eye sunglasses. None of the women are fooled by the book tucked under her arm; it's only a prop. Chances are, she hasn't even opened it.

Kathryn invites everyone to go upstairs, excusing herself for a moment. While waiting, the women take in a new array of framed photos lining the top of a grand piano propped in the entry. The pictures on display are of friends in group settings, but most are candid scenes on holiday. One frame features her parents, yet it's hidden amongst photographs of Kathryn as a child, touting her talents as a competitive equestrian and avid sailor. There are some father-daughter snapshots, but none pair her with her mother. The few shots of Joel stand out as unnatural in their placement. Dana observes the horses, yachts, and swanky Euro vacations before sarcastically stating, "Life must've been rough for Kathryn as a kid."

Laurel interjects, "Well, if you call your sister falling off a cliff to her death and your mother killing herself 'rough,' then yes, you could say she had a rough childhood."

Dana's head swings around faster than her body can follow, releasing a resounding, "What?"

Flat in her delivery, Laurel relays the story. "Her mother took her own life right as we entered our preteens."

Shocked by the news, Dana snaps, "Why didn't anyone tell me this?"

Margo shrugs. "We assumed you knew."

Laurel keeps talking as if no one else is speaking, "Life came to a screeching halt during one of those so-called fancy European retreats somewhere in Switzerland, a family getaway, Dad, Mom, Kathryn, and Kara. Kara was Kathryn's little sister, a.k.a. the golden child. Their mother never missed an opportunity to make Kara the princess and Kathryn the odd girl out. Who witnessed the torment made no difference. Their mother would embarrass Kathryn and dote on Kara."

Dana interrupts, "Obviously, this is not proper book club banter but good Lord, one of you could have briefed me before dropping this news into casual conversation. All this time, I assumed her parents were deceased since she never mentions them. But how would I know her sister was dead? Hell, I didn't even know she had a sister. I thought Kathryn was an only child. The few scattered photographs propped on top of the piano are of her alone, and if it weren't for a couple of shots that included her parents, they, too, would be a mystery. I am so frustrated right now."

In a haunting voice, Laurel recaps the story, "Simply told, it was an outing that went terribly wrong; the family went for a hike, and the next thing you know, Kara went out too far on a ledge, slipped, and fell to her death.

"Their mother never recovered. She blamed Kathryn; she never came out and said those exact words, but she didn't need to. Her mother didn't hide her genuine disdain toward her oldest child. She took delight in her relentless ridicule. The persistent badgering ends each time with her mother asking, 'Why didn't you try to save your sister?' Kathryn, just a kid herself, couldn't have helped her sister. It was awful. Their mother killed herself six months later, sending Kathryn down a path of intense therapy. Her father ensured she had access to the best medical care available, often exposing her to risky trials still in the developmental phases. Several experiments and methods resulted in some bizarre remedies, but nothing worked. Sparing no expense, her dad called in every favor; renowned specialists from around the country flew in to reassure the traumatized child she was not to blame. Yet, all the attention intending to help scarred her. Something in her changed. People always described Kathryn as extreme; sometimes, if they wanted to be polite, they used the word 'extraordinary,' but this was different.

"The time dedicated to Kathryn's mental health amounted to thousands of hours and an undetermined amount of pro bono appointments. The retreat de jour passed off as 'camp' always seemed sketchy. Of course, everyone was suspicious of 'the camps,' but the exposure to all those doctors and sessions made an impression on Kathryn. I'm sure the clinical aspect of treatment played a significant factor in her becoming a shrink."

Dana presses for more, but Kathryn enters, toting a cheese tray, causing the inquiry to close prematurely. Still baffled, Dana puts a pin in this discussion for future investigation.

Olivia pours wine at the bar, thirsty to enter an altered state. "Tonight, I need sedation; my kids, those lovely little financial drains, drive me to drink. How will I survive with two of them in college in less than a year? And to add insult to my already frazzled being, I was denied the increase I requested today. Unfortunately, my employer and I are not on the same page."

Dr. Bob Flanagan is Olivia's handsy boss, who rides as close to that uncomfortable line as he can without crossing over. Convinced if he stops short, he can skirt a sexual harassment suit— undoubtedly a strategic maneuver to dodge a "me too" bullet to the wallet.

The inappropriate office conduct is wearing on Olivia.

"Can we meet this doctor? I want to turn the tables on him," inquires Dana.

"Is Dr. Bob married?" asks Laurel.

"Funny you should ask," Olivia giggles.

"Oh yes, he is married, and his wife, Cynthia, is a crazed fan.

Every time she comes into work, all she can talk about is 'Laurel Stanhope' and drills me to prove we're friends. Cynthia would lose her shit if the celebrity gods graced her with an introduction to the famous Laurel Stanhope. She questioned me about my footwear and choked when I told her my Jimmy Choo hand-me-downs belonged to the one and only you. To view the shoes on my feet didn't suffice. She made me take them off for closer inspection. They were too small to try on, so she resorted to petting them."

With no more convincing, Laurel settles the debate; we will invite "The Dr. and Cynthia Show" to our next party. Olivia cringes; although she would enjoy torturing her boss, feeding innocent Cynthia to the wolves didn't seem fair. With a refilled glass in hand, Olivia professes the need to keep her job until she can find a better one.

"I would like to share some exciting news." Margo proudly beams. "My son was invited to join a baseball program for the entire summer. A relocation and physical activity will keep him away from video games and his persistent father. Frank's sole purpose in life is to entice Tyler into his world of game development. I'm still trying to persuade my single-minded husband to get out of his la-z-boy and into a real job, but to no avail."

In a questionable intonation, Laurel adds, "I'm still waiting; Frank is supposed to bring me a new joystick. I texted him to come over, but the parts are on back order, and some other instrument is needed to upgrade my unit to revive the play in my game."

Laurel laughs but is the only person who finds her distasteful jokes funny. Margo ignores the innuendos and instructs her to keep calling.

"I don't call people repeatedly," barks Laurel. "How about you inform your husband that he must come over and service me to receive compensation."

Margo bites her lip to suppress her frustration as repulsion sets in for the others. Then, without skipping a beat, the diva babbles about electronics and how she can't manage a day without Siri or her iPhone updating her itinerary.

To change the subject, Kathryn extends an offer to Olivia, "I could use your assistance in my office if part-time work helps. I won't need someone full-time until later in the year, but I have a trip planned to visit France at the end of summer and would like someone to field calls while I'm gone."

Olivia is beside herself. "I'm in!"

Kathryn tells her excited new assistant she can start as soon as she likes. The hours are flexible, a couple of days a week, and she can work around her schedule at the dentist's office.

"Olivia, I hope you know how to take notes and make bullet points," cracks Laurel. "Kathryn, you can stop with your paper PowerPoint pages and turn over that tattered alligator binder you guard with your life."

Sensing that Kathryn isn't pleased by Laurel's observation or intentional jab, Olivia enthusiastically blurts out, "OK then, today is officially my first day as an employee of Dr. Kathryn Kane. I will advise Dr. Flanagan of the new terms of my employment first thing in the morning. And if he doesn't want to work with me on this, that's ok, I don't want to work with him either."

Dana sighs, "France sounds like a dream, I'm dying to go anywhere where I could be alone for a while."

Olivia concurs but adds, "I'd like to travel, but the only trip I'm taking is to the Bed, Bath, & Beyond to shop for dorm supplies. Did you know you can pick out your items locally and pick them up at the store near your college? No packing, no sending. It's genius. Oh God, this is my life."

"O," Dana says with sincerity. "Enjoy this time in your life. My two kids are in college, and you are right to be worried; I'm glad you're preparing yourself for the financial hurdle. But please take my advice and change your mindset. Don't focus so much on the money; it will work itself out. Instead, concentrate on the bigger picture, an empty nest! It's a thing, and it's a wonderful thing. Think this through; you will come home to a house in the same condition as when you left. Imagine no dishes in the sink, no underwear on the floor, and no locker room odors emanating from your son's room. Empty nesting is not overrated! And worth the price of tuition. I advise jumping on board with this way of thinking, adjusting your thought process, and keeping your sanity. The best part is that your kids are happy to see you when you visit. Now, that's what I call genius."

Margo chimes in, "Ladies, can we talk about the book? We read A *Piece of Cake* by Cupcake Brown; you should have finished it by now."

"I found this read disturbing," says Olivia.

"Listen on audiobooks, and you'll find the story fascinating," adds Laurel.

"My heart goes out to Cupcake; parents and adults who are supposed to care for kids can do a number on them." The words leave Dana's mouth before she can stop them. She hopes Kathryn doesn't think she is referencing her childhood situation. Dana's wine-soaked mind forgot the recent conversation; although it referenced Kathryn, it didn't include her; therefore, there was no reason for concern. Still nervous, Dana continues talking until Margo saves her.

"Ms. Brown went through a lot, more than any young person should. But the point is, after being dealt a lousy hand, being exposed to dreadful guidance, and making some bad decisions herself, she turned the tables. Despite her ordeal, Ms. Brown overcame the chaos and became a strong, accomplished woman. I admire her tenacity and self-awareness, not to mention that she's written a bestseller. She will go on to inspire other young people. Her accomplishments are huge, and she should be extremely proud."

Margo continues but switches the topic to the bookstore. "You avid readers would benefit from coming into the store; I have some spectacular collectibles which won't last long. A war currently rages between rival collectors to distinguish who owns the city's finest collection of literary works. So, I'm constantly searching to provide my competing customers with rare and unique editions. You can have the first peek if you like."

"OK, enough about books, let's talk about adventures," Margo says as she turns her attention to Kathryn. "Can I talk to you about France? Would you consider a tagalong for the Paris leg of your trip? A visit to les librairies (bookstores) to restock my French section would be one business venture I would like to take."

Of course, Kathryn would like nothing more than to travel with her friend, but this time away is about her, and she intends to take this excursion solo. With a slight strain in her voice, Kathryn asks if they can talk about this later.

This tone pricks Laurel's ear, "Ooh, that's a hard no, Margo."

To justify her response, Kathryn begins, "Please let me explain; I would love your company; however, I need to take this trip alone."

And without further ado, the bomb Kathryn's held a death grip on all night is ready for release. Her speech is loaded, the timing is right, and the bombshell drops.

"Joel and I have decided to divorce." A quick whiplash wave circles the room in Kathryn's direction.

"Stop before you all react." Kathryn puts up her hand like a crossing guard. "I want to explain without interruption. Our marriage ended long ago, and this decision is a mutual agreement. The love we share for one another isn't the issue; we don't want to be married to each other anymore. We are sincere in working together to maintain an amicable and straightforward split. Sympathy is not what we are after; no taking sides, no anger. The marital aspects of our union are over but not our lives together. We are OK; this is what we want. I need you to be OK too."

No one said a word, so Kathryn resumed talking, "I am aware I'm not getting out of here without divulging specifics, so here you go; these are the only details I will be sharing, and I will ask you not to pressure me for more.

"Again, how we've elected to handle our division is amicable, with no theatrics, and as respectfully as possible. We agreed to liquidate and divide everything equally. The house will go to me as our residence serves as my office, and I will keep my Range Rover."

Laurel interrupts, "Randal dropped off my new SUV the other day, and what a marvelous machine. Girls, if you are looking for a new set of wheels, I recommend this one."

The comment shakes Dana. *So why did he say she came to the dealership to pick it up?*

The activities following the delivery date make more sense now. Any lingering doubt is now gone. This "little" announcement may or may not have been intentional, but Laurel confirmed someone was lying.

The unexcused occasions are piling up, with Randal's whereabouts growing more suspect by the day. Additional confirmation only complicates the matter. The clarity she craves is brushed aside; what's the point?

Any questions would become a confrontation; she would be the instigator who provoked the scene. The predictable conclusion would be a well-rehearsed, drama-filled denial by the actress. So, rather than ask for an explanation, she remains silent for now but will keep a watchful eye while plotting airtight revenge on her theatrical friend.

While Dana digests her betrayal, Kathryn recites the scripted arrangement she and her soon-to-be ex will release as public knowledge. Pretense is not Kathryn's forte; she detests the obligation to divulge private information. Nevertheless, she says, "Joel will keep the townhouse in the city and his Tesla."

Another auto-related outburst from Laurel erupts before she can stop herself. A spokeswoman in a commercial couldn't sell the intricate details described or convey her love for the automobile any better. She spews this information while making a cuddly motion with her body.

The attention shifts to the actress, who expresses a pathetic, whiny "What?"

She follows up, "Cars are my passion, and I am fond of this particular model."

This statement isn't generally speaking; she's referring to a specific Tesla, Joel's. The tasteless comments hang in the air for far too long. The sting of the callous remark is visible on Kathryn's customarily stoic face. This hurtful conversation confirms that their dear friend's strange behavior isn't imaginary nor unique; Dana relaxes and smiles.

Margo redirects the focus to salvage what remains of the evening and their friendships by announcing she would love to introduce them to the 4MK thriller series by J.D. Barker. A psychological thriller that is a must-read. She also recommended buying all three books up front as purchasing the others is inevitable and will save her time. However, the next read will be, *Where the Crawdads Sing* by Delia Owens.

"The bookstore is supplying a copy of the book for this read. But I will ask you to return them to me when you finish. The crusade behind this philanthropic exercise is an opportunity for everyone to give back."

Margo explains her quest to start a reading club for women who want to partake but can't afford retail prices. "It's a community outreach program (hence the genre change) requiring little effort from the patrons, and anyone can contribute. My humble vision starts with a grassroots campaign. So, helping me spread the word to other clubs will, with some luck, bring customers into the shop to buy what they need from me. After reading their purchase, they return the books to the store. Then, we will redistribute the gently used titles to those who would otherwise not participate."

The "Reread Project" is a fabulous idea; too bad no one is listening to a word this charitable book master is saying.

The wheels in Laurel's head spin in simultaneous circles of delight and dismay. She fears Kathryn may know about her escapades with Joel. More confused than ever, Laurel wonders if she caused their breakup. The euphoria vanishes when the thought of their split being for her slaps her in the face. After all, half the fun is the chase, the thrill of the hunt, and the hiding in the shadows. Laurel does not intend to be in plain sight with her therapist/friend. The thought of a relationship with Joel outside the realm of sex therapy is repulsive.

Going on and on about what an idiot her husband is for letting her go isn't fooling anyone. With forced empathy, the actress insists she will no longer require his services, either.

Either? Is she kidding?

Such remarks only confirm that the other Dr. Kane provides more than licensed "services."

Adding, "To resume seeing Joel would betray their friendship," pushes everyone over the edge.

The other ladies aren't sure how to react; the hole Laurel is digging draws her closer to the abyss with every word she speaks.

Anyone still wearing blinders, refusing to believe the doctor and patient had previously or are currently participating in some unethical servicing, is now a believer. Kathryn would like to remove the knife from her own back and stab Laurel in the face with the sharp dagger but elects to keep her composure. The years of concealing her emotions while listening to others for a living are put into practice again; the world will only witness what she permits and nothing more. No one in the room can fathom her controlled yet twisted thoughts, nor could they comprehend what Kathryn is truly capable of. Not a clue.

The doctor, consummate professional, and strong woman no one ever took head-on accepts the challenge. Private humiliation is one thing, but belittling in an open forum won't be tolerated. Everyone detected the faux Freudian slips, each syllable dripping with malice, intentional and meant to inflict pain. Maintaining calm is crucial and somewhat debilitating, but she lets Laurel continue and hang herself with a verbal noose.

Attempting to divert the attention away from herself, Laurel extends an olive branch in Dana's direction.

"So, Dana, you said earlier you wanted some alone time. I will be on location on the weekend of May seventeenth to nineteenth. My house will be vacant if you want to stay, you're more than welcome. It will make for a nice little staycation if solitude is all you need. Come by tomorrow, and I'll give you a key and the codes for the alarm. I'll be gone two to three nights tops."

Grateful, Dana states, "This staycation couldn't have come at a more opportune time."

The shutters barring Dana's window of good fortune, just blew wide open.

Kathryn prepared a gourmet meal for this gathering, but the evening went so far south that the several bottles of Merlot on the table may not be enough to revive the night. Margo trails Kathryn into the kitchen.

"I'm sorry, Kat. Laurel is stirring the pot and trying to insert herself into the drama."

"Case in point. We don't want drama. I want this to be as easy for our friends as it is for Joel and me. We aren't upset, pathetic, or lonely; we want to avoid the predictable mess. Separation is what we want; to be apart is what we need. So please accept and respect our decision. Now for Christ's sake, can we talk about something else?"

Back in the living room, the conversation is slow to regain momentum. The topic of discussion slowly switches to the vintage plates and stemware Kathryn collected from antique stores around the city and abroad. The hodgepodge array of fine china and crystal is by design; the mismatched display is thoroughly planned. As it turns out, the eclectic oddities couldn't be more fitting for a night like tonight.

The dinnerware, irregular and unique in a strange way, reflects their friendships, every place setting tells a story, and each piece is prettier than the next. Each discovery generates enthusiasm, but with any accumulation, the time comes when every cherished collection verges on hoarding—time to thin the herd.

With too many place settings, Kathryn acknowledges that some housekeeping is in order. But, for now, the undesirable dinnerware will be reserved for Laurel's use only; she is sure to detect she is the only one with a chip.

Chips, so to speak, don't go unnoticed; she scrutinizes everything. For instance, what you're wearing can't be newer or nicer. To be caught wearing an inferior outfit will result in her personal shopper getting a workout as soon as she can separate herself from you. Likewise, your husband or boyfriend can't be more handsome or successful. This absurd conduct also applies to cars and homes, she'll compete for options, and imported furnishings can't come from a further away land. Laurel's pursuit of the best with the most isn't the worst part. The unsettling component is that she demands that you acknowledge the hierarchy. This lunacy is one of the main reasons she landed on a couch in the first place. Counseling, unfortunately, is not without its pitfalls.

For mental health care to be effective, one must be honest. Therefore, most appointments never went well, as that involves telling the truth, preferably the whole truth. Unfortunately, this part of reality will continue to be foreign forever. The number of couches the actress has unsuccessfully sought help from over the years is unknown. So, this time, she thought she would test the springs on the sofa belonging to her best friend's husband to gain perspective.

In the beginning, the treatment practice was ordinary. Laurel would talk, and Joel would listen, issue prescriptions, and repeat the process the following week. Session frequency increased to a minimum of twice a week toward the end. Yet, the billing doesn't accurately reflect the number of visits to the doctor's office. The statement includes appointments but does not include unscheduled pop-ins, which often occur depending on her mood or stress level. Several scenes would play out; Joel's job is determining which Laurel showed up for her appointment.

Each visit began customarily, but the predictable outcome went down a much less traditional path. The patient lies down, talks, and cries until the doctor hands her a tissue; she pulls him down on her, and the unconventional part of treatment commences. Sometimes she would come in and sit across from him, *Basic Instinct* style, and they didn't utter a word. One can assume they both fantasized about Sharon Stone the entire time.

How Laurel copes with Alan's death may be a prelude to a breakdown. Joel keeps in regular contact to make sure that doesn't happen. He monitors her environment and reinforces that her outward appearances resemble a normal grieving process. She isn't sad or showing any signs of loss to those closest to her and appears to be adjusting well. However, the world witnesses the star's bereavement; they pity the solemn woman, dressed in black, doing her best to deal with the horrible tragedy thrown her way.

Sleep, in Joel's expert opinion, is what is needed. "Just take some time off to rest and escape the media."

But Laurel will have none of that kind of talk. So, this is where the prescription comes in; the little helpers assist in getting the actress the rest she's fighting.

Their involvement is toxic on many levels, and he is diligently working on distancing himself from his fifty-minute girlfriend. His ultimate goal is to terminate their personal and doctor-patient partnership, but this has to be Laurel's doing, completely her idea. A woman scorn, a woman like Laurel Stanhope, would be the final straw in his relationship with his wife, not to mention the end of his career.

In their later sessions, Laurel wanted to talk about Curtis. Initially, Joel eagerly anticipated discussions involving her gentleman friend, never believing Curtis existed. Her imaginary suitors and sensational escapades were common, so he wrote off the fantasy stories as an attempt to make him jealous or hot, one of the two, perhaps both. The humiliation of meeting Curtis mimicked defibrillator paddles to the chest. Embarrassed, the doctor admits his insecurities got the best of him; Curtis is young, fit, and much more attractive. The aging actress's arm candy is the stereotypical boy toy; he is the perfect man until he speaks.

Laurel demonstrates a distinct pattern; when boredom creeps in or she fancies someone new, she kicks the current plaything to the curb, and that relationship, whatever it was, is over and done.

Her actions are unhealthy and unsafe, and as much as Joel would like to help his friend with her issues, he'll be relieved when he is no longer one of them.

The Kane marriage is beyond reconciliation as their lives stand today; any attempt to repair the damage would be insulting. Quickly and quietly conceding is in Joel's best interest; he can walk away unscathed by not contesting a divorce. Kathryn isn't taking him to the cleaners; she is more than reasonable; she just wants out. He will miss both women, but right now, his first concern is self-preservation. Laurel continues to book a few more appointments; again, Joel allows this for one reason; any termination must come from her. Sooner or later, everyone will learn that Kathryn initiated the breakup with Joel, leaving his mistress holding her leftovers. To Laurel, this equates to social suicide, tabloid gold if word leaks to the press. This inevitability didn't escape her, expediting the need to sever all ties with her therapist-turned-lover in a quiet manner.

SIX

Friday, May 10

The day following the disastrous book club meeting, Dana stopped by Laurel's to pick up the house keys for her staycation as instructed. But a few rules needed to be discussed before handing over the keys to the castle. Dana paid close attention as the home's inner workings were explained. Soon the discussion turned to the protection system protocol. Viewing the outdoor camera angles, Dana notes that no indoor monitoring exists before the tour concludes with a lecture on keeping the doors locked.

Laurel belabors, "Famous people must take extra precautions for their safety and well-being."

"Without question," replies Dana, fighting back an eye roll.

After accepting the key ring, Dana recites the security instructions and the alarm codes. Laurel stands bewildered; no notes were taken; her friend didn't write down a single word.

"Easy peasy." Dana smiles.

She reaffirms what a treat staying in such a beautiful home will be. Of course, the homeowner is pleased with her generous deed, as she views this sacrifice as helping the less fortunate.

"Madeline doesn't work weekends, but I will ensure she stocks the Sub-Zero; all you need is your toothbrush. The car service is confirmed; they will arrive next Friday, May seventeenth, at nine a.m., you're welcome any time after I'm gone."

Dana thanked Laurel again for her thoughtfulness, stating, "This opportunity is a blessing."

Oblivious to the meaning behind the words, she agrees her friend is lucky. Stopping at a coffee shop to catch her breath on her way to the office, Dana worries she may have come off as overly enthusiastic. The line for a café au lait is slow moving, which provides a moment to pick up the newspaper lying on the counter. And there splashed across the front page of the entertainment section is Laurel. The paparazzi interrupted her meal; two half-eaten lunches sat abandoned on the table behind the smiling diva. But being the gracious starlet she is, she stood to greet the press and answer questions about her upcoming film project.

The photo captured the backside of a man running away. A face shot of the escapee wasn't necessary; Dana recognized the suit as the clothing she dropped off and collected from the dry cleaners. The clear image of her husband's frozen stride identified him in black-and-white print for everyone, including her, to see. They didn't bother mentioning Laurel's insignificant lunch companion; they only wanted gossip and spoilers about her current gig.

Dana isn't sure how long she can keep up this friendly façade without her lying friend and cheating husband discovering she is on to them. Eliminating her "problem," however, will require more information. But, collected data can't reside on her computer or her phone. So, she will use her company computer to locate stores to shop for a new laptop and mobile device before next weekend's staycation.

A client presentation in Sacramento scheduled for Monday morning provides a safe distance between Dana and her equipment purchases. She plans to utilize the travel time to hatch her plan. Life without Randal is hard to imagine, and doing away with him may not be the correct answer. She struggles to bring herself to say the words to describe her intended action but falls short every time. A quick review of the available options only emphasizes her limitations and reinforces the solution. Leaving him amounts to nothing, and what will Laurel and Randal lose?

Her?

Those two stopped caring long ago. Dana sternly reminds herself that their lack of impulse control got them here and to stop rationalizing their behavior.

Surprised and almost impressed, Randal spent the past two days at the dealership and didn't venture too far from home. Dana busied herself cleaning the kids' rooms, a welcome distraction. Anything to keep herself away from the ladies, as they are sure to detect her mood swing. Those women can smell fear, and they can sniff out a scandal from miles away. So, as a precaution, Dana ditched her phone and didn't check her email or social media accounts Saturday or Sunday.

After an uneventful weekend filled with anxiety-laden chores, Monday morning finally shows up. Dana can't wait to get going; she started preparing for the trek to Sacramento last Friday morning immediately after picking up the newspaper featuring her cowardly husband exiting his lunch date. This commute will bring much-needed quiet time; the self-soothing therapy session begins when the car door closes.

A starting point is a challenge and much more complicated than expected. Frustration is becoming apparent in her daily routine, and she can't control her outbursts. Her calming technique didn't last long as she careened down the highway, yelling at herself to focus. The drive wasted precious time, accomplishing a mild headache and not much more. Painting on a brave face will require retouching her makeup before entering the building. The sound of her voice delivering reassuring messages of composure and professionalism repeats as if a motivational speaker is in her ear.

All the people contacted today must recall that she acted like her usual self; she can't come off as distracted or preoccupied. Remaining present during the meeting is a struggle, but she passes as alert and engaged. Nevertheless, she can't stop wondering if the people sitting next to her at the conference table can secretly transcribe her heinous thoughts.

The appointment ended with nothing notable to report. As anticipated, Dana's audience soon forgot her mundane presentation. Accepting that her fear is legitimate and that her emotions shouldn't be discounted helps maintain her composure as hysteria threatens to dismantle her. With the day's character alibi complete, she freed herself from the office; she can now commence with the activities she's been suppressing.

A Best Buy fifteen minutes away is the first stop. There she purchases a laptop, discreet spyware, and a burner phone. These products bought simultaneously and with cash will look suspicious, but it's unlikely to be traced back to her so far from home.

Reruns of *Law & Order* play in her head, reminding her that trouble follows when people hang on to the evidence. That is one mistake Dana won't make; all receipts and packaging will be disposed of in the dumpster behind the store. There won't be a paper trail connecting her to the merchandise, leaving nothing but the items for her to dispose of later.

The visual aspect of this little endeavor is her driving force. With Laurel's place wired, spying on them will be a click away. Buying cameras is simple enough; installing them in your friend's home is another issue. If Laurel's staycation promise holds, the plan is golden. Every item from this road trip will remain in a gym bag tucked in the car's trunk until Friday. Then, the three-step process is ready to be set in motion: watch, hear, and ruin them. Easy peasy.

SEVEN

Friday, May 17 — Staycation

Randal comes downstairs dressed sharply for the workday; he enters the kitchen to find his wife still in her pajamas. Dana informs him that she is taking the day off.

According to Randal, the money-making hours begin on Thursday morning and run through late Sunday night, so he isn't likely to miss her. But oddly, he didn't detect anything unusual, not the random day off or the flannel at 8:30 a.m. on a Friday.

That is until Dana says, "I'll be spending the night at Laurel's tonight; actually, I'll be gone a couple of nights. She will be away on location and asked if I wouldn't mind house-sitting. Some me time will provide a quiet opportunity to catch up on my reading and much-needed sleep."

"OK, until Sunday." He kisses her good-bye and, as usual, departs for the dealership.

Disappointed but not surprised, her husband didn't ask to join her. Dana did not want companionship but would have appreciated a simple inquiry into her weekend away. The benign "OK" is what you expect from a teenager attempting to conceal his excitement after being told the house is his for the next few days. However, not the response you anticipate from a spouse. Deflated, she refocuses her attention on the mission at hand.

With her bag already packed in the trunk of her car, changing her clothes is the only thing left to do once her husband leaves the house. Donut and coffee in hand, she checks all the hallmarks reserved for an undercover cop on a stakeout. From her unassuming parking space down the street from Laurel's house, the clock on the dash reads 8:55 a.m.

Relieved, talking aloud is still helpful, and as of late, her authoritative voice aloud is the only effective way to gain control of herself. Although, these single-sided debates and all-out arguments are now more common than she would like to admit. Today's conversation has gotten out of hand. "Calm the hell down" is the phrase presently bouncing off the windows inside the car. She chants, "Slow down; you have the house all weekend, RELAX! You planned your work; now work your plan."

A town car arrives on schedule at 8:59; a young man in a black suit gets out, knocks on Laurel's door, and waits patiently on the stoop. Lord, she'd astonish a royal with her travel ensemble; the hat, sunglasses, sheath dress, coordinating coat, and handbag. The spitting image of the 1950s movie icon emerges into the sunlight, minus Ms. Hepburn's personality and social graces.

The man cautiously tucks Laurel into the backseat before loading her luggage. It will take him a moment to pack the twin Louis Vuitton suitcases, a matching train case, and a garment bag into the trunk. The sidewalk display depicts the rank of Marilyn Monroe on holiday rather than a B-lister off on a three-day stint in Los Angeles. A sigh of relief escapes Dana's chest as the black sedan drives away from the curb. To ensure Laurel won't notice her stalking the house, she positioned herself in the passenger seat while she waited. A forced time delay, so she won't jump the gun and leave her hiding spot before the limo is out of sight.

Now in the driveway, the clock reads 9:05; nervous but excited, she opens the door to the beautiful empty estate. Wishful daydreams play in her head as she absorbs her surroundings. A colossal wave of envy gets the better of her when she surveys all the endless amenities, none of which exist in her home. But she reminds herself that eliciting this property was for one reason only, and until that task is complete, the relaxation staycation is on hold. The mission manages its way back to the forefront when her overnight bag hits the floor, and the purpose of why she is standing in the foyer becomes all too real.

A thorough sweep of the perimeter is paramount before getting settled. First, she takes a leisurely walk around the house with a bug detector in her pocket. One can't be too careful, considering the occupant's constant paranoia. Recorders are tiny nowadays; one can hide a lens almost anywhere. So, Dana surveys the house as she may not be the only voyeur present. Nothing registers on the first pass. She is looking for any microphone or video recorder installed before her visit while hunting for a place to conceal her devices.

The upstairs being videotaped makes her stomach turn; her imagination in this department will be plenty. Any visual will be hard to watch; seeing her husband enter the house will be devastating. But she can't think about that now; she needs to concentrate. The miniature spy cam in her hand must be undetectable, positioned for removal without being apparent when the time comes. This process is daunting yet vital; whether seeing and hearing firsthand brings any peace of mind doesn't matter. Respite will only come after ensuring the inevitable punishment fits the current crime.

After scouring the house several times, she is confident that no other eyes or ears lurk besides what she intends to plant. One more view of the security footage monitoring the outside to ensure no one catches her searching the house. The system used is child's play for someone with Dana's technical skills; she can easily manipulate the programs.

All passwords and the alarm code were confirmed when Laurel surrendered her house keys. After logging in, each camera's ID is buried in the internet settings. If Laurel is smart enough to check what is running on her system, only her devices will be listed; all the new equipment will remain in the shadows.

The newly purchased laptop shines bright as the screen comes to life. She envisions herself as a female Jason Bourne, and the suspense races as she swiftly connects the two systems. OK, the action hero is a stretch but exhilarating, nonetheless. A device test reveals a clear view of the living room, kitchen, and dining space. The first spying eye rests on top of a framed work of art. Thoughts of poking a hole in the canvas crossed her mind. However, the unit would be too difficult to retrieve later. The thin black devices are sure to go unnoticed. No one ever looks up; people are like deer in this respect. They look around, not up, the same reason hunters perch themselves in the trees. The unsuspecting animal walks under the hunter without knowing they're being hunted. Here, the clueless people will walk under the cameras, not realizing they, too, are being stalked. The second spying eye, strategically placed on a shelf in the den, captures the entire room and the entry. The battery charge in each unit set should last weeks, so no wires or electricity are required.

Acknowledging that her agenda goes beyond an obsessive fantasy is a continuous struggle. A boisterous battle rages between an angel on her right shoulder wanting to rethink the course of action while the devil on the left is gung-ho; the discussion echoes in the empty rooms.

Our life is OK.

Would I like more?

Of course, I would, but we must consider our children who must finish college. Then there is the financial aid and guidance necessary to set their lives on a positive path to their futures. All the costs, financial and otherwise, needed to be evaluated before you decided to change your lifestyle.

And for the love of all things holy, why Laurel?

Convenience?

For how long?

How long have you been sleeping with my friend?

Unfortunately, those questions, and many others, will never be answered.

Defeated, she says, "You two are being monitored now, and I will get the verification needed to greenlight my operation."

She glances over her right shoulder to brush the rational angel to the floor. A cork pops on what one can only assume is a pricey bottle of champagne. This luxury will soothe her nerves enough to start the project. Early morning light illuminates the kitchen; therefore, adding orange juice to the bubbles seems appropriate. A devilish smile erases all concerns of tainting a glass with OJ as criminal. Further justifying her actions, she tells the bubbles she counted several more where they came from, so spoiling one bottle won't matter.

"Why can't leaving you be easier, Randal?" says the wary wife to her crystal flute filled with streaming bubbles. "Sorry, not possible. No, a big fat NO! Divorce is out."

Little comments under her breath squeak out as she fills one of the monogrammed ice buckets with frozen shards to keep her liquid courage cold for the rest of the morning. She continues her rant, her voice escalating with each sip, "I can't imagine having to pay you alimony. And what consequences will you suffer? I'm guessing you would use my money to take that snob out to dine at five-star restaurants, where I presume you will be showering her with lavish gifts. You don't take me on dates, and where are my presents? Let me guess, the privilege of preparing your dinner and doing your laundry is rewarding enough. Best of luck getting Laurel to do your bidding, sweetheart. You are such an idiot; you can't afford her. Funny, I can no longer afford you. So, we will be making other arrangements for you, my love. How and with or without your side piece is the dilemma."

In her tormented state, she convinced herself their entanglement had been long-term, but the actual longevity of their union is a mystery. Patience is the frustrating aspect and the key to gathering the incriminating evidence needed. Her gut, or the devil on her left shoulder, tells her to sit tight as there is more to discover. *Welcome to your latest role, Laurel; you are playing a fancy fish in a fancy bowl for an audience of one, me!*

With a grin, Dana toasts her endeavor.

Tired after her weekend in Los Angeles, Laurel returns to an empty house late Sunday night. The place is spotless, with a proper thank-you note on the kitchen counter. The drained remains of her host's beloved bubbles stacked in the trash are the only indication anyone stayed in the house.

Monday morning can't arrive soon enough for Dana. The anticipation of viewing her handy work from the safety of her office is almost unbearable. Her reluctance to use the new laptop in front of Randal forces her to wait. However, her cautiousness in this area may be futile; if all goes well, he will take all knowledge of this to his grave.

EIGHT

Tuesday, May 21, 10:00 a.m. — Eric Harper's Office

When dealing with Ms. Stanhope, it would be fair to say that fashionable and late are expected; however, others must be punctual. Eric's receptionist, Lilli, greets their new client with a cheerful salutation, offering coffee or tea while respectfully conveying that she enjoys the actress's movies. Without responding to the compliment, Laurel sets her purse on the chair, and while removing her gloves, she tells Lilli she would like a "grandé vanilla latte with nonfat milk, extra hot."

Lilli excuses herself, saying she will alert Mr. Harper of her arrival. Laurel inserts, "And is waiting."

The door flings open as Lilli bursts into her boss's office without knocking and spits out, "*She's here.*"

Then, with an extended hand, she says, "I need to run down the street to Starbucks to fill 'Her Highness's coffee request."

With a grin, Eric stands and reaches into his pocket, pulling out a twenty-dollar bill; the frenzied receptionist grabs the cash, ripping it from his grip, and runs out of the office.

He is left to retrieve his friend from the lobby himself; airy cheek kisses followed by obligatory pleasantries start the morning meeting on the right foot. The purpose of this consultation is to review the star's current and future financial situation in hopes of bringing her on as a client. Laurel didn't disappoint, bringing a thumb drive containing institution names, account numbers, and dollar figures.

Upon taking her seat, Laurel begins complaining that everywhere she goes, an uproar follows. She is stern in her reminder to him that she is used to overzealous fans, but one would expect an office environment to be more professional. Eric retracts his previous thought about starting right, as this morning has taken a sharp left.

Intimidation is this woman's forte, drama her passion, voicing displeasure her right, well, if you ask her. To state "everyone" in the office pestered her to the point of complaint is absurd. One must first consider that "everyone" equates to Lilli, who, by the way, is terrified. Eric reassures his friend that he will talk with his staff about harassing the clients as he takes his seat across the desk. Again, he extends his services regarding Alan's affairs if she needs him.

An hour passes; the meeting is painless so far and quite productive. The portfolio is sizable, and the paperwork indicates she is in line to gain millions more. Eric understands working with Laurel will include challenges, but this arrangement will be a win for them both in the long run. After careful consideration, she is pleased with the recommendations to maintain and grow her investments.

Wanting to make their business partnership official, she requests that he take over her assets. Laurel then indicated she would notify her current adviser of the change and inform them her new consultant would be in contact to collect whatever information and files he requires. Lilli is the only one who disapproves of this new arrangement; after she delivers the coffee requested, she doesn't come out of hiding until the car service hauling their new client pulls away from the curb.

NINE

Saturday Morning, May 25

The day is shaping up beautifully, although the sun won't burn through the foggy marine layer for at least another hour. Olivia and Eric are shuffling back and forth between whatever sporting events their kids are into these days. They only have a few precious childhood years left, so they embrace the chaos and enjoy every second of watching their kids play.

Margo is hustling about doing housework before heading to the bookstore. Saturdays are the best days, the store is abuzz with families, and kid-friendly activities to occupy the children are ready. Of course, whatever organized fun will feature a book the children will want to add to their private collection. The young readers are encouraged to keep their favorite treasures but recycle the ones they've outgrown, to share the adventures of reading with others.

An incentive chart hangs on the wall listing the titles recycled by each child's name.

The parents appreciate contributing to community pride while offering a learning experience for their children, cleverly disguised as bragging rights.

To be truthful, those moms want a couple of kid-less hours during the week to drink free coffee and sit around with other grown-ups discussing adult topics without being interrupted. Then they justify their guilty pleasure by treating the kids to an educational playdate on Saturday. This part of her world is fulfilling and restores some joy in the shopkeeper's otherwise lackluster life. Frank, King Lusterless, enjoys his "Margo-made" snacks and is busy typing away doing whatever he does on his computer. Porn surfing is the likely guess.

Laurel is pouring herself a mimosa as Madeline won't show her face on a weekend unless given advanced notice of a change. Almond croissants and plenty of fresh-squeezed orange juice were pre-made, so her majesty is adequately nourished in the housekeeper's absence. Alone in her kitchen, casually sipping from her flute, she contemplates her day. With no plans and no one to go shopping with, the internet will pacify her for now. The first click reveals a gorgeous pair of Prada sling-backs. Instantly declaring this item a must-have purchase, she clicks the "Reserve for In-Store Pickup" button. Next, a message is sent to her personal shopper at Neiman Marcus to make an appointment for the afternoon. A fitting area will be reserved to try on her new leather friends in private. She considers this her preferred method of boosting the economy. Plus, upscale shoppers receive champagne if requested. The next couple of hours are allocated to a camera-ready appearance; looking beautiful doesn't just happen. Laurel takes her mimosa to her dressing room and selects what the world gets the privilege of viewing today. After debating with herself over Gucci *or* Gucci, both black, she chooses a dress and orders a car service.

Kathryn, only a few blocks away, spends the lazy morning sifting through old photos. But rather than cherish the mementos; she tosses what some would consider the last of her family's memories into the trash. If the goal is to make her house less intimate, if that's possible, she's succeeding. Even the framed pictures on top of the piano appear staged. Add some fresh-baked chocolate chip cookies and a real estate agent to the scene, and one would almost expect an open house to commence.

As usual, Randal is front and center at his dealership on a Saturday. Dana will use her husband's predictable routine to her advantage; she takes this opportunity to scan all the prior alerts from Laurel's devices back to the start of this endeavor. The footage is boring but reveals Frank came by earlier in the week to set up the new gaming system. She will keep her eye on him; sure, he is doomed to go down the same lurid path as Randal. Shockingly, the installation is uneventful. Perhaps she is wrong; maybe Laurel's feeling generous by giving Curtis a new toy and providing employment for her jobless friend. A moment of guilt for thinking the worst soon vanishes when Frank attempts to demonstrate how the console works, and the snake makes her move.

"This woman is relentless," Dana shouts to herself.

The attack on the unsuspecting victim is calculated; you can almost predict the strike. She didn't waste much time before she pounced, either. Yet surprisingly, Frank stops her, but not before she shoves her tongue down his throat. The slithering seductress has Frank by the balls, not figuratively. The crotch grab eliminates any ambiguity on her part, underscoring her objective. Call it a backup maneuver in case her blatant tonsillectomy wasn't clear enough.

Wait a minute! Rewind, replay. "Was that a rejection?"

Clear as day. This player forfeits the game by hitting the pause button. The shock on this queen's face proves she didn't anticipate being denied or humiliated by the likes of a pawn. Dana watches the screen intently; what she has recorded is priceless and oh-so-satisfying, so much so that she replays the encounter on a loop for a while before moving on. But not before reserving a copy of this section of the tape for future use.

Well, this is unfamiliar territory for the prima donna. However, Frank did take his time to react, letting the inappropriate behavior linger a bit before shutting her down. In his defense, she did catch him off guard, and if you consider he is a bit slow on the uptake in general, his lag time is justified. Unsure of his words, he tells her, "I would like nothing more than to be with you, but we can't do this. I'm going to go now before I change my mind."

Wow, Frank! No one would have bet on you to be the last man standing with the bag of morals. Bravo, Frank, bravo.

Few things are more gratifying than witnessing the self-righteous face humiliation, but the daydreaming must stop; Dana needs to concentrate. Knowing Randal isn't the only target gives her more incentive than ever to stop their crazed friend. A legitimate strategy is the only thing standing in the way. Unable to control her anger Dana creates slow and merciless end-of-life scenarios for her husband and friend before deciding jail would be the ultimate revenge. But how to get them there is the issue. Regretfully you can't incarcerate someone for being a slut. And the law doesn't view a depraved woman's life choices as a punishable offense.

On the other hand, Randal is just as guilty, but not for anything that would land him in the slammer. Imprisonment also leaves the ability to one day be released. He would still win, punished by time served, but half of their assets would await him. A criminal record would follow the condemned man, leaving him to live a simple life, but it's the same lifestyle afforded her—a vicious circle for sure.

Other alternatives rage through the defeated wife's brain, but each scheme is seemingly more ridiculous than the next. And every plan is accompanied by pitfalls. An anonymous tip to the media would surely do some social damage but could also backfire. Her husband would be labeled a loser. In contrast, his mistress would relish the unwarranted attention, not embarrassed or disgraced. The script would flip as always, and she is once again the victim, not the enemy. Headlines would read, "Starlet Used by People Closest to Her in Her Time of Need Following the Tragic Death of Her Husband." These lines are the few of many guaranteed to surface. And for everyone's sake, stop referring to the dead man as "her husband." *Alan! The dead man's name is Alan!*

All the lies swirling around the actress somehow transform into her truths. A pity party will soon ensue, and everyone is welcome; this is where she convinces everyone that she is the one wronged yet again. But, of course, this only reinforces that the actress is always the casualty or the hero but never the villain.

Unsavory ethics are a way of life. As this is her muse, there won't be any sleepless nights wasted obsessing over etiquette to justify her conduct. Thoughts like these only validate the crusade to destroy or, at the very least, expose the real Laurel Stanhope.

Now is the time to move from fantasy to reality; Dana is determined to make strides to manifest her imaginary storyline from the infancy stage toward something executable. She reviews the intelligence gathered ad nauseam and verifies who is doing what with whom. However, this is where the project comes to a screeching halt. Talking to herself isn't helping. It only emphasizes the true means to an end. The end was to get out of her situation, but the playing field expanded. Too many players have been added, and now this is a monumental task with no acceptable outcome. *Two people who are supposed to love me have me contemplating, worse, truly considering the unthinkable. Am I really capable of taking someone's life?*

Murder isn't something Dana ever entertained; she isn't a murderer. Well, not yet, anyway. Switching gears, she focuses on the process, working things out, engineering, after all, is her strong suit. No longer allowing her brilliance to stop when things get messy, she begins. *Every methodical element must be plotted, rehearsed, and performed with precision. Mistakes are how you get caught. Stupid, careless, fixable errors are the missed details that will land me behind bars.*

Wouldn't that be ironic? Randal dies, I go to the clink, and our unscathed friend lives happily ever after. That cannot happen; it will not happen!

TEN

Eric's Follow-Up Call

Anxious to jump-start her week, Laurel opens her email early Monday morning to find she still hasn't received the expected insurance payout. The claims adjuster refusing to return her calls only makes matters worse, magnifying the sourness in her mood. Finally, in her frustration, she decides Eric should take care of this and picks up the phone.

"Can we meet? I want to go over the life policy one more time. The company is giving me the run-around, so I want you to pry an estimated payment date out of them."

Cue the eye roll as he thinks, *here we go,* but also reminds himself of her value. "Sure, when do you want to come in," asks Eric.

The pertinent question is used to her advantage as she redirects who is going where. "To avoid running the risk of another unpleasant incident in your office, can you come to the house?"

Much to his dismay, he concedes to meet at her home later that afternoon.

Eric elects to tell Lilli he has some work to attend to outside the office and won't be back for the remainder of the day. Tact in place of the truth is cowardly, yes, but sparing Lilli's feelings is the kind thing to do. More accurately, the spineless approach eliminates any conflict or backlash his assistant is sure to inflict on him even though he is in charge.

As he knocks on Laurel's door, a shiver runs down his spine; this visit is overkill, but managing her portfolio will move them closer to his wife vacating the job she finds inappropriate. Some fuck-you money would come in handy right now, freeing them so neither would be obligated to work for idiots anymore. The thought of buying a lotto ticket and hoping for the best is pathetic, yet winning is a reoccurring dream these days.

Madeline opens the front door on the first ring, ushering Eric into the foyer before excusing herself for the day. Laurel chirps from the living room, "Come in here, come on, where we can relax."

Laurel's consonants slur together as she speaks. A charcuterie tray displayed in the center of the room is an odd offering for a quick late-afternoon discussion. Before taking a seat, he asks why there's a fire burning in the fireplace.

The day is overcast but not flaming-hearth worthy.

"I'm setting the mood."

OK, the third red flag is waving. Finding the alcohol-induced fireside happy hour strange, he doesn't wait for a rehearsed rebuttal and does his best to ignore her antics. Attempts to dive straight into the finance issue are interrupted by a glass of Chardonnay passed to him before he can decline. Attached to the stemmed crystal are the words, "I like a little buzz when reviewing my assets."

Wine spilled on the floor is ignored as she takes her place beside

Eric on the couch, intentionally encroaching on this tentative man's personal space. Without skipping a beat, he sets his glass on the table, using the reach to his advantage, and slides away. Sitting oddly frozen, he calculates the striking range as his friend entertains herself with this bizarre game of cat and mouse. The open folder in his lap closes as his client's stare pierces through him. Next, he senses her hand slipping under the file and up the inside of his leg. He leaps to his feet without hesitation, letting the paperwork fall to the floor. Standing with his crotch in her face, Laurel glances upward and smiles. The seductive smirk dissipates when it dawns on her; he didn't rise as a matter of convenience; he's offended.

Humiliated, he shakes while berating his friend/client for her inappropriate advance, stating he is no longer interested in her assets. The papers spread over the carpet crinkle under Eric's footsteps; he grabs his briefcase and shows himself out.

On the drive home, the realization of what Olivia endures floods his thoughts—disgusted and brokenhearted as he acknowledges the scenario his wife anticipates daily. In the past, Olivia did complain about Dr. Bob. So much so that her words became routine, disregarding her discomfort and not understanding how degrading being preyed upon affects you. He is sick as he recalls many conversations where he pressured her to stay in a situation she thought she couldn't change or escape. Anger takes over, but not at the actress or the dentist; he is mad at himself. Not taking the time to listen was one thing, but more importantly, not reacting or acknowledging his wife's dilemma was unacceptable. Olivia's world is about to become much more manageable. He will no longer turn a blind eye, wanting his wife to "get over it."

A ping-pong match rages out of control in Eric's head. He

wished his commute lasted longer. But he's home already, parked in his driveway, unable to decide between an apology or a reenactment of the day's events. Either way, it's time to face the music. Upon entering the house, Olivia senses trouble. Tears well in his eyes as he looks at her; holding her tightly, he begins a heartfelt confession.

Olivia listens to her visibly shaken husband as he recounts his afternoon with his newest client. She wants to scream at him but accepts his apologetic remorse for not taking a stance on harassment until the tables turn. There's something to be said about not responding with an indignant "I told you so."

Sometimes the silence of calm acceptance, letting the emotion sink in, is more effective.

After what can be called a contemplative meal, while they put the dishes away, Olivia says she will handle this crisis and tells Eric exactly how this will play out.

Intrigued by his wife's commanding lecture mode, he listens as she dictates, "You will keep Laurel as your client."

"She won't keep me as her adviser, not now."

"Let me finish. We need her account as much as she needs you to remain silent. It would be a shame but media gold to publish her drunken indiscretion, not to mention the perfect time to declare our true thoughts regarding Alan's death. Remember, she is in the middle of a project and can't afford a negative scandal right now. I will transition to Kathryn's office by the end of the year, quitting Dr. Bob once and for all."

Instructions spew from Olivia, who directs, "You will only meet Laurel in your office during regular business hours, and Lilli is to be present at all times. Now, sit down; I need to make a call."

Impressed and somewhat frightened, he follows her orders, wondering what will happen as his petite little firecracker of a wife whips out her phone.

The phone rings, and Laurel reads Olivia's name in the caller

ID. She lets a few seconds pass while deciding whether or not to answer the phone. Then, not having the time or the inclination to listen to what is sure to be a whining reprimand, she stalls.

Deciding to get it over with, she picks up. "Hello, Olivia."

The droll salutation barely leaves her lips before Olivia cuts her off, "After discussing the afternoon's activity with my husband, we believe the best course of action going forward would be if Eric continued as your financial planner. However, you are only permitted to contact my husband at his office during normal business hours for all future business transactions. Write this down; I don't want any misunderstandings. After all, you can't just trust anyone with your finances and image. Perception is essential, don't you agree?"

Taken aback by her friend's audacity, the actress announces that "she" decided this arrangement is acceptable and convenient. Furthermore, she doesn't want the hassle of shopping for a new agent.

Oh, but wait, Olivia is far from finished. After all, if you've got the tiger by the tail, you might as well enjoy the ride.

"You also stand to collect millions from Alan's settlement, correct?"

Laurel cautiously answers, "Yes."

"Well, share your wisdom, be considerate with a caring gesture, won't you? You will recommend to our group of friends the benefits of life insurance. One can't deny the timing is perfect, right?"

Olivia gives a reassuring nod to Eric before boldly stepping out on a limb that is likely to snap along with their friend. "Also, that extensive contingency of wealthy friends you're always carrying on about, we will need to talk to them. I'm sure they too, could benefit from the professional services of your trusted money management team. So, add them to the to-do list.

"Let's start with a casual impromptu conversation at our next book club meeting to enlist our close friends first. We can use this gathering as a rehearsal. Say you've arranged a little seminar for them. Something you are passionate about and consider important enough to discuss. Acknowledge that some are uncomfortable with the topic, so you found a way to breach the delicate subject in a casual environment. But, again, you're kindly opening the lines of communication, so your dear friends are covered with the protection they may be unaware they need. Am I making myself clear?

"The last item we need to nail down is when you will be hosting a dinner party with your well-to-do friends so you can introduce them to Eric. Would you please invite guests with actual money?

"Then, you can give them the performance of a lifetime. Oscar-worthy, perhaps. Check your calendar and confirm by Monday."

Without waiting for a response, Olivia sends a kiss over the line, then presses the button ending their call. Of course, the dramatic slamming of the phone is much more rewarding but difficult to do with a cellular device. Laurel is left with a dial tone buzzing in her ear. A shell-shocked Eric beams with pride as he stares at his wife. The dominance exhibited is scandalous yet a welcomed surprise. His children's sweet, passive mother just made Laurel Stanhope her bitch.

The words "crybaby" pass the diva's lips, yet she remains unfazed by the encounter. Instead, she picks up her wine glass, flips open her laptop, and trolls Siren, an exclusive dating app, for her next conquest. No one of interest pops up while scrolling, but her phone vibrates, and a text notification flashes across her screen.

"I picked up a game you and Curtis may like, buzz me when you are available; I'll drop by, Frank."

A new stimulant erased any negativity lingering from earlier this afternoon.

"Thank you, Frank, for the stress relief," says Laurel.

She switches gears as intriguing new images of Frank tickle her fancy. Frank's initial rejection is a fantasy, and the challenge takes this particular game to a new level.

One can assume Frank knows his way around the sheets, and she suspects an experience with Eric would be similar to throwing down a virgin. Yet the thrill of having your hand slapped for attempting to take something that doesn't belong to you is intoxicating.

Further, amusing herself with thoughts of teaching her finance guy new tricks to take home, she giggles, replacing the fantasy with provocative visions of her pending playmate.

ELEVEN

Book Club Meeting —
***Where the Crawdads Sing* by Delia Owen**

Tonight, Olivia takes her turn as the book club host. It's only been a few days since her run-in with Laurel, but if the actress sticks to the script, the evening should be a success. Dinner, dessert, and lots of wine are customary at these shindigs, with the discussion landing on the read sooner or later. Homemade tortilla soup and lemon blueberry cake are on the menu, all from scratch, all made with love, despite the incident with Eric.

There is a crowd-pleasing display made out of books artfully arranged down the center of the dining table to create the most adorable centerpiece, similar to something showcased on Pinterest. *Thank you, Dana, for cutting off Laurel before she inflicted her opinion on their host's creativity. The diva has no appreciation for the imagination or effort necessary to accomplish such a clever design. How can a woman with so much class be so inept when it comes to charm?*

All the other women conceded to being outdone. Laurel will forgive Dana for her rude interruption when the sound of praise floats her way. Gratitude and heartfelt thanks for using the actress's beautiful home grant forgiveness. Adding how relaxed she is after the experience of lounging in the lap of luxury wins her back into Laurel's good graces.

Margo chimes in with, "We will be checking out the baseball camp next weekend; we'll only be gone for one night, but I need someone to feed and walk the dog. So, if you are interested in a mini staycation, you are welcome to stay at our house. You would be helping me out."

"I'm available," says Dana, jumping at the opportunity.

"Wonderful, let's sort out the details later," adds Margo.

Sounds emanating from Laurel's cell phone are relentless. The constant beeping is annoying; fifteen to twenty message alerts ring out before they are declared intolerable. Kathryn instructs her to answer the damn thing or turn it off. Laurel pulls out her cell and taps violently at the screen. Dana comments, "You should really use a better password than the number one repeatedly."

Margo snidely remarks, "We are all here, so what is so urgent?"

Without missing a beat, the star responds, "Siren dates."

Margo bursts, "You put yourself on a dating app? Are you crazy?"

"Yes and no, I created a fake profile. I didn't use my real name or image. Instead, I uploaded a picture of my sister. You wouldn't believe the number of views; I'm thrilled with the comments saying she resembles me. My screen name is Candice Moore; I didn't reveal too much, but I did insist on excitement, no commitments, must love yachts, and seasickness is a deal-breaker. Full disclosure, this is how Curtis and I found each other; he is also a water enthusiast."

"Wait, I thought you met Curtis on a project?" inquires Dana.

"Well, he became a project, hence the name of our relationship, but we hooked up online. He makes for fantastic arm candy but not much else."

Margo whispers to Kathryn, "Do you find her behavior unbecoming?"

Kathryn can only respond with, "Doesn't everyone."

They giggle at the thought of Laurel's sister finding out her photo generates hits on Siren.

Dana makes a mental note of all the freely divulged data, facts about her, and personal details about Curtis—an intellectual treasure trove to be analyzed and used against her later.

Margo blurts, "All right, back to why we are here. We cut the month short by a week, so did everyone have a chance to finish the book?"

The question leaves an opening for Laurel to contribute to the conversation; she jumps in straight away with her excuse, abusing the time factor as her get-out-of-jail-free card, but not before asking, "What's the title again?"

Naturally, no one appreciates the disregard in her stab at humor. Dana continues, "Where the Crawdads Sing was a slow burn in the beginning for me, but I enjoyed the adventure."

"Listen to the audiobook; this one will entertain you," states Olivia, who says she admired the character's connection to nature, declaring the book worthy of a listen or read.

Amused by the sweet revenge, Margo also rates this month's novel with a five-star review.

Laurel sighs. "I should lie and say I opened the book, but this one went unread like all the others. Some of us interpret the written word for work; you might say it's an occupational hazard. So, more reading is just more time-consuming reading."

"Oh, right, I forgot; you're only here for the alcohol," giggles Margo.

"Girls," Laurel whines, "we're stagnating, and I'm bored; we drink and discuss stories, go to lunches and dinners. Don't you crave a thrill, something fun, something adventurous?

"Come on," she pleads. "We're in a rut; I can only go on so many meaningless hookups and subject myself to a limited number of jaunts with a joystick. But I have to tell you, gaming is my new guilty pleasure. I now understand how playing video games can become habit-forming."

Dana detects something sinister in the delivery of Laurel's last line. Something sinister, indeed.

The sarcasm drips from Olivia's words as she fails to disguise her anger toward Laurel. "What type of risky escapade do you suggest? Mountain climbing, motorcycles, or perhaps scuba?"

"Yes, like scuba, something out of our comfort zone," insists Laurel.

Margo picks up on the bicker in Olivia's suggestion and diverts the group's focus by interjecting, "So, with diving in mind, our next read should be *Something in the Water* by Catherine Steadman."

"Do you mean Catherine Steadman, the actress?" Laurel questions. "She's a writer? How did this news escape me? Add her story to the lineup. I like to support my friends on their projects outside of acting."

"So, you two grab lunch together?" asks Margo.

"Well, I wouldn't say we're intimate, but acquaintances."

Everyone looks at the actress, but no one speaks.

"Fine, we attended the same function. All right, I've never spoken to the woman," admits Laurel. "Nevertheless, I would like to read her book."

Dana pulls out her phone and searches Goodreads for reviews.

"She is receiving positive feedback, five stars, and no one gets eaten by a shark. You're in luck, Laurel; you can participate this time without committing to reading. You will be pleased to learn that Ms. Steadman is not only the author but also the narrator of the audiobook. Her accent will be a bonus."

"Now you're talking," says Laurel.

Everyone retreats to the living room for a slice of cake when Laurel announces she's set up a little surprise. Enter Eric. Olivia gives him an encouraging shove to the middle of the room. This sneaky technique is out of his comfort zone; he doesn't like the shifty sales guy approach. He takes great pride in his work but prefers his clients seek him out for his expertise, not crash a book club to scare ladies into potential customers.

"Attention, please, ladies. I want to share something important to me; all of you know my late husband, God rest his soul, provided me with a favorable life insurance policy. I can't thank him enough for wanting to ensure I'd be well taken care of in the event of his death. Of course, I would rather Alan be here now, but his thoughtful parting gift was not only gracious but a game-changer."

Her choice of words registers on the faces of her friends, so she changes her tone.

"Oh, lighten up, girls; this topic is hard to brooch, so sprinkling a bit of levity helps soften the subject's harsh reality. But all joking aside, I am serious. I can pay off my house and boat because my love took the time to plan. And now, my trusted wealth manager will see that I continue to live a very comfortable lifestyle without worry," Laurel says this as she motions everyone's attention toward Eric, so they understand he is in charge of her fortune.

"OK, enough about Eric, back to me. Believe me when I tell you, the wound of losing the love of your life is devastating; to go through this ordeal penniless would be unconscionable. Funeral expenses alone are staggering. Have you priced caskets? Throw in a decent reception, and the whole thing spirals out of control in a snap. My adviser will assist me in making wise decisions to ensure financial stability from now on. So, I will never have to work again if I don't want to."

Laurel doesn't come up for air until she says, "Do yourselves a favor, take the information, and consider the options. We're all going down the same road, so elect to travel with an expert to navigate a safe path to a secure future. It's never too late to start; at the very least, take the information."

Everyone takes a business card out of courtesy to Eric. Participating in this little charade borders on torture for him. The red-hot embarrassment radiating from the man is palpable, and like an animal caught in a trap, he would bolt from the room if released.

The presentation is finally over, and he tells the women to call him if they wish to speak privately. Again, apologizing for the ambush, he reassures them that although Laurel's methods make for bizarre business practices, she means well, and her heart is in the right place. He says good-night and goes upstairs without further ado, relieved his part in this charade is over.

Margo's interest is peaked at the prospect of some security. Dana is more than intrigued; however, her enthusiasm is motivated by an entirely different agenda.

"I imagine Frank is more valuable to me dead," says Margo. She shares a wry grin with Dana, knowing what she says is true.

Oh, say the word, my friend, and I will fulfill your wish. These unspoken words fight to be heard behind the faint smile she wears. The second reason Dana is smiling is the timing of the unsolicited advice. This unexpected turn of events is the affirmation she needed to boost her confidence and drive her forward. The benefits suggested by Laurel, with the aid of Eric, leave her hands clean.

Several witnesses will confirm that the insurance coverage for her and her spouse was not her idea. Oh yeah, Randal and Dana Lucas will be signing up.

Kathryn declined with no real need for coverage, confiding she lacks beneficiaries. However, they all agree Laurel's intentions are admirable and therefore write off her unorthodox method of enlightening them as another bizarre display of affection.

Something's not quite right; as Kathryn analyzes the sales pitch, she can't shake the notion that her concerned friend may be camouflaging an ulterior motive. Laurel is not one to spend time worrying about the well-being of others. To brag, yes, sincere concern, no. The financial planner is no doubt being taken advantage of by his new client, and somehow, she has decided to make this worth his while in the process. Kathryn is correct in her assumption; more is at play here. The players are simply out of order.

The evening is winding down, and everyone is content with the assigned read. Although not agreed upon, a date for their next gathering will be moved due to summer vacations and Kathryn's trip to France.

Discrete but not unnoticed, Kathryn hands something to Laurel and whispers something in her ear. Dana and Margo witness the exchange and let their imaginations whip up an array of wrongdoing.

Laurel says thank you and goodbye, expressing her thoughts on the night as lovely, giving their host an extra tight squeeze on her way out. Olivia concurs, absolutely perfect, and the start of something big.

Dana and Margo corner Kathryn on their way out and ask what's with the sleight of hand.

The doctor explains, "On occasion, our exhausted friend finds sleep elusive, requiring a little assistance. More so, as of late. Your faces indicate you disagree; you assume this may not be the right thing to do, but trust me, this is the best solution for the current situation. She lost her husband, is working through her trauma, and sleeping well keeps her moving forward during the day."

In disgust, Dana begs, "Do whatever you need to do but return that woman to normal. I can accept her actions are peculiar and offensive, and I can deal with outlandish and sometimes freakish, but I can't handle the person she is now much longer."

Frustrated, she says her goodbyes and goes home. Uneasy and rightfully so, Margo asks Kathryn if Laurel's obnoxious remarks about Frank are innocent or a valid concern.

"The flirtatious maneuvering from Laurel is to mask her grief," reveals Kathryn.

"Remember, Alan is no longer around to take orders, so she's inserting our husbands' in his place. A new replacement will come along soon. Give her time. Laurel isn't as strong as she wants you to think."

In the city somewhere, Curtis's phone rings incessantly but goes unanswered. He's ignoring Laurel's call or perhaps is engaging in a late-night rendezvous with someone else. She tries the next best thing and visits her Siren account but loses interest within minutes. The remote is within reach, but the television won't cut it. Some gameplay would be titillating; the gaming console is staring at her from across the room. She wonders if Frank would like to come out.

Scratch that, as there is no logical or acceptable reason to explain the call.

System maintenance, perhaps?

She realizes how suspicious this sounds and decides against calling. A fear-based decision, no doubt, as a service request at this hour guarantees an infuriated Margo will show up on her doorstep. So, moving on to her next best friend, the orange pill canister on her nightstand. One dose supplied by the other Dr. Kane should do the trick, and before long, the little helper works its magic, and Laurel's out like a light.

TWELVE

Time to Go to Work

Dana checks her laptop from home, no longer caring whether Randal knows about her purchase. Nevertheless, extra precautions such as passwords and encryptions guard her prized possession. These safety hurdles aren't there to lock out her husband, as he can barely open an app on his phone. Instead, they exist if her device falls into the hands of authorities.

An icon on her desktop titled "coupons" springs to life with a click. This unblocked tab contains pages of grocery store ads. The market's weekly specials are programmed to update, automatically keeping the advertisement file current. The video stream of Laurel's house is running in the background. It's an elaborate well-encrypted rabbit hole too deep a dive for most to undertake.

After viewing the "coupon" folder in painful detail, nothing out of the ordinary is deemed noteworthy. A notepad, also easily hidden, is open alongside Laurel's streaming window, where Dana keeps track of the highlights. Everything gathered so far goes into a file; it might be important later, so even the nothingness is cataloged.

Laurel sat at the table the other night bragging about how she created her digital personality; by doing so, she unwittingly provided a savvy tech geek with enough intel to infiltrate her electronic world.

Online dating, however, is foreign to Dana, making Siren her next project. Logging into the app takes a few keystrokes, and creating a phony account for herself is accomplished in minutes. Once in the system, the simplicity required to find and hack Laurel's internet presence is an insult. A couple of clicks and a familiar face fills the screen. "Well, isn't this interesting?

Laurel, a.k.a. Candice Moore, assumed her role as a vixen long before Alan's death. The rest of Candy's character is as described by Laurel.

"Let's find Curtis, shall we?"

Curtis Thompson pops up; one can presume this is also an alias. The sparse details presenting this man read as follows: Loves boating, avid yachtsman seeking a special someone to share in adventures.

"So, tell me, Curtis, do you like older women or only rich and famous dames?"

Dana converses with her monitor as if she expects it to reply.

The next step is to assemble Dana's virtual persona. She does so by copying Laurel's profile almost verbatim. Next, an old photo of Laurel is uploaded, but some necessary Photoshop edits manipulate the picture to make it unrecognizable yet invitingly familiar.

A few more keystrokes alter the dark hair in the snapshot to a short blond bob. Another click changes the eyes to green, and she ends with some verbiage indicating a stunning body awaits a similar person, ready to partake in no-strings-attached experiences. A name is selected, and presto, Sherry Newman is born. Dana, masquerading as Sherry, discreetly slips in with all the other love-seekers as a viable contender in this easily accessed cyber-dating community. A chilling society of which the actress and her gigolo are card-carrying members. Both are active participants, both trolls; the only difference is the criteria in the search. It's only a matter of time before "Sherry" registers as a compatible prospect for Laurel's man, and he will be none the wiser.

Now, to wait for Casanova Curtis to reach out to her, never realizing he is about to be catfished. In all of Dana's mental plotting to do away with Randal and potentially Laurel, she never entertained adding anyone else. But Mr. Boy Toy Thompson does lend a creative option to her project's construction. "Sorry, Curtis, you may need to take a bullet, so to speak, for your insipid proclivity toward women."

He might end up the guilty party or an accomplice or dodge involvement altogether. Either way, he aids in providing incriminating evidence against the actress. More players bring additional detective work, so some associated groundwork is underway.

Diligent in her notetaking, Dana jotted down everything that happened at book club the other night for later review. Then, retracing her steps, she runs across a line she wrote: "overly enthusiastic gaming comment," and underlined it twice. It may be overkill, but she recalls Laurel expressed excessive giddiness over her new console. Toys or electronics, in general, are of no interest to the starlet. Hardware won't amuse her, the only exception being a vibrator, which may elicit a similar response to the one she expressed regarding gaming the other night. An entry-level player's learning curve would bore Laurel right into a bubbling flute. OK, we can assume she is drinking; she's always drinking, and sliding a man next to an intoxicated seductress leads to a predictable outcome. The unsuspecting man finds the moment pleasurable. Soon, however, shame and humiliation are sure to follow. An encounter with Margo's mate would be no different.

Unable to ignore Laurel's veiled remarks, Dana audits the period during the day she earlier classified as irrelevant. Her husband's car placed him at the dealership, so there was no need to review that part of the tape. Of course, her slippery husband may add a new plot twist by simply borrowing a vehicle from the lot to avoid detection. Another new car out in front of the Stanhope home may be risky, drawing the attention of her neighbors. A fender bender would be another consideration; being on the other side of town is hard to explain without a client connected to the drive. All of this is nonsense; Randal can't be bothered with details. And excuses won't be necessary; he owns the business; he answers to himself. The least likely of all scenarios is Laurel picking him up. Don't be silly; she is too self-righteous to collect a man she can order like takeout.

Confident the driver is where his car is parked, the remainder of the film previously went unchecked. Dana makes herself a cup of tea and dissects the unedited footage searching for overlooked clues. Several days of nothing abnormal pass, only to conclude detective work is not for her; surveillance is brutal. Eventually, the weight of her eyelids begins to win the battle when the sight of Frank returning to Laurel's front door snaps Dana back to full consciousness.

He's back, but Laurel's demeanor indicates she is not expecting him. True to starlet fashion, she is camera-ready, even in a housecoat. This lady of the house has a different version of the 1960s flannel button-up; hers consists of a YSL pant set with a matching robe and slippers. The footwear is for appearances only, featuring a teetering kitten heel and a feathery puff serving as a toe strap. Now visualize a tall glass of champagne in hand and a soft "who is it" coming from behind the double doors.

"It's me, Frank. I brought you something."

Visions of the woman he once only thought of as a friend plagued the man, who eventually succumbed to the crippling power of her allure. His playmate's curvy image was ingrained, and the kiss mixed with his resistance to her advance amounted to foreplay. But, of course, he blamed shock for the delayed reaction. The one not forceful enough to stop her for several moments haunts him but in a wanting way.

The thought of straying had never crossed his mind before that day, so to quench his frustration, he worked out his newfound fantasies on Margo. Unbeknownst to her, she had become nothing more than a prop. Her playful banter is unappreciated, and her latest purchase from Victoria's Secret goes unnoticed. A whipped cream–covered Margo suspended from a chandelier won't alleviate his craving for Laurel. The forbidden fruit factor is the problem. The small taste only increases the appetite, and he won't stop until he's savored a full bite. The seductress is under his skin; she is the symptom and the cure, wrapped in slippery smooth silk with fluffy slippers.

Desperate, after several texts went unanswered, Frank took the chance and dropped by the house. "Well, who pray tell is at my front door, but a lonely game boy. Did you perhaps change your mind and decide I may be a worthy opponent?"

Frank stutters, "I developed a new program I think you might like."

Laughing, she gestures for him to enter and closes the door behind him. Idle chit-chat is a waste of her time, so she dives right in, telling him the only game she is interested in playing is naked in her bed.

———

Fixated on her screen, Dana witnesses the two ascend the stairs and come back down a little over an hour later, disheveled. Sick to her stomach, she can't believe this is happening—first Randal and now Frank. The nagging question of "why" resurfaces. Laurel doesn't want their husbands. As friends, the men are fine, but she would loathe them as lovers. No, she thrives on the hunt, the insatiable desire to covet what isn't hers to take and reinforce dominance over their wives.

Ultimately, all that remains is a trail of ruin and a cantankerous smirk. That menacing grin hides the gratification of manipulating the people she cares for the most; again, why?

Every encounter where their spouses were alone with the actress needs to be analyzed.

"What about Alan? He wouldn't condone this, or did he?"

The suspicion clinging to Alan's death not being an accident resurfaces. From the start, the "accident" never sat well with Dana. Likewise, the accidental death ruling never sat well with anyone, yet no one discussed an alternative possibility for his demise.

The timing of Kathryn and Joel's divorce can't be a coincidence. Laurel's recent conduct and the convenience of being under Joel's care leave little to the imagination. What a cliché, the doctor alone in a room with a patient, revealing her deepest and darkest secrets to him. Of course, the men's behavior offends Dana, but Joel's held to a higher standard; he should know better. He is a doctor, trained to spot a seductive manipulator and help her, not take advantage of her insecurities.

Kathryn never let on if she suspected or acknowledged an affair, or at least didn't confide in the ladies; they would have shared that information. Not one to discuss her feelings, Kathryn can be hard to read. She is often mistaken as cold for internalizing her emotions, so her true thoughts are often a mystery. However, she did crack at their last meeting; an ever-so-slight fissure emerged after Laurel made several inappropriate comments about Joel. One would expect the actress to be more discreet and not so inclined to lead her audience in the doctor's direction.

Each man fell for the same setup; all willing participants, not victims. Laurel's involvement is somewhat redundant, but the men are unaware of the other's indiscretions. So, while Dana plots her map, she reserves a pin for Alan. But for now, she will mark Joel as the first man to fall, with Randal second, followed by Frank, leaving Eric as the final piece of Laurel's twisted puzzle—the person conveniently recruited to take over her finances. Soon enough, the temptress will be alone with him, and she will strike if she hasn't already done so.

The hours of monitoring cryptic messages and the constant parade of men betrothed to others who fulfill Laurel's sadistic fantasies begin to wane. She is embarrassed for her friend and these pathetic men who believe they're special. She takes an aspirin, but it doesn't stop the throbbing.

During the past week, Curtis comes by often to play games, all sorts. Randal also makes an appearance, and now Frank visits. The assortment of misfits in between sends Dana's brain into a tailspin. Those other men are not her concern, and she needs to stop dwelling on their involvement; her focus is on Randal and now Frank. She also has to figure out how to run interference for Eric.

All she can think of is Olivia. Should she bug their house? Showing up at the Harper's home unannounced would undoubtedly be random. With little to be gained, Dana decides against another installation. The risk is far greater than the reward in this case. After

Margo's installation, recording devices will be installed all over town, from Presidio Heights to the Outer Sunset area, which will soon need to be collected and disposed of, each fulfilling its purpose and disappearing without a trace. The Harper's house is therefore scratched off the to-do list.

Dana wanted information, but now she possesses too much data to process. So, once again, she reaches for the aspirin.

THIRTEEN

June 5 — Bar Night 1

Dana calls the girls and suggests a night out on the town as an excellent way to kick off Laurel's new "adventure" campaign. A little push to get the star's witty way of putting a pulse back into their lifestyle started. "Wednesday is lady's night at Roman's, that hot new bar in the city; let's go!"

A night out is what Laurel lives for, sought after and desired always wins. This may even compensate for her current string of rejections. Thanks for the memories, Eric. Laurel dismissed him as spineless after he declined her advance. But his high moral stance or devotion to his wife didn't put her off. It was his repulsion to her. He didn't find her the least bit attractive—a devastating blow sure to leave a mark.

The offer to provide car service, courtesy of Laurel, makes the night-out decision easy, and everyone is on board. Dana will be last in line for pickup, but she doesn't mind as this will allow her time to send Curtis a message, asking if he would like to join her (as

Sherry) at Roman's. After the fact, Sherry Newman will apologize, stating she experienced an emergency, causing a no-show on her part. But it won't matter because, much to Curtis's surprise, Ms. Laurel Stanhope will be holding court in the center of the room. His presence may not amount to anything, but placing Laurel and Curtis in public together may. Establishing a bond between the two before Alan's death, at the very least, will undermine her credibility.

The ladies step out of the town car, dressed to impress. And these women, well into their forties, are turning heads. Once inside, Laurel flags down the man in charge, who panicked when he recognized her. He merely snaps his fingers, and a server appears to escort the women to a semi-private booth, so they are obscured but still very visible. Of course, champagne appeared without the slightest suggestion.

A crowd is filing in, but Curtis isn't here. The other patrons in the bar gawk and whisper; some fans are tentative, unsure if they should approach the table, but Laurel waves them over as the night progresses. She didn't stop until she spoke to every person in the place. A night out with the actress is exciting, but Kathryn and Olivia are ready to go home after an hour or two. Laurel, on the other hand, is showing no sign of slowing.

To encourage the star to stay right where she is, the manager signals for more bottles of bubbles. He insists they are welcome to drink for free any night of the week as long as their famous friend is in tow.

Social media exhibited its strength by spreading the word, as Laurel's location lit up Snapchat, Instagram, and Twitter in rapid succession. The buzz branded Roman's the night's hot spot, and the line to enter wrapped around the block.

Well into the evening, Curtis finally makes his debut, failing to locate Dana, well, Sherry. Once his focus lands on Laurel, the rest of the world falls to the wayside. Although the actress pretended otherwise, the tall man with a handsome physique didn't go unnoticed. The standoff will press Curtis's buttons. To satisfy her craving for attention, she turns up the heat by laughing too loud and taking the liberty of touching the surrounding men and some women. Her female fancy has been kept at bay, and she hasn't acted on her impulses. But she leads her boy toy to believe differently. The mere thought drives him crazy with jealousy.

For Curtis, competing with men isn't a challenge. Backed by youth and an athletic build, his Adonis posture radiates confidence. A touch of arrogance establishes his dominance, leaving no room to be intimidated by others. Women, however, pose a new set of obstacles. The rules are different, creating a shift in dynamics that makes competition impossible. He's been polite, but he is done playing an extra in this little show and makes his approach. He is only feet away when Laurel turns to Olivia and places a soft kiss on her lips. Olivia doesn't have time to react before Curtis loses his composure and shouts in Laurel's face.

The damsel in distress retreats into a group of men who are quick to defend her. In seconds, two giant bouncers throw Curtis out onto the sidewalk. The night was playing out better than expected. Not a month since her husband passed, the actress is seen fighting with a jealous younger man. The other patrons who happened to be taking photos of the diva captured the outburst on their phones. The episode should be trending by now. A scene like this is what Dana had hoped for, but she leads the others to believe she is just as disturbed by the blow-up.

Anxious to go home, Dana proposes heading out. She can't wait to save the video clips that are sure to be airborne by now. Curtis also provided Sherry with a convenient alibi. She will text, "Where are you? I waited for you."

Curtis may not check his messages or think of Sherry again tonight; he will undoubtedly assume she showed up after his untimely departure.

Laurel's anxiety lends to a sleepless night, anticipating what will be published tomorrow; she loves the thrill, good or bad, it's publicity. The rest of the party finds the nighttime rendezvous exhausting and are relieved to go home.

The breakfast Madeline prepared waits next to the morning newspaper on the dining room table. Disappointment is served first as her face didn't make the entertainment section. There are several mentions on social media, but the thrill is different. Words on a screen don't produce the same gratifying feeling as holding the paper in your hands and seeing your picture in print.

Rather than wallowing in her depressed state, she concludes that a new outfit may lift the funk. A purchase is always the perfect remedy for any down day. She asks her dutiful housekeeper to arrange a car and informs her she isn't sure how long she will be gone, but she doesn't expect to be out all day. Madeline hopes the latter doesn't hold true.

A car arrives within the hour to collect the pensive diva. The shopping district isn't far, but the quiet drive is used to reminisce about her rendezvous with Joel. His office is only a few blocks from the best shops in the city. The proximity sparks a change of heart; she instructs her chauffeur that they will be making a stop along the way. Under the guise of depression, she decides to drop in on the doctor.

Caller ID alerts the receptionist at the front desk precisely who is on the line. Laurel skips the customary salutation, replacing it with the declaration of an urgent matter requiring Joel's immediate attention. She then announces her ETA is in ten minutes. Not interested in confirmation and fearing a rebuttal, Laurel hangs up and conveys the detour's address to the driver.

The woman guarding the entrance to the practice is a seasoned veteran; it's her job to wrangle the misguided, so handling the likes of Laurel is not a problem. Upon the actress's arrival, the receptionist's firm tone reinforces, "Dr. Kane is with a patient, and under no uncertain terms will he be interrupted."

The following "suggestion" is barked out military-style, "If you intend to visit with him, you will wait here for fifteen minutes."

The cold, unyielding stare relayed to this drive-by patient denotes that this situation is nonnegotiable and to reconsider any thoughts to debate the issue. Not in the mood to argue, Laurel concedes to the instructions and accepts the water offered before sitting in a replicated Barcelona chair in the waiting room.

After a brief, albeit frustrating wait, the doctor welcomes his patient but keeps his demeanor clinical this afternoon. The atmosphere in the office is as gloomy as the gray sky outside. Occupying her usual seat on the couch, the session begins with whining about trouble sleeping and demonstrating anxiety and fatigue as the general symptoms prompting her visit. He listens without saying much of anything yet takes copious notes. Annoyed by his detached attentiveness, she gets up and stands too close, insinuating, as in previous experiences, that she expects to be intimate. With only a folder between them as a buffer, Joel shuts her down by telling her to sit. A command delivered to a dog in training would have been less direct.

The session continues on an analytic level; the doctor dispassionately conveys to his patient that their relationship, all of them, are over. Laurel sits motionless, contemplating the physically uncomfortable sensation that seems to revolve around her with some regularity these days. Overly sensitive due to the recent negative trend, she lashes out at the unreceptive man before her, insisting he misinterpreted her actions, and storms out of his office.

As Laurel passes the desk, a shout rings out, "Same time next week?"

No other words are exchanged, only an evil glare as the actress exits before the rest of the temper tantrum she's suppressing erupts.

"Take me home," is shouted to the only man listening to her.

The altercation crushed her spirit to shop; retail therapy can't help her now; she needs something more reliable. As instructed, the town car turns around and returns her to the house as requested. After changing into her sleepwear, she takes a few pills and sleeps off the ugly afternoon.

FOURTEEN

Ladies Night, Take Two

A group message from Laurel pops up on phones all over town, pinging simultaneously, "It's Wednesday, girls!"

Margo replies, "And?"

"Let's go out again but somewhere a little more upscale. The rumor around town is that The Dirty Olive is the new hot spot. The reviews are off the charts, and it was recently rated the best new establishment in the city. A rooftop bar with a twinkling view of the downtown cityscape on one side and a moonlit bay on the other is something we shouldn't miss, and I'm dying to go. My treat, and I'll provide transport. Who's in?"

Dana chimes in, "Why not? Let's live a little."

Olivia declines, using kid stuff to attend as her excuse not to be near Laurel. Kathryn says she wouldn't mind going out but would rather skip the single scene.

Margo suggests, "Let's go eat, stay for one martini at the bar, and call it a night."

Everyone, except Olivia, gives the thumbs-up emoji.

The following message reads, "Pickup starts at 7:00."

The workday is over for Dana by 2:45; she can't concentrate on anything but the evening ahead. So, she commences with the math: pickup at 7:00 to 7:30, dine between 8:00 and 9:15, landing them on the rooftop by 9:30 to 9:45. OK, it's time to make some calls.

The last lady's night drew some sparks, but Dana is going for full fireworks this time. Curtis loved the residual side effects from last Wednesday. The viral chatter is one thing, and seeing an image or two of himself online is a rush, but it's not enough. Common knowledge dictates he won't pass up a photo opportunity if one arises, which makes manipulating him too easy.

The random still shot no longer satisfies the aspiring actor; he strives for real stardom involving live action. The more chaos, the better his chances of appearing on a newsfeed. Television, however, is the next level; apparently, scandalous reality shows are the chosen road to "making it big."

An altercation with someone famous will increase his shot at airtime exponentially. But whatever the occurrence may be, it must last longer than ten seconds.

Dana, acting as Sherry, texts Curtis from her burner phone, revealing gossip. "OMG! I heard actress Laurel Stanhope will be at The Dirty Olive tonight. We should go. The talk around town hints that TMZ is tailing her; we might get on TV."

The thought of exposure is all Curtis absorbs from her words before jumping into the shower while the water is still cold.

He texts back, "Sorry, I've made plans. Can we try for later in the week?"

The last reply reads, "Let me know when you're available."

"Sherry" and Curtis are engaged in an ongoing text exchange since their failed meetup, each with their convenient excuses to be unavailable.

Next call: TMZ. The same spiel is recited, "Reservations are booked for Laurel Stanhope at The Dirty Olive this evening at ten p.m. if you're interested. Rumors are circulating; the guy who started the brawl last week at Roman's is stalking her. Those two colliding should make for some outstanding entertainment." Click.

Only time will tell if anyone follows the trail of breadcrumbs. The anticipation of what is to come amounts to exhilarating torture. All her traps are in place; nothing is left to do but hope the egos at play won't disappoint.

The chaos involved in this game occupies Dana's every waking moment. The displays of affection, the mundane investigating, and the collection of incriminating evidence ward off accepting her close friend is sleeping with her husband. An odd diversion tactic, but she needs to stick with whatever propels her forward; any more idle moments, and she will snap. Sarcasm and mood swings are frequent and harder to suppress with each passing day. She doesn't know if she should be offended or relieved that neither her husband nor girlfriend pays her enough mind to detect a shift in attitude.

The self-soothing conversations are something Dana depends on to maintain control, utilizing whatever means necessary to keep her off the ledge. Earbuds double as a convincing prop; she always wears at least one at all times, so if caught talking to herself, she touches her ear as if she is on the phone. No insanity here; look away.

The black town car pulling up in front of the restaurant catches the attention of a few people standing outside. The women file onto the red carpet as if attending a fancy premiere. They all admit to deriving a particular guilty pleasure from Laurel's celebrity.

Selfies replace the sought-after autograph of old, but both are regular occurrences when out on the town with a star. For the most part, the groupies are polite and not too pushy. Reactions to the presence of a starlet differ depending on the venue and the amount of alcohol involved. Kathryn favors the devotees who smile or wave from a distance or the others who whisper to each other, assuming no one notices them staring.

All in all, the excitement surrounding fame is phenomenal, even if the experience is somewhat predictable. Once recognized, a welcome and gracious greeting goes without saying. A table is always open, the drinks are free flowing, the cuisine is prepared to perfection, and the decadent dessert divine. But, of course, the price for all of this pampered treatment is determined by the buzz Laurel generates. An appearance earns the photographers and influencers hassle-free content; in trade, they ensure each establishment's name receives proper accolades in print and cyberspace. But one can expect these evenings to be fun, filling, and free. Yes, one can quickly become accustomed to the perks of the pampered and pretentious.

Through martini-soaked eyes, Dana reclines, surveying the room. She wonders if she will miss this lifestyle when realizing what this privilege costs her. She fishes olives from the bottom of a stemmed V-shaped glass while signaling the server for another—anything to mute the painful images of her husband intertwined with her friend.

Laurel finished picking at her dinner and now seeks to replace the serenity of dining with friends with something more exciting. She thanked the restaurant manager for a lovely evening, kissing his cheeks while promising a rapid return. Each full-bellied lady slides into the back of the town car for a short ten-minute ride to their next destination. The clock on the console reads 9:40; Dana impressed herself with her spot-on ETA calculations.

A utility van is parked across the street, attempting to be

inconspicuous, but everyone immediately eyes the obvious indicators. There are no visible call letters; it looks like something a sex offender would drive, stark white with windowless panels. The satellite dish and drapes blocking whatever is in the back of the commercial vehicle scream paparazzi.

They no sooner make their way inside the establishment when Russell, the proprietor, rushes over, welcoming everyone as he escorts them to the VIP table. The accommodating gentleman reassures them that adequate temperature controls monitor the entire rooftop for optimum comfort. Dana half expected Curtis to be waiting, but no sign of him yet. She crosses her fingers and prays that the man of the hour will make an appearance.

The Dirty Olive is a pleasant surprise. The walls are sparse yet skillfully decorated, with modern furnishings displayed to be appreciated. The bar is a showpiece with art deco accents and a mercury-mirrored backdrop. This place will do well in this part of the city. The bars with the loud music and overcrowded dance floors served their purpose back in the day. But they all concur to aging out of "clubbing" years ago, handing the disco ball and ear-piercing techno noise to the younger generation.

The cocktail lounge gives off a country club vibe, geared to an older demographic who still wants to be out and seen yet expects more than sticky parquet and a gas station lavatory. A king's table in the center of one wall is cordoned off, reserved for high-profile guests such as Laurel. The spacious accommodations present a magical view of the city lights, which is not an unpleasant way to spend an evening. However, the rest of the patrons are too close for Kathryn's liking; she prefers a little buffer between her and the others. Dana glances around the room; she appreciates the design, and how they've packed the space while minimizing any sense of claustrophobia is genius.

A fellow patron interrupts to gush over his luck in meeting

"The" Laurel Stanhope. The man doesn't say much more before shaking the actress's hand and returning to his table across the room. The starlet loves the attention but loves complaining about the interruption more.

A smile crosses Dana's face as she sips her third martini.

"Hey there, gorgeous," leaves her lips as her knight in shining Armani walks up the stairs.

Enter Curtis, dressed to impress, dawning a summer suit with an open shirt, drawing the attention he anticipated. Everyone can see why Laurel is attracted to this man. He is beyond good-looking, and his body belongs on the pages of *Fit Magazine*. He takes his time walking over to greet them. Laurel pretends to control her temper, insinuating that speaking to him is a chore. This anger management routine is strictly for show; she has slept with him twice since last week's outing. Of course, Dana is privy to this information because she's been viewing the dramatic albeit intentional arguments for the sake of makeup sex repeating on a loop emanating from the Stanhope home. Watching her friend be intimate with her boy toy is uncomfortable, but the other assorted strays who make their way to the porch are extremely disturbing—dubbing the Red Light District activity on her computer screen her own private Amsterdam. The voyeurism is titillating and repulsive, yet she can't turn away.

"What do you want, Curtis," hisses Laurel, in her best "you're boring me" voice.

"Good evening, ladies; I just stopped to say hello to the most beautiful women in the city. Nothing more. Enjoy the night."

And with that, he walked away.

No, don't go yet! Dana silently yells.

It's a massive relief when the departing player only ventures as far as the first vacant bar stool. This man has no intention of going anywhere; he stakes his claim, so to speak, and orders a drink. His back is to the group, but the reflective wall provides a clear view of the table and his madame. She is ruthless in the way she toys with his fragile ego. The jealous, volatile people have taken their marks as the curtain rises on the second act of this potentially disastrous little vignette.

Two handsome men walk over to the table and introduce themselves. Laurel invites them to join the party; she doesn't bother to check the mirror as she can feel the seething heat generated by her boyfriend from across the room. The men accept, and everyone scoots over to accommodate the new bodies at the table. One man slips next to the star, and one borrows a chair from another table. Nervous and agitated, Curtis shifts in his seat. Clairvoyant messages from Dana beg him to hold it together a little longer.

A woman in her mid-thirties approaches, begging forgiveness for the intrusion before sheepishly requesting a picture with Laurel. The poor darling is visibly trembling like a star-struck teenager, expressing that she is a longtime fan. Margo takes pity on her, saying, "We can do one better. Come on in, sit with us."

The man seated in the booth moves to allow the woman to slip in beside her idol. He slides another chair alongside his friend at the head of the table. This little lady is in store for an experience she won't soon forget; Laurel takes the nervous fan's hand and places their clasped hands in her lap. The woman calms down, losing the accelerated, incoherent speech pattern resembling a shrill only a dog can decipher, and settles into a more normal tone of voice. She attempts to retrieve her hand, but Laurel doesn't let go, giving the woman a wink, adding that she likes her.

Well into the night, several other people make their way over to ooh and ahh. But, the novelty of entertaining stargazers wore off, and nothing is happening. So, finally, having had enough, Dana declares she works in the morning before informing everyone it's time for them to call it a night.

Margo, who consumed a few too many cocktails, says, "We all work in the morning, and she's a doctor," pointing to Kathryn.

The crowd of admirers is displeased with the ladies' decision to leave. Laurel begs them to stay, refusing to vacate the booth, but she understands she can't be left unattended with people she just met. Not caring to wait any longer, Dana announces, "It's time to go."

Laurel assures the fans she will return and hopes to run into them all real soon.

While walking out, Dana tells the unhappy supporters, "If you want a selfie with Laurel, you can do so on the curb out front."

The mass of people disbursed and let them out. Laurel pulls out her phone to alert the driver to be ready for them curbside.

Dana says, "Tell him to take five minutes; you have an audience to please."

The star reapplies her lipstick with a smile, and everyone makes their way downstairs to the sidewalk.

Russell escorts the women to the entrance offering an open invitation anytime they'd like a night out. In the middle of the curbside crowd stands Curtis. Laurel takes note of his placement, intending to use it against him.

The chain reaction Dana waited all night to witness is about to be set in motion. Each person in the congregation waits for their turn for a photo with the star. The cameras eat her up as she poses with her enthusiastic worshipers, hugging bodies and kissing cheeks. The film crew, hiding in the van, springs into action, fueling the frenzy. A microphone is in Laurel's face in an instant. She mentions where they dined without skipping a beat and acknowledges the appropriate people by name. She touts, "The best meal in town, and what better way to end our night out, but here at The Dirty Olive, if you haven't experienced the splendor from up top, you should treat yourself; you won't be disappointed. Russell, my dear friend, thank you for a marvelous evening."

What starts as an innocent yet lingering kiss on the cheek of the blushing bar owner quickly erupts into a flurry of activity. Again, cue Curtis; his chiseled frame comes out of thin air and grabs Laurel by the arm. Of course, she recoils, screaming in terror as the panic ensues.

A film crew, a couple of photographers, along with several bystanders record the pandemonium as the town car pulls up and the women jump in to make their escape.

"Never a dull moment, just once; I would like to go out where we don't conclude the evening in a mosh pit," sighs Kathryn.

"That was terrific," slurs Margo.

Dana agreed, "The whole ordeal was unbelievable."

The previous Wednesday date night didn't make the print tabloids. Tonight, however, is sure to reap a much different reward, as they were quite the spectacle. Kathryn isn't happy, and Dana does her best to feign disapproval by playing along. The only upside is that their identities remain anonymous; the label attached is "Laurel's entourage," which is the generic description in most cases.

Kathryn and Dana concentrate on keeping their faces obscured from the ever-present telephoto lens, along with an alias if asked. On the other hand, Margo appears to be wallowing in the limelight and gets a kick out of a snapshot of herself showing up online and in magazines. Exhilarated by being referred to as "Laurel's companion."

Margo teases she is the Jezebel causing the rift between Laurel and Curtis. The instigator in a love triangle gone awry. She makes up fantastic headlines, but no one else finds this amusing.

Olivia declined to participate in the second brouhaha, so no photos or mention of her being a part of the clique surface. The only notable names divulged to the public belong to Laurel Stanhope and Curtis Thompson.

The bold headline across the media outlets read, "Laurel and her jilted lover." The papers regurgitated the events of last night as if invited to sit at the table. Dana's upset; they rarely, if ever, acknowledge Alan; it's like he never existed. No one notices the widow's husband hasn't been dead long enough for her to take on a lover, let alone jilt one. Technically, anything is possible; the diva is quick and undoubtedly capable of being in and out of a relationship in twenty-four hours. Laurel's public display as a grieving widow conflict with her role as a combatant lover, but no one seems to pick up on this or care for that matter. Regardless, the seeds are planted; whether something grows is anyone's guess.

FIFTEEN

Thursday, June 20

All survived the "Wednesday girls night out," although most found sunglasses were required the next morning to combat the elements even indoors. They're conflicted about whether to be jealous or baffled by Laurel's continued enthusiasm to behave like a college freshman who discovered booze and boys for the first time. The semi-suppressed inhibitions of the others are no doubt connected to their respective responsibilities the following day. In stark contrast to the actress, her friends will report to a desk, patients, or customers first thing in the morning. No legitimate reason forces Laurel to draw back her blackout curtains before noon, so she will sleep in while the peasants go to work. The others can only hope the kid on the other end of the drive-thru speaker isn't too loud and can deliver a bacon, egg, and cheese biscuit with an emergency Pepsi tout de suite.

Across town, a spa staff waits at the ready for the movie maven, who's yet to grace them with her presence. Among the beauty treatments on the menu are IV fluids, accompanied by all means necessary to put the actress's face back where it belongs.

Laurel's schedule indicates another location shoot next week. Last night, the mention of this trip put Dana on edge as she wasn't offered another opportunity to house-sit. But her worries dissipate as she sifts through more video footage of the Stanhope home. There is no need to be paranoid; Laurel doesn't suspect anything, nor did the diva find the cameras; if she had, she would have ripped them from their perches while concocting a merciless hunt for the person responsible.

Dana gagged when an old pattern emerged when comparing the days the actress was preoccupied with the data gathered from Randal's tracker. Her husband is still soliciting companionship in the objectionable strip clubs of the seedy side of North Beach. But what made the scene utterly revolting was knowing upon his return home, she'd be obligated to fulfill one of her many wifely duties by pretending to be interested as the man of her house recounted his rough workday, slaving away at the dealership. A concerned onlooker, she is not; the bullshit Randal spews is loathsome. Every word he verbalizes is an outright lie spoken with conviction and promise. Tightly pressed lips trap bitter words and refrain her from spitting facts in his face. He is testing her sanity daily; ironically, the thought of killing him is the only thing keeping her sane.

Dana dials the phone; Margo answers to the sound of her friend's voice, "Hello, my almost celebrity friend."

Margo delights in the compliment and screeches, "My face is in the paper! I swear I'm reliving 1999 all over again; I look hot. Thank God I kept my hair appointment. Who knew we would end up in print?"

Me, I knew, Dana thinks to herself.

"Not to divert from your newfound stardom, but I wanted to ask if the offer to dog-sit is still available. I need a break."

Margo senses more might be happening with her friend, prompting her to ask if everything is all right at home.

"Yes, yes, home is fine; work is the issue. But I need a change of scenery. The weekend at Laurel's gave me the 'refresh' I needed, and I want to keep the momentum going."

Margo agrees and moves on but adds, "All right, but I'm here if you want to talk."

Dana thanks her for her concern and reassures her that some "me time" is all she needs.

"OK, then, Milo will be thrilled for someone other than us to be here to play with him. He's a low-maintenance beast; one walk per day is enough, although he may beg to differ. Keep his water and food bowls full, and he won't be any trouble. We are scheduled to leave Saturday afternoon and be back late Sunday. I'm excited for my son to be out of this house for the summer. 'A change of scenery,' I understand, now," says Margo.

The environmental escape Margo covets for herself is getting lost in the bookstore she inherited from her father. Its walls are saturated with the scent of Wessex Burley Spice from his old pipe, which lingers in the aisles of one of the last remaining independent booksellers whose doors are still open. Dark wood walls stacked with stories guided her on an enchanted journey through childhood; she grew up in the pages of fantasy, drama, and mystery. She absorbed as many editions as possible, never taking the time allotted for granted. While other young girls enjoyed sleepovers, Margo crawled up in the tiny loft above the back shelves with her fictional friends, lovers, and ne'er-do-wells.

To inquire about her preferred genre will provoke one reply, true crime. So, when her turn rolls around to select the next book club read, no one is surprised when she suggests something spine-tingling. Of course, they all protest, but once they explore the workings of a criminal mind in a novel, they can't set it down. The engrossing tales generate intense feedback sparking stimulating conversations, which keep them coming back for more.

Podcasts are another thrilling way in which she satisfies her slightly morbid appetite. Be forewarned; once Margo starts talking about her passion, grab a mug of coffee and hang on; you'll be here a while. You'll find podcasts playing in the store with some regularity, and for your listening pleasure, the current rotation includes three female duos, a southern belle sans the mint julep, and one Aussie gent.

A sign hanging on the old wood-framed glass door indicates a crime drama is in session, and "discretion is advised."

The warning, although read, is heard in Erica Kelley's sultry southern drawl. Ms. Kelley hosts *Southern Fried True Crime*; her voice alone will pique your curiosity. Her masterful tone will suck you in and hold you in place. A disclaimer also hangs on the door indicating the staff will be happy to turn off the program if accompanied by children. Or if you are offended by distressing circumstances, traumatic torturous behavior, or find the overall experience too "murdery."

"Murdery" is a word taken from the book club's next read, *Stay Sexy and Don't Get Murdered*. The authors, Karen Kilgariff and Georgia Hardstark, also host the *My Favorite Murder* podcast. They are real, use profanity (another reason for the warning on the door), and they "fuck politeness," another term you'll recognize after reading their book. They take pride in what they do; if you don't like it, they will tell you to "get the fuck out." These two colorful, comedic geniuses supply much-needed levity to an otherwise wicked world. Karen and Georgia generated quite a following in the bookshop, so their book debut is a fucking win-win!

Margo also introduced her patrons to *RedHanded*, hosted by the dynamic duo of Suruthi Bala and Hannah Maguire. British broadcasting perfection from across the pond, proving those with ill intentions walk amongst us everywhere. Their point of view is authentic, and they will not sugarcoat anything for you. So, put on your big girl panties, poke your head out from under the duvet, and ditch your AOL address, or perhaps you should take up piano; it's safer.

On the lighter side, the neophyte may elect to start with *Moms and Mysteries* with Mandy and Melissa. These insightful mothers serve up murders and mayhem with a virtual side of milk and cookies. The episodes are informative, dramatic, and nonetheless horrific, but the motherly aspect provides a sense of security, and you're not likely to hear an F-bomb dropped here.

The only male in the lineup is *Casefile*, an Australian gentleman who wishes to remain anonymous. He keeps everything about himself in the shadows, focusing solely on the story. Laurel would benefit from this man's example.

Terrifying experiences about real people aren't for everyone. But Margo will insist, "If you listen to any of these podcasts, I bet you'll be bingeing by the end of the day and jonesing for another episode like a crack addict who missed a fix by tomorrow. In the bookstore, podcasts air from ten a.m. to noon. This time frame works as most kids are in school, and the moms who come to my little shop would prefer their families remain in the dark about their morbid obsession."

The influx of women with empty strollers in tow signals the conclusion of morning drop-off, and the coffee pot is about to earn its keep. Upon the arrival of the last "murderino" (another term from *Stay Sexy and Don't Get Murdered*), the classical music stops and the real-life drama commences.

True crime isn't just about a chilling story involving someone's gruesome demise or the entertainment value of the chosen hosts. The dissection of a twisted mind enthralls most and is generally enough. They like to debate the whole nature-versus-nurture argument. The bookstore hostess spends countless hours analyzing her risky experiences; the number of times she disregarded the internal warnings or brushed off blatant danger signs is mind-numbing. Why is she so fortunate?

How did she stroll through life unscathed when others suffered unspeakable fates after being much less careless than she?

Margo is fascinated by her clientele, connecting to different yet like-minded people respectfully discussing the preyed upon in the tales they explore. She likes to think her people serve a purpose; they acknowledge and commemorate the victims of foul play while appreciating the resilience and raw vulnerability of those who survive the unthinkable. These are actual people; the topics are not fictional, solved, or unsolved; these cases happened. This community exists to ensure that the lives taken or destroyed remain relevant and not forgotten.

The rest of Margo's world lacks that type of authenticity. Frank's laissez-faire attitude toward her and Tyler is palpable. He says he is concentrating on developing his most incredible creation, but something's not quite right. The unaccounted-for afternoons and late-night rendezvous don't add up. He pitifully insists that the extra hours she demands he works are paying off only exacerbates her frustration. Margo can't believe he is spinning the conversation to use her own words against her. Classic flipping the script 101. After concurring, she asked him to contribute; she promptly explained that work equals pay.

Frank stares at his wife, her speech is audible, but he fails to respond. Wanting to make sure she is understood, she dumbs down her reasoning to a sharper point. The additional hours worked should reflect a substantial increase in their bank account. Yet, so far, she is mistaken. Of course, realizing he now must justify his unpaid absence ignited Frank's cue to start yelling and storm out. Classic loser 101, take two.

The predictable outburst guarantees alone time will follow any discussion in which Frank's actions require an explanation. Margo wonders, *If he isn't working, what's he doing?*

Where is he going?

Who is he seeing?

The podcasts aren't helping; they only reinforce her paranoia. After all, the husband is generally guilty, or the butler did it. But who employs one of those these days?

So yeah, it's the husband. Frank is a good guy but is better described as immature, lazy, and entitled. These traits seemed endearing in their youth, but she detests them as adults. Margo regrets her part in enabling her husband; what you allow, you encourage, and that could not be more apparent. She helped create this unsustainable life they've built. Now, she wants him to step up and be the man she *wished* she married, but that may be too big an ask this late in the game.

The realization that a transformation isn't in her immediate future causes Margo to do some soul-searching. But she isn't the only one at fault; Frank's mother initiated the pattern. The senior Mrs. Reed never made her boy do anything for himself. Not a single responsibility, and as one would imagine zero accountability. But at some point, everyone recognizes the difference between being loved and taking advantage of a loved one. Margo embraced her matronly role initially; now, she resents the position. She doesn't understand how to make her husband realize their actions are a blueprint for their son; they reinforce that this is an acceptable way to live and, worse, a proper way to treat women.

Frank's stronghold on denial and his reluctance to admit an issue exists in his household isn't his biggest problem. But, much like all forbidden things, Laurel's image haunts him. He craves her touch; the scent of perfume cripples him, even if the fragrance doesn't belong to her. His muse turned into a problematic distraction of epic proportions. In the past, Frank used distractions as his go-to excuse for not completing a project. Now thoughts of his newest game hinder his actions; he can't function. According to his wife, another woman may hold a tight grasp on his attention, but so does a bag of Cheetos. This man-child needs to grow up, stop fantasizing, and focus on his work.

Frank Reed isn't complicated; he is a creature of habit. So the sudden metamorphosis from disheveled couch potato to showered, shampooed, and shining didn't go unnoticed. A typical day resembled roommates who work opposite shifts, saying hello and good-bye as they passed in the hall. So, the abrupt swing to seductive suitor provoked suspicion. But something else didn't go unnoticed; the behavioral changes began after the game system installation at Laurel's home. He now possesses an insatiable need for sex.

So, what happened?
What did she say?
Better yet, what did she do?

Not addressing Frank's altered reality is where Margo loses most people. On the contrary, Margo likes the blinders she's wearing, but the ostrich approach to her relationship is difficult for others to comprehend. The one-sided strained dynamic frustrates their close friends as they can do nothing but watch the Reed couple flounder as they coexist. This desperate wife knows her faults but won't give up on her family. Instead, she will use whatever Laurel said or did as a last-ditch effort to improve her relationship with the man she married.

Thankful would be overkill. Willful ignorance is closer to the truth. Margo didn't care; her inattentive roommate wanted her again. She misses her husband, but Margo doesn't suffer fools, and any fool can see that he is with someone else in his mind. So, regardless of how demoralizing the circumstance is, she will freely trade dignity for a bit of affection for now.

The Reeds both recognize their expectations are different. She's not fulfilled but tolerates the bizarre affection as she delights in the thought of being touched by something that doesn't require batteries. On the other hand, he reacts to any physical activity void of clothing, followed by a sandwich. They are as harmonious as pickles and ice cream.

One might assume Frank would at least ask his wife if she enjoyed her evening out with the girls, but no, he opted to ignore her straight through breakfast. Without excusing himself from the table or bothering to clear his plate, he retreated to the family room as if to start his workday. Within a few minutes, he resorted to working on himself rather than his latest project. One tends to forget their manners when left unattended for too long. So, whoever is home or which part of the house he "plays" has become irrelevant.

An unpleasant surprise awaits Dana when she eventually witnesses Frank's disgusting practices for herself. After the spyware installation in his home, she will watch his self-servicing live from her laptop. Viewing from her desk at the office will become interesting; she will need to monitor her surroundings to make sure no one in the office detects the inevitable horror that's soon to cross her face. Her coworkers will demand an explanation for her humorous yet disturbing choice of viewing material.

Dana accepts her marriage to Randal is no Cinderella story, and it turns out her prince charming is a womanizing liar. But his portrayal of a seventies porn star is done elsewhere and not in her living room by himself. Justification doesn't dismiss the behavior, but it's less painful.

How Margo can stand living with that man is something only

she can explain. His refusal to abandon his teenage years and her resistance to evolve only perpetuates their downward spiral. The pandering doesn't help; she lays out snacks for a grown man each day before heading to work. The kind of plates your mom would prepare for you when you returned home from school. Yet every day yields more of the same pathetic habitual enabling; despised, frowned upon, and repeated.

Today, however, a pouting husband and a pounding headache won't slow Margo; she can't wait until ten o'clock to open her shop. The podcasts are bringing in more and more customers who seem to be telling their friends. Thursday is when *RedHanded* comes out, a fan favorite guaranteeing a line will be forming at the door when she arrives. Today, raspberry scones wait on an antique tray next to the bestseller stand; the tasty pastries will be a welcomed treat for her loyal patrons. These women like their hot cup of Joe so much that Margo contemplates putting out a tip jar to help defer some costs before concluding that begging for gratuities is tacky. Instead, she continues to provide refreshments if they buy books after the java and confections.

The day will press on like any other; the hangovers will fade, sending the women to neutral corners until this evening's book club meeting, when the pretense of adoring friendship again takes center stage.

SIXTEEN

Book Club Meeting —
Something in the Water **by Catherine Steadman**

Laurel's turn in the lineup is always eagerly anticipated, and this evening's event is no exception. Most are still nursing the ramifications of last night's outing, so it's safe to say everyone may scale back on the alcohol tonight. They elect instead to focus their attention on the literature and what is sure to be a splendid meal.

Hosting parties is where the actress shines. However, to be cast supreme hostess is not for the faint of heart; an undertaking such as this requires confidence and skill. A true entertainer must be able to throw together a soirée, large or small, at a moment's notice while exuding little to no effort. The invention of the favorites list on the iPhone reduces hosting any occasion to the press of a button. Availability is never an issue; most in the service industry jump at the opportunity to work for anyone in show business. The honor lends clout to the resume, and those who decline risk being blackballed. The few caterers Madeline prefers have cooked, cleaned, and served Stanhope events for years, leaving Laurel with little more to do than dress herself. In truth, Madeline is the brain trust; she calls vendors and executes the host's duties, whereas Laurel assumes the role of a heavily jeweled greeter.

Excitement swirls through the air as the friends arrive. The mysterious buzz surrounding Laurel is electric. Although they generally reserve some time for the evening's topic, these meetings tend to be an excuse to drink with others, tonight being an exception. However, the overzealousness of their hostess prompted Olivia to ask if she had started drinking without them.

A striking table awaits the guests in the dining room. The glow from an enormous candelabra is overshadowed only by the aroma of some gastronomic delight emanating from the kitchen. The runner in the center of the table boasts a plethora of silverware and stacked dishes. Flowers arranged amongst the ornate candle holder, cutlery, and bone china resemble a mad-hatter experiment. A spectacle is typical, but this is an extravaganza. On each placemat rests a beautiful box, a gift designed with a removable lid, so there is no need to unwrap the package and make a mess of the paper.

Wide-eyed, Olivia wonders out loud, "What's all this?"

"Don't touch! We will begin the evening by discussing our reading assignment," insists Laurel.

And with a snap of her fingers, she summons Madeline to fetch drinks. Annoyed by Laurel's signaling methods, the ladies opt to serve themselves. Olivia quietly asks Madeline if she would like a glass of something red or sparkling. To accept a cocktail from a guest while on duty would cause her boss to have a conniption fit. Madeline winks at Olivia but declines the offer.

"OK, what is going on," Margo inquires.

"First, we are slapped with the wafting smell of pure deliciousness, presented with a lavish gift amidst buckets of bubbles. Well, that's not that unusual; but what is unexpected is a table worthy of a gala in the middle of the week, not to mention you volunteered, no, insisted on reviewing the book. Who are you, and what have you done with Laurel?"

An evil eye shoots across the room as their host adds, "I'm serious; you loved this story, right? A thriller with a twist, what is more exciting?"

"So, you read the book?" interjects Dana.

"No." Laurel grimaces. "All I do is read scripts. Audiobooks, darling, audiobooks are the way to go. This story captured me, and Catherine Steadman's voice is perfect for storytelling."

The women's eyebrows raise like caterpillars trying to escape, but they are pleasantly surprised by Laurel's involvement in this novel.

Margo informs the group, "Since you liked this story, we should add Ms. Steadman's other titles, 'Mr. Nobody,' 'The Family Game,' and 'The Disappearing Act' to our rotation. Olivia interjects, "I've read 'The Family Game' It's good, but I need to warn my 'Psychological Thriller Readers' Facebook group that someone releases a breath they didn't realize they were holding."

The ladies stare at Olivia, bewildered by her comment. "It's an inside joke."

"O" adds, "Laurel, I believe all her books are also available in audio format for your listening pleasure."

Laurel, almost giddy, says, "Great, let's read or listen to the whole lot."

All nod in agreement, 'Something in the Water' was a five-star read, but their focus has shifted to their gift.

A kid waiting for Santa exhibits more restraint than Olivia, who can't wait to peek into the decorative present. As everyone approaches the table, Margo attempts to lift the box, asking, "Did you buy us bowling balls?"

Appalled at the thought, Laurel snaps, "Just remove the top."

Each lady then unties the bow to open the fancy gift.

Olivia remarks she's happy the unwrapping doesn't involve tearing the paper. "It's too pretty to destroy."

Each lady dismantles the box with care, with no real intention of reusing the gift wrap in the future.

The lids come off, and inside they find a hundred pieces of tissue with what appears to be a black strap with dense silver squares attached.

Margo admits, "I have no idea what this contraption is about."

Laurel barks, "Do you mean to tell me none of you recognize a weight belt?"

Dana barks back, "Are you calling me fat?"

Laurel laughs, "No, silly; you wear them in the water while diving. You will also find an envelope enclosed containing a certificate for scuba lessons. We wanted adventure, and since you won't go to bars with me anymore, I thought we would take up scuba diving in honor of our most recent read. I won't take no for an answer, and by the way, our first lesson is this Saturday."

"I'm going out of town," Margo says with a tilted head and faux disappointment.

"Nice try, sweetheart; you mentioned earlier that you are leaving in the afternoon. So, plan ahead, and your morning will be open. But, again, any negative response is unacceptable," says the unwavering host.

"Our scuba class will take place in the Yacht Club pool," says Laurel.

Olivia objects, expressing her inability to carry around something that weighs as much as she does. Laurel reassures them they won't be schlepping anything; she will arrange for the equipment to be brought to her boat and stockpiled in her dock box.

"The cabana boys will do all the heavy lifting, and you will never carry anything. Come on; we deserve some fun."

Dana whispers, "We will never set foot in the ocean."

"I'm counting on that," says Kathryn.

"Laurel won't make it past the introduction," adds Dana, who then states, "She does realize her hair is getting wet, right?"

Giggles are interrupted when Laurel insists on a show of hands. "Who is in for the adventure?"

Reluctantly, everyone concedes to try the first session, but only because the pool is heated and they can enjoy the spa amenities afterward.

"Who is the band leader at our next soirée, and what book are we reading?" asks Kathryn.

After tossing around a few options, Dana chimes in with, "O, I'll punch you in the throat if you choose historical fiction."

Red wine spurts from Laurel's lips, blocking a laugh, and she quickly dabs a dribble with her linen napkin. Margo suggests holding the next meeting in the bookstore after hours for old-time's sake. She proceeds to announce the two titles she selected for their consideration.

One Day in December by Josie Silver or *The Silent Patient* by Alex Michaelides are the choices.

Margo proudly quotes Reese Witherspoon, "*One Day in December* charmed her."

She adds that she and Reese Witherspoon share similar tastes in titles.

"I'm never disappointed with her picks," said Margo.

"Then *The Silent Patient* it is," shouts Laurel.

Margo leans over to Kathryn and repeats a common question these days. "Do you find Laurel's behavior unbecoming?"

Kathryn's reply is always the same: "Doesn't everyone."

"Swing by the shop if you want a copy of either or both books, or text me what you want, and I'll bring everything with me on Saturday," says Margo. They all agreed one book would be sufficient until the end of summer vacation. The evening ends with a coconut cake, coffee, and a slight fear of getting wet.

SEVENTEEN

Yacht Club Scuba Lesson

Early Saturday morning, Laurel's snapping fingers echo through the Yacht Club, where she assumes the role of head maître d' rounding up the staff at a Michelin star restaurant for a pre-game huddle. The thrill of a celebrity in their midst wore off some time ago for the employees. What remains is the indignity of being treated like a servant for the amusement of other members. Her demands are such when she speaks; she speaks at you, contempt radiating from her lips. Similar to being spit in the face with venom.

The snake can come out of nowhere, ejecting poison into the air, paralyzing her victim with fear. Be warned; her contentment is worse; coiled and calm is a trap. Keep in mind that this woman is never content, and an improper greeting is a slight, a glass half full, a faux pas. Yet the scandal of all scandals resembles insincere enthusiasm upon her arrival, especially in the presence of her guests. Keeping your excitement level high is beneficial if you value your employment. The slightest dip in tempo results in a humiliating reprimand, or worse, if offended, she may bear her fangs, penetrate your skin, and inject her venom into your bloodstream. At this point, she owns you; you are helpless and will suffer.

The wicked snake scenario slithers from the receptionist's head as Laurel moves closer to the hostess stand. On duty is Alison, who snatches a pen and pad of paper before scrambling behind the imaginary serpent like an obedient little soldier. The python marches on, her hood fully fanned and forked tongue whipping at lightning speed. The only saving grace, this she-devil tips well; she takes pride in maintaining a reputation for taking exceptional care of those who are loyal.

"Is my table set?"

A nod and a slight smile indicating affirmative are barely discernible on Alison's petrified face.

"Are my bottles chilling? Is the kitchen informed of my menu?" Laurel rattles on without waiting for an answer. "Send an attendant to retrieve the dive gear from my dock box and bring everything to the pool. Now, please! It's gangway M; my yacht is at the end. But I'm sure you know that already."

The barrage of questions seems endless as the hostess hurries to keep pace, scribbling mixed with "yes mesdames" when appropriate.

Then, to demonstrate she hasn't missed a trick, Alison states, "I, myself, verified your requests, confirming all requirements are to your standards. If you or your guests require any further assistance, please don't hesitate to call on me."

Laurel refrains from unleashing the pocket full of insults she never leaves home without. Instead, she says nothing, only offering the confident girl her infamous nod of approval before walking away.

The day is bright; Laurel's oversized sunglasses shield her from the sun, as does her headscarf fluttering in the breeze. Laurel stops in the locker room to trade her heels for deck shoes. The recommended footwear is not optional. To ensure Olivia didn't show up in knockoffs, Laurel donated a gently used pair for her to wear.

The ladies overindulge in the amenities one would expect in a members-only establishment. While changing into their swimwear, they joke about the lifestyles of the rich and famous.

In a mocking tone, Olivia says, "Oh, come on; membership life can be fabulous."

"You meet people with like interests, lie about what you own, brag about who you're jumping in bed with, and a diet Coke appears at the snap of a finger. It's magical."

Laurel walked in to catch, "It's magical."

A flash of pity strikes Laurel when it dawns on her that Olivia will never truly understand how the other half lives.

She is proud of herself for offering her friends a glimpse into her privileged life. Kathryn can venture to guess the pending assault and interrupts the process before the thought forms into hurtful words, instantly killing the day. She asks if all the equipment is the same size, a ridiculous question but the only thing that came to mind.

Dana jokes, "Laurel's mask won't fit over her scarf."

"Wonder Woman, you're going poolside naked," Margo jabs.

"You must remove your force field and bracelets before the dive."

Laurel shakes her head and reminds everyone that remarks like these from anyone else would result in a slow and painful death.

Dana whispers under her breath, "One can only hope."

Divemaster Todd's well-rehearsed and enthusiastic welcome for Ms. Stanhope and her crew brings smiles to the nervous faces. A voluntary boast highlighting Laurel's gracious offer to introduce her friends to the wonders below the surface earns Todd an acknowledgment.

The deep-sea attire is awkward and tight initially, but he assures them they will move freely once they are in the water. Next, they are herded like seals to pick out fins and other aquatic essentials.

Olivia whines, "This is a lot of work. We should consider the aquarium. The sea life is the same, and staying dry sounds better and better all the time."

Laurel informs the instructor that they would like to utilize the belts she brought. This guy's got game; he's buttering her up like hot, toasted sourdough. He compliments her expert selection, but the praise is followed by the legal reasons why they can only use what the diving school supplies. However, he explained that the pro shop stocks the latest and most expensive accessories; "our members would accept nothing less." The patient instructor promises to take the unused equipment back to her dock box for safekeeping to appease her further.

Custom everything from head to toe is provided, of course, as a personal favor to Laurel.

All the pandering makes Margo seasick, saying under her breath, "'Custom,' it's all the same, 'black,' how can you tell the difference?"

The girls giggle as they make their way out of the staging area. The crystal turquoise water sparkles against the pale sky, but the best part is that the water is warmer than expected. They all prod Laurel to go in first.

"Suck it up, sister, and get in," says Dana.

The opportunity to float around eased the pressure; they all agreed swimming would be enough; no one cared to participate in class. A while later, Todd introduced a snorkel to give them more freedom. They are starting to come around, discovering something about being in the water that lets the world drift away. The weightlessness is exhilarating; submerging their faces underwater while continuing to breathe sparks glee. The session for most of them is euphoric. But panic engulfs Margo the minute her foot loses touch with the bottom of the pool, but lucky for her, instructor Todd is on hand to comfort her. A little individual instruction had her trusting the snorkel, and she was reassured she wouldn't drown on his watch.

The lecture portion of the day is over, but Todd invites everyone to stay as long as they like. The water is soothing, and to their surprise, no one is ready to leave. Still, Laurel pouts. Disappointed they didn't use tanks today until Todd pulled her aside. He expressed he didn't harbor any reservations regarding her ability; his concern was with the rest of her party. The thought of introducing everything at this time would be overwhelming and unsafe. Todd sprinkles in that she's a natural, and the others will acclimate soon enough, but they need time and some practice now. His goal is for his students to anticipate the next lesson with joy and not be afraid. To earn his gratuity, the instructor added that his job would be easy if all students were genuine yacht people like her. She took to the water like a mermaid.

"Oh, please," says Dana.

"Are you hearing this drivel?"

Margo barks, "Tip the man and let's eat; I'm starving. What is it about swimming that makes you so hungry?"

The requirements to be a staffer at this prestigious establishment are complicated. One must possess the skill to read Laurel's mind or acknowledge what she isn't saying when it's clear she's saying something. The dining room only offers three tables Laurel deems acceptable. She always calls beforehand to allow time for adjustments. Table number one, "the grand table," is for entertaining groups and resides in front of an expansive floor-to-ceiling window. Table two is an intimate nook where the couple isn't visible to other diners. Option three is also for two but is reserved for those occasions when Ms. Stanhope expresses she adores her fans and wants to make herself available. All three vantage points share the same panoramic visual. But before you can appreciate the spectacular view, you will "view" Laurel; then, it's up to you whether or not you "appreciate" the picturesque scene.

Today the table arrangement imitates the cover of a bridal magazine, decorated more for a shower or wedding than an after-scuba brunch. Once again, Laurel spared no expense to treat her friends to a beautiful afternoon. Each nautical-themed place setting is gorgeous. The dishes are not standard flare; they belong to the Stanhope's collection. The off-white plates trimmed with a thick marbled ribbon of blue lapis lazuli and finished with a fine line of gold at the rim are stunning. Kathryn recognizes the distinct china and the stemware as belonging to their host. Each side of the table boasts a monogrammed silver ice bucket perched on a matching stand. Each is stocked with a vintage selected from the Stanhope's private liquor locker. The display is impressive, yet the nautical embellishments come off as a miserable attempt at what Laurel interprets as charming.

"Bless her heart," says Margo, "She's made Martha Stewart seaworthy by putting a spin on Olivia's centerpiece."

"The little fins are hilarious," laughs Dana.

Kathryn comes to Laurel's defense, "Leave her alone; she's entitled to some credit for trying."

Laurel pulls up a chair facing the water and asks what's so funny. She was off browbeating the chef to ensure her preset menu presented as planned. The question asked is dismissed under the accolades surrounding her gorgeous arrangement. A server approaches the table and asks permission to pour, and he waits with a bottle in hand wrapped in a crisp white cloth until he receives an approving nod. The starched uniformed men glide around the table in a choreographed routine. Each server in the cast executes his role in the performance with panache. The afternoon is sheer perfection, from the ambiance to the imperial treatment. Dessert tops this lovely meal with light raspberry sorbet and chocolate truffles.

Delighted with her efforts, Laurel beams until her eyes land on Curtis, who is dining with another member. The couple isn't seated at a discreet table; they are on display. This spectacle won't go unnoticed by the other members, turning into juicy gossip before she can drain her flute. Mr. Thompson is a plus one to a trust fund tart who inherited handsomely, married well, and divorced fabulously. The trifecta of a hated woman. Her being more suited for Curtis and doubling as Laurel's younger sister only adds the final ingredient in a recipe called "scandalous disgrace."

No one else recognized Curtis until Laurel stopped speaking mid-sentence and stared into space. They follow her gaze, prompting a frantic conversation to transpire in complete silence. Instantly, a nonverbal yet unanimous agreement takes shape; they need to go and go now before an unpleasant incident erupts in the middle of the noon rush. With a loud voice, Kathryn thanks Laurel for outdoing herself. The others chime in with more accolades as they surround their speechless friend and usher her to the exit. Ample congratulatory praise, which would delight a host under normal circumstances, spurs agitation and is ignored. Olivia quickly stuffed a couple of truffles in her napkin and dropped the wrapped treats in her bag before leaving her seat.

The capacity to conceal her emotions is not Laurel's strong suit; they only have seconds before she explodes. As if on cue, the actress hisses, "The audacity to entertain that adolescent in MY CLUB."

Kathryn thinks the obvious, *this is her club too and her boy toy as well*, but she thinks it best to keep her opinion quiet.

Olivia says she would love to stay and witness the beheading but wants to go home to her kids. Saturdays are filled with an organized sport happening somewhere without her. Margo hands Dana her house key and invites her to accompany her home. She wants to reintroduce her to the dog Milo and show her where she keeps his supplies. They all bid each other farewell and reinforced their enjoyment of the day.

Far from ready to go home and in no condition to drive, Laurel balks as Kathryn does her best to convince her to leave. She insists they go for a boat ride to prove she isn't affected by Curtis and his little exploit.

"Come on, let's go cruise around. No one is waiting for us; we can't go home this early."

Kathryn concedes only out of fear that her tipsy, frustrated friend will likely go out alone. From where Curtis and his pretty companion dine, they will surely notice the yacht and all her splendor as she glides past the big bay windows. So, Kathryn finds a seat out of public view, wanting to avoid being associated with the drama. They idle out beyond the breakwater, and the skipper abandons the helm to go below to pop open more bubbles.

The new captain uses the "I'm driving" excuse as her reason not to partake in the upcoming stupor. However, after the diva consumes a few more glasses, the ugly effects of alcohol present themselves. Kathryn decides it's time to return and heads in the slip's direction.

The quiet vessel glides against the dock with ease. All the high-tech options assisted by the current keep the boat against the mooring long enough for Kathryn to secure the boat by herself. The change in course nor coming to a halt registered with the first mate. She is still ranting about Curtis and his juvenile playdate.

The lockup sequence is simple; they've all witnessed the procedure several times. After securing the cabin, Kathryn places the key back in its hiding place. The half-empty champagne bottle gets tossed in the trash at the end of the gangway on their way out. Laurel only agrees to go home after being promised she'll be brought back to collect her vehicle in the morning. Of course, calling Uber or Lyft is an option, but this famous starlet considers such an act cruel and unusual.

Once at home, safely tucked in bed, the woozy star lays motionless, appearing at peace amongst the satin sheets as Kathryn examines her—thoughts of pressing the pillow over her resting friend's face dance through her head. But the realization of showing up on the security tape assisting her intoxicated sidekick into the house erased the fantasy.

While Laurel and Kathryn went out to sea, the valet retrieved the remaining cars; Dana followed Margo home, where Frank and Tyler sat waiting to start their road trip. A reintroduction wasn't necessary, as Milo, the happy Labrador, loves everyone. So, with farewells exchanged, the Reeds are off on their adventure. This welcome and overdue getaway for the family came at the most opportune moment for everyone involved.

The rare sunny afternoon fades into a vibrant sunset, but enough daylight reflects against the incoming fog to enjoy being outdoors a little longer. Milo woofs at the door, indicating he would like to go out. Not knowing where to go, Dana allows the dog to take the lead as he reveals his usual walking route. Milo sits at the curb and won't go into the street; he doesn't need a leash, but Dana is nervous, so the dog remains tethered until they are almost home. They walk for a long while, allowing the family to travel a safe distance, eliminating any chance they may return. A point exists in any journey when a forgotten item's importance constitutes returning home. There is also a point when the car is not turning around, regardless of the left article's significance. Dana and her furry walking partner agree that forty-five minutes is sufficient, and Milo is let off the leash to roam and relieve himself on everything in sight.

Back at the house, Dana unpacks the cameras from her gym bag one at a time. Disposing of the packaging weeks ago behind Best Buy in Sacramento alleviated any mess. She reminds herself to wipe down the unit, leaving no trace evidence behind. Art is the perch of choice again; she stands on a chair, careful not to touch anything. The frame is boxy and black. The camera will lay hidden, remaining unnoticed unless, of course, someone goes searching. Dana tests her reach for quick removal, ensuring she can grab the device from the top of the picture without the chair. She only uses the seat to mount the recording stick without touching anything else.

Fingerprints won't matter when she removes the unit; prints left behind will only come into play if someone other than she discovers the recorder first. It isn't necessary to sweep the house for bugs or spyware. Margo would've shared a sneaky undertaking of this magnitude with the group. And why would she need to bug her own home? She knows what goes on here during the day.

The home's layout is a small open concept, requiring only a single recorder to survey the living, dining room, and kitchen. Those are the only rooms, other than bedrooms and bathrooms. The hardware installation is declared complete without reason or desire to capture what transpires in the remaining locations. Dana is still tossing around "the master plan" in her head but hasn't found the proper outline yet. She's always watching, hoping something will come to her. An idea better reveal itself soon; masking her despair is becoming more complicated. Sharing a home with Randal is daunting, and the pretense of friendship with Laurel will become transparent sooner or later. Right now, the plan is to make some coffee, eat something, and check the spyware is functioning.

Not wanting to cook, Dana finds cereal in the pantry, a sugary treat not stocked at home since the kids went to college. After consuming two bowls of Cap'n Crunch, she notes to purchase Tyler another box because this one will not last. Then, with the roof of her mouth in shreds, she takes her coffee and laptop to the sofa. Opening her computer, she confirms one device in the Reed home is more than adequate. Three windows now fill the screen; one is Laurel's house, the second image is Margo's place, and the other is the world wide web. Finally, Dana logs into Siren, which illuminates the third panel. Several interested suitors left messages for her, much to her (Sherry's) surprise. But she doesn't bother with them; she focuses on her mission. Laurel will be along soon enough; if she is one thing, she's predictable; Dana's only task is to sit back, lurking in the background, and wait.

Unbeknownst to Laurel, her "Candice" Siren file plays alongside a voyeuristic peek into her home. Margo's panel is closed now, as Dana does not need to watch herself.

Too angry to rest, Laurel didn't stay where Kathryn left her for long. A little power nap restores her composure to marginally functional. The altered state won't hinder her trolling ability, she grabs her laptop, and from under her soft covers, she logs on to the dating app.

Humiliation is not something Laurel will forgive, and Curtis's minor indiscretion this afternoon won't go unpunished. How ironic. She'll punish her boyfriend for the same reason she is being punished. A plan percolating in the actress's brain involves manipulating another man resulting in the infliction of sweet revenge on Curtis, sending him into an uncontrollable rage. Dana can work with that.

Unaware of the counted keystrokes, Laurel taps out her desires. Only a few clicks and a swipe before the vixen hones in on her target, lays the bait, and bingo, she lands a hookup for tonight. This woman's stamina and devotion to the payback are admirable, but Dana wishes the torment could wait until tomorrow.

While observing the animated actress carrying on an entire conversation with her monitor, the audio detects irritation in her voice. The following discussion, although one-sided, is between Laurel and her publicist arranging the evening's paparazzi. The topic revolves around photos that have yet to be taken and when they will appear in print.

To be the public relations representative for this high-maintenance client would be a nightmare from which one wouldn't wake. The first nonnegotiable demand requires TMZ to be on-site, as they receive the best ratings for reporting B-list shenanigans. One would think the desperate star might reserve that resource until she hits rock bottom. Today, however, she'll take any attention, favorable or unfavorable. Her sole agenda is visibility; it matters not how images surface or who acquires them as long as the actress is in the public eye.

Dana, as Sherry, sends Curtis a text from her burner phone, relaying that she knows where several celebrities are dining tonight and that he owes her a date. After all, he shouldn't be required to wait for tomorrow's newspaper to learn of the diva's indiscretion. He is entitled to the same experience he afforded her; he should witness this with his own eyes in real time. Fortunately, his angry antics are escalating; he can't maintain self-control when confronted. Public scenes cultivate an online mention, but outbursts secure newsfeed content and hopefully an appearance on the 11:00

news, where he will be featured tonight if all goes according to plan.

The next phone call is to the television station. It's time to plant some seeds. The pre-screened plea connects her to the Channel 7 entertainment desk, where she states, "I am an inside source with information regarding Laurel Stanhope's whereabouts this evening. The location is the Regency Lounge; her escort is an unknown male, someone other than Curtis Thompson. The tabloid relationship featuring Ms. Stanhope and Mr. Thompson, as of late, although considered toxic, is riveting. They spar publicly at bars and restaurants around the city, creating a social media frenzy.

"Why have the police and the masses ignored this volatile relationship? It should be apparent that the courtship began before the late Alan Stanhope's body was even cold.

"How do you develop a bond worthy of epic battles with someone you just met?

"You don't!

"Yet no one has shown any interest in this angle, not even his family."

Dana's ranting is palpable, and she ends with, "I can't say if Curtis Thompson or Mrs. Stanhope were participants in her husband's death, but what if they were?

"You should be held accountable if you covered the story but didn't bother to investigate the matter as a crime. Review the facts; Curtis flies off the handle whenever Laurel is with another man. How did he control himself around her husband?

"How will he conduct himself this evening at the Regency Lounge?

"All I'm saying is someone should take responsibility here and dig deeper. The station has an obligation to its viewers to do what is right, investigate!"

Click.

Dana planted the thought process while Laurel unwittingly took care of the internet. Now tabloid TV or the local news should broadcast Laurel's date with the Siren guy. Curiosity will provoke Curtis to appear, and a guaranteed shitstorm will follow. One can only hope the insecure boyfriend, who repeatedly proves his temper is explosive, doesn't disappoint. A domestic altercation should generate enough attention to motivate someone to investigate the claims about Alan. Regardless, if nothing else, the word is out. Public opinion should fuel some outrage.

The excitement has taken its toll; Dana falls asleep to the only light in the room, the flickering blue glow of her screen. The last thing she remembers is Laurel going upstairs to dress for her evening out. She can no longer keep her eyes open, and with Milo cuddled up next to her on the bed, she doesn't budge until dawn. Her hairy sleeping buddy takes up half the mattress. The king-sized bed can't accommodate Frank, Margo, and an extra hundred pounds of dog, at the same time. She lets the big dog know she's aware of being played. Then again, she isn't them, and it's only one night. So, she grabs handfuls of skin around his jowls, conveying she has no intention of telling those Bambi-brown eyes to sleep on the floor.

EIGHTEEN

Lazy Sunday with a Dog

The light of day seeps eerily across the bed; any attempt to fall back to sleep is a losing battle. Milo is anxious to go out, and the small amount of Cap'n Crunch left at the bottom of the box is all the incentive Dana requires to force herself out of bed.

With half a cup of coffee consumed, Milo runs Dana through the usual paces during the walk routine; she again considers the mental and physical benefits of having a canine companion. Milo proves to be a great sounding board, and he never argues, only obligingly agrees. The hound objects to the number of cookies provided, but other than that, his behavior is predictable. After sufficiently watering the neighborhood, Milo guides Dana back to the house. She pours herself the remainder of the abrasive cereal and fills her oversized mug with more coffee.

Java and bowl in hand, Dana settles in at the kitchen table with her laptop and her new warm, fuzzy friend resting on her feet. She will be visiting the local shelter when her current predicament is over.

"OK, what awaits us today, big boy," she says to Milo.

The first task is to locate the point on the video where she stopped watching before conceding to the weight of her eyelids the night before. Uninterrupted slumber may sound unambitious to some, but it's an accomplishment for an overactive mind. The last thing she remembers is Laurel confirming a hookup and going upstairs.

She clicks the arrow key while the video jumps forward in thirty-second increments until she catches sight of a refreshed woman in a tight red dress. Something pricey, no doubt, with a small handbag and heels which don't match yet blend, pulling together an outfit you'd expect on the runway during fashion week. Envious of the starlet's dressing area, she considered converting her son's room into her personal space, but that project will remain on hold until she wears something other than work attire and sweats. But, of course, trading her husband for a designer wardrobe would require zero consideration. Sorry, Randal.

The doorbell rings, and an image of a handsome older gentleman standing in the doorway appears on her screen.

"Well played, Laurel."

Dana detects the strategic move straight away. A senior, as the chosen escort, is sure to upset her boyfriend. Distinguished is a better description of this new man; he is far from old, fit, and well-dressed in his late fifties or early sixties. It matters not; jealousy trumps the current situation rectifying itself in a dignified manner.

The camera's sightline doesn't capture the parked car, so Dana can't determine the type, model, or license number.

What is Laurel thinking?

She clicked on this man only hours ago on the internet and invited him to her home.

Doesn't the cardinal rule of online dating dictate the initial meeting transpire in a public place?

The thrill of the hunt and throwing caution to the wind with reckless abandon supersede self-preservation. One can only pray that this guy doesn't discover his famous date's true identity, or this situation may go sideways quickly. But, of course, this whole thing may go sideways, regardless. He enters the house and kisses her on the cheek, introducing himself as Dale Warner. The name flowing fluently off his tongue may very well be an alias.

After all, Laurel is pretending to be Candice Moore, intentionally omitting her name during the introduction by simply saying, "Welcome" and "Won't you come in?"

Her guest stands posed just inside the threshold. They exchange pleasantries while Dale assists his date in putting on her coat. Panic for Dana subsided somewhat when Mr. Warner remained in the foyer, not venturing further into the house.

Laurel and her dashing companion complement each other. They resemble an attractive Hollywood power couple. But, unfortunately, this poor guy, pleased at the moment, lacks the foresight of what is in store for him. Reality will be slapping him in the face soon enough. Until then, Dana's only option is to sit and wait for their return.

Crossing her fingers, she hopes Dale is sincere when he voices his dinner arrangements and goes directly to the Regency Lounge as intended, not a predetermined dumpsite prepped to hide her lifeless body.

What Dana doesn't see on the tape is the couple arriving at the restaurant, where the car pulls up in front of the valet stand. A young Ryan Gosling lookalike approaches the passenger door, extending his hand to help the actress out of the vehicle.

The attendant recognizes Laurel, greeting her, "What a pleasure to have you join us this evening, Ms. Stanhope."

Dale grabs her by the elbow, escorting her to the door; he whispers in her ear, "I knew it was you."

Laurel giggles back, "I know, but it's part of the fun," winking to lighten any tension.

A doorman in a sharp suit also addresses the actress by name before ushering the couple inside. She smiles, lightly touching his arm as a delicate thank-you gesture.

The hostess is equally gracious, steering them toward a private table.

Not in the mood for seclusion, Laurel asks, "Would you mind if we sat there?" She points to a table positioned in the center of the room.

"Of course," says the embarrassed young woman, seating them without hesitation.

Two servers appear; the men place cloth napkins across the couple's laps while handing Dale a wine list, which he refuses.

Instead, he requests the finest champagne for "his lady."

Dale asks Laurel if he may take the liberty of ordering oysters and caviar for her. She says nothing, but her signature nod signifies her approval.

A thought accompanied by a strange sensation presented itself this evening. Happiness, and the sudden flood of joy, felt foreign yet wonderful. So much so that she almost didn't recognize the signs.

Could this be more than a one-night stand?

An authentic relationship may be developing. Future possibilities coupled with grandiose ideas swirl like a tornado in her head. Realizing she is coming off like a love-struck teenager, she blames exhaustion from the day's events for her momentary delirium.

A courtship had never entered her mind; any actual attraction to this guy wasn't on the menu. Entertainment is always the primary hope, but she never expected much or cared before now. The intention for this outing centered around revenge. The strategy entailed sipping bubbles, dining on fine food, and devastating Curtis. However, the simple plot derailed upon opening the front door. The man before her presents as charming, sophisticated, and well-versed in the proper way to treat a woman. If he ticks a few more boxes, this woman is in a world of hurt, the insatiable kind.

Anxiety is beginning to surface; it's too late to alert her publicist to call off the dogs; she noticed the press waiting when they arrived. Of course, the photographers won't pounce until they finish their meal, but they are ready in the event drama unfolds. For now, they will lie in wait, hoping the boy wonder crashes this intimate setting, causing a newsworthy disturbance featuring this lovely unsuspecting man.

The evening is progressing remarkably well, with no glaring red flags or minor annoyances to pick apart.

So, why the need for a Siren account, and why is he still available?

Not one to hold back, Laurel comes right out and asks him.

"Why is a man like you single?"

He states he's lonely before flipping the script back to her, adding, "You're beautiful, smart, and talented, so why the need for online dating?"

Laurel is ecstatic that he didn't describe her as sexy. To refer to sex appeal would mean he only wanted one thing, sex, followed by a disappearing act in the predawn hours, never to be seen again. That scenario, of course, is what she planned to do to him until she found him to be a worthy suitor. They both agree that this semi-blind encounter turned out to be a pleasant surprise. Having finished their meal, Dale asks if she would like to split a piece of cake or chocolate-dipped strawberries.

Laurel replies, "Only if we can take it to go."

The server is tasked with selecting two treats to be wrapped up, preferably something that won't melt on the way home. Then, a sleight of hand transfers a valet ticket and a black American Express card to the maître d', who stops by to ensure everything is to the couple's liking.

Dale reassures the man that the experience was divine, but he doesn't want to keep his lady waiting. Although more for Laurel's benefit than the manager's, the comment force-feeds the notion that chivalry is alive and well. She acknowledges his refined etiquette by squeezing his hand, but she wants to get out of there, so they can share some dessert and whatever is in the to-go bag.

The blissful twosome steps outside to a wild scene. The paparazzi snap away as Dale opens the car door for his date while shielding her from the attacking crowd.

"That's an adrenaline rush. Does this happen often?"

Laurel laughs, "Sometimes."

He, too, is contemplating "long-term" here; this is exciting and a fresh start for both of them.

Headlights trip the security system as the car rolls into the driveway not long after they leave the house. Concerned by the hasty return, Dana assumes something went wrong and continues watching the tape.

What if this guy is trouble or a bore, and Laurel called it off?

He wouldn't be the first Siren troll to suffer this fate. She will drink his expensive libations, be recognized, and after a few photos, she's had enough, insisting he take her home. Alternatively, if no one is there to adore her, she will excuse herself, call for her car service, and vanish. But instead, an instant connection is on display —the very definition of a guy who is about to have his cake and eat it too. Too bad he hasn't the first clue he is about to be kicked to the curb before he can put his pants back on. Either way, this is not safe. All Dana can do is sit waiting in frustration, praying this affectionate man is genuine in his search for love and not stalking a victim.

Laurel tells Dale to select something to drink from the fridge, and she will be right down. He rummages through the kitchen, finding everything needed to plate the cakes. Excited, he found a bottle of champagne he was familiar with but had yet to sample. A romantic setting awaits when the lady of the house returns in a two-piece silk pajama set with a matching robe and slippers.

"I like being comfortable when I enjoy a late-night snack."

They retire to the couch, where they hand-feed each other decadent confections. The discussion flows from vintage Grande Cuvee to pale pink rosé until he takes the glass from her hand, asking permission to kiss her. She said she's been waiting all night to taste his lips. How he holds her arms causes the robe to slide off her shoulders and land at their feet. She takes him by the hand and leads him up to her bedroom. The second floor is out of Dana's sight line, but that is best as Randal would be who she sees entangled with the seductress, not this random stranger. The visual is too painful, not to mention repulsive.

Dana isn't privy to Dale being pushed onto the bed, nor does she see his shoes being removed and tossed aside. Only with a blind eye can Dana predict the acts that follow. Yet, images of the dominatrix climbing on her conquest invade her thoughts. Finally, the lights go out, but no one is sleeping.

Dale spent the night, which is unusual. Laurel often brags that its customary that as soon as she finishes, her playmate is asked to vacate the premises, whether he is finished or not. Cuddling is not common practice, and her makeup removal routine is mandatory. It's assumed that no one but Madeline could identify the actress without face paint, but the bigger concern is ample time to moisturize and hydrate.

Still shocked by what she's witnessed, Dana can't relate to the possible dangers to which Laurel subjected herself.

And where is Curtis?

This new fellow is moving in fast. A replacement for the boy toy wasn't previously an option.

"What could this man possibly say that would warrant a sleepover!"

Dana shouts profane words to the ceiling in disbelief.

Confused over what to do, she sits for a while. Milo is also bewildered; they are in the kitchen; therefore, he deserves a biscuit. She informs her furry friend she's been with one man for the past twenty-one years. Laurel went through more men in the previous twenty-one days than she had entertained in her entire lifetime. The dog lost interest and laid down.

Enough, for now. It would be nice to use this quiet time to relax, but shutting off the computer won't stop the wheels from spinning. Although an excellent companion, Milo offers little in the way of input. He does, however, provide plenty in the form of support.

Somewhere in the information gathered thus far hides a blueprint for a murder or two; there has to be. *Think, Dana, think!*

NINETEEN

Waking Up to a New Man

The smeared mascara on Laurel's face unveils the ramifications of a successful night out. Early dawn creeping through a slit in the curtain is her cue to refresh before her actual appearance sends the bare bum of her new man running into the streets to escape her clutches.

Catlike, she sneaks out of bed and into her dressing room with plenty of time to put herself back together before Dale wakes up. Of course, he's aware she left the bed, but he's a good sport and plays along.

Madeline is off on Sundays, so there's no one to make breakfast, offer pastries, or pour coffee, so she needs to make arrangements. She slips back into bed as Dale rolls over, pretending to wake.

"Hi, beautiful."

"Hello, sunshine," whispers Laurel in a Listerine-fresh voice.

"Looks like the sun is out, and it appears to be a lovely day. Would you like to join me for brunch at the Yacht Club?"

Dale, almost confused, says, "Sure."

He assumes he has exceeded his welcome and starts getting dressed; he indicates it will take him an hour before returning to collect her. Laurel insists on driving, telling him she will meet him at the Club. She asks if he needs the address; he shakes his head and smiles at her as she lies in bed, surrounded by her overstuffed pillows.

He kisses her forehead, saying, "In an hour, my lady."

The time factor and the unknown flood Dana with frustration; the surveillance covered nothing for the past nine hours; she only witnesses the two arriving home and her date coming down the stairs, grabbing his suit jacket, and driving away. The diva comes down twenty minutes later and makes herself a cup of coffee.

This acquaintance must be extraordinary; Laurel is never up this early, not to mention showered and shining. She steps out in cute capri pants and a flowing blouse. Her hair is in an updo, and the scarf over her shoulders will soon wrap around her head to complete the ensemble. The hall mirror confirms she is still capable of star quality at a moment's notice. It appears she plans on meeting up with her new man to continue this romance in the light of day.

Opening the door to the garage presents a slight setback; it's empty. Her car is already at the Club. A quick call to her car service will remedy that mental lapse. She then calls the Club to notify the staff of her arrival. There is a noticeable difference in the message delivered this morning. The politeness applied starkly contrasts Laurel's typical means of communication. The instructions advise that the gentleman accompanying her is a special invitee requiring some privacy. After a few routine requests, she verifies the use of her monogrammed champagne bucket filled with ice and specific details, denoting a unique vintage from her private collection.

"One final touch, if it's not too much trouble, please provide a carafe of fresh-squeezed orange juice as my guest may prefer a mimosa."

A firm thank-you spilling from Laurel's lips shocks the hostess, who replies, "The pleasure is mine."

Accustomed to shouted orders followed by a dial tone, this interaction leaves the staffer smiling and saying to no one, "Today will be an interesting day."

As expected, the Yacht Club is commanding, although the modern architecture is a bold yet commendable choice. The usual nautical ornamentation is missing, which is a pleasant surprise. Aesthetics aside, Dale is nervous as the flurry of activity last night left him apprehensive; he can't help but anticipate the same attention today. However, his stress dissipates when he pulls into the empty valet. Parking attendants are available to take your car, limiting outside access and ensuring protection from unsolicited parties. Besides, the imposing marquee clearly states members only.

The day shows promise; Laurel looks fabulous, comfortably residing as the queen of her element, and he is most grateful the conversation flows without the awkward dead zones. They both boast that freshly fucked look as they gaze at each other lovingly over eggs benedict. All indications point to Dale liking Laurel for Laurel, a delightful yet uncommon circumstance.

Laurel places her napkin on her plate and stands, stating, "I'm full, let's walk off our breakfast. Plus, there is someone I want you to meet."

They walk along the boardwalk and stop when they reach the end of the dock. "There she is." Laurel points to her yacht.

"I'd like you to meet *'Lady,'* well, *'The Leading Lady,'* to be precise. She is the only one I will willingly concede that title.

"When you suggested bringing a book to read while we relax on your boat's deck, this is not what I had envisioned, she's gorgeous." Says Dale.

The sunny weather didn't last, so reading time quickly turned into a naked stateroom event, where they stayed well into the afternoon.

Their impromptu online introduction sparked something new in both of them. With a gentle kiss, Dale bids his new sweetheart farewell for now but suggests getting together for dinner in the coming week. He tells her to select the restaurant; better yet, he would like to prepare a meal for her at his home. The invitation thrills Laurel, but for anyone else who took the time to listen to any podcasts, this is hell no 101.

Laurel met this man on the internet yesterday!

Please DO NOT go to his house. Or, at the very least, tell a friend the location, so they can alert the authorities on where to start searching for your dead body.

TWENTY

The Workweek

Monday morning rolls around, and Dana is back in her office at Skyhill Technologies. Her small laptop glows from the side of her desk. According to the tracker on Randal's car, he is present and accounted for at the dealership where he is supposed to be. Frank works hard from his La-Z-Boy on his latest project, complete with snacks. Kathryn's twenty-second commute down the stairs should have her in her home office, seated in her comfortable chair, waiting for patients to arrive. At the same time, one can presume Joel and Eric wait patiently in slow-moving traffic toward their workplaces. Without an agreed-upon schedule, Olivia pushes the boundaries with the dentist. Today she has elected to work for Kathryn. Olivia is taking great pleasure in making Dr. Bob wonder if she is coming back. Since Olivia informed her boss of her additional part-time job, he's kept his distance and given her a slight pay increase. Nothing he does will keep Olivia in his practice long-term, but both jobs are necessary for now.

Margo is on her way to the bookstore, anxious to open. The 10:00 hour is the only thing this wary wife anticipates with any joy these days. Customers filter in, thirsty for an escape, while drinking coffee with the other neighborhood moms. Today's podcast is *Trashy Divorces*, with hosts Stacie and Alicia. These two enchanting ladies will leave you wanting more by delivering well-researched and witty commentary on the demise of your favorite couples.

Stacie and Alicia dish the dirt on current relationships and go back to the past to take a deep dive into history's most fabulous breakups, from Ernest Hemingway to Sonny and Cher. *Trashy Divorces* allow for a break from criminals, but sometimes they cross over. For instance, the episode featuring Erica Kelley from *Southern Fried True Crime* is fascinating.

The podcasts remove Margo from the personal misery encompassing every fiber of her being. Of course, learning someone else's marriage is worse doesn't make her situation any better, but the hope and support generated by the community make her life livable.

On deck for today's event, Stacie and Alicia cover episode ten, "Double Fantasy," the trashy divorce of Brad Pitt and Jennifer Aniston. And if that's not enough "trash candy," they doubled down on Brad's next matrimonial adventure with his second wife, Angelina Jolie. Margo wishes she had time to print "Team Jen" T-shirts for her patrons, then wonders who will be on her team when the time comes for her split from Frank.

On the other side of town, Madeline serves Laurel her breakfast. Their morning displays few exceptions from any other day of the week. The quasi-robotic routine begins with coffee, followed by Laurel reading the activities in her day planner.

Next, the mother figure, Madeline, spouts instructions, "Your Pilates instructor will be here in forty minutes. After your workout, take a quick shower; you have color scheduled, so don't shampoo."

A glare screaming, "I can read," crosses Laurel's face as Madeline dictates the rest of the itinerary from memory.

The hairdresser, among others, is required to come to the house. Laurel fears someone will catch her in foils and sell the pictures to a tabloid. She occasionally makes an appearance in a salon for styling or trim, but only if guaranteed she'll be stunning while the stylist works their magic. Most essential services require privacy. Anything with potential side effects, such as embarrassing or unflattering photos, happens behind closed doors. The mani-pedi, dry-cleaning, and shopping for clothes are serviceable tasks that can be taken care of from home or delegated. Madeline does all the grocery shopping, cooking, and housework. Dana wonders what Laurel does all day. Well, she is about to find out.

After Laurel reviews her day, she flips open her computer; Dana can tell what she is doing from the swiping action. The dating scene baffles Dana; *how does one derive satisfaction or meaning from so many blind encounters with anonymous men?*

Dana whispers, "God, I would hate to be single."

The minute the words leave her lips, the reality of her marital status changing overwhelms her. *That will be me! I'll be out there!*

She understands she is alone in her relationship now, but having someone and being lonely is different from being on your own. Dana's next thought makes her smile, *I'm getting a dog.*

A more significant realization comes moments later. *I'll be a...*

Dana can't bring herself to say the word to describe who she will be if she eliminates her husband and friend. Thoughts of seeking guidance cross her mind. But confessing the actual reason for her visit may put her in danger, so she sticks to the topic of anxiety as a layer of protection while searching for help.

Dana laughs as she is confident lying on a therapist's couch and stating, "Hey, I'm thinking of killing my husband, and I'm sure if I talked with someone, I'd feel much better," would prompt a physician to call the authorities.

Then concluding the session won't be covered by a confidentiality agreement, or her medical insurance makes her laugh harder.

A chat with Kathryn sounds promising, but the pressure she is about to put on their friendship may be too tall an ask. These secrets are dark, illegal intentions, some of which should and should not be shared. Besides, Kathryn would also be obligated to talk her off the ledge. Perhaps if she only divulged Randal's extra-curricular activity. The "activity" being Laurel will be omitted.

The next voice Dana hears is Olivia answering the phone.

"Hello, O, it's Dana. I didn't realize you started working at Kathryn's office already."

Olivia beams excitedly. "Yes, I'll be here a couple of days a week until Kathryn returns from vacation. Dr. Bob freaked out, but I told him I needed the money. So, he reluctantly concurred."

Dana interrupts for fear Olivia will retell her entire life story right here. "Is Kathryn available?"

"She is finishing up with a session. Do you want to wait or call later?"

"I'll hold." Knowing if she hangs up, she won't call back; a few minutes pass before Kathryn picks up the line.

"Hi, Dana; this is a pleasant surprise. How are you?" asks Kathryn.

"Are we on speaker?"

"No."

"OK, I need to talk about Randal; I have health coverage and can schedule a time like a regular patient."

Assuming the acknowledgment of her PPO card or name written in the appointment book makes their conversation officially confidential, Dana confides she needs a professional opinion on Randal.

Kathryn glances at her open planner, inquiring, "When would you like to come in?"

Dana replies, "As soon as you can make time."

"Is everything all right? Do we need to speak now over the phone?"

"Well, I'm not sure where to start. I'm afraid Randal is seeing someone."

Kathryn inquires if she is assuming this or knows it for a fact.

"Fact," said Dana.

"Let's stop here before we get in too deep. It would be best if you came to the office. Olivia goes home at five. Can you swing by tonight after work, say 5:30?"

Dana says she will be there and arrives at the office at 5:15, in time to see Olivia pulling out of the driveway. Kathryn stands in the doorway, watching the women trade places. Tears begin streaming down Dana's cheeks before she's through the threshold. Then, after a warm embrace, they go upstairs, where they can talk in a less formal setting.

Hot tea steeps in front of the two friends seated on bar stools at the kitchen counter.

In a motherly doctor's voice, she says, "OK, start at the beginning and tell me what prompted your suspicion."

Dana confesses her husband's mid-life crisis is embarrassing and ridiculously textbook. "Randal lost interest in me and started going to strip clubs to fulfill the desires he lacks at home. His philanthropic efforts are unconventional; he enjoys funding wannabe college students, one dollar bill at a time. The first red flag was intimacy, his pursuit teetering on the edge of aggression. But his insatiable quest is for the physical act itself; I'm just a convenience. I faintly remember the last time he took me anywhere or expressed affection toward me. I wouldn't be shocked if he accidentally left a tip on the nightstand."

Kathryn holds back from asking if she's genuinely taken aback by all this and steers the discussion to how she feels. Dana may retreat immediately if faced with direct questions, so she lets her drone on without interruption. But the conversation bores the doctor. She finds herself fading in and out, trying to decipher the order in which the men fell victim to the star. It's clear to Kathryn Dana suspects Randal of surrendering to the foreplay their friend so freely dishes out. She just can't admit to herself this could actually be happening. But with Laurel's never-ending quest to commandeer each of their husbands, you'd have to be one rung below complete denial on the reality ladder not to see the florescent graffiti spray painted on the wall. It's baffling how fame and beauty can disable someone's defenses enough to leave oneself vulnerable to the evil lurking under a thick coat of makeup.

In most cases, Laurel exploited people for no other reason than to see how far she could sway them. Men and some women appear easily coaxed by the implication of sex, the suggestion of drugs, or both. She embraces her stardom and wealth; thus, you benefit or should at least feel privileged by association. Elaborate tales of erotic encounters are never in short supply. Her own belief in her lies is the hook. The goal is to convince you the lies she is spewing are truthful. That's the magic; you will hear similar stories repeatedly, and soon you won't remember what is real or made up. Dana was stuck in this purgatory for far too long, but she can discern fact from fiction now. Openly discussing her findings is the hard part.

After thirty minutes, Dana continued to babble on about her philandering husband but never revealed he delivered much more than a car to his mistress. The whining is nauseating. In the interest of everyone's time, if you're experiencing an issue important enough to seek counsel, for goodness' sake, tell the doctor the actual problem. The deceptive half-story laced with ill intentions prompts Kathryn to suspect her new patient may be concocting a plan to do away with Randal. She also considered whatever scheme this crazed wife was cooking up would be over-planned, with no real intention of implementing said plan.

To say Dana may be over her head is an understatement; Kathryn doesn't need to be a doctor to recognize a disaster in the making and decides her friend isn't capable of embarking on this adventure alone. She will need assistance moving on with her life sans Randal or any knowledge of his demise.

While listening to Dana describe how she went so far as to install a tracker on her cheating husband's car, only making matters worse, the other men in the friend group and their escapades with Laurel drift into Kathryn's conscience. She won't hold Joel's moment of weakness with the actress against him; his penance will be life without her.

But Frank, on the other hand, is another story. Laurel's conduct confirms she is playing with him, and he appears to have lost this game on level one. Looking the other way while Margo supports her deadbeat man and adult son is no longer acceptable.

So, Franky, your pathetic existence is over. You jumped at the first opportunity to fall in your lap, or, in this case, on your dick, and you played this new game like a mad Mario Brother. Sorry, sir, your death will be slow and painful, you prick.

One has to assume an assault on Eric is forthcoming if it hasn't happened already. Or maybe the serial slut skipped Eric out of fear he wouldn't fulfill his future obligation if she crossed the line. Either way, Kathryn won't apologize for Laurel's actions; but she is sorry if he had to endure an unpleasant experience. Rethinking the "obligation" regarding the Harpers brings an untimely smile to Kathryn's face, which she quickly readjusts. The obligation came in the form of asset management for the actress. Laurel insisted everyone take out a life insurance policy, so she also took out coverage on herself to show good faith. Naming the Harper family as her beneficiaries wasn't as charitable as it was self-serving. However, they shouldn't hold their breath as it may be a while before they see the light of day on this generous offer, but eventually, it will be a game-changer.

This unique arrangement came after a lengthy conversation between Laurel and Kathryn. The discussion revolved around the actress being family deficient, with no heirs to carry on her legacy or leave her fortune. Convinced her assets needed to be in the hands of someone who would memorialize the Stanhope name made the Harpers the clear choice. Their reward is a secure retirement. For Eric, being labeled the good guy finally has its advantages.

Although the recap in Kathryn's head is loaded with helpful information, the internal discussion the doctor is having with herself won't be shared with her patient. Who she realizes is still talking.

Careful not to appear distracted, Kathryn composes herself before reverting to the standard "How did that make you feel" to cover for her brief mental absence. The question will allow enough time for her to catch up and continue through the hour without further interruption.

To dissect the mindset of those who are troubled is Kathryn's passion. A real-life puppet master, formulating life-altering changes for her subjects to obey is her calling.

With a calm voice, Kathryn starts, "Have you considered what you would like to do going forward?"

Dana takes a moment before answering, "You mean legally?"

The doctor instructs her patient to slow down, adding, "Let's review your options before we go straight to divorce."

"Divorce? He's not getting off that easy. I would have to pay him alimony, not to mention two tuition payments; I can't lap dance away. Include bills, cars, expenses, and our mortgage; there's no room for him on the dole. And my beautiful house, I won't be able to afford our home by myself."

An expression unlike any other sweeps over her as she sobs, "I would lose everything."

Intrigued, Kathryn presses her to go on.

With a blank stare, Dana confides, "I'm contemplating something more along the lines of utilizing his life insurance policy and avoiding the legal aspects of separating."

Mouthing words under her breath but loud enough for the doctor to hear, "Simply submit a claim and be done with him."

She continues, "Lucky for me, we both bought equal policies simultaneously, with the help of our very own home-wrecker—I mean, friend—Laurel."

"We've discussed this already. She is messing with your head. The inappropriate comments are intentional, her twisted way of extracting a reaction from you. We don't have any proof Laurel is hooking up with your husband other than her provoking comments."

All the blood runs from Dana's face.

She stares at Kathryn and says, "You're mistaken."

Kathryn tries to explain away Laurel's promiscuous antics when

Dana stops her mid-sentence. "I'm not talking about misinterpreting Laurel's behavior."

"I said, 'You are mistaken.' I've never spoken to you about Laurel, so you're saying I'm not the only one. Your professional oath won't allow you to betray the others, so I won't put you in a position requiring you to lie to me about who else is having similar issues. But that's OK; in this case, the process of elimination will be short-lived.

"We can disqualify Eric; he is a gentleman and loves his wife. Laurel's involvement with Joel was never confirmed but assumed. So, this leaves fucking Frank. She probably hooks up with Randal and/or Frank on the evenings we hold our book club meetings or before we go out on our girls nights. All right, these are the cards being played; deal me in. Be warned, though; this is going to get ugly."

The remainder of Dana's diatribe rattles through tightly clenched teeth, branding Laurel as the instigator, the enemy, and now the intended target. The next step is determining appropriate sanctions for the tart's latest charade. A slanderous strike on her celebrity is easy enough, but not a real sport. No, this must be memorable, requiring a specific and unique punishment to fit this personal crime; by whom and when is the question.

Dana finds talking out her issues with someone other than Milo and herself quite therapeutic.

The knowledge of Frank's involvement with their friend would never come from her, but learning that Kathryn is already privy to playtime with the game master adds an unexpected new level. Her obligatory confidentiality is the only thing stopping her from sharing the details.

The intertwined players turn this situation into a convoluted mess; Dana hopes Kathryn can keep up as she clears her mind on the sofa. But it's not long before she is exhausted and quits talking, but her doctor/friend insists they resume therapy regularly in the confines of the office.

"I want you to promise me that if you experience any motivation to harm yourself or others, you will call me regardless of the time of day or night. Do you understand?"

Dana can't make eye contact, ashamed of her rant. Kathryn informs her troubled new patient their conversations will become more intense as she releases her stifled emotions. Then reassures her that this is all part of her journey through therapy. Before the session ends, the doctor reiterates calling or coming by anytime.

Under these circumstances, managing sleep and nerves is often an issue, so a prescription was offered but quickly refused.

Dana snaps, "Like the pills you supply Laurel?"

The doctor glares, "I can't talk about her with you as I can't and won't discuss you with her or anyone else, ever."

Picking up on the message hiding inside Kathryn's comment sends a flushed sensation through her like a hot flash.

She apologizes for the outburst, cringing as she responds, "No, I don't think I need chemical help yet."

A tear slides down Dana's cheek as she shares how much talking this out, put her in a better place. She then lets herself out.

No one is exposing their husband or the issue openly; they each think they are the only ones. That is why they are not comparing notes, which is good. So now, several people harbor enough resentment/motive to want to harm their beloved friend. Toss in the hordes of men manipulated beyond the point of invoking irrational impulses, and a substantial suspect pool emerges.

"Thank you for being 'mistaken,' Kathryn."

Dana would love to talk to Margo but doesn't dare. For now, the fewer people who link her knowledge of Randal and Laurel, the better. Dana will plead ignorance exhibiting devastation if their affair ever becomes public. After all, Kathryn is the only person who can confirm the connection, and she isn't talking.

———

Today at 5:30 began a doctor-patient relationship between the two women—a rendezvous that will stand every Tuesday. After-hours work in Dana's favor; no one knows she is receiving treatment, and she's home before dinner. Kathryn doesn't charge her for visits, nor does she write her friend's name in the calendar, so no record exists; Olivia suspects an arrangement as she sees Dana arrive, but since she wants to hold onto her new job, she doesn't ask too many questions.

TWENTY-ONE

Boat Party Invites — Ahoy There, Matey

Surprised by how enamored she is with Dale, Laurel's gut impulse is to alert the media, but she decides to run her newfound love interest past her friends first, which might be a better idea. As a rule, relationships are not her preferred arrangement, but this guy fills all requirements, some twice. A red flag is waving somewhere, but she'll ignore the vigorous flapping.

"Could this be too good to be true?"

Those words stop most women in their tracks or, at the very least, spark concern. But not Laurel; she will blindly parade and follow this man anywhere. (Stay away from the woods, nothing good happens in the woods.) Any smart "murderino" understands the importance of performing a background check on potential suitors; the bare minimum entails a criminal and financial report. He may not be who he claims to be. Laurel's notoriety dictates using a qualified private investigator; one should've been vetted and put on retainer by now.

Anyone who entertains strangers needs a fact-checker, and their sleuth's phone number should be a single digit on speed dial, especially if you're famous. That's not to say one should live life assuming all acquaintances are psychopaths, but one should live life as if the man you met online yesterday could be. But this time, no investigation will be necessary as the women in the inner circle are well-versed in trapping a rat.

A group text requesting everyone's presence on the Sunday following the Fourth of July for a sunset cruise and a night of fireworks at the club.

The teaser will ensure that everyone attends: "This will be your chance to meet my new boyfriend."

A second invitation, sent only to Olivia, suggests Dr. Bob and his wife Cynthia are welcome to come along.

"Your turn for the hot seat, Dr. Bob. Let's see how comfortable you are when outnumbered by women out of your league."

Laurel tells Olivia, "Time for you to earn a bonus."

The bonus, however, is self-serving. She wants Dale to witness Cynthia be star-struck by the movie maven.

Olivia isn't thrilled with this idea but only concedes knowing her occupational safety net, in the form of Kathryn, is secure and intact. And, with her posse in tow, she feels empowered and accepts the challenge of remaining calm while these ladies put screws to her boss.

Not taken aback by much of anything the actress does these days, Dana quickly reviews the men who will attend. Three of the five have already carved a notch in their friend's bedpost. Eric is a sitting duck, and Dr. Bob is in for the ride of his life. Of course, nothing will happen with the dentist, but the diva will lead him to believe a possibility exists, only to humiliate him for thinking he is worthy of a shot.

This heartless ego-filled scenario occurs often; the plot consists of four acts. First, the actress flirts with a man belonging to someone else. Whether the target reciprocates is irrelevant, the game has begun.

Self-gratification checks the initial box. Public humiliation ticks the second box, devastating the couple and destroying a relationship. Such an embarrassment leaves the girlfriend or wife single like Laurel, ticking box three, and the coup de grace, number four, is crossed off when Laurel appears to be the coveted victim.

The message concludes, "The rocket's red glare over the water guarantees a spectacular event; the finale for the Fourth of July weekend is always fabulous." The RSVPs come in one after another. Yes, by all.

Out of consideration, and with no excuse not to attend, the soirée will commence after Independence Day, intentionally leaving the Fourth open for other obligations. Nobody has other plans; they'd simply prefer to stay home and avoid the mayhem. The crowds in San Francisco during any three-day weekend can be daunting. Residents no longer consider the masses who flock to the city in the summer amusing. However, mocking the lobster-red out-of-towners who believe themselves impervious to the sun's rays never gets old. The Club keeps the fireworks on display well after Independence Day, so celebrating a couple of days after the holiday is appreciated.

TWENTY-TWO

Boat Party, Please Welcome Dale

True to form, Laurel will squeeze her money's worth out of the Yacht Club during this Fourth of July extravaganza. A few basic details include a personalized menu, Stanhope fine china, and the ever-present monogrammed ice buckets, even on the boat. Next to the liquor locker bearing a brass nameplate is a second branded cabinet reserved to accommodate place settings for sixteen and glassware for every occasion. Extra dinnerware resides on the yacht; paper or plastic reeks of shabby without the chic.

The evening will commence with hors d'oeuvres and cocktails, followed by the entrée, with the servers retiring for the night after dropping off dessert. A tray is tucked away in the galley to store the used dishware for collection in the morning. All aspects of the evening are orchestrated and performed to resemble opening night at the Met in a miniature format.

Positioned toward the bow, Laurel and Dale stand on the dock to receive their guests as they walk the gangway like a never-ending red carpet. The couples exchange introductions and cheeky air kisses as they make their way onto the yacht. Each guest is welcomed with their preferred beverage and enough hors d'oeuvres to feed an army.

Last to arrive are Dr. Bob and his wife, Cynthia, escorted by the Harpers. The schoolgirl giggles are hard to contain as the star-struck fan catches sight of the actress. Olivia hides her nerves by attempting to finish the story of last Saturday's scuba lesson and opens the dock box to show Cynthia their diving gear. The contents are in perfect order; boating supplies and five new weight belts lay unused. But Cynthia ignores Olivia, not hearing a word, as she reaches for Laurel's outstretched hand to shake.

Once everyone begins mingling onboard, Laurel introduces her date and the newest couple to the group one more time. Dale is a man's man who exudes charm. He's comfortable and relaxed in the presence of other men; blending in comes naturally. Dr. Bob is sixty-something, attractive once; his money makes him believe he still possesses the ability to rely on those attributes. He couldn't be more wrong.

Sporting their boating attire, the women double as a Talbots commercial featuring Hampton-Newporters dressed in almost identical outfits in various colors. Capri pants and high-collar shirts, a sweater draped over the shoulders. Top off the ensemble with sunglasses; there you have it, an instant ad. The matching deck shoes are a given; Cynthia offered to remove her footwear as she missed the memo. The dentist's wife is on cloud nine when Laurel expresses that she is pleased they accepted her invitation to join them for a night of fun.

Their conversation skips along with the diva gaslighting the dentist's wife, hinting Olivia often speaks highly of her. The compliment is taken as a gateway to chat, and Cynthia talks nonstop for what seems like an eternity. Laurel, however, never acknowledges a single word, leaving Olivia to interject so her boss's wife doesn't realize she is talking to herself.

The clock is ticking, and it's time to cast off. Laurel abandons her chatty guest mid-sentence, not waiting for her to come up for air. Instead, she instructs Randal and Dale to untie the ropes and takes her seat to guide the vessel away from the dock. Once in deeper water and far from the other boats, she lets her new man take the helm. By all accounts, everyone gives the appearance of enjoying the evening. But, of course, each has hidden demons and agendas lurking beneath the surface.

Randal does his best to divert his attention away from Laurel. Olivia nervously entertains her assigned guests by refilling their drinks. Eric is impatient as he waits his turn as skipper of the ship; he will do anything to avoid interacting with the host. Unfortunately, his plan of a wide berth in a confined space is impossible. Dana observes the others while sipping champagne alongside Frank and Margo on the backbench.

Appearances alone don't indicate Joel and Kathryn are in the process of a divorce. He is very attentive to her and her to him. Oblivious to the eggshells underfoot, Dale proudly wears the sailor cap and a huge smile. But he overplays impersonating Captain Fantastic, and Eric cuts in for his dance at the wheel.

The evening, although lovely, is off. Joel can't put his finger on what is going on, but something is happening here. Observant by trade, he studies the other attendees; the men, in particular, are on edge. Something is up.

His initial thought centered on the wives telling their men he slept with Laurel. But, on second thought, divulging intimate fine points is uncharacteristic of his soon-to-be ex-wife. Moreover, she's a private person, not prone to sharing her secrets. So, he doubts she would expose her humiliation. Joel struggles to turn off his instinct to analyze the partygoers and relax, but he can't. The cramped space aids in the visible discomfort, but it's not the balancing act to avoid spilling a drink or inappropriately bumping a body creating the tension; something is wrong.

Jealousy grips Frank by the throat; to witness a frumpy dentist consume Laurel's affection is about to send one of them overboard. Margo senses her husband's frustration and fears a scene will unfold, so she reels him in with a plate of food and a fresh Manhattan. The hint of rough sex later is implied. The momentary distraction is enough to defuse her preoccupied mate. But he can't stop himself; every time he sips his cocktail, he steals a glance over the rim of his glass and watches Laurel incessantly flirt, which everyone views as nauseating. Creepy as this sounds, Cynthia appears to be turned on by this performance.

A fixture at the helm, Eric won't relinquish his post. Dana is also unwilling to surrender her position on the backbench. She takes advantage of the situation by snapping her fingers, directing Randal to fetch her more liquid courage and another round of small bites. The pyrotechnics rivaled the nightly presentation at Disneyland; the humongous pops of color and crackle lit up the starless sky. Each projectile launched draws oohs and ahhs from the people lining the parkway to take in the free show.

With the sunset gone, the refreshments depleted, and only the trail of smoky streamers left in the air, Laurel takes the helm and her guests back to port.

She glides the yacht effortlessly back to the dock like a bird landing in a nest. Owning state-of-the-art equipment does have its advantages, as the craft practically parks itself. From the bridge, Laurel barks orders, instructing Frank and Randal to jump off and tie down the boat. Her command over the situation excites Dale and makes him happy he took a chance with online dating. He never imagined one blind encounter could be so life-changing.

The proud couple repositions themselves at the bow as the

arrival procession replays in reverse. The couple bid their friends farewell, thanking them for coming and accepting warm thanks from the attendees in return.

Margo puts the leftover cheese in the fridge as Kathryn stacks all the dishware in the tub provided by the kitchen staff. Then she tells Margo to ask one of the men if they wouldn't mind removing the trash. Responding with a giggly aye-aye, she goes above deck to retrieve someone to take the garbage to the dumpster. With her deck mate's attention averted, Kathryn wraps Laurel's champagne flute in a linen napkin, careful not to touch anything with her bare fingers, and slips the glass into her handbag.

Laurel's cell phone lies on the counter, which Kathryn slid into her purse beside the flute. The staff will undoubtedly take inventory, so a flute from the back stock on board will complete the item count in the bin.

The rubbish is handed out the doorway to whoever answers the call. Personal effects are next up the ladder. Laurel's Louis Vuitton Neverfull—the term *never full* is somewhat debatable—goes out first.

The cabin entry is a conveyor belt of outgoing handbags, the last of which belongs to Margo. This little purse parade successfully blocks Margo's path and her reason to reenter the galley. Finally, Kathryn's exit pushes her helpful friend further out on the deck, allowing the door to be closed and locked. Kathryn carries her bag with her jacket and gloves lying on top, concealing the stolen items. As the lights go out, Laurel takes the keys and hangs them in their hiding place.

Well-orchestrated indeed. The ladies allow Dale to escort them down the gangway while Kathryn quickens the pace toward the gate, raving about how Laurel outdid herself—once more, providing her loved ones with a fabulous evening. Margo jokes she wouldn't be surprised if Laurel arranged the fireworks for their entertainment.

With Laurel beaming, Dale says he's honored to make their acquaintance, and he looks forward to spending time together again soon. Margo squeezes him by the arm, whispering they are all happy to meet him too, and they are thrilled their friend finally found someone to whom they can relate.

More kisses and all go their separate ways. Once in the car, Joel asks about the tension surrounding the men.

Kathryn brushes off his concern insinuating they seem different because Dale and the Flanagans changed the dynamic. She then laughs at Laurel's expense stating the excessive flirting tonight amounted to quite the performance. Joel can't conceal his annoyance. Kathryn eventually lets Joel in on their secret, explaining the flirtation was intentional for how he treats Olivia. She pokes fun at his jealousy, asking if their interaction made him uncomfortable.

Perturbed at the accusation, Joel spits, "Oh please," in disgust. As they pass the Stanhope residence, Kathryn reaches into her bag and turns off Laurel's cell phone.

Joel drops his date off at the house they once shared, walking her to the door and kissing her cheek. Kathryn thanks him for bringing her home and says good-night. Joel's been living in the city condo ever since the breakfast breakup. Time apart allows them some space to rekindle their friendship. They are both disappointed they hadn't thought of this arrangement years ago.

———

Frank and Randal experience a different drive home; both rides turn ugly quick. Dana brings to light her knowledge and disdain for his relations with their friend. The way Laurel's every move consumes him is humiliating. She informed him that she would no longer tolerate his behavior. Randal refuted the accusation, responding with the standard, "What are you talking about."

Sorry, Randal, you're not getting off easy this time.

Dana doesn't come off as mad in her delivery, which he finds hard to combat. You can't play defense in an argument if the other person doesn't argue. Instead, she took the opportunity to deliver her message in simple terms, her voice filled with disenchantment, conveying he is the one in the dark. Neither spoke a word the rest of the way home.

On the other hand, Frank took a beating. First, his wife, the enabler, took his balls out of her purse and beat him over the head with them in a manner of speaking. Then, in an authoritative tone, she states she doesn't understand where tonight's performance came from, but she's had enough.

She said she was tired of covering for his childish conduct and warned if he didn't move off the couch and stop behaving like a spoiled teenager, she would be calling it quits.

A list of demands and corrective actions quickly follow. The requirements were laid out as law and stamped nonnegotiable. The statement stunned her husband, as he believes their current home life is to everyone's satisfaction.

For the first time, it dawns on him that if she leaves, so does his bank account, housekeeper, and cook; no more ready-made snacks, clean laundry, or ATM card. His lifestyle, his very existence, flashed before his eyes. The expression on Frank's face speaks volumes. She knows what he is thinking. But, sadly, in those thoughts, she never saw the part where he considered it was her he would lose.

On the way home, Dale confesses, "I'm falling in love with you. I hope that doesn't scare you off."

To his astonishment, Laurel admits, "I haven't felt tugs on my heartstrings like these in a very long time.

"Until now, with the exception of Alan, of course, men were toys to be played with and discarded. I never wanted to be humiliated by an unexpected breakup, especially in the media, so I dispensed with the others first.

"This situation, however, is much different, remarkable even."

This man is incredible; he can read her mind and instinctively knows what she wants and needs. She confesses she, too, is captured by their undeniable connection. The length of time since Alan's passing notwithstanding, and the absence of a looming breakup, open up future options with her new love interest. Not wanting to appear desperate or demanding is a fine line when you are a widow unwilling to gamble with the opportunity for a genuine relationship.

Laurel is considering the next step with Dale, even contemplating the need for a commitment soon. Lucky for the starlet, the feeling is mutual. Alan's replacement arrived, planted his flag, and announced he was here to stay.

The gentleman, always cautious in how he plays his cards, takes his new love in his arms and kisses her softly. He thanks her for a splendid evening indicating the night is over. The busy work week ahead is his justification for departing early. However, he does extend a dinner offer, letting her choose the time and date according to her availability.

Well-versed in the art of finesse, he knows she needs to want and miss him. So, saying good-night left his date shocked but also intrigued. She stands in her entryway until he gets into his car; she blows him a kiss before closing the door. His intuition is spot on; she can't wait to see him again.

For the first time in a long time, Laurel doesn't grab a bottle of bubbles or pills. She doesn't log on to her computer to check Siren or try to find Curtis or any other boy toy in her stable. She instead changes into her silk pajamas and goes to bed content.

TWENTY-THREE

Making a List and Checking It Twice

Monday, everybody should be en route to their respective workplaces by nine. Well, everyone but Laurel. She prearranged a plethora of spa treatments to alleviate an anticipated hangover and erase any other ill effects that may linger after a party weekend. These services will occupy the star for most of the day and leave the actress exhausted and talked out from over-socializing with her staff. She's misplaced her phone, but she doesn't care; she didn't even miss it. All she wants now is a shower and a nap. Besides, two can play the unavailable game. Dale can leave a message, and she will call him at her leisure. Knowing he wants her as much as she wants him gives her an advantage, and she doesn't want to appear needy.

Not caring to face the day with the dentist, Olivia opts to cement her future career at Kathryn's practice. So, she calls in sick for the time being. Something Dr. Bob is dead set against. But she couldn't waste the day talking to Cynthia, who would find an excuse to visit the office. Thus, the day will be spent rehashing in painstaking detail every second of last night's boat party. One day of "let's pretend" was enough.

Margo is busy previewing a new podcast some regular customers recommended: *Let's Not Meet.*

A true horror podcast that revolves around firsthand accounts of frightening events. In this format, the victim survives a harrowing tale, and the storyteller is often the person who was stalked or randomly assaulted. The short vignettes showcase those who got away or, at some point, didn't ignore the little voice in their head. So, on today's docket is *Let's Not Meet.*

Kathryn never pays any mind to her commute; she enjoys her short walk down the stairs to work. But before leaving the comfort of her kitchen, she takes a moment to review a vital pending project. Equipped and well-rehearsed, her preparation for this venture nears perfection. All to-dos on her list are verified, tiny pencil dots perforating the paper next to each item reinforce her due diligence, yet she goes over it once more to be sure. The workday will be like any other; patients will come and go, keeping her occupied. All the while, innocent Olivia will be oblivious to the maniacal scheming swirling about the home office.

The process is quite simple; when an unacceptable predicament arises, especially one plaguing Kathryn or anyone in her inner circle, she fixes the issue by pulling out her worn, once crimson-red alligator binder and devises a list. Her listing is a macabre coping mechanism to deal with undesirable situations. The method is meticulous, writing with vigor until she can execute her mission from memory without fail. Mistakes, especially minor infractions, aren't tolerated. Any deviation from the original plan hurls Kathryn into a manic state. She becomes an unstoppable force obsessed until she rectifies the ordeal to her satisfaction. A task, once accepted, is completed regardless of the danger or risk to herself or others.

The current "list" consists of two parts; part A has been years in the making, and its execution is long overdue. However, part B only became necessary after a recent string of unfortunate circumstances.

Last night after Joel dropped Kathryn off at home, she took the liberty of packing some essential items into her Louis bag. Each object finds its place in the order of appearance for the big reveal. The doctor includes three packets of crushed tranquilizers, a rock from the garden, duct tape, zip ties, everything required for cleanup and disposal, and a firearm for her protection. Don't fret; she is a responsible gun owner; the gun isn't loaded. The purse also contains the champagne flute wearing Laurel's fingerprints and the actress's cell phone.

Earlier this morning, Kathryn laid out tonight's ensemble on her freshly made bed; each article selected duplicates Laurel's fashion sense. The required deck shoes, black jacket, and matching gloves positioned next to the clothing complete the costume. And, as expected, the final touch: a dark scarf and sunglasses.

After a seemingly uneventful day, the final patient confirms next week's appointment. Kathryn calls down from the second-floor kitchen, requesting her new assistant finish her work upstairs. Poised on the kitchen's island are two stemmed glasses. The one containing wine is positioned in front of Olivia, while the other remains empty, begging to be filled.

Scattered on the countertop are the ingredients for supper. Kathryn focuses on washing lettuce, asking Olivia if she wants to join her for dinner. The wife and mother will predictably decline; her family is waiting at home, eager to be fed. Regret drips from her words as she refuses a hot dish she didn't prepare and shies away from the tempting intoxicant sitting before her.

On this note, Kathryn excuses herself, returning moments later in sweats, with her bright-red hair pulled back in a tight ponytail. The professional doctor switched to house mode, ready to settle in for the night. The conversation turns to Kathryn's chosen entertainment; she reveals she's been watching foreign movies with French subtitles to aid her communication skills. Her anticipated summer in France will be here soon, and she would like to be able to communicate when she gets there.

Kathryn lifts the declined glass of Merlot and takes a sip before resuming her meal preparation. Finally, the last file is complete, and the tired assistant announces she is done and is off to start her second job for the day, lovingly referred to as the family.

After their good-byes, Kathryn takes Laurel's phone and gets in her car. The destination, for now, is in the vicinity of the actress's home, where she turns on the phone, using the password Laurel so freely exhibited; the number one repeated six times.

Parked on the quiet street behind Laurel's home, with a well-lit screen in hand, Kathryn sends three invitations. Two men receive the same memo, the time being the only difference. A third man gets a slight twist. The time is different, and the vocabulary requires altering, as the harshness of the invite may scare him away.

Message one to Frank: "Quick fuck my boat tonight at 8:00 SHARP; Park on the street, NOT in the lot."

Message two to Randal: "Quick fuck my boat tonight at 9:00 SHARP; Park on the street, NOT in the lot."

The language is appalling yet compelling. Frank and Randal will be hard-pressed to think of anything else once they read the request.

Message three to Dr. Bob: "Quickie, my yacht tonight at 10:00 SHARP; Park on the street, NOT in the lot, LS." LS makes the text idiot-proof if he can't figure out the name of the only seaworthy person he knows.

All the men should be wrapping up their day in their offices or driving, so she doesn't anticipate an immediate response. Ten minutes after the final text, she turns off the phone and goes home.

The car isn't halfway into the garage before she hits the button closing the door behind her. The headlights shine on the tools hanging above a workbench in front of her. With a screwdriver taken from its outlined mount, she removes her car's license plates and replaces them with paper temporaries from Randal's dealership. Upon receipt of the permanent plates, Joel tacked the dealer souvenir to the garage wall. Now time to change into the outfit waiting for her on the bed.

Dusk looms in the sky, affording twenty-five minutes of limited light. The darkness and the doctor should arrive at the dock simultaneously. Disguised and equipped with her bag of tricks, Kathryn gets in her car and returns to the parking space behind Laurel's house. Once there, she again turns on the stolen cell, illuminating her face; she sighs in relief when "no new messages" is the only announcement.

The scarf, an integral component in her disguise, shields Kathryn's distinct hair color, but more importantly, the signature styling will generate an instant assumption. After replicating how

Laurel wraps her head, she pulls away from the curb and heads toward the marina. Stepping out of the car, she walks from the dimly lit parking lot to the dock, mimicking every detail, from how she holds her bag to the actress's distinctive sashay. The access code grants entry, allowing Kathryn to waltz down the gangway unimpeded.

The dock box is the first stop, where she'll gather three of the five weight belts and a tarp. Second stop, collect the key from its hiding place and climb aboard. The rolled tarp will rest on the side of the backbench; the gray mass blends in well and should go unnoticed. A swim platform attached to the stern provides space to lay out the dive gear. The belts appear to be decorative accents, perfectly bordering the step.

Methodically, everything on board is tracked and checked off the list. Anything used goes back into her handbag; nothing can be left behind. Next, three scotch tumblers from the galley cupboard, one for each man, are filled with enough liquor to dissolve the powdered tranquilizers covering the bottom of each glass. Then two of the three cocktails revisit the cabinet; the other lingers on the bar.

Mounted on a stand is a silver monogrammed bucket now overflowing with ice. An expected vintage takes its place nestled amongst the frozen crystal cubes.

Unhurried, Kathryn unwraps Laurel's glass cautiously, careful not to smudge any prints. A small linen finger towel is left to absorb dripping condensation from the champagne bottle. A fingerprint is more likely to adhere if the surface is dry. One would presume at least one of these gentlemen possesses enough etiquette to wipe the moisture from the bottle before filling a waiting flute. For kicks, a splash of alcohol on the counter is blotted with the napkin leaving residue on both. The soiled cloth will be tossed under the table as if overlooked.

The Neverfull stocked with emergency essentials, sits within range for easy access if necessary. The stolen phone rests off to one side of the bar. After reading each text sent to the men, she carefully deletes them, leaving their previous exchanges with Laurel untouched—a treat for the authorities to uncover later. The only incoming calls listed are the repeated attempts from Laurel's house phone to locate her cell. She's apparently unaware of how to use her laptop's "find my iPhone" feature. There is a message from Dale and one from Curtis, but that is all. Now the only thing left to do is wait. Frank's libation is prepared by adding more scotch to the tumbler; the powder disappears with a stir.

The gold Cartier timepiece dangling on Kathryn's wrist reads 7:55; she grunts, "I pray you fathom the meaning of the word SHARP, Frank."

Kathryn is focused on her mission, waiting in dark silence with the creaking of the dock and the fog slithering across the bow, which would otherwise have her hunkered down under the covers below deck instead of peering through a slit in the drapes anxiously awaiting her first guest.

The gate is left ajar in the event her suitor isn't privy to the combination. Now, all he has to do is show up. The time is 7:59, and the sound of someone approaching cues Kathryn to turn on some classical music as she slips into the bathroom.

Once inside, the stateroom is a clear shot from the cabin's doorway; dim lighting invites a glimpse at a bed turned down and waiting—an undeniable mood enhancer.

Frank enters and surveys the small room; he hears a muffled voice say, "I mixed you your favorite. Toss back your cocktail; I'm dying to make you another."

Her voice is breathy, asking him to signal when he's finished. The words are audible yet muffled; any sound coming from behind the door will be indistinguishable over the instrumental music.

"Done!" shouts Frank.

The door opens, and to his surprise, Kathryn stands before him. Seeing the empty glass perched between them, she pours him another, careful not to touch the rim.

Frustrated, he grabs the drink from the bar as she says, "Let's step outside; we need to talk."

Confused, he asks, "Where is Laurel?"

Propping herself on the stern's ledge, she rests her feet on the bench. She pats the space beside her. With no alternative place to sit, he complies.

He positions himself on the ledge before attempting to spew some feeble explanation of why he agreed to meet Laurel at 8:00 on a Monday night. Not caring to entertain his nonsense, Kathryn talks over him.

She explains, "Your better half came to me regarding her concerns about you, as did Laurel. So here is a little tidbit you may not have expected: our friend described all the intimate aspects of the games you two are playing to your wife."

Stunned, Frank scrambles to assemble a coherent thought; he strains to focus as the medication invades his bloodstream.

"Are you OK?" asks Kathryn.

Impaired, he struggles to answer. A vacant split second allows enough time for her to put on her gloves before taking the toxic elixir from his hand.

He slurs, "What the fuck did you do to me?"

"Nothing yet, but I plan to fix the mess you made; think of this as a little payback for upsetting my friend."

Frank's faculties are fading, but he still tries to grab her. He attempts a strong-arm advance, which she deflects with ease and a laugh.

"Oh, sweetheart," she whispers, "don't fight the unpleasantness. After all, Margo didn't. Take a rest, darling; this will all be over soon."

Another minute passes, and Frank's immobile but wide awake. "Time to go, Franky."

He will fall forward onto the deck if she stalls any longer, making moving his lifeless body impossible. Kathryn grabs his shoulders and pushes him hard, causing him to tumble to the swim shelf below. For a lean man, he is cumbersome but not unmanageable. Unfortunately for him, his arms are useless; they don't reach out to break his fall or soften the blow before his face smacks the rough ledge with a thud. A faint "sorry" is heard, as the impact was undoubtedly painful and sure to leave a nasty mark.

Catlike, she climbs over the edge and shoves her friend's limp body against the transom as she slides the weighted strap around his waist. All the subdued man can do is stare at her, wide-eyed, like a snagged fish.

After hiding his body with the tarp, she goes back into the galley, unaffected by his pathetic gaze. With gloved hands, the tumbler is gingerly washed out and patted dry. Special care is taken with the exterior to preserve any DNA left behind. All the glassware from Sunday is gone, collected by the staff this morning. Therefore, all the barware in the cabin should be unused and devoid of evidence.

The second glass exhibits patience in the cupboard, waiting its turn in the game. Kathryn prepares another beverage with the same care as making a cup of tea for a loved one. The minutes are slow in passing, and she wonders if the gate is still unlocked, but the risk of confirming is too high. Besides, Randal will text Laurel's phone if he is locked out.

The rhythmic thump, thump, thump of footsteps on the dock become louder; the time is 8:53. She's relieved her second suitor is punctual, but again, one can assume his dick is making the decisions tonight. An enticing cocktail awaits him as Kathryn retreats to the tiny bathroom.

The same act plays out, but Randal is overzealous in this scene, expecting sex before chit-chat.

"Relax," is heard from behind the door. "Drink up and let me make you another so you can slip me out of what I'm slipping into."

The two-inch frozen block bounces inside his empty tumbler as he jokes, "Make me another, wench."

She lets a few seconds go by before opening the door. Randal's backpedal routine resembles a cartoon character on a unicycle.

"Stop; everyone knows what you're doing."

Her tone is dismissive, bordering on disgust. But she has to be careful. The need to convey trust is crucial; she can't anger him, or he may storm out. Her voice indicates she possesses information of interest to him, enough to lure him in, but the sprinkle of concern will make him stay.

"Laurel informed your wife that you are the flavor of the week; my position here is damage control. Let's get some fresh air and discuss how we can save your skin."

Grateful for what he interprets as a lifeline, he complies. Again, Kathryn sits on the back ledge with her feet on the bench, and Randal follows suit.

He asks, "Why the charade?"

"Reassurance you are a willing participant, and Laurel isn't manipulating you and your better half."

Randal concurs; the double ruse sounds like something Laurel would instigate.

The concoction takes longer with this man, but the signs begin to show.

"Did you drug me?"

He asks this question with Frank's identical fat tongue slur and an expression worn by a deer about to be struck by a semi.

"Seriously Randal? I'm here to help you. You made a fool out of your wife. So, you need to make things right."

He listens while grappling to make sense of what is happening.

"Are you all right?" inquires Kathryn.

His demeanor indicates he is about thirty seconds away from being immobile.

The few brief moments left are used to enlighten this disoriented husband. "Your wife is an intelligent woman, a woman you underestimated. Your lack of finesse or sheer stupidity made tracking you a breeze. She has suspected you for a while. The tracker she installed on your car only served as a confirmation method. The frequent and unnecessary trips to the Stanhope residence leave little to the imagination.

"To think your biggest mistake involved a car, not bothering to coordinate your stories. Imagine Dana's embarrassment when Laurel announced you delivered the car to her home. How ironic, your considerate gesture rapidly turned into a conflicting account— a monumental faux pas, so innocent yet so incredibly damning. The despicable, seemingly innocuous announcement revealed her intent. Shameful, really. She counted on you lying to your wife, so to prove her point, she inserted some drama. Your blatant disregard for the intelligence of a woman you have been married to for decades is astounding. Not only is she tech-savvy, she is painstakingly diligent. She told me she cataloged your every move, including your brazen lunches and home visits. Let's not overlook the strip bars. I expected more from you, Randal; gentlemen's clubs are such a degrading institution. Tacky, even for you."

Overwhelmed that his secrets are common knowledge, coupled with the effects of the drugs coursing through his veins, cause his eyelids to collapse. His dulled awareness provides his abductor the time needed to reach over and move the tarp. She takes his glass with her right hand, and with one hard shove from her left, over he goes. He lands on Frank with a thud before settling in behind him. Kathryn pokes fun at the two men spooning. Both men are still conscious but motionless, they want to scream, but no matter how hard they try, no sounds emanate.

"Here is something else you may not have guessed; you two are taking turns in this filthy dance. Say hello to Frank."

Understanding his friend is what he falls on fills Randal with mute terror. Respectfully, Frank now realizes a body is what landed on him, and that body belongs to none other than his buddy Randal. Escape scenarios run through their heads, but their bodies won't obey. Motionless, Frank listens to the familiar clanging of whatever was tied to him now being strapped to his friend.

"What you're wearing are dive weights intended for our book club to use in scuba class; Laurel wanted to add some adventure to our dull existence. She hit the nail on the head with this one, didn't she, boys.

"So, let me explain 'our adventure.' I'm pleased you both possess the wherewithal to comprehend what's about to transpire. I do apologize for the immobility aspect of this excursion. You must understand my need for full cooperation, and this way guarantees your only option is to participate.

"All right, gentlemen, we are waiting on one more guest to complete this little party, at which point we can commence with the festivities."

The stowaways are covered with the tarp as Kathryn initiates the cleaning process. She isn't sure if Bob will join them but readies his refreshment anyway. Next, she double-checks that all her accessories are ready. Another glance at her Cartier as the time ticks away, 9:55, 10:00, 10:05, 10:10, 10:15.

Peeking out the tiny galley window, Kathryn hopes to catch her last guest on the dock or the road leading into the Yacht Club. But, with no one in sight, she concludes the giddy dentist isn't going to grace them with his presence this evening and decides they should move on.

"Well, Bobby, today turns out to be your lucky day."

The boat's ropes are untied, casting the craft into the darkness. The men are terrified as the motor comes to life. A rumbling vibration from the engine and the water bubbling beneath them changes the atmosphere from horrific to silent hysteria. A weightless motion indicates they are moving away from the safety of their mooring. Pressed together, they dispense little comfort to each other as all they can make out from the underside of the tarp is blackness. The cold rushing water only intensifies the reality of what is to bestow them.

"Location, location, location" are the only words they hear Kathryn say as the forward motion slows to a stop. They traveled out far enough; it would appear the men entered the water further out only to be swept back in by the tide. Google provided the essential data needed to calculate the specific drop site for this dirty deed.

Currents and tides are not something anyone assumes the actress will understand. The authorities will also suspect Laurel believes the increased weight is enough to sink a full-grown man to the bottom of the ocean, never to be seen again.

They idle as Kathryn takes the baggies that contained the narcotics and rinses them in the saltwater before placing each one, along with the rock from the garden, in a big plastic bag. Then, after squeezing the air out of the zip lock, she drops the incriminating evidence overboard. Kathryn rolls up the tarp and will return it to the storage box later. The men lay still while her intentions rage loud and clear.

Newer boats come equipped with everything. An electric platform meant for divers is proving to be a convenient amenity. Panic escalates every time she pushes the button, descending them deeper into the water. To ensure this outing is fulfilling, Kathryn describes how the rest of this little caper will play out.

"Boys, you're going for a little dip; calling your plunge a swim would be presumptuous."

She explained with glee that they would stay put for a few more minutes, hoping the cold water would sober them up.

"You must admit the sense of hope, albeit false, is exhilarating; if you are curious, the diving accessories aren't props; they will be quite helpful. The extra pounds will ensure your faces wade under the water line until you drown. This exit seems humane, considering how you two have conducted yourselves as of late. Even without the weights, the distance alone eliminates your chances of survival, and that's if you could move, which you cannot.

"With your remaining few minutes, I want to discuss your families. Please don't concern yourself with their well-being; take comfort knowing that your beloved's saving grace will be the new life insurance policies you signed. They will all go on to thrive in a life they deserve—comfortable, happy lives, the life you failed to provide. As your wives spoke of your relentless insipid conduct, I often wondered how they didn't kill you themselves.

"The same narration depicting your self-absorbed behavior came from both women. Each episode contained minor variations but not enough to make the outcome, in either case, any different. Your expressions indicate you're experiencing a self-centered moment right now. Of course, your primal instincts should take over, so now is the precise time to think of yourself. By all means, you are allowed this last self-serving indulgence."

The men have no choice but to listen to this maniacally calm woman, someone they consider family, act out of character. This person before them isn't their friend; this ruthless being is a psychiatrist turned psychopath.

Her quiet rant is unending as she steers them into the night.

"Did either of you take into consideration how this affects me? I understand if I'm not top of mind, but did I creep into your heads?

"An incident such as this should provoke all kinds of unexplained thoughts and emotions in all of us. And although the circumstances here are much more traumatic for you than for me, the effect is still profound.

"Rage, hatred, and blame should cover a few of your feelings. But I certainly hope you two don't hold me accountable for your current state of affairs. Let's not forget that I manage culpability for a living. So, I see through your masked self-loathing and appreciate your dedication to depravity. Yet it bothers me not."

Kathryn is enjoying the sound of her voice echoing off the water. Sadly, most of her friends and associates believe she likes to keep to herself. She keeps emotional cards close to her chest, never tipping her hand. However, the assumption about her privacy is incorrect; the doctor would love a turn to open up and talk about her feelings. The opportunity to analyze her delirium with someone else over coffee and muffins would be delightful. Yet, the laws against such logic and actions curb those conversations. But a captive audience grants the freedom to speak the truth with reckless abandon without criticism, scrutiny, or imprisonment.

"I'm sure you're wondering if this is my first rodeo; I can assure you several bodies are buried deep in my barn. So, again, rest assured, I've thought this through, from your demise to the care of your loved ones."

Kathryn reveals, "As a young girl, my father equipped me with the tools to compartmentalize issues deemed unbecoming. I'm sure we can all agree your behavior designates you a place in this specific category. So, we must blame "attention" if we are casting judgment. Attention is the root of all evil. My younger sister Kara loved attention; her selfish demands exhausted all my mother could spare, leaving nothing for my father and me. After Kara's unfortunate death, my mother implemented the same self-centered tactics on my father, taking his attention away from me. This adverse turn left me alone, emphasizing my loveless sad reality, prompting her demise.

"Do you see the pattern?

"Every incidence reverts to attention. Earlier, I told you my father gave me tools to recover, but that's a lie. What he gave me was an alibi. My father is also a psychiatrist and, like many professionals, harbors an aversion to anything discrediting. The problem with being a prominent Doctor of Psychiatry is that you can't spawn a bad seed. It's bad for business.

"The social rejection would humiliate and humble my father. The unsalvageable career damage would cripple him. But the inevitable ex-communication from the mental health community would destroy the man. The fallout, although exaggerated, made divulging the truth an impossibility. So, he ensured I and everyone else understood that the tragedy befalling my family was not my fault. He summoned teams of renowned physicians who labeled the ill fate my sister and mother suffered as an accidental fall, an unfortunate circumstance, and nothing more.

"Many specialists and colleagues went to great lengths to assist the doctor and his 'troubled' daughter. They saved me, the poor traumatized child, so I wouldn't grow up burdening myself with the responsibility for the mayhem surrounding me. But to be honest, I am the mayhem. Daddy knew fact from fiction, but admitting or acknowledging the magnitude of who and what I am, would ruin him. So, he made all the attention go away."

Glaring into the eyes of her motionless captives, she abruptly ends her rant.

The confession time is over, and Kathryn returns to the current situation. But, not to hold the men solely responsible, she attacks Laurel, "Our dear friend is an attention-seeker; as of late, the word *whore* attached itself to the phrase; I must say a rather vulgar display.

"Your ego's neglected to acknowledge she presented you two suckers with an exciting opportunity strictly out of boredom. The timeline in which you both surrendered to her advances speaks volumes. So desperate to satisfy your penises desire, you dismissed all you hold dear to take advantage of a fleeting tryst.

"The diva must've crossed your mind by now; after all, she is the villain in this story. But don't worry about her, darlings; she isn't going to die. Death is far too mundane, too forgiving. A headline or two, and Laurel will be a distant memory to the press. There's no fun in that.

"Her most sought-after role in life is the constant need for attention. You two contributed to her overinflated delusion. What I still find absurd is you, idiots, actually thought she found you attractive. Think this through for a second; she can be with anyone she wants. So, what do you two bring to the table?

"Nothing about your relationship with Laurel revolved around you."

The light bulb doesn't appear to be illuminating, so Kathryn explains, "What Laurel covets most is at your wives' expense. She's not interested in you; none of this was ever about you; jealousy is the prize. Inflicting her warped sense of entitlement on those closest to her is somehow gratifying. The sad thing is, she truly believes saying 'my apologies' and letting a few days pass grants her forgiveness. Not this time.

"Fear not, my friends, we are taking the high road, and

collectively we will bestow upon Laurel her greatest wish. She will be the 'star of the show' for the rest of her life. And come to think of it, our loving friend's cause of death may very well be attention."

Kathryn shivers, saying, "I am getting cold, so I'm going in. Time to bid you two a fond farewell."

She presses the lever from the helm, setting the men free as the boat glides forward. Coherent yet unable to move, Frank and Randal slide into the icy cold water. Their bodies float a foot below the surface—she stares as the last bit of life dissipates from their eyes. Kathryn is wondering if they think Laurel was worth the price of admission.

The boat glides away and circles back; a faint silhouette of the lifeless men is visible under a moonless night in the murky, black water. A steady stream of bubbles escapes, foiling their last-ditch effort to stay afloat. Water will replace the air they breathe, making them less buoyant. They won't stay submerged long. The gases percolating in their corpses will soon send them to the surface. Although introduced as more than a prop, the belts are, in fact, for vanity; they aren't heavy enough to make any real difference.

Kathryn relies on the authorities putting little stock in Laurel's intelligence, believing she intended the weighted men to sink. Unlike the "unweighted" Alan Stanhope, who floated, making his discovery fast and noticeable.

The journey back is peaceful; she takes a moment to close her eyes, feels the damp air on her skin, and breathes in the salty mist. Kathryn's boating experience proves invaluable as she glides the vessel against the dock without making a sound. The fancy features and the current in her favor made the return almost too easy.

Memories bubble up as the turbulent water from behind the boat becomes calm. Reliving family moments bring a half-smile. The summers the family enjoyed together, playing in the sun on sailboats and yachts. They would cruise the Channel Islands on weekends or travel down to Catalina off the Los Angeles coastline. Yet, behind the picturesque façade of her seemingly perfect family resides a lonely little girl with a twisted childhood.

Kathryn reminds herself to stop daydreaming and quickly recaps. Dr. Bob's glass is scrubbed and returned. Next, drop the leftover belt and sink the champagne bottle into the water. The police might send a diver down to search for clues. Any fingerprints may dissipate in the saltwater, but they also may not.

Moving along, the bed is remade, and the light is set to full strength before being turned off. Then the ice is dumped overboard; check, check, check. Then everything used gets wiped down before being stowed. Although handled with extra care, the same procedure leaves Laurel's glass clean to the naked eye.

With her tote bag repacked, Kathryn gives her apparel a concentrated once-over to confirm her costume is impeccable before venturing out. Her actions border on an obsessive-compulsive disorder as she scans every inch of the cabin and stern one last time, checking and rechecking everything is as Laurel would demand: pristine.

The drill keeps replaying in her head; lock the cabin, refold the tarp, and return the key to its proper place. Last, she rechecks the knots; the cleats are tied precisely as the men were instructed on Sunday. Now to exit, preferably unseen.

Disguised, her resemblance to the star is undeniable as she casually walks to her vehicle and vanishes into the night. She parks in a dark space around the corner from Laurel's house. Then, with the stolen phone still powered on, she walks as close to the front door as possible. The ladies sat through several demonstrations where Laurel boasted about the security system guarding her fortress, so Kathryn stopped before the cameras could detect her.

The driveway side of the property is out of view, which provides an avenue to move closer. Now within striking range of the porch, she tosses the phone onto the grass by the stoop. Then casually strides back to her car to avoid bringing attention to herself.

Cautious as she drives the few blocks home, again to discourage unwanted interactions that could cause an issue. She quietly pulls into the garage, the door descending before the car is fully inside. She runs through the remaining tasks, switches the license plates, and returns the screwdriver to its holder. Next, pinning the paper dealer plate back on the wall is imperative. Everything must be correct and the placement perfect; following the recognizable dust outline is helpful. Each pin lines up to the original hole. Nothing is left to chance; something as simple as an extra set of pinholes may result in a smoking gun.

The capri pants worn twice go into the outgoing dry-cleaning bag along with the blouse worn Sunday; the dark silk scarf and non-descript button-up top that every woman owns and worn tonight is steamed and pressed. All items are accounted for and replaced in the wardrobe. The deck shoes resume their position in the seldom-used section of the closet; duct tape and zip ties go back to the utility drawer. The bullet-less weapon is secured in its case and put back in the safe. She surveys her room; every item from Sunday and used again today is where one would predict.

At this point, Kathryn goes downstairs to resume cooking her dinner, though she is much too excited to eat, the leftovers in the refrigerator tomorrow will aid in the ruse of a night spent at home. While she was out, her phone remained at the house, confirming her location; every meticulous detail was planned and executed.

After consuming the wine left on the island, she pours herself another. Two glasses on a movie night go without saying, and after finishing half a bottle, one might be considered too intoxicated to drive around town committing a complicated murder.

Another showtime staple is popcorn; what better to promote a "stayed-in" scenario than the unmistakable aroma of popcorn? The first bag is sacrificial, burned beyond recognition; popping another to consume will accomplish the mission. The smell of fresh-popped corn may not linger, but the stench of cremated kernels will last for days.

Amelie, a French romantic comedy, was the movie chosen for her viewing pleasure. Amazon Prime history will validate a record of the purchase, but she is unsure whether anyone can verify if the movie was viewed. So, to be safe, the film played while Kathryn entertained the men.

If questioned, *Amelie* is a film Kathryn can recite verbatim with effortless enthusiasm. A small notepad with scribbled French words lies on the coffee table, indicating she took notes. The wine was recorked, and the glass went into the dishwasher, but most importantly, the leftovers were in the fridge to reinforce an alibi if needed. Kathryn goes over the list once again before going to bed.

The time is 11:47 p.m.

TWENTY-FOUR

Tuesday, the Morning After...

This very ordinary Tuesday is about to become anything but ordinary. For the second day in a row, Olivia elected to work with Kathryn, deferring any interaction with Dr. Bob and Cynthia, his star-struck wife.

The Kane house is quiet when Olivia lets herself into the home office. She announces her presence as she goes upstairs to find her new boss in the central kitchen wearing the same sweats she wore the night before. A French twist accompanies the women's obligatory salutation this morning.

Instead of the usual "Good morning," Kathryn says, "Bonjour, mon amie."

Having taken French in high school, Olivia responds, "Bonjour, comment vas-tu?"

The volley is returned, saying, "Tres bien, merci, et toi?"

"Hello" and "How are you" is the extent of the conversation aujourd'hui (today).

But Kathryn will continue to reinforce her dedication to her bilingual quest. As intended, the inescapable pungency eventually assaults Olivia's senses.

She crunches her nose, asking how many kernels perished in the fire.

Kathryn fills her in on the battle with the popcorn, confessing the first bag met a tragic end, forcing a watchful eye on the next one. Persisting with the farce, it's explained that she wanted to enjoy a showtime snack, but while refilling her Merlot, she ignored the warning pops, or lack thereof, and almost set the house on fire.

Olivia giggles, amused by the evening's tale, as she puts her lunch in the refrigerator, moving the leftovers from last night's supper to the side. An inquiry regarding the meal's success is met with a dismal rating. However, the review was admittedly marked as an unfair assessment as the focus gravitated more toward the movie than attending to her culinary creation. She points out that watching a foreign film with French subtitles is helpful; viewing the words while spoken is most beneficial.

"I'm tracking familiar words to gain confidence. I'll try anything." Kathryn sighs as she eyes her study pad on the kitchen table.

Olivia helps herself to a mug from the cupboard and pours some coffee. The doctor apologizes, confessing she was so engrossed in her studies that she neglected to review the schedule. Then casually asks, "So, who is coming in today?"

"OK, Mrs. Morris is coming in at nine. I'll leave her file on your desk. You better get moving. She'll be here in twenty minutes," says Olivia.

"OK, time to shower; I'll resume my language learning plus tard" (*later,* said in a practiced French accent).

The notebook claps shut, and with coffee in hand, she goes to prepare herself for the day. Olivia had barely finished pulling paperwork when Mrs. Morris walked in the door. She is led to the office while being offered a beverage. Mrs. Morris opts for a piping hot Earl Grey but sits confused as to why Kathryn isn't present; Dr. Kane is always seated in her chair when she arrives. Olivia assures the unnerved patient that it will only be a few more minutes. Then, with a comforting smile, Olivia tells Mrs. Morris to make herself at home while she makes the tea.

The friends, now colleagues, pass each other in the hall; Olivia gestures toward the kitchen and takes her boss's empty coffee cup like a well-practiced NFL hand-off. Upon returning, she sets the serving tray on the coffee table and closes the door signaling that the doctor is in session.

The files for the day's remaining clients lay on the credenza. Today's calendar is light, with only two sessions in the morning and two in the afternoon.

This is perfect, Olivia thinks; she will use the vacant openings to organize the neglected storeroom.

The time is 9:45 when the phone rings; oddly, it's the house phone. All mobile devices are silenced out of courtesy, and the business line isn't blinking. Olivia quickly picks up the handset to stop the disturbance.

"Kane residence, Olivia speaking."

"Hi, O, Dana here. Is Kathryn available?"

"No, I'm afraid not, she is with a patient, and appointments this morning are back-to-back. Can she call you later?"

"No," shouts Dana in a panic, prompting Olivia to ask if she is all right.

"No, I'm not. Randal didn't come home last night. I need to talk to Kathryn."

"Hold on; she's almost finished with her first session."

The inability to accept the inevitable in-your-face confirmation keeps Dana from tapping the keystrokes necessary to initiate the tracker pinpointing her husband's exact whereabouts. She also considered checking the cameras she installed in Laurel's house but couldn't bring herself to look. Exasperated, Dana admits her marriage has unraveled. But her husband's failure to come home was the last straw. He finally crushed what dignity she had left, as well as any desire to reconcile. Admitting defeat is one thing; however, witnessing the end is too much to conquer on her own. She needs backup for this discovery.

The small talk is strained as the sound of call waiting clicks in their ears. "Hold on, be right back," says Olivia.

"Kane residence, Olivia speaking."

Margo expresses the same panicked tone and skips the pleasantries, demanding to speak to Kathryn.

"OK, but you'll have to wait a minute; she should be wrapping up in a few minutes, but Dana is on hold. Can she call you back?"

On the verge of tears, Margo says, "No, no, I need her now."

"OK, OK, hold, please."

Mrs. Morris takes her sweet time making her way out into the reception area. Olivia tries to attract the doctor's attention by holding her hand in the shape of a phone against her head. But Kathryn can't decipher Olivia's crazy antics.

"Is everything all right, Olivia?"

"Yes, but two lines on the house phone are holding; you may want to take the calls in the kitchen."

Before shoving the older woman out the door, Olivia escorts Mrs. Morris to the front desk to confirm her standing time slot for the following week.

At most, two minutes pass before the next appointment arrives. Olivia informs the hypersensitive gentleman in plaid pants that Dr. Kane will be a moment, she is tending to an emergency but shouldn't be too long. The man is ushered to his chair, and she retrieves the coffee he requested. Her hurriedness is more in hopes of catching the crisis than servicing the waiting customer. Olivia crests the top of the stairs, giving the "what's going on" face, but Kathryn waves her away before she hangs up the phone.

Desperate for details, she asks, "Tell me what's happening!"

"Margo and Dana are on their way over. You better make more coffee. Who do we have booked for the rest of the day?"

"Your ten o'clock is ready and waiting. The other two appointments are later this afternoon, at one and another at three."

"OK, reschedule our one and order lunch. When the girls arrive, tell them to wait for us upstairs and interrupt me if I go long."

Fifty minutes later, the second session for the day confirmed his routine time slot for the next week. Not pushing but applying pressure, Olivia wishes the man a lovely day before ushering him onto the porch.

The ladies arrived ten minutes ago, so she takes the stairs two at a time, fearing she missed out on an important detail. A simple glance calms Olivia as Kathryn commands the room. "OK, let's start over. Dana, you start with Monday morning and work forward to today."

"Well, the day seemed like any other day, with nothing noteworthy; Randal and I both went to work, and we came home."

Olivia asks, "What time?" as she scribbles the details in Kathryn's homework folder.

"About five thirty, I guess. I changed clothes and made us something to eat. Randal said he had to drop off some keys and a contract later. He indicated he would only be gone for a couple of hours. So, we had dinner together; he left but didn't return."

Olivia asks, "Is it customary for him to conduct business with buyers at night?"

Dana's reply starts condescendingly, "Some people require after-office hour deliveries, but he always comes home. So I went about my night; I washed the dishes, poured myself a chardonnay, and called my daughter. We chatted about her school, a new boy, etc."

"What time did you call your daughter?"

"Would you stop?" pleads Dana. "I'm not sure, eight-thirty, eight-forty. I hung up sometime after nine-thirty; I know this because I searched for shows starting at ten. Don't you dare ask me what show. After some television, I went to bed. The alarm went off at six thirty; I rolled over to discover Randal wasn't beside me. I checked the house; nothing indicates he ever came back. His car wasn't there either."

The next reenactment unveiled eerie similarities. Margo started her day at the bookstore.

"I would say I was busy, but everything was normal. I got home a little after six, and no, my househusband nor my son prepared anything or bothered to start dinner. So, I cooked, and we all ate together. My mistake was inquiring about my husband's day. He heard, 'How did my good-for-nothing husband spend his day while I worked making money to support our family?' OK, that's what I thought, but not what I said. Of course, he used this as his opportunity to ignite an argument, then, in turn, stormed out. The faux fight and bolt routines are not uncommon; he will take 'nothing' comments, blow them out of proportion, and bingo, an excuse to leave. Even Tyler gave him an eye roll before retreating to his room.

"Time is a luxury for my lazy mate; he is accountable to no one all day; he can come and go as he pleases. So, is it entitlement, or am I being punished for some reason? His whole day is wide open; why does he wait until I'm home to go out?

"Regardless, he took off around seven thirty; I didn't note the specific time. I cleaned up and did the same as Dana. I chose a Pinot Noir, a hot bath, and listened to a podcast instead of TV before bed.

I woke up alone this morning; Frank's side of the bed was untouched."

Margo's next question swings open the floodgates, "Did anyone talk to Laurel yesterday?"

A knock at the door prompts swear words to sneak out of Olivia. "The delivery guy. Ugh, hold your thoughts; not another word until I return." Olivia runs down to collect her order.

"Thank you, sorry, and keep the change" is all the guy can make out before the bag's snatched from his hands; money is tossed in the air, followed by the door slamming in his face. With the to-go bags in hand, she bounds back up the staircase. Olivia invites everyone to the table, spreading the sandwiches and chips out so they can make their selection. She then asks everyone what they would like to drink as if this were her kitchen. Usually, Kathryn wants to be in charge; however, this is not one of those times. Today, she is happy to sit back and watch her assistant run the show, taking full advantage, opting for lemonade with lots of ice.

Dana responds to Margo's earlier question, "No, I haven't heard from our friend, nor am I aware of who she entertained last night. Has anyone talked to Laurel since the boat party?"

The consensus is no from everyone.

Kathryn asks, "You tried calling your husbands, right?"

They both tried several times, but the calls went to voicemail. The doctor wonders if their pant pockets light up when a call comes in or if the devices are as dead as the men.

The thought of confiding in each other regarding their husband's newfound playmate didn't seem appropriate. At least not yet. But the discussion quickly turned toward the actress anyway. The fact that she is in question leads one to assume she is the common thread. Another oddity is that Olivia and Kathryn don't give the impression that this news is new or shocking. On the contrary, their reaction indicates they are well-versed in all parties' indiscretions.

Kathryn recommends involving the authorities. However, Margo demands that they call their friend first. Dana agrees with the latter, which thrills Olivia. The self-appointed queen is about to be crucified by these two angry wives, and she gets a front-row seat.

Olivia checks herself, realizing that containing her excitement at this time would be prudent. After all, two people are missing.

Posed as a legitimate question, Olivia asks how Laurel could have lured and then convinced both men to stay out all night.

Kathryn shoots her a disapproving glare, which shuts down any further questions.

Margo confesses her gut instinct guides her, not actual proof, but all arrows point in Laurel's direction. Finally, the pieces are coming together, and she can no longer bury her head in the sand. The non-compensated consulting gigs late at night, and the number of outbursts have become as subtle as a flashing neon billboard.

"Frank's angry demeanor when Laurel flirts didn't go unnoticed either. His annoyance was unmasked for all to witness when she pursued the dentist, of all people. His humiliating behavior reeks of jealousy. I'm so embarrassed, but again I have nothing solid."

"Oh, Frank isn't the only one; Randal's performance borders on despicable. His blatant attempt to ignore Laurel yet position himself to capture her every move reached a new low. I am insulted to think he finds me so clueless," cries Dana.

"I guess she tried them all," Olivia grunts in disgust.

Aghast at this remark, Margo shrieks, "Eric too?

"Eric slept with Laurel?"

"No, but not for her lack of trying. She propositioned him, but he rejected her advance and walked out."

They all stare at Olivia in silence.

"She called him to discuss her portfolio but didn't want to come to his office. She made up some story about Lilli being an aggressive fan. So, Laurel suggested counsel at her house, and you can guess the rest."

"The glaring difference here is that Eric declined and left with his pride intact," said Dana.

"Now Eric will only work with Laurel at his office, and Lilli's attendance is mandatory," adds Olivia.

Dana interrupts, "Did Laurel answer yet?"

"No, it goes to voicemail." Margo then tries the house phone, and voila.

"Hey, Laurel, it's Margo, we are at Kathryn's, and you may want to come over."

"Why the clan meeting?"

Not finding the inappropriate comment funny, Margo yells, "Get over here," and slams down the phone.

"Well!" snaps Laurel into the dead line.

Being spoken to in such a manner should have indicated something was amiss. But she is strangely fascinated by the hostile summons.

Madeline's name echoes through the house; she appears, pretending to be interested in what her employer has to say. Laurel dictates she will be going to Kathryn's, presumably for brunch, so the itinerary must be adjusted. While scribbling out a list of items required for a location shoot later in the week, she reinforces the importance of purchasing the precise necessities, no substitutes, and, dear God, nothing generic.

The working conditions may seem harsh for Madeline, but don't underestimate her; she embodies the Rosario character from *Will and Grace* sans the members-only jacket. She is much more than the indentured servant Laurel would like you to believe. Madeline is also quick to put the madame of the house in her place when she's gone too far. A stark reminder that life without her involves doing one's bidding tends to restore peace at the residence.

No sooner is Laurel out the door when she hears the distinct sound indicating an incoming voicemail. The noise stops her dead in her tracks and draws her attention to the grass.

While reaching for her phone, she says, "I've been looking for you."

Only three messages are registered: one from Dale, one from Curtis, and another from Margo. The other twenty or so calls she made to herself. Disappointed in her popularity, she drops the device into her bag and moves on. The actress drives the two blocks to Kathryn's, admiring the few streets with manicured lawns in front of the homes she wishes she had walked. The trip is faster on foot due to parking, but who is she kidding? Walking is out of the question.

Moments later, she stands on the steps of the Kane home, incessantly pressing the doorbell. Olivia answers the front door that swings open as their impatient friend barges into the house without as much as a hello.

Upon eyeing the depression in the room, Laurel crudely asks, "Who died?"

In a dismal attempt at humor, she adds, "You gals look like shit."

"Laurel, come in and sit down," says Kathryn, offering her something to drink.

Nothing provided in this house before noon will benefit the diva, so she barks back, "Nothing for me."

No one is surprised a thank-you doesn't follow at the end of her statement.

Irritation sets in as Laurel fears an intervention is in her immediate future; she insists they tell her what is happening.

Margo starts, "We know about your relations with our husbands. We are also aware you propositioned Eric."

"Who refused her," Olivia proudly interjects with a slight smirk.

Laurel pushes back in her chair and, through pursed lips, says, "I'm not sure what your idiot husbands are trying to pull, but I'm appalled. And after everything I do for all of you."

A manila envelope is pulled from Dana's bag, slapping pictures of Laurel and Randal together onto the tabletop. Several printed screenshots of google maps hit the table next, showing his car at her house, with occasions outnumbering excuses for his presence. The evidence showcasing Frank's performance is in her possession but withheld for now. After all, what legal justification or explanation can she produce for possessing photos from inside her friend's home?

Dana explodes, not waiting for a response, "Explain this to me!"

"Why are you deliberately destroying our lives? Your involvement is painfully apparent, and why the hints? Why would you ever want us to entertain the thought, not to mention the risk of us all collectively confronting you?"

Margo cuts in, "Don't bother answering. Whatever you say will be a self-serving lie anyway."

At this point, Dana doesn't care to hide her exasperation. "You are a sick woman; you're sick."

No one can conjure up anything constructive to say, so they all sit staring at one another for what feels like an eternity.

An incoming call from Margo's phone breaks the deafening silence. She doesn't recognize the number, so she doesn't pick up. Dana's cell begins to vibrate; unknown caller, so she lets it go to voicemail. Both phones ring again; they all swap concerned looks, and Dana answers hers. "Hello."

"Hello, Detective Ken Freeman of the San Francisco Police Department speaking. May I speak with Dana Lucas?"

"This is she."

"Are you at home? If so, can you open the door?"

Startled, Dana says, "No, I am not."

The detective says, "Mrs. Lucas, we need to speak to you immediately." Before Dana can decipher the reason for the call, the detective strongly suggests they meet in person at the station. He tells her he will not release any other information over the phone. Dana asks for the precinct's address, grabs her purse, and instructs Margo to answer her phone.

TWENTY-FIVE

At the Station

The phone in Margo's hand rings again; she answers only to receive the vague yet alarming instructions given to Dana moments earlier. The call ends, but Margo can't move; panic sets in as her worst fears gain momentum.

"Go home, Laurel; we can talk later."

Kathryn's words are not a suggestion but rather a polite order. Compliance accompanies theatrics as the diva storms out, offended. She is more put out by being excluded from the drama unfolding and not so much for being called out on her cavorting practices.

Before anyone unravels, the doctor again takes command of the room; she first dictates to Olivia to cancel the patient scheduled at 3:00. Her professional demeanor projects trust, comfort, and an element of safety. Knowing what is to come allows her the freedom to orchestrate the scene and manipulate the actors with little effort. Next, she encourages Margo and Dana to ride to police headquarters with her and Olivia.

"Something out of our control is happening here; one can predict this won't be pleasant. A chauffeur may prove useful."

The precinct is anything but welcoming; Detectives Sophia Torres and Ken Freeman introduce themselves and indicate they would like to speak with Dana and Margo separately. Kathryn instantly steps on the cordial manner in which they attempt to divide the women.

"I would like to remain with my patients," suggests Kathryn.

"I am their doctor; Ms. Harper is my associate; our presence may be beneficial at this time."

Permission to stay is granted but comes with a condition, and they agree to vacate the room if asked. The interrogation room is small; the walls are covered in ceiling tiles, and the tiny holes in the padded panels give the room a soundproof vibe. A scratched steel table and chairs resembling props from countless 1980s cop dramas invite them to sit.

Detective Torres reveals she needs to formally notify them of the accident. Dana jumps in, demanding, "What kind of accident?"

With sympathy, Torres resumes, "I'm sorry to have to inform you, but Frank Reed and Randal Lucas were found this morning in the bay."

Confused, Margo asks, "Found?" Her voice drops, "What do you mean by found? I'm sorry, what were they doing in the bay? And you said *accident*, what accident? Can you *please* tell us what is going on?"

Troubled by the detective's misguided tactfulness, the women want facts. Torres, in turn, delivers the whole story.

"Your husbands were discovered by the crew aboard the commuter ferry early this morning. Preliminary results indicate drowning as the cause of death, but confirmation will require an autopsy."

Margo screams in disbelief, "They're dead?"

The delivery method meant to soften the blow of bad news wasn't received as intended and erupted into a spontaneous outburst of bitter rage.

"I don't need an autopsy. I can tell you the cause of death."

All eyes in the room fixate on Margo.

"Laurel did this! And you want us to believe this drowning was accidental? No, more like coincidental. You may want to take a second look into how her husband died! This incident, like Alan's, was no accident." The screaming is deafening, her high-pitched shrill bouncing off the bare walls as the new widow rages inconsolably.

"We can't be sure of anything yet; let's settle down and think this through," whispers Kathryn.

Olivia requests some water, although no one is sure why. Furious, Margo yells, "I will not calm down; that bitch killed my husband."

Hysteria takes over, but that doesn't slow her; "That woman couldn't be satisfied by using him to humiliate me; no, the thrill for her is in my absolute ruin. The goal here is to ensure we, 'her friends,' are just as lonely as she is."

Visibly shaking, Margo breaks down sobbing.

Motionless, Dana sits staring into space. The glass of water offered is refused; Olivia stands with two paper cups in her hands; unnerved by the silence, she asks Dana if she is OK.

"OK? No, no, I'm not OK! First, digesting proof my husband is cheating on me with one of my best friends was bad enough, and now I'm being told he is dead! So, no, 'OK,' I am not."

Fearing the wailing won't subside anytime soon, Detective Freeman pulls Kathryn aside to clarify what they are talking about and who is this Laurel person.

More than happy to oblige, Kathryn enlightens the detective on the morning's events.

"Both women called my office this morning, informing me their husbands failed to return home last night. Besides being my patients, we are all close friends. So, I invited the ladies to my home, which is also my practice. Dana confided that she suspected Randal of being unfaithful. So, she investigated, only to discover he often sought entertainment elsewhere, ultimately entertaining our friend Laurel. The pictures Dana produced today replaced any misconceptions with sobering reality. Our conversation took place right before you called. However, a hunch and uncharacteristic mannerisms are the basis of Margo's fear; Frank's infidelity is undoubtedly in question, but it's all speculation. The infamous women's intuition is what fuels Margo's suspicion. Until now, nothing substantial indicated who the woman might be until Dana revealed her findings."

The convincing particulars of the affairs continue to flow as the detective speedily takes notes.

"Margo declared Frank was preoccupied with checking his messages all evening and picked a fight providing the justification he needed to walk out. She's uncertain whether he received a text or just expected one."

Kathryn continued, "Randal arranged to deliver a car to a client. He owns an auto dealership, so this appointment didn't raise any red flags. He didn't divulge the sale specifics, as they aren't relevant to his wife."

"Who is Laurel?" inquires Freeman.

"What is Mrs. Reed referring to when she said the death of Laurel's husband wasn't an accident?"

Kathryn constructs a tale guaranteed to pique this detective's interest, "The Laurel she refers to is Laurel Stanhope."

The surprised detective says, "You mean Laurel Stanhope, the actress?"

"Yes, the actress. Her husband, Alan, experienced an

unfortunate circumstance where he drowned a little over a year ago. The authorities found Laurel asleep in the cabin of their yacht about fifteen feet away. She claims to be aware he left the bed during the night but denies knowing what happened to him."

The detective excuses himself, instructing officers to pick up Laurel Stanhope and bring her in for questioning. Following Detective Freeman into the hall, Kathryn tells him she should be home. Of course, she provides the men with the address to be helpful.

Detective Freeman turns and gestures to the doctor to return to the conference room to finish their discussion, where she recaps the morning.

She takes the opportunity to embellish, "A noticeable shift in dynamics between the men toward Laurel became evident at a party thrown last Sunday night. She takes pleasure in manipulating men, more so with an audience. Of course, nothing happened, but as I said, everyone noted the men's behavioral changes.

"So, when their husbands didn't come home, each assumed their man spent the night with Laurel. This morning, both wives called my office, describing the same scenario.

"When the ladies arrived, they relayed their stories, and collectively we decided now would be the opportune time to bring Laurel into the conversation. Immediately upon entering, she was confronted with physical evidence that she and Randal were meeting for no plausible reason other than the obvious. The photos were revealed, but there wasn't time to discuss them before the phones rang.

"We acted per your instruction and came down to find out what this is all about, and I sent Laurel home," said Kathryn.

The detective asked how the actress responded to being told to leave. "Insulted, equivalent to being uninvited to a social event. She pouted, grabbed her purse, and went home."

Watching the detective assemble the information in his head is comical. The intentionally long pause inserted before continuing has the desired effect.

"She seemed agitated, but she is always perturbed about something."

Then she stopped talking; the lapse in cadence carried in the doctor's voice didn't go unnoticed by the detective, who added, "And?"

Careful in her choice of words, she concludes, "After witnessing two disturbing phone calls requesting her friends report to the police station, she left. No dispute or curiosity, just cooperation. You need to understand this woman; she prides herself on being a bit of a bully; you can't tell her to do or not to do something without an argument. So, in retrospect, I find her compliant departure odd under the circumstances. She's told to go, and she got up and went."

A puzzled grimace crosses Kathryn's face as she lets her words sink in.

Detective Freeman, excited for the possible lead, asks, "Would you excuse me, Dr. Kane? We'll need to speak to Mrs. Reed and Mrs. Lucas now. I hope you understand."

"You're welcome to wait. Ronda will gladly provide you and your assistant with coffee or a soda if you like."

A dark-haired woman behind the counter peers over her readers with a glare indicating, "To serve you is not in my job description; hospitality is not my strong suit."

The ladies pass on the beverage. "We will wait here; thank you."

Kathryn and Olivia select a seat on the uncomfortable bench reserved for loved ones waiting for the accused or interrogated. Freeman walks off to interview the newly widowed in separate rooms.

Detective Torres recites the obligatory and well-rehearsed

condolences, "I'm sorry for your loss; please understand I am required to ask you some questions."

Margo is up first. Torres starts, "Can you account for your whereabouts last night?"

Exhausted, Margo recaps her night. "I went home after closing the bookstore. Together we ate dinner as a family, my son, husband, and I. Frank seemed to be waiting for a message. He was agitated, and when I questioned him, he stormed out. So, I took a bath and went to bed, a typical evening, other than Frank not coming home."

The audible truth highlighting the relationship between Laurel and Frank pours salt into Margo's open wounds.

"Confirmation of Frank's actions came to light this morning. I believed he was involved with someone, but I never entertained that 'someone' was Laurel until today."

Torres pressed for more details, "How or who confirmed your suspicions?"

Margo said, "Dana, she had been following our friend. She suspected her of hooking up with Randal. On one such stakeout, she caught Frank kissing Laurel in the doorway of her home."

As the process wanes, one question, particularly, strikes a chord with Margo.

Freeman joined the conversation late and asked if they could name anyone who would want to harm their spouses.

Margo glares, "You mean other than Laurel? Let's face it; both men are dead simultaneously and embroiled in an intimate relationship with said slut, so do the math! She is always the common thread; you can bet if someone or something is ablaze, that woman will be found somewhere in the vicinity holding a match. It's standard protocol; she creates the chaos she will later ride in to fix."

Dana recounts her evening from the cold metal chair. "We both came home from work, shared a meal, then my husband left to conduct business with a client. I called my daughter, and we spoke for about an hour. I then went to sleep and woke up to find Randal never returned."

The festivities from Sunday night are recited verbatim by both women: they were invited to a gathering on the yacht to celebrate the Fourth of July and introduce Dale to the group. The celebration, as anticipated, went off without a hitch. Everyone ate, drank, and enjoyed the firework display; everyone appeared happy. One officer had to fight the urge to write blah blah blah in his notebook; first-world problems of the rich and famous are such a bore. The only marginally interesting detail jotted down was alleged that both husbands seemed irritated by the host and that Laurel did her best to ignore the men, which fueled stifled tantrums only their wives detected. Margo and Dana divulged discussing their unacceptable behavior with their respective spouses after the party. An identical list of attendees is the last piece of information supplied by the widows.

The current dialogue spins on a continuous loop going nowhere. Neither of the men appears to have any enemies; they seem decent enough if you discount their extra-curricular activities. Everyone could use some coffee and agree it's a perfect time to take a break while waiting for Laurel to arrive.

Across town, a hard-knocking sound emanates from the Stanhope front door as the officers wait for a response; for no apparent reason other than it's a bother, the occupant is reluctant to give them one.

Law enforcement knows Laurel's reputation and wants nothing to do with the upheaval she can inflict on them. The officers decide to employ a voluntary approach to avoid a confrontation. They do so by persuading her that her assistance is requested.

"Would you mind coming with us; there's been an accident."

The words *assistance* and *accident* capture Laurel's attention, but then they inform her that her friends are "waiting" downtown completing the trifecta.

The late invitation won't relieve the sting of being left out, but she will reserve punishment for their error later. Without hesitation, she voluntarily accompanies the uniformed men to the precinct. A swift updo, a quick change into a sheath dress, add a Prada bag with matching shoes, and you have an instant celebrity. Of course, a hat, dark glasses, and gloves shield her from the sun and supply the final touches to her picture-perfect appearance.

The spectacle, Laurel Stanhope, waltzes into the station anticipating a reception, expecting her friends to run into her open arms to be saved by her embrace. Whatever the tragic occurrence, she has arrived to resolve the issue, making any unpleasantness disappear with a wave of her gloved hand. But, much to Laurel's dismay, she is accosted by Margo shouting across the precinct, "That bitch killed my husband!"

Taken aback by the outburst, Laurel doesn't object to being escorted into a small room, but she expresses her disapproval when the interrogation commences before she's properly seated. Perturbed by the uncouth treatment, Laurel begins a separate investigation.

Detective Torres poses the same question for a third time today, "Can you account for your whereabouts last night?"

Laurel says, "I was at home," as she removes her hat and glasses.

The detective asks, "Can anyone confirm your alibi?"

"No, I live alone. And why on earth would I need an alibi?

"Before I say another word, I would like to discuss the pretenses used to bait me into coming here today. Then I want to know what this accident is about."

The stone-faced detectives finally reveal the fate of her friends.

"You can't seriously believe I had something to do with this?"

Her unempathetic rebuttal is an instant and somewhat defensive response to being told someone close to her is dead.

The detective doesn't react but asks, "Can you tell me the last time you spoke to these gentlemen?"

Unsympathetically, Laurel states, "Sunday evening on my yacht."

Her reaction is emotionless, and she displays zero regard for the seriousness of the current situation. She even volunteers a statement without hesitation.

"Everyone came out for a cruise on the bay to enjoy a firework show. A fantastic event, if I do say so myself. Ask anyone in attendance; a lovely outing indeed."

The detective asks for the guest list, which she recites without delay. Tension escalates when asked if she contacted either of the men after Sunday; an unwavering Laurel again insists, "I stayed in by myself. I did partake in my scheduled spa treatments yesterday, but I utilized most of the day rehearsing for a table read scheduled for the end of the week."

One more time, they asked if there was any communication from Monday until this morning.

Beyond frustrated, Laurel snaps, "How many times must I repeat myself? It was common knowledge within the friend group that I would be at home and was not to be disturbed this week. So again, no, I did not speak to anyone in person or on the phone, only my housekeeper and staff. As a matter of fact, I didn't take any calls, as I couldn't locate my cell."

"Is your device in your possession now?" asks the detective.

"Yes, I found it this morning on my way out to join the ladies; the phone was lying on the lawn outside my front door."

"So, you're saying you took a call on a phone you couldn't find?"

"No, you idiot, Margo called the house phone. My cell must have fallen out of my bag on the way into the house Sunday night. You would not believe all the…"

The detective cuts her off. "May I look at your phone?"

"No, you may not! Why are you speaking to me like this? What do you want with my phone? Do I need my attorney?"

Quickly changing his accusatory tone, the detective tells Laurel they will ask everyone when they last spoke to Mr. Reed and Mr. Lucas.

"We are trying to establish a timeline to determine when and who spoke to the men last."

He demands the phone again, exerting too much authority this time.

Laurel stalls, trying to think. Nothing from Sunday to today is damaging, but what are they hoping to find? She realizes they'll find a series of correspondences between Randal and Frank that will paint an unsavory picture.

So, she holds her ground. "No, nothing on my phone is of any importance to you, and due to my profession, I must always be reachable, so again, no."

"We can obtain a warrant," the detective threatens.

Laurel doesn't blink before a straightforward "go ahead" spits from her lips. Followed by a dramatic, "Are we done here?"

"Not yet, Ms. Stanhope," says Detective Freeman.

This line of questioning infuriates Laurel, who refuses to partake any longer and demands to speak with her lawyer.

Detective Torres initiates obtaining the paperwork needed to search Laurel's phone, boat, car, and home. A judge grants the request but expresses with clarity, no media. The circus Laurel is about to generate and the havoc she leaves in her wake is imminent.

With permission, they now possess the legal recourse to dissect the phone and the yacht; access to the house and car will soon follow.

Torres returns with the necessary documents in her pocket; she politely asks Laurel to surrender her phone again. Once more, the actress resists cooperating and, through a thin veil of abstinence, states she must be available to her agent and producers. Not impressed by fame, Torres places the tri-fold warrant on the table. This action took the diva by surprise. And without further ado, she's ordered to relinquish her device.

Defeated, she hands over the phone but requests her attorney's contact number before surrendering the cell. Laurel is allowed to place a call, and as predicted, she is told not to say another word.

The distraught widows are free to go after their alibis are verified. The same questions regarding their whereabouts required an answer from Olivia and Kathryn, but more as a formality.

Kathryn stated that Olivia left the office a little after six or so. She then made something to eat, watched a movie, and went to bed. Olivia corroborated Kathryn's night in, adding that her boss asked her to stay for dinner or at least relax with a glass of wine, but she needed to get home. "I'm not certain, but guessing sometime after six is when I left." Olivia continues by stating that she had dinner with her family and remained at home for the rest of the evening with her husband and kids. They are free to go without further delay.

Detective Freeman stops Kathryn to ask one more question.

"Why did Laurel keep the yacht after her husband died?"

Unsure if he intended his remark to be sexist or morbid, Kathryn answers, "Laurel uses the yacht as an escape, for quiet solitude and to rehearse uninterrupted. She often goes out on the water alone, a floating sanctuary, if you will. The yacht didn't belong to Alan, the boat belongs to her, and he was not the yachtsman; she is."

Embarrassed by how he posed his question, the detective thanks the doctor and excuses himself.

According to the call log, it appears Laurel did lose her phone. The register indicates a few missed incoming messages, most from the house phone, but nothing outgoing. However, upon closer inspection, they discover older explicit text exchanges between Laurel and the men.

Dana and Margo are pacing while waiting for the others to come out. Laurel elects to make herself comfortable on the wooden pew in the reception area, deciding it's best to wait for her attorney so that he can retrieve her phone. Everyone assumed she wouldn't leave without her cell. Yet her friends didn't think twice before leaving without her.

TWENTY-SIX

Time to Process...

Not much is said on the ride back to Kathryn's house. Olivia is counting the trees protruding from circular holes cut in the sidewalk to keep herself from asking a stupid question and potentially offending someone. Kathryn graciously invites them all to spend the night, but everyone declines; they want to go home and process what has happened alone. Margo and Dana promise to call later if they need the friend/doctor's help.

A fleeting moment of peace floods Dana as she silences the world by closing her car door. But the temporary respite is short-lived; she picks up her phone and dictates an action plan to voice record; her life now depends on the decisions made in the next few hours; she can't leave anything out. So, starting in priority order, she begins a clean sweep to eliminate her presence all over town. Not allowing herself to falter, she deflects the hysteria threatening to engulf her as she travels to Laurel's residence.

The task is simple, get in and get out, with no mistakes. But time sensitivity applies pressure that resonates in her ears with every heartbeat. *Hurry, but don't rush*, she chants, as she worries how long it will be before the authorities discover the interaction between players. The entangled relationships expose their deceit, eventually creating enough motive to dispatch a CSI unit to the Stanhope estate.

The authorities should arrive soon, and the electronic force field requires attention. Date stamps and facial recognition will identify Dana as an intruder, with no justifiable reason to let herself in while Laurel is still at the precinct. An unauthorized intrusion would be difficult to explain, and an argument strong enough to validate uninstalling spyware doesn't exist.

Gaining access to the actress's protected lair might prove challenging, yes; impossible, no. The front and back entrances are not options; the security system will alert Laurel's phone. A warning message indicating someone is on the Stanhope doorstep, complete with an image of Dana "breaking and entering," will pop up on her screen. The only option is a kitchen door that isn't visible from the street and is the only entry point without video coverage. The alarm is engaged but won't initiate a notification if the passcode is entered in the time allotted. Staycation recon and a duplicate key allow undetected entry through the side door. A silent thank-you is mouthed to the lazy homeowner who fails to update her codes. Safely inside, Dana hesitates and listens to make sure she is alone.

The momentary break to compose herself is interrupted by a mortifying oversight that smacks her square in the forehead like a puffy white animated hand wielding a mallet. All recordings from the cameras reside in the cloud!

She asks herself, *For an intelligent woman, how can you be so stupid?*

The files backed up to Laurel's hard drive are easy to get rid of, but everything stored in the ether is another issue. There is no time to deal with that now; she will have to wait until later.

But her tentative itinerary is immediately adjusted, as Laurel didn't bother to hide her laptop; it's lying on the counter, an open invitation to a hacker. Dana keeps a note in her phone listing Laurel's passwords and usernames for repair and maintenance. The diva sends all her electronics to Dana for servicing; she doesn't trust the Geek Squad with her private intellectual property.

The plan was to come in, grab her hardware, erase today's activity, and go. Instead, the second error of the day bleeds into her brain, erasing only the current data, hands Laurel an airtight alibi. She is sitting with the detectives as the destruction of evidence takes place. This action will surely omit the actress as the one who tampered with the recordings.

A modification is necessary, everything after the last backup needs to go, and the record button is switched to the off position, eliminating a start and stop timeline. She stalls momentarily in frustration, wondering what else she has forgotten.

Finally, unable to resist, Dana presses play before hitting delete. She fights nausea and kicks herself for not monitoring the footage from home. That marks the third mistake today; she shouldn't risk spending this much time here.

Throbs of pain shoot through her mouth as she bites down hard on the inside of her cheek; she can taste blood as the scene unfolds. She watches the happy couple arrive home after the Sunday evening boat party. Dale helps Laurel in but doesn't stay. Laurel escorts him out, and she goes back inside. Monday, Madeline shows up on tape at 7:45 a.m., and the spa personnel arrive at 8:25 a.m., departing at

11:30 a.m. So far, Laurel's recollection of events is surprisingly accurate.

Madeline went home at the end of the day, and no one else went in or out. She reviews the whole night; nothing, no movement in or out. Today, Madeline clocks in as usual; Laurel exits the house to go to Kathryn's, then returns less than an hour later. Madeline leaves to run errands with a list in hand, and the officers show up to take Laurel to the station.

"Shit, Laurel never left the house. OK, back up and absorb every detail before deleting the file."

Dana rewatches, confirming that everything from Sunday to the present happened. One more time, she hits play, but this time she makes a copy with her burner phone, the quality will be useless, but she has something to review.

After much thought, Laurel's actual whereabouts are removed from the system. So, in theory, investigators will believe this is where the diva keeps her history and won't look for internet storage.

The record feature is in the off position, eliminating the chance of being recorded coming or going today. Fingers crossed, the investigators will believe the homeowner intentionally turned off the recorder and will move on searching for other clues.

One saving grace is the diva's predictability. Once she registers or creates a profile, she assigns her password, never bothering to revisit or change it; this practice will become a fatal flaw.

The cloud is the next hurdle; one can delete the past, but it's never entirely erased. So, Dana logs in as Laurel and creates a portal to hide the stored files elsewhere. She leaves only the very first camera recording and nothing else. Her original account linked to the system now appears set up and ready but unused. Multiple layers of code will deny or impede the discovery of the second location, but she hopes it won't come to that. The intention is for the police to attribute the empty online space as a failure to maintain an adequate archive—nothing in the trash; therefore, nothing to chase. Firewalls and encryption are Dana's wheelhouse. A forensic team may figure this out, but she wishes them luck; they won't live long enough to penetrate all the barriers she constructed.

The external sterilization commences, and the place gets a thorough Silkwood scrub down before replacing the Clorox towelettes under the sink, keeping the used wipes. The last step is to clean the laptop's keyboard of all fingerprints. Any prints discovered can't be explained as residual leftovers from the house guest's recent staycation, as the actress would have taken her laptop.

Upon Laurel's return, everything is in its proper place. The actress will presumably attend to her email straight away, leaving only her DNA to be lifted from the computer when it's searched. The final look around is bittersweet, believing this will be the last time Dana graces this beautiful house. With everything in its place, she reactivates the security system and locks the door behind her. The next hurdle is processing what she witnessed before experiencing a breakdown.

Paranoia joins the equipment, riding shotgun on the seat beside her; the neglected hot potatoes she is convinced will cart her off to prison, where she will live the rest of her days. Too many *Law & Order* episodes play out in real time. CCTV units pepper the street corners, glaring like the prying eye of big brother.

Dana asks herself, *How did I forget to include disposal as part of the operation?*

Then, she refers to herself as a terrible criminal, noting that the deep breathing exercises she's been practicing are no longer helpful.

The authorities will watch her, and she expects they will retrace her every step. The husband doesn't always commit the crime; sometimes, their partner is the guilty party. None of this matters now; she anticipated being high on the roster of suspects. Interrogating those closest to the victim first is standard procedure, regardless of the circumstances. The anticipation of their arrival will be a test of wills, but if she plans to survive, her story must remain consistent with fluid responses, with a dash of fear disguised as grief.

Again, driving encourages talking to oneself, and she yells, "Dispose of the electronics today, now! If—who am I kidding, *when* —they ransack my house, finding surveillance paraphernalia, although not illegal, tends to raise suspicions."

One can also presume to install spyware in someone else's home without their permission or knowledge is frowned upon and likely a punishable offense. Not to mention, the content supplies motive.

Upon returning home, she's anxious to watch the coverage recorded on the tapes from a different angle. The alternate camera angle is disappointing and reveals nothing new; the entire timeline is uneventful. The actress recanted her version of the past two days with precise accuracy, like reading from cue cards. She is that good.

The phone sticks to Dana's sweaty hand, so she switches to her computer to replay the past few days, again paying close attention to Monday night. Something triggered the motion detector, but no one appeared on the monitor. She watches one more time, and during this viewing, an ever-so-slight flicker of light streams across the yard, causing the activation. The tiny glimmer went unnoticed, as she was only looking for people, allowing the indiscernible flash to fly under the radar.

When Laurel left the house this morning, she stopped on the pathway to collect something off the grass. That "something" was her missing phone. She is telling the truth. She didn't leave the house, and she did lose her phone.

Who brought it back? Better question, who did this?

A conflict commences over how to proceed; a war, so to speak, is waging on Dana's shoulders. Those miniature versions of herself appear again, whispering in each ear, one is her conscience, and the other wears the red cape of self-preservation. Neither side will concede.

The data collected should be handed over to the authorities, but the outcome is predictable, resulting in jail time. The video omits Laurel as the murderer but doesn't discount her as the instigator or clear her involvement. But chances are no one will investigate or further accuse the star. On the contrary, Dana is sure they will implicate her as the killer or accomplice using the same evidence she provided. The detectives may not follow this path of least resistance, but who is to say they won't be satisfied with a quick resolution and call it a day? The digital proof would set the starlet, otherwise referred to as the nuisance, free and get her out of their hair.

It's all too convenient. But, unwilling to take any chances, Dana starts over, committing as much of the timeline as possible to memory. She reformats her laptop, confident she can recall at least the facts. No trace remains, but the electronics themselves are without question a liability.

In the privacy of her garage, every item is thoroughly cleaned before being stuffed into a small but heavy canvas duffle bag. Next, the hammer-wielding widow exerts her pent-up frustration on the tote containing the spyware and computer until the rubble is unrecognizable. After the therapy session, she searches the floor, using a shop vac to vacuum any rogue pieces that might've escaped the tote bag. Then hides the sack in the trunk before stating, "Time to visit Margo."

The persistent knocks on the Reed family's front door almost went unanswered. No one in the house is in the mood for condolences, so the commotion is ignored. Tyler finally gives in, opening the door to find Dana standing on the porch, longing for a hug, which he extends. The young man welcomes her in before excusing himself to deal with his struggle alone.

Dana apologizes, "I'm sorry for the unexpected drop-in, but you are the only person on this planet who understands what I'm going through right now."

"Take a seat," says Margo.

"Would you like some coffee or perhaps something stronger?"

"Some hot tea would be nice."

When Margo retreats to the kitchen, Dana jumps up and snatches the spy stick perched on the painting, stashing the gadget in her purse. Returning with some robust Darjeeling, the two newly widowed ladies sit and sip in awkward silence. The company or solidarity, although comforting, lacked relief. They both agree a nap would be beneficial and reassure one another that they will reach out later in the evening. Conscious of her movements, Dana takes her friend by her hands, thanking her for her kindness. The devastation in her voice is authentic. Being seen pulling out of the driveway and heading toward home should provide an alibi regarding her whereabouts. But that's not where she's going.

Her destination is the recycling center, ten miles the opposite way. A broken bag of tricks and one tiny spy stick still intact are on a ride-along. The refuse station is an old brick building that isn't equipped with CCTV cameras anywhere, which is a bonus. A bored young man leaning on the collection table is in his late teens; Dana smiles and says hello as she approaches the counter. The guy hands her an empty container to deposit her recyclables. Dana pours the plastic debris into the bin, tossing the bag on top, representing the proverbial cherry. She says she found her son watching porn while spying on his sister and her girlfriends. Stunned by this customer's choice of words, the attendant accepts her explanation as more than sufficient and wonders if listening to old ladies say such things are in his job description. Dana then blurts out, "But we must recycle."

Fixated on the smashed garbage as the scraps jiggle on the

conveyor belt into the crusher. She must be 100% certain every bit of damning evidence no longer exists.

The backstreets are the safest route home; the road is much prettier through the trees, and there is no CCTV to coincide with her journey. The aimless travel will be attributed to shock if someone broaches the subject. She'll claim she couldn't comprehend her predicament, and sitting at home alone only worsened the situation. Her statement isn't a lie, thus granting some leniency while drawing sympathy for her delirious state of being. After all, she *is* a distraught wife and mother who must now inform her children of this devastating event.

The time to speak to her kids is overdue; if she waits any longer, they will learn their father's gruesome demise is also the lead story on the evening news. In her desperation to gather enough courage to make the call, explaining that their father is gone, she realizes this is something else she failed to consider. In all her planning, plotting, and fantasizing about life without Randal, she not once entertained the notion of having the conversation in which she tells her kids their dad is dead. Not only dead but murdered. Reprimanding herself for being so selfish, she bypassed one of the most heart-wrenching aspects of this scenario, her family.

Out of time, she decides to rip off the Band-Aid, for lack of a better term, and she dials the phone to deliver the crushing news. Devastated and worried about their mother, the Lucas children book the first available flights home.

Bewildered by how her agenda materialized into an executable plot without her, more accurately for her, is unnerving.

She awkwardly chuckles, "They took Frank too. He never played any part in my objective, indicating something much bigger is at play here. I can't imagine who would do this; I can't imagine who would do this *for* me."

TWENTY-SEVEN

Dr. Bob...

The afternoon's effects take a toll on Kathryn and Olivia, who decide they need a stiff cup of coffee before rehashing the day's events. As she passes the cream, Kathryn asks Olivia if Laurel truly hit on Eric.

"Yes."

Looking like the cat who ate the canary, Olivia said, "Let's say our friend and I came to a little arrangement, a mutually beneficial pact. We agreed that if I promised to keep my mouth shut regarding her questionable behavior, she, in turn, pledged to honor her agreement and retain Eric as her financial adviser. Why else would Her Highness go out of her way to invite us to her parties? Did you ever wonder why all of Laurel's 'friends' are lining up to work with Eric?"

Kathryn laughs, "Well played, O, well played."

Out loud but just above a whisper, Olivia questions, "Do you think Laurel is responsible for what happened to Frank and Randal?"

After contemplating, Kathryn responds honestly, "No, I don't, but if you had asked me if I thought she was capable of sleeping with the husbands of her closest friends, I would've said no to that too."

An incoming call causes Olivia's phone to dance across the table with each ring. Dr. Bob's name illuminates the screen. A reluctant hello doesn't get past her lips before Dr. Bob starts screaming. Words spit from his mouth at lightning speed. A word edgewise would come in handy right now, as she doesn't have time to fix whatever office catastrophe he's created. Her boss's audible yet disturbingly unintelligible speech comes across the line, but not a word he says makes any sense.

"Bob, settle down," shouts Olivia.

The abruptness of her comment alerts Kathryn to trouble on the horizon. A twinge of morbid curiosity rushes through her as the anticipation dissipates and the adventure evolves.

Olivia interjects between bursts of babble, "I understand you're upset, but I can't make out what you're saying."

He takes a second and clears his voice, "She wanted to kill me too!"

After regaining enough composure to tell his story, Bob begins again, "Your friends from the other night are on television. They're dead! She called me! Not a phone call, a text. She texted me and asked me to meet her at her yacht last night."

"Who texted you?"

"Laurel! And you can't tell me it's purely coincidental that I received an invitation to join her on her yacht, and two of her friends happen to be found dead the very next morning in the water in the same harbor as her boat. This is the message she sent me, 'Quickie, my boat ten o'clock tonight, LS.'"

He added he never gave Laurel his number, and how she got it is a mystery to him.

"I was taken aback by who would send me such a racy request, but Laurel is the only person with the means and nerve; the letters LS further narrowed my choices."

The voice of a shaken man pleads, "You are my witness; you saw how she behaved with me on Sunday; she pursued me. Of course, I didn't mind at the time, but I assumed she acted this way with everyone. I mean, my wife stood right next to me the whole time.

"Then this happens. I swear the thought of meeting up with that woman never crossed my mind; after all, what plausible excuse would render permission to go out on a Monday night at ten? A maneuver so bold would amount to marital suicide. Sorry for the wrong choice of words, but you understand where I'm coming from."

The desperate swing at dignifying his non-compliance to the invitation as a noble gesture defies logic. They both "understand" the unspoken truth; the dentist would've been on that yacht in a heartbeat if he could've concocted a viable reason to escape his wife.

A resounding "NO! I most certainly did not!" follows being asked if he replied to the temptation. "I disregarded the text altogether." He inserts a slight hint of disgust for added effect.

"Is the message still on your phone?"

All he says is "Yes."

"All right, don't do anything; wait for a detective to contact you. One more question before we hang up. Is your screen open now?"

Again, a one-word answer, "Yes."

"Take a picture using Cynthia's phone." She also advises him to take a screenshot so multiple records exist. "Do you need me to tell you how?"

"I'm not a child" is heard before the distinct sound confirming he knows the trick rings out in the background.

Olivia thinks to herself, *No, Bobby, a kid would've thought to do so straight away while simultaneously posting to Instagram and Twitter. The tweet would be trending, gone viral, and forgotten.*

Olivia, however, refrains from belittling Dr. Bob's phone skills and directs his attention to a call coming his way. Kathryn pulls the business card Detective Freeman gave her at the station from her purse.

A cursory once-over of Laurel's device reveals nothing but what she stated. The call log shows Dale left a message regarding dinner. Curtis left a two-word message, "Miss me?" followed by an awkward yet impressive dick pic. Margo's text instructed Laurel to come to Kathryn's house; the remainder were repeated hang-ups from Laurel's landline. No other alerts, nothing else on Monday or today. The phone is returned to Laurel and in her possession when Detective Freeman excuses himself from the interrogation room to answer his cell. After Kathryn enlightens him, he contacts Bob to hear firsthand the account of the past evening.

Bob retells his story, but the investigators want his device to review for themselves. A formal statement is requested downtown, and he is advised that they will confiscate his mobile device as evidence. The need to ask twice wasn't necessary as he deemed his phone cursed.

The new information prompts the need to reevaluate Laurel's phone. Resistant by nature, she isn't quick to comply with the detective's demand, but fearing her rights are limited, she relinquishes her cell again. The detective passes the device to his partner, who doesn't wait for instructions. Instead, Torres bags the item; her rank encourages forensics to perform an immediate and thorough search while she waits.

Some strings are pulled, and some may or may not follow proper protocol but a full report displaying current and erased data prints out in thirty minutes. With papers in hand, Torres asks Laurel to explain removing the activity sent to Randal, Frank, and Bob yesterday. The actress's reaction is disturbing. "Bob? Bob isn't dead."

"You're certain of this?" asks Detective Torres.

"You distinctly said Randal and Frank are dead. You didn't mention Bob! So, one can assume Bob is still with us," snaps Laurel.

The attorney flailing his arms does nothing to cut off his client even though he insists she stops talking. All attempts to silence the chatty diva go unnoticed; she can't help herself and continues reiterating her lost phone story. Finally, having heard enough, the attorneys stand and announce they are leaving. No one believes Ms. Stanhope is being truthful, and his lack of control over her emasculates him.

Speculation and a phone are the only clues gathered at this point, nowhere near enough to stop Laurel and her team from walking out. The only way to detain her is to charge her with a crime, but charging their only suspect with homicide may be premature. So, for now, they can only watch as their primary person of interest collects her hat and dawns dark sunglasses before parading out the door. A warning to stay close to home is conveyed, emphasizing they will be in touch.

The detectives convince Judge Hurst to grant the remaining warrants, along with instructions forcing the surrender of Laurel's passport.

Regard mixed with suspense prompts Kathryn to conduct a welfare check on her dear friends. A man's voice surprises Kathryn when she calls the Reed home. Relief washes over her when she realizes the husky tone belongs to Tyler, who isn't a young boy anymore. He informs Kathryn that his mother is lying down and would prefer not to wake her.

After hours of crying, Margo fell asleep, and waking her to ask if she was all right would be cruel. Hesitant to persist, she hangs up and reaches out to Dana, who picks up after the first ring.

"Hello."

"How are you holding up?" asks Kathryn.

"OK, considering the circumstances" is the only reply that's deemed appropriate. An alternate would be admitting her actual status teeters on the verge of a nervous breakdown. The concern is appreciated, but she isn't in any condition to talk to anyone right now. Her kids will arrive soon, and she wants some quiet time to think.

Nothing adds up. The burden of knowing Laurel stayed home during the tragic incident is tiresome and brings zero satisfaction. Dana's need and want to discuss the matter amounts to self-sabotage. To speculate with the others would not be effortless or guilt-free. The stress of inadvertently divulging something she should not know will indeed cast suspicion her way.

Understanding the process of elimination requires time and more than one suspect; the widows nervously wait their turn to be interrogated. After all, they both possess motives for killing their spouses, but why the other man? A romantic connection to all the men may or may not be Laurel's motivation to eliminate them, but Dana takes comfort in the actress emerging as the front-runner.

A self-confirming alibi won't aid in Laurel's innocence. Even if someone did confirm she remained at home, that only proves she never left her house but doesn't exempt her from any wrongdoing. Every movie star establishes a fan base consisting of hundreds if not thousands of loyal fans, all vying for a bit of attention from the star. Sheer numbers alone dictate that locating a few star-struck individuals swimming in the shallow end of her groupie pool wouldn't be difficult.

Encounters with the actress's devotees are often exhilarating yet sometimes frightening. But one can't overlook those rare occasions which force security to intervene. The ladies witnessed at least a dozen crazies willing to accommodate their idol in whatever fantasy she made available.

Second-guessing the destruction of the video is dismissed as the tape only releases Laurel from the physical act but doesn't exclude her from the possibility of assigning her dirty work to a gullible worshiper. An accomplice, if nothing else, offers an alternative scenario, and the show still revolves around the queen.

Guilt drops in the form of tears from Dana's eyes as remorse seeps into her core. Her friend was to take the fall in the original proposal, so why the flip-flopping mind games now?

The little voice in her head won't stop over-analyzing her involvement, even though she wasn't involved.

I wasn't ready!

The implied plan wasn't real, at least not yet; it was more of an idea or a concept still in the developmental stage. Regardless of the label attached to this premeditated wish list, the execution transpiring without her blurs the lines of sanity.

A call coming in from Olivia brightens Eric's face. But in a split second, his cheerful voice loses its optimism when his wife delivers the devastating horrors of the day. In a panic, Eric sprints from his office, instructing Lilli to cancel his appointments for the rest of the day before bursting out the door.

On the ride home, his brush with evil haunts him; what if he conceded to Laurel's advances?

Would he be in the bay too?

Eric hyperventilates as his old gray Audi comes to a screeching halt in the driveway. Somehow the topic of Laurel Stanhope tends to invoke difficulty breathing and the taste of bile. All conversations centered around that woman never end well. This time the discussion will be no different, only magnified. Those thoughts dissipate at the sight of his devastated wife; he hugs Olivia so hard he's crushing her. Eric breaks down. "Something is grievously wrong with her. I don't understand how or why she did this, but I'm sure of one thing: Laurel is the mastermind."

TWENTY-EIGHT

Strip-Searching *The Leading Lady*

A CSI team takes their time to examine every inch of *The Leading Lady*.

The hazy light of day doesn't offer much assistance in illuminating the yacht's cabin; the dim, cramped space will conceal incriminating fragments that will surely go unnoticed. Black fingerprint dust, however, didn't need proper lighting and soon revealed a riveting tale.

The task force anticipated discovering markers from everyone who attended Sunday's gathering, but that was not the case. All the surfaces tested initially presented as freshly washed until little black outlines began to emerge, and those images are an exact match to Laurel, Randal, and Frank. Two tumblers in the rack indicate the men handled the glassware, and one champagne flute produced a smudge belonging to Randal and Laurel. No fingerprints matching anyone else from Sunday's guest list appeared anywhere.

"The cleanup effort is a job assigned to a professional service after each event," says Laurel when asked who tended to the vessel's maintenance.

But not before adding, "My friends took care of the china and stemware."

The detective peers over his readers; he doesn't ask specifically about the dishes. Freeman made a note to inquire about the dishware cleanup. When questioned later, Margo and Kathryn answered that they had placed everything they used into the provided bin. A Club employee was to retrieve the tub the following day. The ladies couldn't confirm what happened to the container filled with dishes after it was collected. They said they wiped down the counters and took out the trash before leaving, but that was all.

"This is Laurel's floating haven; she will ensure the crew scrubs it to perfection; anything less than sterile is not allowed," barks Margo.

More damning evidence emerged on the Club's surveillance footage; Laurel's car pulled into the parking lot Monday evening. However, she didn't select her usual space in front of the well-lit gangway; on this particular night, she chose to park along the back row in the dark. Frank entered the area at the top of the hour; he walked in as instructed. Then he traveled down the walkway along the dock's edge and let himself in the gate.

Next, approximately an hour later, Randal also appeared on foot and followed the same pattern. No other cars showed on the recording other than Laurel's. She returned to her vehicle at 11:03 p.m. and drove away. The men never reappeared.

The lab finishes its analysis on Laurel's phone. As documented in Laurel's statement, an almost scripted discovery confirms that the phone went to the marina on Sunday and back to the Stanhope residence.

Adamant about staying home on Monday is also somewhat verified by her phone. The cellular device remained at the house or, at least, didn't ping another tower throughout the day. So, all is copacetic until three outgoing texts are sent to the men Monday at 6:14 p.m. The ping from the phone indicates the texts came from Laurel's house.

As the evening progresses, the phone travels to the harbor, goes out on the water, and returns to the Stanhope home before midnight. The phone remains at the house until the following day, presumably on the lawn.

The messages are another crushing blow as each typed word implicates Laurel and establishes premeditation. The security tapes validate two of the three men received and accepted the invitation.

Armed with enough probable cause, Laurel Stanhope will be brought back for questioning. She will most likely be taken into custody and booked for a double homicide, among other charges.

Reaching out to Kathryn left Laurel less than comforted when it was suggested that she tell the truth; the words delivered in a condescending professional tone struck a nerve.

A snarky retort flies from Laurel's lips, "Would you like me to tell them everything? Should I mention I slept with your husband too?"

Kathryn ignores the sting of this specific truth, but not before adding that she thought they worked through her husband's indiscretion.

"This ordeal will work out much better if you are cooperative and truthful. Be honest; disclose your involvement if you are inadvertently or otherwise responsible for what happened to Randal and Frank."

Laurel screams, "I didn't do this; someone is trying to frame me."

Kathryn calmly asks her friend, "Who would want to frame you? And for what reason?"

A collective of angry housewives was a thought, but Kathryn kept that to herself.

Deliberate in her speech, Kathryn chooses emotionally provoking words to elicit a dramatic outcome. But keep digging, Laurel; the hole is getting deeper. If the police are listening to the conversation, which is highly likely, all buttons need to be pushed in the appropriate order. Then she can sit back and observe as the diva unravels, becomes entangled, and hangs herself with silk rope.

Kathryn offers her services as a physician and friend, making herself available even though the actress insists on complicating the matter. She also asks Laurel if she would like any of her medicine, explaining that she would only dispense individual doses to monitor her usage. And for a good reason. Before this incident, there was no need to entertain the notion of self-harm. The administration of drugs now is intended to prevent the suspect from doing anything stupid. The starlet won't be given the opportunity to check out early if the going gets too rough.

On second thought, the drama queen is too self-absorbed to kill herself. Photos of her lifeless body appearing as tabloid fodder, unflattering or tasteless poses, would be too much, even after death. A tarnished image is not how Laurel Stanhope desires to be remembered by her fans.

Smiling inside at her spontaneous wit, Kathryn dreams up a headline spouting, "Starlet Found Naked Sprawled on the Bathroom Floor, Dead from an Apparent Overdose."

Although it has a snappy ring, this star will go out with more dignity.

The detectives secured a warrant to dismantle everything

associated with the actress. They find fingerprints matching Randal and Frank in her home, demonstrating they explored every room in her house, including her primary suite. Unfortunately, the prints only confirmed her inappropriate entertainment practices with married men; nothing indicates she killed anyone. CSI found DNA from Madeline and Dana, but they anticipated those findings.

Pill canisters displayed in clusters about the rooms resemble decorative accent pieces rather than narcotic reciprocals. An uncapped container discovered under the bed indicates it was handled only by Laurel, but the bottles in the kitchen and dressing room reveal they were in Kathryn's possession at one time. The detectives return to Dr. Kane and ask her why her fingerprints would be on their suspect's medication. Quick to explain, she tells them Laurel doesn't trust herself.

She demonstrates several scenarios: "Sometimes, Laurel gives me the containers to hold, and I dispense the medicine as needed. This practice reduces the possibility of a rehab stint in her future. Sometimes she self-medicates and doesn't give them to me; other times, she requests the entire bottle."

Detective Freeman went on to ask Kathryn if she had written the prescription. This line of questioning is infuriating; his juvenile strategy insults her intelligence. Freeman already mentioned they found the mind-altering stockpile. A genius IQ isn't required to presume the first thing an investigator would do is read the label, making this inquiry redundant.

"No," replies Dr. Kane. She takes her time and adds only, "I did not."

Detective Freeman pauses, anticipating more, but she prefers to let him stew. He breaks the awkward silence by asking, "Are you familiar with Laurel Stanhope's doctor?"

"Of course."

Again, she momentarily holds on to the remainder of her reply, implying she may not tell him who that doctor might be.

"As you gathered by reading the bottle, the MD writing the prescriptions is Dr. Joel Kane."

Kathryn elects to stop here, leaving her thoughts to the detective's imagination. The detective insinuates the association between Dr. Joel Kane and Ms. Stanhope is an exclusive doctor-patient relationship. Kathryn commences by delivering a well-thought-out narrative about those two. A story convincing enough to deconstruct the diva further as a decent human being begins to take shape and expose her true self, a serial destroyer of humanity.

"The association between Joel and Laurel, personally or professionally, went on unbeknownst to me initially. Laurel was dismissed by her previous therapist, at which point she received referrals and searched for a new doctor to torment. That list referenced Joel Kane's name alongside mine. Often people seeking help shy away from confiding in someone with whom they are acquainted or have an intimate connection. Some find they can't be open or reveal private struggles, yet Laurel enlisted Joel. She finds men easier to manipulate and aims to use the doctor-patient privilege to her full advantage. The first appointment was scheduled under an assumed name, knowing Joel would never agree to counsel her. In his defense, all the paperwork regarding his new patient revolved around a fake name and profile. He would be oblivious to the client's identity until she showed up and sat on his couch. They agreed not to share this arrangement with me or the friend group. I was not to be the topic in session, and Joel was not to bring up his patient at home.

"About a year ago, Laurel executed a well-crafted sidestep in their pact, allowing her to enlighten me that my husband was, in fact, her doctor without breach or conflict. But first, you must acknowledge her claim of being plagued with anxiety, accompanied by a self-diagnosed sleep disorder.

"Several conditions were conveyed to Joel, who prescribed medication to alleviate these symptoms. However, self-control is often an issue, so Laurel asked me to hold her pills, a childish ruse to ensure I became aware Joel is her doctor and secondary to prevent her from becoming a statistic.

"Actresses tend to go down the same euphoric path when bored. Ms. Stanhope utilized me as her personal dispensary to prevent an accidental addiction. Nothing is more embarrassing for the famous than an unorchestrated stint in rehab. Laurel refers to those glamorous institutions as a last resort for the B-list celebrities who hit rock bottom. That sort of desperate plea involves a new level of self-sabotage, reserved and only initiated when all other means of attracting attention are exhausted.

"The 'ask' is two-fold. First, by design, soliciting me to be the administrator would prompt me to validate the prescription. Second, I am a doctor; therefore, I would verify the drug as appropriate and the physician as credible. So, I am abundantly mindful, thank you, that this fear of being an addict is for my benefit. But the drama was easily avoidable if Laurel had bothered to verify our marital status before manipulating my spouse and, in turn, me.

"Our partnership ended years ago; the decision to live separate lives is the only recent change. We are still close but better together if we are apart. I hope this makes sense. Joel and I are still in one another's life but as friends. For instance, he escorted me to the Fourth of July party. Unfortunately, failing to do her due diligence resulted in unrewarded efforts; she couldn't derive any pleasure or satisfaction from ruining a non-existent union.

"To prove my theory, Laurel stopped seeing Joel, at least in a private setting, soon after we announced our separation."

The detective went on to ask how Laurel's behavior didn't

bother her. Unfazed by his tactic to prod her, she retains her composure and moves on.

"Those are your words and your interpretation. A failed marriage is a life-changing event with unavoidable and profound effects on both parties, even if the separation is mutual. We respect each other and remain close, catching our friends off guard. As previously stated, our partnership dissolved some time ago; we lived together out of convenience. The divorce came as a shock to our friends but not to us."

TWENTY-NINE

Confirmation

The autopsies performed on both Frank and Randal revealed what everyone already knew; the cause of death was drowning. But, to be specific, a drug-induced drowning. Their bodies contained a high dose of narcotics, alcohol, and saltwater—a larger dose than Alan's cocktail if anyone cared to compare the files. Seawater in their lungs concludes they were alive when they entered the water and, most likely, conscious when they drowned. The type of medication used would render them immobile but presumably wide awake to experience their deaths.

The heinous and meticulous detail involved reflects immense patience. This killing took intricate planning, which points to this not being the first go-around for this perpetrator. A random crime produces errors, of which they have found none. Nevertheless, authorities can't dismiss the possibility of dealing with a serial killer. In the meantime, they will wait for Laurel Stanhope to slip up, wondering if the murderer and the actress are the same person.

Margo returns to the station for another round of questions. Torres and Freeman are curious about her and her husband's recent life insurance purchase. Snapping back with a vengeance, the angry widow explains, "Laurel also instigated this endeavor. Now this all makes perfect sense."

She screams at the detectives, "Laurel pressured us to sign the papers because all of this is part of her sick charade; she knew the outcome all along."

Detective Torres excused herself from the interrogation room and contacted Dana to validate the new information before posing similar inquiries to Olivia and Kathryn. They all concur; Laurel insisted on obtaining policies. Olivia interjected, wanting to get her story out first, "Laurel pressured my husband Eric to facilitate the meeting to guarantee everyone followed through with signing the paperwork."

Olivia further seized the opportunity to lash out at Laurel, saying, "She was relentless about our coverage, bragged about her husband Alan's gracious policy that provided her with more than adequate funds to keep her in the lifestyle to which she's grown accustomed."

Then, for good measure, Olivia added, "You may want to investigate the timing of her husband Alan's policy."

Margo said, "Frank and I signed up to cover expenses, college, the house, and a little leftover to survive, not to thrive."

Dana's conversation and details of the policy she and Randal purchased show they too insured to care for their family in the event of an unexpected death, not to win the lotto.

Kathryn declined coverage, as did Olivia.

The good fortune in the form of a payout is circumstantial, and its orchestration almost works in Laurel's favor. Her husband did as responsible partners do; he ensured she remained financially stable if he were to pass first. So why wouldn't she want to share the protection process with her closest friends?

The fact that they bought coverage and, soon after, their husbands passed too is undoubtedly a coincidence. Some argue this is more suspicious than coincidental, but they can't prove malice aforethought. Not yet, anyway.

The authorities pinpointed Randal's car near the Yacht Club entrance after being alerted that vehicles from the dealership come equipped with locators. Unfortunately, Frank's car didn't have a tracker. Still, it wasn't long before a couple of uniformed officers walking in opposite directions from the entry discovered Frank's car parked half a block away.

A sudden chill runs through Dana. *What if they find her tracking unit, the one she installed?*

She calms herself, deciding to own the installation if asked. She'll declare it was a proactive response after excessive auspicious occasions put Randal where he didn't claim to be. Dana initially intended to keep her honest man honest. It turns out he wasn't honest at all.

The parking arrangement is an odd choice when an empty lot sits in front of your guest's destination. Laurel selecting a space in the back row rather than her usual spot went unnoticed by her invitees. She would want the men to see her car, and besides, walking in is for others.

The text messages sent to the men instructed them not to park inside the Yacht Club grounds, perhaps so their vehicles wouldn't be found by the staff the following day. In hindsight, maybe she should've let them; the valet would have the cars towed without a valid parking sticker.

Interference from the unwarranted parking issue clouds

Kathryn's day; she confirms that she did not make a mistake and moves on. Her planning proved spot on; the instructions and car location established forethought, which is crucial, and she couldn't risk one man identifying the other man's car before making his way onto the boat.

The police suspect Laurel didn't count on Randal having a tracker in his car or Frank finding a parking space so close to the gate. The current situation is beginning to look rather grim for Ms. Stanhope.

THIRTY

Breaking News

LAUREL STANHOPE ARRESTED today on suspicion of murder. As reported earlier this week, the bodies of Randal Lucas and Frank Reed were discovered Tuesday morning by passengers and crew aboard the Harbor Bay Ferry in San Francisco Bay. Sources close to the victims confirmed that both men were close personal friends of the actress.

Instant scrutiny by the community prompted law enforcement to announce they would petition the court to reopen the investigation into the demise of the late Mr. Alan Stanhope. Unfortunately, nothing about his death was considered suspicious; therefore, the incident was hastily characterized as a tragic accident, and the case was closed. Yet, the similarities between the two cases are undeniable, forcing officials to reconsider their initial findings to determine whether the circumstances are, in fact, coincidental.

At home, accompanied by her lawyer, the actress waited for the authorities to arrive to take her into custody. Notifying Laurel's counsel of her impending arrest gave the accused the satisfaction of surrendering voluntarily. Laurel Stanhope arriving at the station without incident is to everyone's benefit. This maneuver gave the actress an audience to play to, ensuring decorum in lieu of kicking and screaming. Despite the harsh "No Comment" shouted by her attorneys, the mass of onlookers barricading the walkway were treated to the overdramatic cries from the star, professing she is innocent of any wrongdoing and that this is all a terrible misunderstanding.

"Nothing to hide" might be what Ms. Stanhope barks, but the detectives are confident her mobile phone will unlock a bevy of hidden secrets. After a complete sweep of her cellular device, the correspondence between her and the deceased confirmed a solid romantic liaison.

Celebrity incarcerations often coincide with the precinct filling with crazies, film crews, and field anchors shouting for a sound bite or video clip. The spectacle of being brought in made no difference to Laurel; she was using this as an opportunity to gain exposure. She didn't kill anyone, so she wasn't worried. This ordeal converted into an energizing photo session, tossing kisses and winks while posing amidst the chaos. However, her photogenic smile dissipated when she was publicly read her rights. She was again caught off guard when swiftly led away to the booking area, and this was by no means a runway catwalk-type saunter. The hurried stride of the escorting officer and the associated grip around Laurel's arm felt excessive. But being manhandled was the least of her worries and quickly forgotten when the walk ended, and she was placed under arrest. The charge, "double homicide."

The word "homicide" caused Laurel to choke. Another string of gag-inducing words rapidly followed: "Standard prison-issue attire."

This phrase was alarming enough, but being told to change her clothes was met with some resistance. However, it was immediately evident that balking at the guard's request wouldn't bode well for Ms. Stanhope, and she quickly conceded.

The imposing gray "inside" contrasts her colorful world "outside," so she decides to comply in hopes of a speedy release. The actress waltzes through the holding cells with her head high and heels higher while the luxury of dressing in street clothes becomes a non-option. Finally, she is stripped of her ensemble, replacing a black St. John pantsuit with a tangerine onesie and slip-on no-brand sneakers until she can post bail. The women in lockup harass the newest inmate by coining phrases about orange; they can't help themselves. It's too easy.

A debate rages behind dark wood-paneled walls regarding a suitable dollar amount, followed by her release or whether the movie star remains in custody. Everyone in attendance does their best to appear shocked, but no one is surprised when bail accompanies a one-million-dollar price tag. Freedom, however, seems to be priceless and very grounding as she must now surrender her travel documents.

Today may be the only time when being a world-traveling person with means is a disadvantage. Judge Hurst's statement resonates clearly; these proceedings are not a joke. He doesn't foresee releasing Laurel on bond as a threat to the city's residents, nor does he believe she will be a flight risk. Therefore, banishing her to her home or restricting her is unnecessary.

Where is she going to go?

Her face is everywhere. Also, his honor remarked, "Allocating surveillance funds for the famous equates to squandering taxpayer dollars." This insult drew an audible gasp from the starlet before being advised to stay in the county.

His parting words were frightening, "I'm relying on you to remain under self-imposed house arrest for your safety."

Every media outlet will secure her exact movements from now through the end of the trial. The world will watch the disgraced entertainer; everyone will be apprised of her location every minute of every day, whether interested or not.

The Stanhope legal team arranged Laurel's release, and she is allowed to leave for now. Pleading calls and messages professing her innocence go unanswered. From this point forward, the only interaction with her friend group will be in a courtroom, and they will be present to assist the prosecution. For now, Dale keeps his opinion to himself, too overwhelmed by the accusations to comment. On the other hand, Curtis had no qualms about cutting ties with the actress. Until Laurel's little misunderstanding with the law, she played a significant role in establishing Curtis as a hot commodity amongst the city's elite. He can't risk tarnishing his reputation by being associated with the desperate and defamed. Therefore, he requested that she not call him and delete all texts, photos, and his number.

Laurel sends out dinner invitations which are left unread, as are requests for lunch at the Club. One would assume the membership agreement at the Yacht Club includes a clause revoking privileges if branded a felon. It matters not; no one will subject themselves to a humiliating confrontation or risk rejection. A rendezvous on the boat would be in poor form, so she doesn't bother to ask. The news sites are contributing to her downward spiral as they forecast her portraying a pitiful woman wasting away in her big house alone.

Laurel got what she wished for; she wanted the ladies to experience the same loneliness she harbors. To her, conquering their men gives her some sick sense of superiority. Ramifications, after they found out, were never a concern. The self-absorbed are rarely bothered by particulars.

Typically, time remedies Laurel's indiscretions. But the same pattern emerges with every assault; most fibs start as minor embellishments to add drama to a narrative. Each deceptive conversation varies from half-truths to outright fabrications; every cut is told with juicy details to dazzle those she dubs as that day's friends. None of her anecdotes produce accolades for the individual under attack—only irreparable damage at the expense of someone she claims to love.

Never contributing anything original or noteworthy, Laurel resorts to shock value to keep her fan base interested. Nothing is off-limits once she's hooked someone's ear; she would sacrifice her entire wardrobe for a moment of undivided attention. Reprimands deflected like gnats are commonplace. If cornered, she'll spit, "My apologies." Of course, the salutation will be delivered under duress and certainly not heartfelt.

The following steps involve a calculated restoration plan to revive the last relationship she torched. After a reasonable amount of time passes, "the process" commences, with Laurel sending a mundane text message about something benign or obligatory. Massaged words aid in regaining a smooth, comfortable rhythm, and before long, normalcy reigns. Until she tells the next lie and the life cycle repeats.

The unrest coursing through Laurel stems from her jealous nature and overwhelming fascination with dominance. Bitter from the realness of never finding true love is proving impossible to conceal. The one reoccurring dilemma is that no one will ever view Laurel how she views herself. The person she honestly believes she is doesn't exist.

Laurel's brief incarceration highlighted the afternoon airwaves; by tomorrow, photos of her marching into police headquarters will saturate the newsfeeds and tabloids. All reports insinuate that Laurel orchestrated and then committed the murders of all three men, making the "Black Widow" the talk of the town.

The San Francisco court system rushed the arraignment to happen within a week. Havoc was taking over and causing problems before the great Hepburn impersonator made her first appearance. But, when she does show up, no signs of weakness are visible; on the contrary, she exudes arrogance.

The courtroom scene resembles organized pandemonium, whispers hushed, and phones confiscated. Poised front and center, Laurel Stanhope stands, ready to speak. Her posture drips with annoyance as the hiss coated in sarcasm delivers her "not guilty" plea to the court. The words "you idiot" almost slip off her forked tongue. Agitated by her righteousness, the judge comments on her disrespect for him and the proceedings. He suggests she alter her demeanor if she expects any consideration in return.

Judging by the expression on Laurel's face, one can presume she thought this was all a ridiculous formality and that the judge would then say he was sorry for consuming her time, apologize to her again for the inconvenience, and send her on her way.

The attorneys appear lost as they implore the actress to remain calm. They didn't expect a fistfight so soon, but wrangling their client's opinion is something they should've practiced. The fear of being recorded is the only thing keeping Laurel from going ballistic in public. She knows everything she says will air before she hits the sidewalk. So, composed and unaffected, she rises, straightens her jacket, and walks out of the courtroom without saying another word.

The doors bursting open initiates the pushing and shoving. Microphones and cameras flail, vying for a spot before the oddly subdued diva to capture her grief. The hoard of people rushing over seems to go unnoticed by her. A bizarre parade of images invades her thoughts instead. The cold sharpness in the air is shockingly abrasive for this time of year. The sun descending behind the skyline distracts Laurel from the roaring crowd, who've assembled like angry bees fighting for their queen.

The possibility of going mad also popped up on her radar. The customarily distracted star now appreciates the breeze on her face but worries that her feet are no longer beneath her. She fears she is hallucinating when the sound of a car door opening snaps her back to reality.

A man's hand squeezes around her arm as he shoves her into the waiting limo. The car pulls away from the commotion, but the voices don't stop. Her attorneys beside her want to ensure she comprehends the full extent of her predicament, but she remains unresponsive.

Initially, the accusations were for publicity and not taken seriously, but the possibility of being locked up is quite an awakening. The realness of today reinforces that this is indeed happening; it's not a publicity stunt, and the beloved movie star is, in a word, fucked. For the first time in years, Laurel breaks down; the tears are real and more painful than expected.

Safely tucked in at the Stanhope estate isn't a relief; it's suffocating. The confines instantly morph into a claustrophobic prison, one boasting better sheets but a prison just the same.

Kathryn pours herself a glass of wine, second-guessing her selection, conceding champagne would have been more appropriate. Laurel's preferred beverage is always bubbles, perhaps a crisp brut.

They won't be popping corks on cell block B tonight.

Kathryn's aware her friend isn't spending the night in jail, but imagining her cocktail-less friend behind bars is a delightful vision.

The "list" requires a final review to confirm that Kathryn conveyed her knowledge of events to the authorities with the style and finesse she recalls. But for now, her homework can wait. She'll enjoy her Merlot and quietly reflect, hoping her self-aware attitude doesn't take over; her conscience should be interjecting here, allowing her to keep an emotionally safe distance from her actions. The notion of empathy and remorse are contemplated, but neither suits her. Those are kind words with no place in her world au présent. Back to reality, she justifies her current state as rational, not self-righteous. She is a task-oriented, trained professional. A situation arose; she accepted the challenge and resolved the controversy. In her mind, the goal accomplished has earned her some well-deserved relaxation time.

Downtime can be a problem for thinkers who find shutting off their brains a formidable task; Kathryn is one of those people. Wine sometimes helps, but tonight, the Merlot consumed to help her unwind only triggered more anxiety. The solution executed to resolve the trouble the men created won't stay quiet and allow her any peace.

Attention, at its core, is evil in disguise, marking the seeker as one to be monitored and hopefully medicated. The person isn't void of feelings, just more likely to be dismissive in expressing their emotions or acknowledging yours. They understand the concept of caring, but it's not enough to curb their conduct, making them unpredictable, not to mention dangerous. By adulthood, Kathryn transformed her disdain for such characters and her lack of empathy into an inner strength. She channels this energy to defend those who, like herself, fell victim to loved ones who didn't love them back—a justified crusader, if you will.

Kathryn often blamed her selective resistance to people on her parents, mainly her mother. She once stated, "My mother understood the gentle art of parenting but made a conscious effort not to exercise her skills."

As a daughter, acknowledgment is all she wanted; Kathryn did all but grovel. Sadly, her mother couldn't even pretend two children lived in the house. Grown-up responsibilities and parental personality flaws are not a burden any child should carry. Yet, the more Kathryn tried to convince her mother she possessed enough love for her and her sister, the more her mother resisted.

The stereotypical experience for the offspring of parents with high standings tends to be one of structure and happiness; this was not the case for Kathryn; she viewed her hypocritical upbringing as fabricated.

Most young children, including Kathryn, are ill-equipped to handle their complex mental well-being. But she was left to fend for herself, struggling to communicate and manage her emotional neglect independently. The family members didn't talk to each other much; the expected open dialogue between parent and child wasn't encouraged, increasing their oldest daughter's frustration.

Resentment replaced togetherness, which led to isolation in an already fractured family unit. Communication and an equal division of affection may have made some situations more livable and far less violent.

In hindsight, through no fault of her own, Kara was punished for their mother's behavior. If Kathryn were to reenact the horrible event in question today, she would eliminate Mother first. Perhaps not having to do away with Kara at all.

To think she missed out on a lifetime of sisterhood is unsettling. Yet guilt doesn't surface, her sister is dead, and dwelling on that now serves no purpose. She chooses to save reevaluating the past for her patients.

After Kara's passing, Kathryn was sure her mother would expel all of her love and focus on her, making eliminating her sister vital. The answer seemed straightforward, remove the problem, and all will be well. But she failed to consider that the plan could backfire, and the unforeseen ramifications that followed were devastating.

The attention she so desperately craved turned to blame. No one can prove Kathryn pushed Kara to her death. Baiting her to move closer to the chasm's edge with promises of viewing treasure at the bottom was known only to Kathryn. One quick shove and problem solved, or so she thought. With no witnesses to the slip and fall, all anyone had to go on was the Grammy-winning performance portrayed by the hysterical older sister. And with that, the accidental tragedy was a convenient explanation requiring no further investigation. Mother, however, was hesitant and not yet persuaded; she wasn't wrong when she detected something more diabolical at play. Life for her other daughter expectedly changed, but not for the better.

Not long after Kara perished, Mother inserted herself in the role of the pusher. Her constant badgering, asking why she didn't try to save her sister, cycled on a continuous loop. The rejection and torment proved much worse than being ignored. Father, unable to control his home's discourse, condemned his now only child and wife to intense analysis. Several physicians counseled them both, resulting in various and somewhat unethical prescriptions to remedy a variety of phantoms.

After six months of grieving and badgering, Kathryn reached her fill with this sort of attention, deciding she only needed her father's love, and all would be right in the world. Her father, suffering himself, always dedicated time to comfort Kathryn, but not her mother; her mother's grudge only deepened the divide.

High tea is where Kathryn's mother found serenity. This old English afternoon tradition became habitual, reflecting her desired lifestyle. So naturally, one must dress appropriately to attend the midday affair, and punctuality goes without saying. The private service commences at two p.m. each day without fail, and the menu never varies. One can expect single servings of steeped leaves, some biscuits, mother's medication, and, last but not least, a well-deserved nap.

One lazy overcast afternoon, Kathryn asked permission to prepare the daily ritual. An affirmative response sparked glee, and her mother obliging made Kathryn very happy. A gorgeous silver tray decorated with beautiful china, Lorna Doone cookies, and mother's meds presented well. However, the teacup teetering on the edge of the tray slid off its saucer, spilling its contents before hitting the floor. The abhorrent etiquette displayed didn't provoke her mother as Kathryn had hoped. So, she rushed to the kitchen, leaving her guest to clean up the mess.

The lack of liquid didn't halt the medication consumption or a cookie being savored as her dutiful daughter reappeared with a fresh cup—profusely apologizing as she placed the new teacup and saucer on the coffee table.

This slight disruption modified the natural flow of the afternoon, leaving the door open for other changes. The conversation during their little soirée revolved around the topic of horses. The plate of Lorna Doones was passed, and the tempting little helpers resting next to the cookies were consumed as they discussed the next horse show on the calendar.

Anything equestrian-related guaranteed a lengthy discussion, captivating her mother's interest for hours. A simple request to retell stories spun a dozen times before engrossed the storyteller in a tale causing her to lose focus on her surroundings.

"More, Mother?" said the polite hostess while pouring hot water through the stainless-steel loose-leaf strainer.

Graciously she accepted another biscuit, and several more pills couldn't hurt. The atmosphere was most pleasant, almost euphoric; she was astonished at how enjoyable this tea, cookie, and pill party with her daughter had turned out to be. So much so that she sat in wonder as to why they hadn't shared more afternoons. Before Mommy could identify her hazy condition, she ingested more cookies than prescribed. Naptime arrived when Mother's limp body slumped over on the couch mid-sentence. With the finesse of a skilled housekeeper, Kathryn cleared her place setting from the parlor, along with any clues alluding to a guest being entertained this afternoon. The gloves she wore were not a fashion accessory but a well-thought-out safeguard. She took her mother's hand and wrapped her fingers around a new teacup, making sure to touch the edges of the saucer. The cup's rim was gently pressed to her mother's lips to leave sufficient DNA should anyone be so thorough.

The now half-filled teacup containing lukewarm untainted Yorkshire regained its proper place atop its matching saucer. Mother only drank a tea of English nature. Yorkshire, to be precise. If you scrutinized the box, you would find a royal seal stamped on the side, as if this ensures better quality—only the best for Mother. Adjacent to the cup sat an overturned medicine canister.

Before jumping on her bike, Kathryn double-checked that everything was in its proper place. Then, she casually rode to the library to check out equestrian books to share with Mother. But, of course, that all depended on whether she was still alive.

Upon returning home, a patrol car and fire truck told the end of the story. The bright red-and-blue lights swirled as the paramedics wheeled a gurney out of the house. The stark white sheet draped over her mother's lifeless body flapped in the breeze. This scene should have seared vivid images in the child's memory like a photograph—well, one would have thought.

Father stood in the front yard with his hands over his mouth as the ambulance driver shut the door before pulling away. Kathryn laid her Schwinn on the lawn, dropping her book bag to console her distraught remaining parent.

He held his daughter's face as he told her that her mother was gone, attempting to explain the meaning of suicide in understandable terms. Not waiting for him to finish, his child broke free of his grasp; she collected her things and cruelly said, "How unfortunate."

He stood alone on the driveway next to her abandoned bicycle, still on the grass, and watched his dispassionate daughter go to her room to read her borrowed literature.

A cold chill ran through his body as genuine emotion so deliberately suppressed bubbled to the surface. His daughter's reaction brought forth a stunning revelation as if someone pulled back the curtains to expose a clear window into his child's troubled soul.

Denial, heartache, and juvenile detention all crossed his mind. How could a doctor, a well-respected medical leader, be so blind?

He wasn't; he wanted his baby girl to grow out of this phase, change, or improve through therapy. He blatantly refused to acknowledge his daughter's disturbing personality traits, the ones screaming she'd exceeded the spectrum. The apparent warning signs were present; her extreme will, oddly reserved temperament in the face of death, and the absence of basic social cues were more than just a few quirks. Mix feelings of abandonment with highly methodical mannerisms made for strange attributes, especially for a young child. But regardless of his suspicions, he never considered his behaviorally impaired daughter capable of murder.

Dear old Dad went into self-preservation mode rather than institutionalizing or admitting his flesh and blood possessed psychopathic tendencies. Everyone believed Mother took her own life due to the depression she suffered after the death of her youngest child. Father concurred with the assumptions of others playing into the sympathy and moved on. He rallied the best psychiatrists in the state to treat his mourning daughter. Amused by the posturing, Kathryn observed and studied, mastering the games designed to fix her. The feedback doctors wanted wasn't hard to decipher, and she would respond in kind. Again, it's as simple as serving afternoon tea.

Kathryn took full advantage of being raised by a psychiatrist and a sociopath. At birth, her parents provided her with a dangerous predisposition. The combination of nature, assorted meds, and basic survival skills produced a clever girl. Dr. Dad forced her to sit on the couches of his professional friends, enduring countless hours of counseling, failing to recognize she's a shapeshifter who finds adapting to her environment amusing. It's too bad their efforts only served one purpose: to hone this child's talents in becoming an emotionless master manipulator.

The system intended to help Kathryn only aided in developing the unique life equalizer, later referred to as "the list."

Like puppets in a show, the egotistical professionals convinced everyone they helped and healed her. Then, fascinated by the human brain, and the game, Kathryn decided to study the behavioral sciences herself. Her aging father is still living, although today, the father and daughter maintain a long-distance relationship. He prefers she stays away, far, far away.

THIRTY-ONE

My Fair-Weather Friend

Proximity within a suburban neighborhood often dictates one's first friendships. Children of the same age and gender almost guarantee an instant playmate. This scenario rang true for Laurel and Kathryn, who lived a few houses from each other growing up. The unlikely pair also attended school together, yet no one considered them inseparable. Nevertheless, they did provide reassurances in the other's time of need. The gestures always seemed heartfelt, but they both knew that any kindness was a superficial habit. But somehow, the questionable relationship endured by ticking several boxes, each girl filled with dark thoughts and deceitful amusement disguised as caring concern.

They never found it necessary to discuss the awkward arms-length force field tethering them; that conversation would only highlight their faults and expose their true intentions. However, Laurel did make a point of being available for her often-grieving neighbor. But more so to place herself in a front-row seat to witness all the trauma Kathryn's family suffered.

Constant contact wasn't necessary as they often drifted in and out of each other's lives. This arrangement suits Kathryn; she doesn't like people getting too close, and she doesn't ever confide in anyone who can't take her secrets to their grave.

In the past, these two fair-weather friends could temporarily push aside their vindictiveness and let whatever drove them to the brink resolve itself. But today, however, each would rather watch the other burn in hell.

Laurel remains under self-imposed house arrest as she can't move past her driveway without being accosted by cameras and microphones. The alternative being a cold cell keeps her in check but won't stop her from voicing the debate between sequestered versus the right to move freely.

The film producers expressed disappointment with the actress's inability to adhere to their work schedule. In addition, a leak in the production company repeatedly fed confidential information to the general public. As a result, their whereabouts went viral, and the press and devotees converged on whatever unfortunate small town drew the short straw. The hoard of onlookers made filming impossible; the diva's presence no longer mattered; the excited fans wanted a peek at the drama.

The movie is near completion; recasting the leading role would be too costly and time-consuming. The studio has no choice but to embrace Laurel and the chaos she creates. Their only hope is that all the free publicity justifies the aggravation. The film's marketing director will use their star's misfortune to their advantage; a scandal of this magnitude will put this production's gross revenue into the record books. They won't need an advertising budget; the media coverage exceeds any exposure they could afford.

The preliminary hearing scheduled for the end of the week causes the first conflict. The reminders in Laurel's calendar indicate a set visit to finalize her project. However, her court appointments are becoming inconvenient, and her new schedule isn't negotiable. Laurel didn't care where she was going; all she wanted was out of the house; the reason for escaping her confines was irrelevant; anywhere but stuck at home would do.

She dresses each day as if she is going somewhere or expects visitors. But these days, Madeline and the attorneys are the only ones who come in or out. Service personnel are instructed to use the side door. No one else is allowed, not that anyone attempts to make contact or visit.

None of the book club members will take Laurel's calls. However, Kathryn toys with the idea of reaching out. It is more for information-gathering than concern for the well-being of their isolated friend. The investigators occasionally pop by the lady's homes to pose previously asked questions, attempting to elicit a conflicting response. Revisits are where Kathryn stays one step ahead. She jots down notes after each interrogation, scribbling what's asked and tracking the answers she gives in return. The doctor's demeanor surprises no one; she is spot on, never wavering in her account of any statement.

With no other workable leads, the detectives are fishing and grasping at straws in hopes of a slipup from someone. The hired gun theory circled the station for a while. But they can't find any clues suggesting Laurel conspired with an accomplice. Instead, all evidence gathered points directly at Laurel acting entirely on her own. So, to date, the actress remains the one and only suspect.

THIRTY-TWO

The Preliminary Hearing

No one was surprised by the media circus packing the courthouse. Before commencing, Judge Hurst warns the gallery that any outburst would result in a closed court. The warning fell on deaf ears as the chaos bounced off the walls, echoing down the corridor. The crack of the gavel striking the sounding block precedes the raised voice of the judge delivering a final decree. Remain and keep quiet, or leave. Failure to comply earns immediate removal, followed by a contempt of court charge. The heavy wooden doors closed, and silence filled the room.

The prosecutor, as expected, started the day by entering into evidence each clue discovered thus far. Their presentation, although short, contained compromising accusations. First, they introduced the cell phone and video surveillance from the Yacht Club, then added the diving equipment confiscated from the Stanhope dock box. Testimony from the dive store clerk identifies Madeline as the person who made the purchase; he also produced a copy of the sales receipt. They traced the ticket back to Laurel's credit card, and the products listed matched the gear found on the men.

Crime scene investigators only recovered four of the five belts. The fifth belt reserved for Dr. Bob Flanagan must have gone overboard with the men when the dentist declined the invitation. The GPS on Laurel's mobile phone pinging a tower only accessible by water will be difficult to refute. Still, the fingerprints found aboard the vessel belonging to no one other than Frank, Randal, and Laurel will be the most damning evidence.

A solid stance is absent from the Stanhope squad; they've neglected to demonstrate a strategic course of action thus far. A bulletproof alibi would come in handy, but one doesn't seem forthcoming. The star prides herself on her word being sufficient; rarely being challenged only encourages her self-righteous thinking. Team Stanhope argues that their client's presence on the boat doesn't prove she killed anyone. Of course, the prosecuting attorney capitalized on the opposition's blunder after they willingly suggested Ms. Stanhope was indeed on the yacht on the night in question.

This banter went back and forth, stopping with the burden of proof landing in the lap of the prosecution. They will now need to convince a panel of peers that the accused wasn't "home alone." Not a noteworthy strategy from the defense, but they will take the advantage.

Another hurdle is combating the CCTV footage of a woman resembling Laurel in the Yacht Club parking lot, driving a similar vehicle. Now would be an appropriate time for Laurel to reevaluate her predicament. But there was no time; in a blink of an eye, what the actress and the friend group assumed would be a lengthy ordeal was over. The case will be bound over to a grand jury for review, and the double homicide case of Laurel Stanhope is heading to trial.

As the proceedings for the day end, Laurel, who should be grateful for the option to go home, sticks her nose in the air and tries not to touch anything as she rises from her objectionable hard wood seat. Her handlers escort her through a side door, and on her way out, she glances over her shoulder, hoping to find moral support. Instead, she glimpses her silent friends in a single file line exiting the room with no intention of offering sympathy. Laurel uses the ride home to reconsider her friendships. Her concerns over what they must be thinking are genuine. Yet, the actress is more put off by the women showing no interest in spending time with her than the incriminating circumstance in which she finds herself.

The restrictions placed on Laurel while out on bail are self-inflicted. Her stifling homebound humiliation is nothing compared to the trauma the three hots and a cot jail would bring. Yet, appreciative she is not; she assumes everyone arrested for unspeakable crimes should be permitted to return to a life of luxury while waiting for the legal controversy to blow over.

Frustrated, Dana flips through the secrets in her head, which have become too overwhelming to keep. A hired hit is the only logical scenario at the moment. The tapes confirm Laurel isn't the killer, but that doesn't exclude her from being the instigator. Assuming that Laurel orchestrated the murders, she shares equal guilt with whomever she coerced. This justification quiets the widow's nerves until they start wrestling again. She vacillates between confessing to the destruction of the video corroborating Laurel's innocence and assisting in convincing everyone the evil diva is responsible. She contemplates divulging what she's done to relieve her guilty conscience. Still, she knows a confession to the police outlining her involvement will only make her a suspect, not an informant.

The tired widow needs to rest; some sleep would be beneficial, but sweet slumber became elusive long before the accident. The word *accident* surfaced again, a word used with careless frequency these days. Someone needs to coin a better term for *intentional homicide*.

———

Steeped in anger, Margo stomps around her house, praying Laurel will be convicted and sentenced to live the rest of her life behind bars. Death is instant and final; it's almost a pass, much too forgiving and not nearly painful enough. This widow's gratification will come from watching Laurel imitate an aggressive dog locked in a shelter cage marked unadoptable. Margo would've forgiven Laurel for her liaison with Frank; as strange as it sounds, Laurel put some excitement back into her marriage. On the other hand, death distorts the fantasy, pushing Margo to vocalize her disapproval.

Meet the new anti-Laurel spokesperson, Margo Reed, she positions herself at the top of the courthouse steps before each hearing, ensuring the world knows her plight. The press is on her side and excellently conveys her message to the listening public. Loud and without reservation, the distraught Mrs. Reed delivers her emotional plea to the masses. No one is left wondering who she's holding to task, not only the death of her husband but also the deaths of Randal Lucas and Alan Stanhope.

Only an intimate friend would be privy to the firsthand knowledge spoon-fed to the gossip rags. Margo may be loud, but she's careful to disburse her classified information in calculated intervals, like a morphine drip, never dispensing too much in one sitting. The goal is to keep Laurel's increasingly pained face splashed across the front page for as long as possible.

As more juicy details and personal pictures emerge, the more damaging the story evolves for the starlet. On a mission, Margo will make damn sure, regardless of the verdict, Laurel doesn't come out of this ordeal more popular than when it all started. Margo's quest is to dub Laurel the most hated woman in America. The only outcome worse than prison would be poverty and shame. Images of the fallen star slinging hash in a diner outside Barstow dance in Margo's head, making her laugh.

With her indifference parked in neutral, Kathryn concentrates on exuding nothing but compassion, offering counsel to anyone struggling or needing to talk to someone. She isn't angry, and without a doubt about who committed the murders, she isn't conflicted like the others. For instance, today's headline painted Laurel as a serial killer, followed by the "Black Widow" moniker in the tagline. Amused by the label "serial killer," Kathryn never thought to give herself this illustrious title.

The prerequisite to achieving this type of status is a deliberate act causing death to two or more persons in different locations. The time frame in which the killings occur doesn't appear to be a factor. One can only assume the body count for the doctor adds up to four: Kara, Mother, Frank, and Randal. That is incorrect.

Full disclosure will require dissection of a few prior incidences. Each will shed some light on Kathryn's very dark past. First, rewind to college; her schooling served as nothing more than a means to an end. Higher education was mandatory to obtain the degrees necessary to become a doctor. The rest of the university experience repulsed her.

But, to advance and gain praise in the eyes of her father, the reluctant freshman needed more than straight A's and perfect attendance. She needed content for her resume. So, with glowing referrals, some fabricated, she weaseled her way into the Chi Omega sorority. A sought-after organization with a stellar reputation for refining the leadership skills and social graces of the campus's bright and beautiful. Everyone in Kathryn's world believed this a perfect fit for a young lady needing a little social refinement.

Despite a diligent attempt to slide through academia unnoticed, many thought of Kathryn as well-liked. She is often referred to by her "sisters" as "friendly with many acquaintances." Not a glowing review, but this was by design. There was no burning desire to be part of the social scene; activities bored her, and this introvert displayed zero interest in becoming too entwined with any group or person. Instead, she deflected attention away from herself, like someone avoiding a sneeze to the face.

The sorority house was a stately mansion, a lovely home to eighty-plus members. Of course, only some women live on the premises, but all regularly gather on-site for meetings and socials. The house is impeccable, colonial in style, clean, and displaying aged elegance. In a place with rules and regulations, the young ladies gracing the establishment exemplify all that is wonderful in the world.

However, a house member occasionally falls short of the chapter's standards. They surface as the bragger, the overzealous cheerleader, and the drunk crier, to name a few. One unsavory sister stood out; Bianca was her name. This obnoxious girl insisted on inserting herself where she didn't belong. She talked over the others while making life a living hell for the shy, introverted young women who had yet to find their voices.

This unacceptable behavior was annoying, but instead of confiding in one of her housemates or confronting the girl directly,

Kathryn jotted Bianca's name in her rich crimson alligator skin journal tightly wrapped shut with leather ties. The sound of the young woman's name made her pull a face, "Bianca," reminding her of a breath spray designed to mask halitosis.

The gracious manor hosting the young women serves as an equalizer for all kinds of theatrics happening behind the brick façade. Yet, the magnificent structure isn't strong enough to combat rumors involving a particular sister cavorting with classmen betrothed to others. In a house full of women, lies are the only thing to spread faster than an STD, especially when they are one and the same. So, cue the fighting as dozens of possible suspects emerge in the unfortunate disappearance of Bianca.

Over time, a clear pattern develops and remains true to form. Consistency being the signature attribute, the marked individual may not exhibit any malice aforethought or be conscious of any direct interaction with Kathryn per se. In general, a sense of ill will might be the only trigger. However, a simple encounter that goes unnoticed by others could have a much different effect on Kathryn, who is paying closer attention. The sensation once evoked seethes with the same intensity as her fingertips held to a flame.

For instance, a decade before college, Kathryn was smack in the middle of her complicated childhood. Soon after her sister's death, her parents and therapists decided Kathryn needed a break from the institutional darkness where she resided. The chosen remedy was a cheerful summer camp where kids make friends, do crafts and swim in a lake. All believed the fresh air would be beneficial—an adventure providing an escape from the clinical monitoring of day-to-day life.

An incident from this vacation warrants recounting. A few days into the week-long excursion, a couple of campers became victims of a terrible accident. The boys, rock-throwing, cannon-balling knuckleheads, were harmless but somehow posed a threat to Kathryn. One can guess they were merely hyper kids doing what annoying un-parented campers do, but they, too, ended up with their names written neatly in pencil.

As the camp's tale goes, the two boys repeatedly jumped off a dock into the lagoon. Presumably, they grew weak from playing yet continued hurling themselves off the platform. One boy struck his head on his way into the water and never came up for air. Everyone assumed the other boy became lodged under the dock attempting to rescue his buddy. Both children left the grounds unresponsive via ambulance.

All the guides and campers in attendance underwent thorough counseling, each delivering a heartfelt, tear-filled statement. This traumatic ordeal scarred most of the kids for life. Yet, when it came time to interview the quiet redheaded girl wearing her hair in braids, she responded with an emotionless, detached account of her day. As a result, her story went unchecked, and her whereabouts unverified.

Years of training helped disguise her antisocial markers, masking her manipulative antics, leaving Kathryn overlooked.

The discussion with a counselor only reinforced her capacity to control an outcome; she recognized she possessed power. The authorities further confirmed her ability to eliminate issues and erase her participation by believing any situation, whether true or false, real or imagined, remained inconsequential. Not running away or making excuses allowed Kathryn to hide in plain sight. Cunning enough to position herself in the peripheral also had advantages; this discovery opened up a fascinating world for a serial personality.

The startling aspect of every dark event in the wicked child's life is that the suspicion never falls on her. Most situations didn't involve her at all, the accidental nature of her family drama is self-explanatory, and there's no link connecting her to the others. Likewise, each case lacked anything physical to connect to Kathryn and no motive to suspect her, so she was never considered.

Law enforcement agencies from different regions had no reason to compare notes, so randomly selecting Kathryn for interrogation or suggesting exploring her psyche would be unwarranted. As a result, each investigator missed the subtle clues needed to expose the fundamental methods of her madness. When Kathryn is entangled, she becomes a victim, a bystander, or a grieving loved one. Continuous comfort rather than confrontation only encouraged her irrational tendencies.

One would expect the routine of a ruthless killer to be more complex; on the contrary, Kathryn prefers a simple itinerary. It starts with a seemingly benign sheet of paper in her notebook, to which she transcribes a deadly recipe that manifests into a storyline. Acting on her plan ends the turmoil, and she moves on as if nothing ever happened.

The tactless art of stalking prey is considered rude; she doesn't take time to sit in her attic with a collection of photos of her intended target. You won't find weathered newspaper clippings of victims tacked to a storyboard in the basement, nor does she save souvenirs. To acknowledge the person as a life lost before or after whatever tragedy they suffered would be a bother. The only crucial component revolves around the execution of the plan; following the "list" to the letter is mandatory for her crazed maniacal mind to lay dormant until provoked enough to pull out her pen again.

Years go by, and her well-organized memory files keep her compulsions at bay. Yet all it takes is the tiniest spark to ignite a brand-new list. What's strange is that this insane fixation never starts with Kathryn; the actions of others cause her obsession to make right what in her mind is questionable. At least, that's what she tells herself.

Another person's need for constant admiration is generally the underlying issue. She doesn't understand or tolerate people's fascination with being the center of attention. She would prefer people stay in their lane and appreciate the life they built or, in some cases, were dealt.

Laurel's name has been scribbled and scratched off the parchment many times over their decades of friendship. Guaranteed entertainment keeps Laurel returning to Kathryn's world, thus escaping a final draft until now. But unfortunately, the latest interference disrupted an otherwise peaceful existence that required rewriting their relationship.

Frank and Randal fulfilled the craving for accountability and the satisfaction of witnessing the end of someone's life as they locked eyes in horror. But, much to her delight, Laurel's philandering initiated a new nonlethal yet equally satisfying way to destroy a person.

A new day brought devastating news; the district attorney sought the death penalty. "First-degree murder with special circumstances" due to the particularly heinous and cruel manner in which the men met their demise. The malice aforethought is abundant, and the intentional infliction of suffering before certain death went without saying, which promises (if convicted) that the accused could receive the same end-of-life sentence in return. Both men lived their last moments knowing they would die. Cruel is an understatement. So far, the plan is to hold the falling star's feet to the fire by proving that the famous actress is solely responsible.

The prosecution and the defense presented pretrial motions to resolve outstanding matters and establish what evidence and testimony would be admissible at trial. The Stanhope group attempted to argue the phone messages, GPS, and the Yacht Club videotapes were inadmissible but failed.

A valid search warrant accompanied every item seized by detectives, guaranteeing everything collected makes its way in front of the jury. Laurel Stanhope will not walk on a technicality, not today.

THIRTY-THREE

The Trial

The usual cast of characters arrives at the courthouse early. The ladies, Eric, Joel, Dale, and many reporters test how many people the courtroom will accommodate. From the bench, strict orders from the judge again advised the animated attendees that he would not tolerate disruptive conduct. A glance over his black horn-rimmed glasses at the actress eliminated any ambiguity as to whom the warning applied.

With the strike of the gavel, the proceedings commence. A whispered "Damnatio ad bestias" slips off Kathryn's lips.

Dana replies, "Seems appropriate."

The two women exchange a snide smirk. The Latin "condemnation to beasts" is a form of Roman capital punishment practiced in the Dark Ages. Visions of Laurel running from hungry lions may be extreme, but both women would purchase tickets to be spectators during her dismemberment.

The prosecutor came out of the box swinging with a solid

opening statement. Precise in her delivery, the Marsha Clark lookalike does her best to convince the jury that the woman before them is a ruthless, manipulative, cold-blooded murderer. The legal veteran is adamant in her quest to prove beyond a reasonable doubt that no one other than Laurel Stanhope could have committed these crimes.

Demeanor is crucial, especially in a high-profile situation; if this is true, Ms. Stanhope isn't helping her case. The flip-flopping between stoic an unapproachable to an actor playing a helpless victim leads the confused panel to believe that the actress thinks this is nothing more than a character assassination.

To add to everyone's bewilderment, the sheer incompetence emanating from Laurel's defense team clouds everyone's judgment. This soap opera performance isn't fooling anyone; it only accentuates the stench of fear wafting from their table.

At times the team hired to defend the star gives the impression they are unclear of their role here. They try to persuade everyone that Laurel is truthful, generous, and a kind, loving ally. It's almost as if no one informed them that the charges against their client are for murdering two of her closest friends. The panel listens intently but remains skeptical; they have to assume the actress's former confidants would not concur with the described attributes. The overall tone is abrasive, resulting in the dramatic dialogue coming off as theatrical and insincere. Ill-prepared speeches become louder with each telling, yet the story doesn't change, just reworded. The tactic resembles a bully browbeating a subordinate through repetition.

The actual turmoil, however, begins when the witnesses start their testimonies. Almost all questions prompted objections, with "hearsay" shouted at any responding comment not tying in neatly with the speaker's working narrative. As a result, several individuals summoned to give testimony felt slighted, cut off mid-sentence, and unable to contribute what they deemed pertinent content.

A knot is forming in the stomach of Dr. Joel Kane when he hears his name called to take the stand. A ghostly pallor washes over his face as his hopes of remaining anonymous flutter out the window. Joel is here in the psychiatrist's capacity to testify for the accused and draws the doctor-patient card at the first opportunity. A maneuver that exempts him from divulging much of anything. Inquiries swirling around Laurel's sanity lifted a few eyebrows, but Dr. Kane refused to confirm or deny anything about her mental stability. Although he volunteered that violent or homicidal tendencies never surfaced as topics of conversation in their sessions. He further indicated his patient expressed her frustration in other ways, and none were lethal.

Ms. Stanhope's sanity and fragility, or lack thereof, won't be an avenue of escape. Her psychological acuity is rendered intact before and during the trial. On the other hand, her loyalty and trustworthiness take a hit along with the discredited doctor. The fundamental nature of their sexual relationship is on full display and documented for the world to see. This juicy morsel of gossip created a dull roar that abruptly halted with the crack of the judge's gavel hitting the sounding block.

A silenced gallery nor doctor-patient privilege will save the shamed man now. But Joel has a separate investigation to worry about, as the code of ethics he so gallantly vowed to uphold yet later amended is coming back to bite him.

Dr. Joel Kane resorted to being open and honest about his different relationships with the accused. When asked, he responded, "Yes, I was Ms. Stanhope's Psychiatrist as well as her friend. We did enter into an intimate relationship, but that liaison ended mutually months ago." The timing of the affair is off, but they ceased interrogating him on the issue. They anticipated some concealment when discussing the intimate connection between the doctor and his love interest, so they let the timing go. In the end, they extracted what they were after. Joel admitted under oath that he, a physician, entered into a romantic partnership with Laurel Stanhope, who was under his care.

Those golden words, "unethical behavior," resonating through the room is what the prosecutors waited for all day—leaving the panel with no option but to embrace the deceit.

The defense neglected to pry anything of value from the doctor; their passive fact-finding drew vague answers. The doctor reiterated his whereabouts on that Monday night and not much else. His colleague previously corroborated his story, validating their dinner engagement, and confirmed they talked until after midnight. The police verified the alibi, thus clearing the doctor of any wrongdoing, at least concerning where he was during the murder. Judge Hurst finally interrupted the redundant rambling, excusing Joel from the stand.

The others who took the stand unwittingly participated in a seed-planting expedition. One side poses a question, while the other can't resist the urge to object, leaving the unanswered inquiry hanging until withdrawn.

The answer isn't what they're after; to suggest an alternative is their quest, leaving some thought-provoking material to contemplate—the sowing of seeds. Tiny thought particles are strategically implanted in hopes of those thoughts germinating into suspicion, thus sprouting doubt. But to the contrary, the defense's probing produced the reverse effect, and speculation grew more toward guilt.

Laurel's advisers call Kathryn to take the stand, desperate to divert their previous stab at a witness. They asked when the involvement between her husband and the defendant became apparent to her. Unfazed by the jagged inquiry, she states, "Several months ago, Laurel gave me a prescription bottle with Dr. Kane's name printed on the label; that was sufficient confirmation."

The attorney hinted at an illicit drug distribution scheme, later implying Kathryn may be disgruntled.

Kathryn deflects the feeble yet personal attack with confidence and grace. Her calm disposition is impenetrable. These men can talk at her all they want; she's not about to be shaken by anyone in an ill-fitting suit. Verbatim, Kathryn recants her testimony, reiterating why Ms. Stanhope's prescribed medication is in her possession.

Laurel's counsel soon realizes their interrogation has flipped on its side. Kathryn possesses the uncanny ability to make people trip over their words as they speak, making their efforts appear shameless and desperate while trying to portray her as a woman scorned.

Dr. Kathryn Kane's straightforward factual retorts garnered the jury's trust rather than the bitter animosity the lawyer hoped to provoke. The prosecutor was beaming as she observed the hearts of the decision-makers sway in her favor.

The prosecution takes their turn and apologizes for the nonsense endured before asking if she consented to a lie detector examination. Kathryn announced she had volunteered. Exhibit A contains the polygraph results, which she hands to her. She's asked to read the report out loud. The first inquiry revolved around the safekeeping of pharmaceuticals, and the second was the return of the medication upon Laurel's request. Both responses were affirmative. The test didn't detect deception, and neither did the jury.

Unsure of where this line of questioning is headed, the Stanhope legal minds flippantly ask for directions. It's apparent in their haste that they failed to review the document presented today. The frantic turning of the pages indicates they are unaware they signed off on the current demonstration as admissible, so the hits kept coming. Again, of course, they objected when the inquisition was reread, but this time the answers were supplied by Laurel. Dr. Kathryn Kane read that Laurel replied "yes" to "Kathryn's custodianship of the prescription" and "no" to "Were the pills returned upon request?"

Laurel responded positively to the first question, but the recorder registered deception on the second answer. Objections throughout the testimony make any final facts hard to follow.

The Stanhope council did succeed in having the lie detector evidence thrown out. But the judge didn't stop there; he scolded the prosecuting attorney, warning that such reporting isn't reliable or relevant. Therefore, all information associated with the polygraph is stricken from the record, followed by jury instructions to ignore that specific portion of the testimony. One can tell the jurors to forget the items discussed, but they won't. Not entirely; they will remember Laurel lied.

The entertainment resumed with a crowd-pleasing slideshow displaying all the deleted messages from Laurel's phone. This presentation only proves the text originated from her device, not that she did the typing. The GPS coordinates came next. They determined the messages were transmitted using her cell from the Stanhope home. This discovery drew an audible gasp from the gallery. The gavel strikes the sounding block, but not before the defense shouts, "Someone else could've sent the messages."

The prosecutor jumped in immediately, using Laurel's words against her by interjecting, "But Ms. Stanhope swears under oath she stayed at home, alone all night."

Let the condemnation begin. The unhappy officiant regains control by threatening both attorneys with contempt.

The introduction of the home security tapes sparked an intense debate. Laurel can't provide a legitimate explanation for the time missing from her network. The defense wants to persuade the court that this is due to a coincidental mechanical error. The opposition fires back that the time frame is a bit too convenient. Laurel claims she doesn't know how her system operates. She has no idea why the recording stopped after the last backup. So no, she cannot explain why the crucial time frame is missing.

Convinced her alibi is solid, she stands firm, again not helping. Laurel's downfall is her failure to connect the link between being home alone with full access to her electronics as a detrimental predicament.

The next item for the court's viewing pleasure is the CCTV footage from the Yacht Club. The video shows a Range Rover pulling into the parking lot and selecting a dark space along the back row. Then, a woman, presumed to be Laurel, exits the vehicle.

The person enters the combination to the gate and proceeds down the gangway toward *The Leading Lady*.

Unfortunately, the camera's line of sight doesn't extend to the end of the dock, so one can only speculate that the Stanhope yacht is the destination; two men who resemble the deceased approach the entrance about an hour apart. The gate is ajar for the first man, but the second enters the passcode and follows the same path. A couple of hours pass, and the woman reappears, walks back to her car and drives away. The men do not make another appearance.

The film plays twice, but the prosecution wants to drive the visual aspect home and asks the jury to indulge her again as the tape starts over. This time in slow motion, the guise of darkness impeding proper identification of the vehicle's occupant is the reasoning for the third run. Along with this last viewing comes a rude awakening. A Range Rover, identical to Laurel's, pulls into the lot in the final showing. But there is one glaring exception; the car isn't black, the vehicle shown on the screen is midnight blue. The same color, make, and model as Kathryn's Range Rover, also purchased from Randal's dealership.

As the car enters the space, the front end passes under a ray of lamplight. The flash of cobalt is quick and easily missed or mistaken for a reflection of light. A flare so minute and subtle, no one but Dana and Kathryn pick up on the clue, not even Laurel.

This sequence of events has been played for the defendant at least twenty times; her remark that "it isn't her" meets an immediate objection. Uninterested in another replay, she studies her cuticles. Kathryn sits one row back, incensed over this minor infraction. She's displeased for underestimating the distance and not considering the overhead lighting. This monumental mistake could cause irreparable damage to a well-laid plan. This faux pas will haunt her, initiating an uncontrollable spiral that won't end well for someone.

Motionless, Dana scans the room with just her eyes. Every ounce of strength locks her head frozen in place. She can't risk making eye contact with Kathryn. A simple glance will confirm that she, too, witnessed the incriminating bolt of blue. Dana is terrified, fearing her friend will extract her innermost secrets with just a look. A seemingly innocent glance from the doctor will have you spilling your guts, regardless of the danger to yourself or others.

Among the remaining witnesses is Madeline, who takes the stand and confirms she bought the dive gear. She is thanked and excused before revealing the purchase's intended purpose. The spa personnel are questioned next. All told similar accounts of spending part of the day at the Stanhope home. Each took their turn and indicated Ms. Stanhope behaved as usual, nothing out of the ordinary. But the lingering conclusion came when the prosecutors posed a statement disguised as a question. Saying to each of them, including Madeline, "Laurel is a trained performer. Playing herself would come naturally, would it not?" A slow retraction follows an objection barked by opposing counsel each time the question is asked. But the suggestive seed is firmly planted. Finally, all testified they concluded their business at different times, but all departed by 5:00 p.m., leaving Laurel alone as she indicated.

The judge again warns against leading the witness before allowing counsel to continue. The parade marched on, which included the Yacht Club staff. They proved to be an outspoken lot. Most of them despised Laurel and painted her as the devil herself. However, a select few remained loyal, fearing the actress might one day return. The head hostess, Allison, stated, "Ms. Stanhope expects excellence, as do all members. Superior service is what they pay for, and, therefore, deserve." Laurel gives the hostess her signature nod, bringing the now staff favorite to tears.

More often than not, the diva is her own worst enemy; her self-destruction stems from her sincere unapologetic view of herself. She is privileged and deserves the riches of the world. She is entitled; if you aren't, that's on you. An attempt to disguise or make excuses for her blatant holiness is not coming.

Apologies are not Laurel's forte; she will not be held responsible for her mistakes or another's misfortune. To fabricate or deny her actions is a predictable scenario; the damning implications for others are commonplace. You are now nothing more than entertainment if you are the chosen scapegoat caught in her crosshairs. Her behavior proves your feelings or ruin are collateral damage and none of her concern.

Warmth and love reside somewhere in the deep recesses of Laurel's steel heart. But few, if any, have witnessed any such authentic feelings. Instead, Laurel's interactions with others revolve around some form of servitude or gratuity-motivated endearment. Often conceding a person's position in life voids their right to possess emotions or experience pain. Most, if not all, people surrounding Laurel, besides the book club, are not her friends; they're employees, which explains a lot.

Generally, legal counsel frowns upon their clients speaking on their behalf. This case is no exception. Against the advice of counsel, their client insists on addressing the court. When questioned, the actress again vehemently denies stepping outside her home, which she still neglects to recognize is detrimental to her case.

Self-incrimination isn't on her radar; she has something to say, and damn it, these people will listen to her. So, it matters not that she will likely shatter her credibility beyond what her already suffering image can withstand.

As one could predict, her time on the stand doesn't go as planned; the few excerpts from her well-rehearsed monologue further cloud this mystery. She couldn't explain why or how her phone moved all over town without her when asked. The device finding its way to her front lawn also defies logic, and for the finale, the videotapes were dismissed as fake news. Faithful to her narcissistic roots, winning over the people who will soon decide her fate doesn't appear to be her objective. It's her voice she wants to hear. But she's immediately confronted with disappointment when not allowed to speak freely.

Frustrated by the invisible gag, Laurel bites her tongue to stop talking when it's not her turn. Forced to play by the rules, she retraces her steps of the night in question. There is one constant; she performs every line word for word. The mastery used to avoid being the villain is noteworthy but won't earn her an Emmy or compassion today.

As the scene unfolds, the gallery, although gripped by the suspense, hoped the actress would say something to sway them, but her redundant performance left some still reluctant to choose a side. Many jurors find themselves caught between believing a beloved screen icon and admitting the person perched before them is an aloof, arrogant stranger. The evidence and testimonies are stacking against the famous diva, making it hard to remain unbiased.

Steadfast in her stance, Margo won't rest until Laurel goes to jail. Holding her opinion becomes arduous; unwilling to keep quiet, she breaks her silence and whispers her frustration to Dana. "Laurel's disposition confirms she believes she's above the law. Even the looming reality of an address change to death row is not top of mind. Look at her, sitting there fidgeting as though made to wait too long for a mani-pedi. One would think waking up behind bars might spark some reaction from the cold fish. Yet nothing."

Sights and sounds are losing shape; the light in the windowless room is painfully harsh, giving Dana a migraine. The thought of circumstantial details brushed aside or falling short of a conviction makes her nauseous. Margo won't shut up and relentlessly rages on, "If this were one of Laurel's movies, she would be in shackles on her way to a hauntingly dark gray asylum covered in dead ivy, but it's not a made-for-TV special."

Interrupting Margo's rant, Dana voices her apprehension to the group just as the bailiff hushes the crowd, announcing closing statements are underway. All of this is happening much sooner than expected. Unfortunately, Dana's concerns will have to go unaddressed for now.

The prosecutor and the defense reiterated their case, each insisting the opposite is true. The life and freedom of Laurel Stanhope hang in the balance, and all she can do is wait. Foolish in her belief that they can't condemn an innocent woman, she stubbornly holds her ground. The posture-perfect starlet continues to project a pretentious air rather than remorse while waiting for her apology.

THIRTY-FOUR

The Verdict

After less than three hours of deliberation, the solemn-faced decision-makers resumed their positions in the jury box. When asked, the foreman states that their vote is unanimous.

"What say you," says the judge.

The man glances down at the paper in his hand, seeking confirmation before announcing, "We, the jury find the defendant Laurel Stanhope guilty on two counts of first-degree murder for the death of Randal Lucas and Frank Reed."

Loud chatter travels across the audience like a wave as chaos erupts; camera flashes and shouts only add to the swirling mayhem. Finally, the gavel bangs the sounding block to regain order. Undeterred, Laurel turns and instructs her lawyers to initiate an immediate appeal.

Early in the investigation, Laurel dismissed a simple solution to end this damning charade, the plea deal. Common knowledge dictates that accepting such an arrangement must transpire before the final verdict. Unfortunately, the actress never gave the alternative much consideration, and all attempts to negotiate died with her knee-jerk reaction to scoff at their suggestion.

The plea deal offered by the prosecution proposed life in prison, eliminating the death penalty from the menu of options and the meager likelihood of freedom someday. However, acceptance did come with strings attached, requiring a full confession, but the immediate release clause was not up for discussion. Therefore, not deemed a bargain by the accused.

It's safe to say that the finality of the latest announcement is not what was expected. So much so that she believes she is entitled to change her mind and maintains she is within her right to revisit the previous offer. She is sadly mistaken. A minor outburst ensues when the disgruntled drama queen receives confirmation that the allotted time to accept any prior arrangement has expired.

Laurel clings to the hope that this is some industry stunt where Ashton Kutcher springs from behind the bench, points, and laughs, telling her she's been "Punked."

Team Stanhope pours gasoline on the already out-of-control fire when conveying to their outraged client that a do-over will not happen today. Any appeals will take time, and she will spend that time behind bars—an officer standing behind the convicted woman gestures for her hands, then slips handcuffs around her wrists. Somewhat out of character, the actress goes silent after her request to speak to her attorneys in private is denied. Unanswered demands are another inconvenience the convicted will soon become accustomed to in her new environment.

The never-ending barrage of articles in circulation turned Laurel's fan base into an angry mob. Publications portrayed the once-beloved star as a sloppy amateur criminal one day, only to credit her with the capacity to concoct and execute an elaborate scheme the next. Public opinion may fluctuate, but the villain angle sells more papers.

Yet anyone who spends enough time in front of the television should realize the errors in the prevailing narrative. These aren't rookie mistakes. Clues so convenient and obvious should be the first indication that Laurel isn't the mastermind behind this crime. Furthermore, the uptick in ratings only increases the media's motivation to condemn her. The theatrics and embarrassment are far more fascinating than exhibiting compassion for the wrongly accused. Out for blood, the entertainment outlets stoke a contagious buzz through the local community and abroad. The Stanhope name may never recover from the scars inflicted.

From the start, Laurel positioned herself as an easy and convenient target—one who put forth little effort to convince investigators or anyone of her innocence. Furthermore, the actress's reluctance to expand on her alibi assisted the authorities in establishing her guilt. But, of course, this is all by design; after all, the behavior of others is Kathryn's specialty, and her lifelong friend is a predictable read.

The detectives jumped at the chance to condemn Laurel while simultaneously forging a trusting partnership with Kathryn; they valued her insight and found her personal and professional opinion useful. The always helpful doctor fulfilled her civic duty by supplying the police with the exact buttons to push to produce the maximum dramatic effect from their suspect. Some clues provided a precise road map; others were fine breadcrumbs prompting detectives to make conclusions independently.

Patience is what Kathryn prescribes to herself. Then, assuming the role of the concerned onlooker, she sits back and admires her handiwork while her dear friend implodes.

Regardless of any presumed guilt, a cursory glance at anyone else for the sake of due diligence seemed prudent. Yet, investigating other leads or additional suspects didn't seem worth pursuing. Instead, the investigators ignored their reservations about Laurel's brilliance and decided to exploit her ignorant arrogance; it was a more viable option. This maneuver resulted in a drastic personality shift in the accused. Without a script to follow, her abrasive combativeness only reinforces her guilt.

Doubt, although thoroughly dissected, never produced enough concrete evidence to sway the population to join the handful of loyal fans waving banners demanding release. As a result, all efforts to free the shamed starlet failed, and the chosen panel of jurors convicted Laurel Stanhope of murdering Randal Lucas and Frank Reed.

The Stanhope legal minds lose hope in the fight to free their client; at best, they pray the sentencing statement excludes the word "Death." A life behind bars would be a blessing. Her glamorous lifestyle may be over, but at least her heart is still beating.

Their client indignantly sits wearing a smug expression, still thinking she deserves an explanation for being treated like a criminal. Of course, she is correct, but Kathryn is the only one privy to the real story. So, the words "we are sorry for the inconvenience" won't be uttered today—or ever, for that matter.

The jury's decision sends the courtroom into an uproar. Reporters are scrambling as if the room were on fire, and people are climbing over the pews to escape with the news. The shouting spectators imitate crazed soccer fans after winning the world cup, and they aren't shy when slinging snide insults regarding orange as Laurel is led away to begin the long wait of the appeal process. Kathryn's grip tightens around Margo's arm, stifling her contribution of obscenities.

The door to the gallows below swings open, a surreal gateway to another world. Amid the stunned crowd, Dana turns to Margo, saying, "Laurel got her greatest wish."

Margo laughs, adding, "The queen does adore a captive audience, but even Her Highness wouldn't wish for this."

"No," explains Dana.

"Laurel insists on being the main attraction; now, she will receive more admiration than she can handle."

Under her breath, Kathryn releases a few simple words, "How unfortunate."

If the doctor intended her comment to go unnoticed, it did not. Dana, as well as Margo, caught the rather offhanded remark. They both find this an odd response after hearing their friend is now a ward of the state. Margo blew off the jab as inconsiderate yet deserving, but not Dana. She can't ignore the unavoidable chill in the air or that tiny bolt of blue. A new aura shines on Kathryn, a terrifying bright light.

The otherwise generous and vivacious actress couldn't conceal the shallow malicious person dwelling inside during the proceedings. An unfamiliar person emerged, a woman devoid of compassion, a cold and impartial being Dale didn't recognize. In court, unable to escape the accusation, Laurel sat exposed, vulnerable, and at the mercy of all.

Dale's only interaction with his new love revolved around a gracious movie star with caring friends and adoring supporters. He became angry with himself for not once detecting any signs of trouble. His description painted the star as fun and exciting but never dangerous. No red flags or sense of fear ever reared its ugly head. So blinded by Laurel's charm, he didn't detect any threat to his safety or cause for alarm. Perhaps he didn't want to.

Still processing his romantic liaison with a murderer, Dale scrutinizes every endeavor with the woman he loves. She often entertained him on the boat, and several late nights turned into sleepovers at her home. He now views each as a missed opportunity. If he had disappeared, he contemplates the time frame before his family or friends realized he went missing; worse, they wouldn't know where to search for him. Dated and dumped to drown are among the crazed nightmares running rampant, so much so that they drive Dale straight into therapy.

Contacting Joel crossed Dale's mind; after all, both entertained the actress, and both men survived her. But, after some soul-searching, he decided a third party would be best; to confess intimate encounters to Joel wouldn't be therapeutic for either of them. Finally, after an exhaustive phone campaign, Dale found a doctor willing to take on a new patient requiring multiple sessions per week.

At the advice of his new therapist, Dale removed his profile and canceled his subscription to all dating sites. His mental health adviser suggested he would benefit from being single for a while.

Margo secretly hopes the condemned is paraded into the public square and hung. But sadly, any retribution issued won't bring her husband back, so in exchange, her only relief is witnessing the woman who ruined her life suffer.

A quiet dinner offered the Kanes an ideal opportunity to discuss the topic they had been avoiding. Kathryn expressed that the humiliation stung more than the heartbreak of their broken marriage. The words exchanged remain controlled yet smolder with white-hot intensity. Joel contributed as little as possible to the dialogue, as he is uncomfortable discussing his side piece with his soon-to-be ex-wife. But his shame isn't the reason for his disengagement in their talk.

He is preoccupied with recounting the missed occasions when his mistress could have hurled his drugged body into the bay. The thought riddles him with anxiety, and the nagging question of why he was spared is equally unsettling. However, his feigned remorse appeases his ex as he listens silently and lets her say what she needs to say.

When Kathryn finishes, they agree that further discussions regarding previous private encounters won't serve any purpose. They also agree that a show of solidarity helps them save face, so they attend the proceedings together as a united front. The arrangement may be essential for their careers, but Joel would like to think they still need each other, just not as husband and wife. They will always consider each other family; however, the trust aspect will take time to rebuild. But for now, they will protect each other at all costs.

The grieving process affects everyone differently. For Dana, the sorrow loomed like the grim reaper. The ramifications of her actions absorb her, and the obsession hinders her ability to mourn Randal. Unlike Margo, who is quite vocal in expressing anger, Dana remains numb to everything around her. Now by herself in her home, emotions depleted, she allows herself to break down and cry, and cry she does.

It's not long before Dana's puffy eyes dry up. She needs clarity and finds a pad of paper, and starts writing. Scribbling what she did and didn't do helps decipher fact from fiction. Somewhere in the details hides an answer to this mystery. Somehow, the frightening yet logical outcome is that Kathryn is behind all of this.

But the million-dollar question is, why would she want to kill Randal and Frank? And you throw Dr. Bob into the mix, and it makes no sense.

The accusation on its own is outrageous. And if she is responsible, why isn't she considered a suspect?

She couldn't predict the detectives would target Laurel and recruit her to help in the investigation. The entire spectrum of events is ridiculous, making the impulse to confront Kathryn plausible. But how does one broach this touchy subject matter, even with a friend?

Questioning or suggesting someone may be behind committing a heinous crime can put one in a precarious predicament. Their sisterhood won't survive this conversation.

Once again, she contemplates contacting the authorities. Yet, any attempt to explain what is sure to be perceived as fictional quickly becomes a non-option. They would all be questioned again, and Kathryn would undoubtedly assume Dana made the accusations. She realizes discussing her suspicions with either party is dangerous, and with no intention of becoming the next victim or suspect, she must stop obsessing. The original plan is playing out before her, and she isn't involved. So, looking at the overall picture, Dana should say "thank you" and keep her mouth shut.

The sentencing hearing took place on Monday of the following week. The news outlets being the driving force behind the outrage adds significant pressure on the judicial system to expedite the closure of this case.

As everywhere you turn, the unavoidable article or trending feed showcases the muted actress's stressed face staring back at you. Most of the "Black Widow" comments don't bother her; however, the remarks describing her apparel are the ones she finds disturbing. Those paying close attention will note Laurel obsesses over her image far more than her pending doom. The reality of her most recent photo being a mugshot should begin to sink in soon.

After lengthy legal formalities and a brief recess, an announcement to reconvene prompts everyone to return to their designated seats. The attorneys resume their positions while Laurel continues to fidget awkwardly. The psychological and physical havoc of incarceration is evident as the once flawless actress sits in the front of the room, looking ten years older. But that's unfair, as anyone without makeup or hair care products would look weathered after a week. The dreaded oversized jumpsuit designed to flatter no one only adds to the stark contrast to the former movie icon everyone remembers.

News reporters, equipped with a cameraperson, take up most of the courtroom. Only seven people occupy the row reserved for Laurel's friends and family. The "friend group" declared they would like to do away with that title; no one cares to be associated with the Stanhope name.

All concerned parties appeared in court to protect and encourage Margo and Dana, not as moral support for the accused. But to be honest, morbid curiosity and a hint of entertainment value aided in the legitimate reason anyone attended this trial. Together, the tight-knit friends lived through this cataclysmic event since its inception, and they are not about to bow out before the fireworks showcasing the grand finale are set ablaze. Dale, not initially part of the friend group, is also present; he still loves Laurel or the fantasy of her. Silently he sits, hoping someone will rise, shouting it wasn't her, and prove his lady friend has been wrongly accused.

New deep, cracked lines take up residence alongside the grimace on Laurel's face. The external deterioration and growing discomfort are why Kathryn is in attendance. A fictitious pen leaves a red circle marking her working list as "unacceptable," she can't let go of the lighting issue with the car.

So, to curb the inclination to manifest a new list, she must extract a certain level of gratification from witnessing Laurel's agony as she acknowledges lockup is now her life.

The demons possessing Kathryn are unnervingly calm. She wickedly waits in anticipation for Laurel to recognize that her demise is not for her conviction. The ultimate prize is when their jailed friend realizes her posh existence ended as payback for interfering in the Kane's marriage. The rest was merely cleanup, nothing more than a means to an end, and more than worth the effort. The fact that Kathryn once toyed with the Stanhope's wedded bliss has no bearing here, as nothing happened between the doctor and Alan other than some questionable flirting. However, she wonders whether her friend will ever connect her to Alan's death or if she still presumes her husband's drowning was an accident.

Alan's fixation with Kathryn was apparent only to Laurel. But the actress knew the trusted friendship with her girlfriend would keep her husband's fantasy in his pants. She also may not have cared as her infidelity is not a guarded secret, nor does she pretend to be anyone other than her true self. Alan, on the other hand, portrayed himself as a devoted husband. He appeared content in his role as Mr. Laurel Stanhope, but his true happiness came from using his wife's fame to attract other women.

To be fair, Alan didn't discriminate; he harassed all women. No woman was off-limits: Club members, coffee shop servers, and even associates' wives were all fair game, particularly redheads. Nevertheless, he practiced restraint with the women in their inner circle; Kathryn was the only exception.

For years, Alan pursued Kathryn; of course, she deflected his advances until the chase abruptly stopped. Just like the old mechanical pony ride at the grocery store, when your quarter ran out, the ride came to a halt mid-stride, as did Alan's unrelenting pursuit. His attention shifted to a staff member at the Club, a much younger, prettier version of Kathryn. The fiery red hair with the thin line of freckles stippled across her nose made his selection blatantly intentional.

Frustrated by repeated denial, Alan decided to play out his redheaded fantasy with a replacement. But his choice of pets proved fatal; a list was born, and he was dead.

The necessary ingredients to bring Kathryn's little caper to fruition took a little imagination but minimal effort. A new bottle of expensive scotch and a bug in Laurel's ear to share her pills with her overzealous husband tied a fancy bow on her suggestion. Sleepovers on the yacht meant drunken sex to Alan, a practice of which Laurel grew tired. She often searched for creative ways to keep him off her, so the doctor supplied a practical solution to help them both.

Intoxication tends to make a person, in this instance Alan, more malleable. And always true to form, Laurel will wash her daily dose down and be out early to avoid the inevitable love and affection her husband expects. This part of the exercise is where the idea of impersonating Laurel first takes shape. In full costume, Kathryn passes for Laurel with ease. The disguise, however, went untested, as no one witnessed her make her way down the gangway to lie in wait.

Some time ago, in a stupor, Laurel shared one of Alan's disgusting habits; he gets up in the middle of the night to relieve himself over the side of the boat. He was going overboard if he came out to partake in this ritual that night. One little-known fact about Alan is that he never learned how to swim. A juicy tidbit Laurel made the mistake of using against him in a public setting, a point remembered.

If Alan had slept through the night and thwarted her plan, Kathryn would have waited for another opportunity. There was no need to rush; with the similar way Laurel and Alan conduct their revolting lives, little time would pass before the next opportune moment presented itself.

The end is near. And with counsel in their prospective places, each side presents their last argument. Each step through the gate with their best foot forward. The prosecution provided factual evidence, and the defense interpreted their version of the facts to create reasonable doubt. Last on the agenda and without question the most damaging is the impact statements made by family members of the victims. The crying pleas from devastated relatives can be a game-changer as they recount the effects of the senseless killings inflicted on their families.

Margo was the first person to approach the stand, and by storm, she delivered her well-rehearsed presentation with humble brilliance. She relayed the painful, haunting ramifications that followed the tragic killings. "My husband and son's father" are the penetrating words peppered throughout her speech tugging at the heartstrings of many. The distressing repetition describing the daily destruction raining upon her family as they struggle to survive hits home to those watching. The widow confidently addressed the panel, but her steel intent focused on Laurel. She is tired but never blinked, staring a hole that would sear a burning ring on the actress's chest if this were one of her movies.

Held together by a thread, Margo takes her time to ensure everyone witnesses the agony in each word spoken. Then, through a weak smile and welling eyes, she expressed her gratitude for the chance to be heard. But the bonding moment lay in her final words, "I am putting my faith in you and God to do the right thing and provide justice for my husband and family."

Some jurors wiped away tears rolling down their cheeks, and some nodded in agreement.

Dana is next to take the stand; her plight mirrors the commentary given by Margo minus the venom. Dana's strategy invokes a more profound emotion; she goes straight for the heart, and the weeping heard from the gallery is merely a bonus. The panel must experience her pain, slip into her shoes, and live this horror with her. In a gentle voice, Dana relays the brutal torment of her every waking moment. The most haunting aspect is the image of her husband drowning, unable to save himself as he inhaled water instead of air. He spent his last moments alive, suffering, knowing he was about to perish. Pausing for effect before continuing, she described her loneliness as unbearable and the financial aspect of her present life as "absolute ruin."

The stress of telling her children they may be unable to continue attending their colleges is tearing her heart out. She expresses how coping without a husband and father is a horrible nightmare from which she cannot wake. Dana concludes, hoping the lasting picture is of her alone, afraid, in their family home, a house the jury believes she can no longer afford.

The declarations achieved the desired effect by leaving a fresh mark. The same material regurgitated by loved ones cuts deep, gripping the courtroom. These heart-wrenching speeches drive certainty into any person who remains undecided, and the sentence will now escort reality straight into Laurel's soul.

The arduous task of weighing all the information and digesting the testimonies to decide on an adequate punishment can be emotionally overwhelming. After all, each juror is held accountable for their individual decision. Understanding the complexity of the guidelines and requirements governing their next move is extremely important, so his honor clarifies one more time.

The instructions read as follows: A person sentenced to life would not be eligible for parole until serving at least twenty-five full calendar years. The remaining two choices are self-explanatory; life in prison without the possibility of parole confines the convicted to jail for the remainder of their natural life. Option number three is the death penalty. With this determination, lethal injection would end Laurel Stanhope's life.

Clarity by way of reiteration didn't make the looming task more comfortable. No matter how you look at it, to hold in your hands the power to dictate someone's life, guilty or not, is a heavy burden.

The jurors leave the courtroom after being excused to deliberate. Everyone else decides that eating will help whittle the time, as no one can predict how long the deliberation will last. Joel asks the prosecutor to text him if and when everyone reconvenes; he also offers to pick up a sandwich for her. The woman agrees to keep them apprised but declines the to-go box. The small eatery adjacent to the courthouse serves its purpose; however, a snack doesn't ease the tension as they sit, picking at their food in awkward silence.

A reporter stealthily follows them, but Dale stops the man at the door and warns him not to speak to Margo or Dana. A true gentleman, Dale's protective stance made a welcoming impression. The reluctant journalist ordered his food and went out on the patio. Everyone's exhausted, having reached their limit in dealing with the constant demands from the media for the past month. They want their anonymity back and the world to return to normal again.

Out of nowhere, Margo snickers, "Laurel's about to enjoy the thrill of being introduced to a whole new fan base."

"Stop it," snaps Dana. "This isn't funny; our husbands are dead, and Laurel will live out her days in a penitentiary, or worse, she could be facing death."

Confused, Margo barks, "She killed Randal and Frank; she deserves whatever she gets, and better yet, I want to watch her rot. The thought of seeing the light of day from a cage or never attending another premier will drive her insane."

Dana rushes out of the café with her purse tightly clutched against her chest. The mounting pressure is getting the best of the new widow; some space to verbalize her torment aloud would be beneficial, but she doesn't dare. A voice, not hers, rings in her ears; Joel is right behind her. He tries to console her, pleading with her to talk to him. His lips are moving, but the only audible sound resembles a monotone wah wah wah. She is grateful for his concern but wants to be alone.

A text alert startles them both; the sound buzzes inside Joel's pocket. He knows who's calling without looking, saying to Dana, "They're coming back." He asks her if she is strong enough to go back inside before confirming the call. Joel understands her fragile state and voices he is willing to stay with her until she is ready.

Dana thanks him for his kindness, then takes hold of his arm and confidently says, "I can do this."

Joel waves to the others in the café, indicating its time. Poor Dale is in shock like everyone else; the only difference is that he doesn't want to lose Laurel; he isn't ready to end what was supposed to be a dreamy retirement. At the very least, he expected a week, hoping for a month, perhaps two, before having the rug ripped from under his feet.

Anxious, everyone files back into the packed room; the man from the diner aligns himself right behind Dana and Margo. Dale exchanges a menacing glare with the columnist as they take their seats. His message, although received, is null and void the minute the sentence is read, then all politeness will be forfeited.

The chatter in the air is weighted, almost suffocating, but the whispers cease when his honor enters the room. Everyone stands until directed to be seated. Then, without hesitation, the jury is asked if their decision was unanimous. The answer takes the room by surprise. The foreperson answers, "No."

Judge Hurst asks if the panel of twelve is undecided on the sentence itself or if the degree of punishment is where they disagreed. Therein lies the quandary; the star's execution became an impassable obstacle. Uncertainty revolved around whether the death penalty is appropriate in this case. After being instructed to go back and deliberate again, the jurors file out of the box. But this time, they must choose between twenty-five years to life or life in lockup without the possibility of parole. All rise again, and most of the gallery vacates the courtroom along with the jurors.

The prosecutor warns the weary group this might take hours or days. She also indicates she would be waiting, anticipating the end is close. Kathryn uses the break to reapply her lipstick in the ladies' room. Dana tags along to wash her hands; some cold water on her wrists will calm the anxiety attack threatening to surface. Everyone else stays seated. Only an hour or so passes before all are alerted to return.

Escorted by guards, Laurel sits beside her lawyers, who stand in her presence. With everyone again in their place, the judge wastes no time, asking if they reached a unanimous conclusion. The foreperson answers affirmatively, handing the bailiff a piece of paper. He passes the note to the magistrate, who reads and returns what amounts to Laurel's lifeline to the bailiff. The bloodthirsty anticipation is palpable as the foreperson reads the results aloud. All attendees stand in a room so quiet a pin drop would be earth-shattering. Laurel's pitiful sad eyes bore into the nervous messenger. A little late to apply emotional tactics, her renewed involvement comes off as desperate and tends to reinforce all perceived notions surrounding her authenticity.

Time stops as the words leave the foreperson's mouth and flow into Laurel's ear with the searing burn of acid. The remorseless Laurel Stanhope receives "life in prison." The diva faints, collapsing right where she stood. Dana slumps down in her seat, and Margo screams. Kathryn, Joel, Olivia, Eric, and Dale don't react; the disbelief leaves them frozen. An officer lays the actress on the floor and calls for a medic. A moment later, she is conscious and regains her composure after the guard lightly slaps her face before helping the newly sentenced convict to her chair.

The press is going wild. A suppressed giggle bubbles up in Kathryn; she is almost embarrassed by the cattiness of her thoughts; all this drama goes to waste if the newspapers aren't made available to inmates. After all, tomorrow's headline is something Laurel shouldn't miss.

The absence of all niceties makes Kathryn giggle harder; Madeline, fluffy slippers, mimosas, and freedom are all gone. One would venture to guess losing her independence would rank higher on the list of must-haves, but we are talking about Laurel. Yet it matters not, as her new accommodations will be without the most basic comforts, making the lap of luxury a thing of her past. The simplicity of this little caper brings the doctor immense joy.

To gloat, however, is of no particular interest to Kathryn; from now on, she will be content with Laurel having lots of time to contemplate what she once took for granted. So, other than for pure amusement, she won't give Laurel much thought from here on out.

Trying his best to be positive, Dale says, "One good thing she can take away from today's outcome is she won't die, at least not by conviction. However, the ability to survive lockup is a story that needs serious consideration. And she won't be eligible for parole for twenty-five years; that's a long time to ward off the other inmates."

Dana does the math. "She'll be seventy years old."

"Remember, eligible doesn't guarantee she will be released," adds Dale.

Arrangements are already in place for Eric to keep track of the Stanhope investments, so she will retain enough wealth to live out the rest of her life without worrying if she is one day deemed fit to reenter society.

Having a change of heart over her preferred outcome, Margo begins to scream louder. She falls into Joel's arms, wailing that Laurel deserves to die between sobs. Kathryn emanates zero emotion while waiting for her condemned friend to sense her glee.

Laurel turns to scan the horror-filled faces of her friends.

The last words, "I didn't do this," leave her lips before being taken away. Her final gaze lands on Kathryn; they lock eyes long enough for Laurel to detect a tiny slow wink from the doctor's right eye accompanied by a slight grin. Then, the "tell" hits Laurel like a shot between the eyes.

The newly convicted woman's demeanor switched instantly from defeated to uncontrollable flailing. No one understood what transpired; they only knew Laurel was screaming, "She did this; she is the murderer," pointing in the group's direction.

The guards quickly subdue Laurel, whisking her away and out of sight. Dumbfounded, the entire gallery scrambles in confusion; the paparazzi snap photos of the spectators, unsure who they should photograph.

Margo screams at Laurel, "Are you serious? So, you decide to point the finger at us now? How dare you!"

Dana avoids eye contact with Kathryn for fear she will read her mind. Dale, Eric, Olivia, and Joel stand in disbelief while Kathryn picks up her purse and calmly says, "How unfortunate," before leaving the pew. Her remark registered with them all this time, although, in the chaos, no one addressed Kathryn's unempathetic statement except Margo. An involuntary "What the Fuck, Kathryn!" spews from her mouth.

No one acknowledges the profanity; they silently follow Kathryn as she exits their row. The cameras flash to capture their initial reactions to the sentencing before anyone goes outside. Joel pushes forward, extending his arm to block the ladies from the rushing crowd. He then assumes the spokesperson's role for Laurel's friends; he announces, "They are all deeply saddened by this event. We are in an unimaginable position; words don't exist to express the monumental effects of this tragedy. Three of our closest friends lost their lives, and we can only presume Laurel will spend the rest of hers incarcerated. None of us will comment further, and we ask you to respect our privacy."

They abandon the reporters on the courthouse steps, head to the parking structure, and say their good-byes. Joel escorts Dana, Margo, and Kathryn into his car. Depleted and unsure of what to say, no one says much of anything on the short ride home.

Dana experiences a rush of panic and needs to get out of the car before she vomits. The rapid spin of the rogue tilt-a-whirl she's riding generates dreadful flashing images that won't stop. The outcome is what she wanted. But she underestimated the toll a death, a trial, and being inadvertently responsible for her friend's imprisonment would entail.

Dana is whining in Kathryn's way of thinking; truthfully, she should be more appreciative. After all, achieving a swimming result with zero participation is a huge win. But, of course, Dana's dilemma is that she didn't consult with anyone, yet all of this is due to her reckless scheming.

Relief is hard to come by, as danger lurks in every question; Dana acknowledges Kathryn's involvement but still wonders how to reference her suspicions without endangering herself. She wants to get away for a while, but her location isn't the issue; her thoughts are the problem. Out of fear of giving herself away or experiencing a total mental breakdown, Dana will keep her distance from everyone for now. She's desperate to talk to Kathryn, but thanking her right now seems highly inappropriate.

THIRTY-FIVE

Post-Trial...

The ladies exchange a few phone calls in the following weeks, but most contact transpires through emails and text messages. The book club is on an indefinite hiatus with no other attempts to arrange a meetup. A break to let the dust settle gives everyone much-needed time to heal.

Communication between Dale and Laurel continued from when she left the courtroom to her new residence behind bars. Any interaction with the prisoner is much to the disdain of his adult children, yet he fails to acknowledge the harm in corresponding via the U.S. Postal Service. He would like nothing more than to hold Laurel in his arms, but the written word is as far as he is willing to venture for the foreseeable future. As one would guess, the letters he receives revolve around professed innocence. However, they also include lengthy rants describing her insipid living conditions.

Life outside the walls topped with razor wire is of little importance to Laurel as of late unless a publication mentions her, at which point she demands specific details. A bit hurt but not surprised by her indifference toward his life, Dale continues to correspond despite her lethargic attitude when discussing how this saga affects him. Their writing evokes a duel-enabling act worthy of dissection by a team of neurology students. Reading into the self-righteous words, Laurel pens pretending she needs him as much as he needs her, willfully reinforcing his dependency, not hers.

Dale understands associating with a psychopathic murderer is unhealthy, yet something about her draws him back. Their attraction amounted to more than a benign romance; he is still in love with the woman he first met. The destiny he envisioned with his new lady friend embodied excitement filled with movie premieres and yacht clubs. But, unsurprisingly, a stint in the big house was never part of the long-term plan.

He admitted this case intervening in their courtship was advantageous as the odds of longevity in the relationship were not in his favor.

Yet, through it all, he never changes his opinion of his love; he still doesn't believe her, no one does, but he is unwilling or unable to cut ties with her yet. They each satisfy a gaping void in the other, providing a sliver of false hope, a match only they can appreciate.

Dale's new therapist must be wondering why he demanded the next available appointment when he presents himself as calm, with no signs of distress and no apparent need for professional help. In the initial consultation, he describes ending his short-lived romance with his girlfriend as a "breakup."

He conveniently omitted the minor detail that the affair ended involuntarily and resulted in imprisonment.

Murder was also excluded, and so was the ongoing correspondence with his convicted ex-lover. He would, however, like to discuss his phobia of open water. The ocean once brought a sense of tranquility, but now he can't go near the coast without invoking the fear of the dark wavy liquid extinguishing his life.

One day he may reveal the truth, but until then, he'll be satisfied conversing with a third party who isn't badgering him for details about his close encounter with a serial killer.

As expected, Laurel is experiencing difficulty adjusting to her new environment, the Central California Women's Facility in Chowchilla. Lockup, after all, is in stark contrast to her former lifestyle, with servants and amenities at her beck and call. Yesterday's chills came from a glass of crisp champagne; today's chills come in the form of frightening stares from a type of evil she once thought only existed on set.

One can only presume the actress will bring new drama to an otherwise mundane atmosphere. As a rule, Laurel enjoys the role of entertainer, but this is not what she had in mind. It's not like her to go out of her way to make friends; the only exception falls to super groupies or those brave enough to call her out on her bullshit. So, Laurel prays that a few fans are on the inside of her gated community to make this transition a little easier; the bullshit to come is unavoidable.

Word of Laurel's arrival spread like wildfire through the whole compound before she finished her orientation. Her nerves are exposed, and the tension is high; too many undesirable people touch her. The sheer number of bodies in her space is suffocating. To be told her placement is not with the "general population" is the first refreshing thing she has heard all day. She envisioned a private room, preferably with a view. However, the "suite" provided is inadequate, but she will keep her dissatisfaction to herself. The decision to play along and take her complaints to the warden later turns out to be the safer bet.

On the bright side, if one exists, joining the congregation must be better than solitary confinement, right?

One glaring complication is the new convict's assignment is to assimilate with inmates who committed similar crimes, murderers. The commotion is such that Laurel's current housing is with the white-collar criminals until she acclimates and everyone else calms down, which may never happen.

The literary world is Margo's escape; the books transport her mind to another place. But the saving grace is her patrons. Some regulars bonded together to create a support network. Others offered to work shifts without compensation if Margo should need any time off. A gracious gesture, but minding her shop and surrounding herself with people who care translates to her version of group therapy.

Several customers suggested developing a podcast detailing the tragedy from the first-person point of view. Some expressed it would be therapeutic, but it's much too soon. Besides, the news stations, relentless in their reporting, didn't cover much of anything else for the past few months.

The distraught widow is incredibly grateful for the loyalty of her customers and friends, but the real help came by way of life insurance, the plan Laurel initiated. The disturbing thought of insuring her husband as part of a deliberate scheme makes blood money hard to accept. But reality dictates she won't get by without receiving the payout, so pride for the sake of being noble is not an economically feasible stance.

The Reed family's intent for purchasing policies for each other revolved around security, not instant wealth. They secured their most significant asset, their home, and established a college fund for their son, Tyler. The surviving spouse would also receive a little extra for health, well-being, and maintenance to live a modest comparable life. The bookstore is debt-free, so the income and personal benefits are bonuses.

Tyler deflects his grief by converting his pain into a shield to protect his mother, which everyone finds endearing. He lacked any genuine interest in the bookshop until his father's death. But lately, he's become a fixture in the little store once owned by his grandfather. You'll find him hanging around the counter after school in case his mom may need a hand.

The young man's visits in the past resembled ATM transactions or bumming a ride home. Today his appearances are akin to welfare checks to ensure his mother is OK. Favors that used to be avoided have been replaced with unprompted assistance. In another abrupt change, Tyler abandoned his dream of attending a university out of state, opting for a school closer to home. This mother-and-son duo quickly transformed into a secure, cohesive team. Together they will survive just fine; sorry, Frank.

Before Laurel's incarceration and at her attorneys' request, Eric and Olivia Harper were named as her trustees. But only after being informed that it's prudent to keep her affairs in order if the result of this fiasco is unfavorable. Naturally, this advice didn't sit well, but the actress reluctantly conceded to a worst-case scenario.

The lawyers assured her that by signing a power of attorney, the control of her fortune would transfer to the Harpers only if she was convicted and only for the duration of her sentence.

Laurel also nominated Eric and Olivia as her joint beneficiaries if anything unforeseeable happens to her. Under normal circumstances, most people find creating a will uncomfortable, citing natural mortality as their reasoning. Therefore, it's understandable if one finds it disturbing to plan for an untimely death out of fear your neighbor is packing a shiv.

The strained conversation stops when Eric reminds the actress that it's better to be safe than sorry.

"Sorry" is the State of California assuming her property, leaving her with nothing when she gets out. Sugarcoating a glimmer of optimistic freedom versus dwelling on the division of assets in case of a shanking seemed to put things in perspective. The preparedness proposal is approved, and Laurel concedes to sign over her livelihood to the Harpers.

Until all the appeals are exhausted, and while Laurel remains incarcerated with an undetermined release date, Madeline will live in the Stanhope residence rent-free. Her duties are to maintain the house and stand guard over the castle. She is not to use the primary suite but can select a guest room. A safe deposit box bearing the Harpers' names will store all jewelry except for a few pieces Olivia fancied. All jewels borrowed are considered on loan. Under this agreement, everything taken must be returned upon the day of Laurel's discharge.

The thought of being forgotten is terrifying to the actress; perhaps having her jewels in public where her signature bling is visible will remind people to think of her.

Besides gold and diamonds, the impressive collection of designer ware resembles a sample sale at Neiman Marcus. Tags still dangle from garments, while other purchases remain untouched, never making their way out of the original wrapping. But, on the contrary, Olivia is pleased with her newfound image and finds it exhilarating to add new apparel to her rotation.

If the verdict stands, all property, contents, yacht, and cars will go to an auction. However, Olivia's well-rehearsed conversation regarding the appropriation of the diva's closet will transpire before any such yard sale occurs.

Separate instructions for all artwork are insisted upon, as each piece will need special handling requiring an appropriate museum-style warehouse. Laurel owns several priceless paintings she doesn't intend to part with as they, unlike her, are sure to grow more valuable with age. Collected treasures will be out of style if and when the condemned is released, so fashioned items will be auctioned or donated. The photographs and keepsakes will go to a storage unit.

Unfortunately, Madeline's tasked with boxing the house she once took pride in maintaining, but she does take pleasure in assuming the role of the madame of the house instead of being the maid.

Olivia arrived at the Stanhope home to meet Madeline with a copy of Laurel's directive. After that, the two of them together will start the tedious dismantling of the estate.

Their famous friend isn't getting out, so the two ladies resign themselves to the actual task. They agree to move slowly and start by separating anything tagged for bidding.

Boxes are brought in, but before assembling the first box, Olivia grabs two crystal flutes and pops the cork on a bottle of champagne. "It only seems fitting to make a toast." And they do so by allowing bubbles to flow freely throughout the day.

"Restitution!" is splashed across the newspaper's front page, anything to squeeze one more headline out of the Stanhope case. No one is sure who instigated these articles, yet the topic of paying damages to the victims reared its ugly head in bold print. If the court decides to pursue this action, Laurel's assets could go to Margo and Dana.

The justice system may also demand a slice of the pie by attaching properties and investments to reimburse the state for her "staycation" behind bars. This decision is much to the delight of the taxpayers but not advantageous for Eric and Olivia.

After Googling what goods the state can confiscate, the inventory list is revised, deleting a few sentimental heirlooms for safekeeping in anticipation of someone knocking on the door to collect Laurel's valuables. The doctored file accurately reflects everything left in the house; all items display descriptions and valid identification numbers.

Along with settling the fallen star's affairs, Olivia works with Kathryn. She plans to quit Dr. Bob's office after Christmas if he doesn't dismiss her first. Seeing his once-alluring assistant creates anxiety; he gives her another raise but regrets doing so afterward. Her presence is a constant reminder of how close he came to drowning.

In all of this, there lies a silver lining for the dentist; he found a new appreciation for his lovely wife. Love notes attached to surprise gifts are commonplace, and he enthusiastically takes her anywhere she'd like to go. Newfound respect, in general, will keep Dr. Bob from straying very far from home ever again.

The once star-struck Cynthia adopted a new standpoint as well. She stopped idolizing celebrities without a full investigation and not blindly believing whom they claim to be. Yet no one, including Bob, dares to inform her that *The Enquirer* isn't her best resource for research data.

As a compromise, she chooses to admire the stars from afar; it's a safe bet since it's not likely an invitation to attend another boat soirée will arrive anytime soon.

The Lucas children soon gave Dana their blessing to sell the family home. They know their mother didn't need their approval, but rallying to make decisions as a family strengthens their bond. After the kids returned to their respective colleges, living in the house she once shared with Randal became too depressing. Relocating will be a healthy adjustment, allowing her to escape the constant reminder of the recent trauma.

The lurking concern over new neighbors recognizing her from the television coverage will dissipate with time; having the generic last name Lucas will allow her anonymity wherever she lands.

Southern California offers several inviting boutique cities; the Carmel area is also a contender. Employment isn't the deciding factor for the first time in her life, giving Dana the choice of where she wants to be and whether to look for work. She is undecided about what kind of job she'd even like, but for sure, something other than electronics. Perhaps a part-time position in a flower shop or nursery. Something grounded to fill vacant hours by keeping her hands and mind busy, but more to provide an opportunity to make new friends.

Although appreciative, thanking Laurel for her financial stability is wrong. She will admit her situation would be much different if buying a life policy hadn't been proposed. But again, life would've been much different if her husband hadn't been murdered. A private jury is still hanging on reasonable doubt, and she is not thoroughly convinced if the actress was to blame.

The grim plot Dana concocted to do away with Randal and Laurel is suppressed but not erased. Thoughts of them both often pop up at the oddest moments. Self-soothing, which translates to talking to herself, is still a thing. Unfortunately, justifying how the whole ordeal came to fruition remains a struggle. Strangely, two undesirable people needed to leave her life, and now they're gone. How they got out shouldn't be her burden to bear. No one is glad Randal and Frank are dead, or that Laurel might as well be. But remembering their toxic existence and thoughtless actions got them where they are today helps deflect regret and guilt for what's happened.

Kathryn's involvement hasn't been forgotten but hasn't been solved either. So much information left undiscovered and so many loose ends. All of which only reinforces the importance of therapy. Conflicted by what she may or may not reveal to someone is the hold-up. Telling her story would put her in danger, so what's the point of counseling if you're going to lie or omit the real purpose of your visit?

The search for peace, for now anyway, will begin by resetting everything. A new address is the first step away from her past, so she'll search real estate websites for another home as soon as possible.

For Kathryn, France is on the horizon; her long-awaited sabbatical is now only days away. Diligently training Olivia to field calls and referring anyone in crisis to Joel while she is on vacation requires no further attention. She is satisfied with this arrangement. Most of her patients are acquainted with her ex and are comfortable seeing him if they need assistance during her absence.

This holiday abroad will last about a month, but being absent in her line of work justifies a reliable backup and someone on staff. In addition, not vacationing with Joel allows them to assist in each other's practices, in theory, a convenient arrangement for both doctors.

The persona for this Francophile adventure is to pass herself off as a writer. Therefore, a woman who prefers to travel alone won't be the subject of discussion for other travelers she encounters. She can think of nothing worse than bored vacationers desperate to figure out her story.

Kathryn's objective is finding isolation. The thought of making friends with strangers is loathsome and unnecessary. She wants to be left alone, not bothered by pesky hotel guests inserting themselves into her solitude. The idea of a nosey hotel employee forcing a bus tour because a companion does not accompany her is repulsive. Being alone doesn't mean you're lonely. She wishes people, past, present, and future, to understand and not interfere with her quiet time.

The timing of this trip is commendable if she does say so herself. Itinerary adjustments would have only been necessary if the court proceedings had lasted longer than expected. Arrangements for this "les vacances" (vacation) were made months before the murders, eliminating any suspicion surrounding Kathryn's departure from the country on the heels of the trial. The thought of negative perception would have caused most to cancel their plans, but not the doctor; she'll continue to rely on her confidence and skill for positive reinforcement and enjoy her much-deserved retreat.

After all, the investigators caught and convicted their suspect, which wasn't her. It's never her.

Kathryn's demons and well-worn cranberry-colored alligator skin journal are prepped for their own sabbatical. The words that once graced the pages are only kept in the notebook until the final list is committed to memory, and the plan is put to rest along with the subject of said list. She stores the binder in the safe as if locking the planner away will stifle its use. But before the journal is stowed, the ratty-edged pad with its cryptically inscribed pages is replaced with a fresh new one. Her pen hovers hesitantly over the crisp white page. The urge to jot Dana's name in dark black ink is met with reluctance. A noticeable lack of eye contact between the two friends provokes curiosity. Kathryn makes a mental note to trace back to pinpoint the behavioral change. A convenient explanation could be grief or trauma. *"Is Dana avoiding everyone or just me?"*

Solitude is another simple justification and something the doctor also craves. But her gut is telling her otherwise. With no desire au présent to dive into another list before her holiday, she will put a pin in her concerns about her friend. So, for now, the soft faded cover concealing the bright, pristine pages is closed and secured with its worn weathered ties. She should use a journaling app for security, but there is something sterile and impersonal about that. Her lists are intimate, passionate, and penned with purpose. The trick is to avoid giving the good doctor any reason to scribble your name inside the pages of her prized possession. Very few people know how Kathryn corrals her twisted thoughts, and no one has ever read her journal; certainly, no one still breathing.

Thank you for reading *Pushing Blame*; if you enjoyed the book, please rate and review it on Goodreads, Amazon, or wherever you purchased your copy of the book. I greatly appreciate you taking the time to do so.

Coming soon, find out who makes Kathryn Kane's list next in *Yourself to Blame.* Dr. Kane finally sets off on her solo sabbatical in France. Posing as a writer, her faux persona allows for the isolation she seeks, but what she finds is far from solitude.

Upon her return to San Francisco, she is offered an assignment working with the detectives from the Stanhope case. She is asked to psychologically profile several suspects to catch a sadistic serial killer plaguing the city. The good doctor will certainly lend her expertise; however, her unconventional method of solving issues may complicate things.

To receive advanced release notice of *Yourself to Blame*, drop me a request at **TSR@TSRubidoux.com.**

Join me on Facebook@ TSRubidoux "Friend Group"

For **"Bragging Rights,"** post a photo of yourself with your copy of *Pushing Blame* from your favorite reading location. I would love to see where you're from.

Book Clubs: If you would like *Pushing Blame* to be your club's next read, quantity **discounts are available**. Email bookclubs@ underbitebooks.com for details. Please include Pushing Blame in the subject line.

Acknowledgments and Shameless Plugs:

Podcasts: Books and Merchandise from all podcasts mentioned are available on the host's websites or your favorite bookseller.

- **Casefile**; Anonymous, Casefilepodcast.com
- **Let's not meet**; A. Tate, Letsnotmeetpodcast.com
- **My Favorite Murder**; Karen Kilgariff and Georgia Hardstark; **Book "Stay Sexy and Don't Get Murdered"** www.myfavoritemurder.com
- **Moms and Mysteries**; Mandy and Melissa, Momsandmysteries.com
- **RedHanded**; Hannah McGuire and Suruthi Bala; **Book, "RedHanded"** www.redhandedpodcast.com
- **Southern Fried True Crime**; Erica Kelly, Southernfriedtruecrime.com
- **Trashy Divorces**; Stacy and Alicia, Trashydivorces.com
- **Wearing Memories Locket**; wearingmemories.com
- **Psychological Thriller Readers**; Facebook page.

I am grateful for the podcasts and the hosts who provide much more than entertainment; you all bring informative levity to the darkest parts of humanity while carefully considering the victims and loved ones affected.

You've normalized the discussions surrounding mental health and pointed out that therapy is simply a gym for your brain, and we all need exercise. The number of people you've helped in this area is immeasurable.

Thank you for respectfully honoring the memory of lives lost and acknowledging those who have been victimized so they and/or their circumstances are not forgotten.

YOURSELF TO BLAME
CHAPTER ONE

France

Visions of art and sipping Merlot solo along the Seine is the only thing Dr. Kathryn Kane entertains herself with these days. Thoughts of freshly baked croissants and tiny espressos will surely hinder emails to her ex-husband Joel and her girlfriends back home once she touches down in France. Food and Freedom are foremost, but contact is essential; of course, this is for their benefit, so she tells herself. It's common for people to create distance between themselves and others after a tragic event or completely detach from their everyday lives. But Kathryn intends to prevent this from happening to her close-knit circle of friends.

Plus, open lines of communication are a form of insurance; she'll be alerted if any pertinent news arises regarding their dear incarcerated friend, Laurel Stanhope. The once-beloved actress is on a much different adventure after being sentenced to life in prison for murdering the husbands of two of their closest friends. Unfortunately for the defamed diva, she won't get a crack at parole for twenty-five years, all for a crime only Kathryn knows she didn't commit.

An Uber pulls in front of the Wedgewood blue row house with its creamy white trim, precisely as ordered to take this anxious traveler to the San Francisco International Airport. Light traffic makes for a swift ride, and thankfully, the newest terminal improvement project didn't impede her on-time arrival. Tardiness, in general, is unacceptable, as are sweat pants or pajama bottoms when traveling. Flight time from SFO in San Francisco to CDG in France is eleven hours and thirty-nine minutes; as one would predict, Kathryn is sharply dressed and plans to remain so for the duration of her journey.

TSA pre-check makes security a breeze, placing the doctor in the lounge with her glass of champagne in hand forty-seven minutes after stepping out her front door. Before her divorce, every vacation with Joel began with a stopwatch. He timed what he referred to as the cocktail run, attempting to break the last trip's doorstep to bar stool record each time. She will miss her partner; they traveled well together, but this adventure is all about her this time.

A stemmed glass is raised in a private toast to Laurel; a slight twist of the wrist sends frenzied bubbles to the surface. The thought of the actress drinking swill from a prison toilet evokes an audible snicker before all thoughts of her friend dissipate.

At last, peace and much-craved seclusion are here. The strain of Laurel's trial has taken its toll over the past few months. Now the only thing left is to relax and let her journey commence.

The call for first-class passengers to approach the gate crackles over the loudspeaker. A flight attendant stows her bag and offers another beverage while they wait for the rest of the plane to fill with travelers. The complimentary flute is accepted with a smile. Two drinks down, Kathryn settles into her seat, ready for a well-prescribed nap, hoping her slumber will last until the wheels touch down in Paris.

Baggage claim and customs didn't take as long as expected, and hailing a taxi required standing at the curb--a fantastic start to a glorious holiday. The trek from Charles de Gaulle to her rented apartment took over an hour. Immediately impressed by the chaotic swirl of cars circling the roundabouts, it's noted that Parisian drivers prove to be savvier than San Francisco motorists. No road rules seem to apply, yet no one gets in an accident; the mayhem somehow works. The thought of driving is nerve-racking, besides walking or using public transport is the preferred method to move about the city.

The rented flat is perfectly Parisian, with floor-to-ceiling shutters concealing long classic French panel windows that provide a view of the road below. A welcome basket, cradling a regional Pinot Noir and a fresh baguette, rests on the kitchen table. After settling in the apartment, Kathryn makes her way to the streets. Meandering for hours, she soaked in the history and the magnificent architecture. Every statue, building, and bridge is a marvel; each structure is more beautiful than the last.

Each arrondissement represents a different part of French culture. Twenty individual districts set in the pattern of a snail's shell make up the Paris city center. The first arrondissement sets the circular design in motion, with each area expanding the circle. She'll need to hustle to achieve the ambitious goal of visiting each district.

Five minutes into the long-awaited excursion, planning her itinerary came to a screeching halt. A local man looking over her shoulder on the metro frowns with concern as the blatantly obvious tourist outlines her intended path on a map. Finding it hard to refrain, he interjects, eventually taking her pen, saying, "Non, non, c'est dangereux," while crossing off the areas to avoid. Kathryn wondered where French people earned their reputation for being rude. Parisians are lovely.

This kind gentleman raved about Paris and took his time

outlining places of interest while underscoring the must-see attractions. He rescued her from miles of unnecessary walking and perhaps an unpleasant encounter. Grateful, she bids her fellow passenger farewell by saying, "Merci pour votre aide, passez une bonne journée," (thank you for your assistance, have a good day) before exiting the train to conquer the city.

To experience Paris fully, you must walk, absorbing each neighborhood one block at a time. Here, Americans can learn a thing or two from the French; they understand the importance of embracing the day; everywhere, people sit in cafes indulging in small bites, a coffee, or a glass of their favorite beverage. Regardless of the time of day, they take the time to appreciate life.

Jealous of their free spirit, Kathryn applies the "when in Rome" approach and stops by a boulangerie to take away a baguette and an espresso. Loaf in hand, she wanders down the stairs leading to the banks of the Seine, where she can sit and savor the flavor of the environment, while snacking on warm bread and enjoying her rich coffee.

Lost in the river's current, she realizes she can't accomplish her lofty itinerary in four days. Pleased, her schedule includes a repeat visit to the city after some downtime in the countryside eases her frustration. But she considers even that might not be enough time to see all Paris has to offer in one trip. Delighted yet exhausted, the jet-lagged traveler returns to the flat and tucks herself in for the night.

The city is even more enchanting in the early morning light. Today begins with a curbside bistro along the Champs Élysées and a cup of coffee. While admiring the steam wafting off her lait, her bliss is interrupted by the undeniable sensation of someone watching her. The café patrons appear occupied with their phones or in deep conversation with the person across the table. No passer-by stands out, but she can't shake the uneasiness.

With her cup empty, she begins her pursuit to find a petite librairie (small bookshop) to acquire a rare foreign treasure for her friend Margo. Without waiting for the server to return with her bill, Kathryn leaves a couple of euros on the table and strolls down the iconic tree-lined boulevard. Unfortunately, a bookstore similar to Margo's boutique bookshop back home is proving more difficult to find than expected; perhaps the tourist area isn't the best place to start.

Window shopping is an under-appreciated pastime; the city boasts incredible fashion from high-end to casual chic, offering something for everyone. However, one can't ignore the museum-sized Louie Vuitton emporium, with its gorgeous array of colorful handbags artfully showcased in the window. Laurel crosses her mind; her fashion-forward friend would kill for any one of those purses. The visual of the fallen star sitting in her jail cell and being told she has a package is riveting. Imagining the puzzled grimace on the inmate's face while she opens the box is beyond suspenseful. The realization of holding a Crocodile Capucines BB in Imperial Topaz is thrilling. The color choice would be immediately noted as an intentional dig, as the hue would coordinate magnificently with her one size fits all tangerine jumpsuit. But the fact that this joy is temporary and soon to be ripped from her unmanicured hands would be priceless.

A pause to grin and giggle, enjoying the moment, understanding her imprisoned friend isn't allowed to receive vanity packages. Yet she can't help but wonder if the warden wouldn't let her hold the luxury item for a moment while telling her the gift arrived via Fed-

Ex from France. The guaranteed torment would justify the extravagant $32,000.00 price tag attached to the purse. Such a gesture would be cruel even for Kathryn, so she scrubs the idea and continues on her way.

A helpful street vendor directs her toward the nearest la libraire. (book store.) The small literary establishment she stumbled upon doesn't possess the same charm as Margo's shop, but it does offer a wide variety of well-aged titles alongside many new books from which to choose.

Leisurely browsing the dusty archives in search of a vintage find is always exciting, but experiencing a chill sending goosebumps from head to toe is a new sensation. Glancing up from the book in her hand, she eyes a man positioned strategically in her path. A red flag is hoisted as he wasn't there a second ago.

The stealth stranger concentrates on locating something specific; his selection coincides with her turn in his direction. Not electing to dance, Kathryn turns again and goes the opposite way. This will eliminate having to excuse herself to pass, which opens the door for unwanted conversation. She thinks to herself, "This guy is embarrassing himself," before dismissing the thought of him.

After finding a book that's sure to thrill Margo, she waits her turn in the queue to make her purchase. The same man blocking the aisle a moment ago is now behind her in line. His hot breath bounces off her neck; he's too close. She reaches into her bag, releasing a hard elbow to his side. They lock eyes, but not in an apologetic way; her glare clearly states, back off.

He excuses himself, saying, "Pardon."

A forced grin is delivered before turning away to discourage any banter. Nevertheless, this exchange fills her with unease. Uncomfortable in her surroundings, Kathryn hands the clerk more than enough euros to cover the cost and a sharp merci, not waiting for a receipt or her change.

The next thought is to get out, and she jets out the door with the book pressed to her chest, hurrying down the street before realizing her faux pas. The man chases her, yelling, "madame, madame."

But she ignores his calls and doesn't turn around until he saddles up beside her; she notes he didn't take the time to pay for the book he stood in line to buy.

"Madame, you left your change," he said in perfect English as he extended his hand, offering the sales slip and coins.

"Merci," is all she says before turning to walk away, but he's quick to ask if she is from the United States. Her reply is short, "Oui, Je suis Americaine. (Yes, I am American).

The abrupt cut in her sentence indicates she isn't interested in talking with an unfamiliar person. But, much to her dismay, the man misreads her not-so-subtle hint. Instead, he assumed conversing "en français" was an invitation to begin a lengthy bilingual discussion.

A scowl marks her second error; this stupidity directly insults her self-preservation. Without emotion, Kathryn snaps, "I speak French, and I am American; thank you for your kindness, but now I must go." He makes the mistake of touching her arm; her eyes focus on his hand, then up at his face. Her expression reads, "To kill you would be my pleasure," but instead, she delivers a harsh, "Please remove your hand from my arm."

His reaction is immediate; he recoils but persists in trying to make friends.

There is no point in being impolite, but she is, yet the man is undeterred. A stern "Merci, au revoir" indicates the conversation is over. The man concedes with reluctance and doesn't force this awkward altercation any further.

Relieved to be rid of the pesky Frenchman, Kathryn is back on track; her next stop is the Louvre. The random route selection diverts away from her actual destination, taking much longer than planned. But it's a necessary precaution in the off chance her persistent admirer decides to be a nuisance.

———————

Excited, Kathryn walks onto the stately grounds encompassing the largest museum in the world. She strolls by the giant Ferris wheel, several arches, and countless statues. The sizable and controversial glass pyramid rising from the ground functions as the museum's grand entrance. Three smaller versions of the massive blue-tinted protrusion don't appear to serve a purpose other than to let light into the subterranean gallery below. The contemporary glass and metal structures are mystifying. The contrast is indescribably provoking, standing out against the grand historical French Renaissance-style buildings serving as a backdrop. An odd choice indeed but beautiful in their own right.

The endless halls boast thousands of spectacular portraits and sculptures. One could spend a month here, and it wouldn't be long enough to capture the beauty in every masterpiece. The Mona Lisa, of course, is a must-see attraction, but after an hour of art appreciation, Kathryn craves the sunshine outdoors.

She makes a mental note to revisit the Louvre; truthfully, she will mark several attractions for another visit. But, for now, she'll walk, which is equally awe-inspiring, not to mention better people-watching.

A long day of touring the city earns Kathryn a well-deserved aperitif in the privacy of her quaint abode. The complimentary bottle of wine graciously left by her host is uncorked before getting settled. Excited to revisit her day through pictures, she patiently waits for the photos to upload to her laptop for better viewing. While inspecting her images, the overwhelming sense experienced earlier in the day returns, the eeriness of someone watching.

The apartment sits on the third floor, and the shutters are open to survey the street below, but someone on the road cannot peer in. People are walking by, but no one is milling around. Against her better judgment, she brushes aside her sixth sense and continues to peruse her photographs. Fixated on a shot of the small pyramids, she recognizes his face staring back at her; he's been with her all day. Kathryn springs off the couch to scan the street again, but he's not out there. The fact that he stalked her undetected infuriates her.

The thought of him being aware of her accommodations is also alarming. Irritation creeps in for being so naive; venturing carelessly about the city is how you get assaulted. How did she overlook someone on her tail?

A better question is, what does he want?

The more she thought about the intruder, the more troubled she became. *"Why is this man so intent on meeting me?"*

Kathryn reexamines her morning. She didn't sense anything unusual. But why would she?

The first attempt to engage happened in the bookstore. That is not to say this is the first time he spied on her.

Rewinding to the beginning, the Uber to SFO, inside the terminal, the lounge, the flight, the taxi, the apartment, nothing out of the ordinary registers. Naturally attentive, Kathryn didn't place much emphasis on her well-being. Traveling alone wasn't something she often did, but being a single traveler shouldn't prompt paranoia. Next, scrutinizing every photo, she recounts the first couple of days in the city. Not the slightest bit amused by the Where's Waldo game in Paris, the agitation set the "listing" wheels in motion.

Now angry with herself for disregarding her instincts and permitting a man close enough to touch her, even after her intuition sounded the alarm. As a doctor, she knows better, and by now, she should have read "Stay Sexy and Don't Get Murdered," a book Margo gave her.

The authors of the book point out the first rule of thumb is, "fuck politeness," call the potential assailant out; if wrong, stand corrected and apologize.

You might be embarrassed, but so what?

At least you're not dead. Failing to abide by this simple rule resulted in some psycho following her because she's too fucking polite.

Today's errors are not all on Kathryn; selecting her as a target will go down as an unwise choice on his part. He should've done his homework, or perhaps choosing the doctor isn't haphazard. It doesn't matter, the turf may be his, but this is her world. To be the victim will never happen, at least not to her.

This unaccompanied rendezvous centers around her mental well-being, unwinding and putting to rest the recent turmoil surrounding Laurel Stanhope's murder trial and subsequent prison sentence once and for all. Stifling the urge to "list" was paramount in regaining her inner strength. But this man, this brazen infiltrator, forced her well-planned itinerary off course. He may not meet the same end as the others, but he will suffer for inserting himself into her sabbatical...

I hope you continue with *Yourself to Blame* coming out soon.

ABOUT THE AUTHOR

T. S. Rubidoux lives in California with her husband but prefers to write in Hawaii.

38042495R00213